SIREN SONG

As she reached the doors of the Bank Trust Building and tugged at one of the massive gold handles she was aware of one thing: it had been a year ago when she had first passed through them as the new head of Floderus Incorporated, her father's company, determined to prove that a young woman with no business acumen but with fair intelligence and fierce devotion could keep it going, and even increase its fortunes. And she had failed.

SIREN SONG

Lesley Stone

W.H. ALLEN · LONDON
1985

Copyright © 1985 by Trevor Enterprises Inc.

Printed and bound in Great Britain by
Mackays of Chatham Ltd, Kent
for the Publishers, W.H. Allen & Co. PLC
44 Hill Street, London W1X 8LB

ISBN 0 491 03404 0

To
Marcia and Randy Peterson

CHAPTER 1

SITTING AT HER ease in the rear of the smoke-grey Lincoln limousine, her body cradled in supple leather and her silk-clad legs crossed at the thigh, Lorraine Floderus felt like a tigress in heat. Luxury went to her head, and from there to her libido, where it throbbed insistently until she did something about it. It had always been this way, even though she'd been born to it; luxury had never jaded her, and she was ready to delight in the touch of raw silk or the taste of champagne or the shimmer of precious stones at every moment of her life. These were the good things, and they were there for her, and she wasn't going to deny them, any more than she would deny a Brahms symphony, or roses, or moonlight.

Also she felt guilty, as the traffic piled up and the limo floated to a halt alongside a bus stop; and she kept her eyes lowered to admire the exquisite emerald calf Guccis she had kicked off so that her toes could nestle in the thick pile carpet. On occasions like this she felt tempted to press the button and lower a window and tell the line of people at the bus stop that they didn't have to look at her this way; she worked a damned sight harder than they did. But then it wouldn't necessarily be true: everyone worked hard in this city. This was Manhattan, where this morning and every morning a half million people had woken to the electronic bird calls of their alarm clocks and got ready for work, while another million and a half came surging through the tunnels and across the bridges onto the island to keep the life in its glass towers running. In these few square miles there was focused the highest concentration of commercial wealth on the surface of the earth, vested in the multi-billion-dollar corporations whose enterprise influenced two-thirds of the world's trade. Everyone worked hard to keep it that way, but even here, not everyone rode around in limousines; and Lorraine didn't think this was fair, though she'd never told anyone, because it would have sounded in her own secret heart like a betrayal of her birthright.

Her father had given her all these things, bringing out of Hitler's Europe the clothes he stood up in, a box of worn books tied with string, and a dream: the same kind of dream that so many had brought to this new land where suddenly everything seemed possible. In a year – he had told Lorraine when she was old enough to understand what he was saying – he had grasped the new language well enough to get a job in a New Jersey soap works and study cosmetic chemistry at night, bringing out the old worn books and translating the gist of their contents so that he could share them with any of his new friends who were interested. In three years one among them – Barry Corbett, a young Harvard man with a little money and lots of ambition – had offered to go into partnership with Wilhelm Floderus, setting up a small cosmetic-chemicals plant not far from the soap works where he was now assistant marketing director. Six years later – the year when Lorraine was born – Floderus Incorporated turned in its first million-dollar net profit and went public, establishing itself in the fledgling ranks of the perfume industry. Its first independent creation, *Picaresque*, was still adorning the shelves in Saks, Bonwit Teller and a thousand luxury boutiques throughout America and Europe.

Thus it was that Lorraine's earliest memories had been of spacious rooms with white walls and gilded panels; of wide lawns and lily-ponds; of silk sheets and fur coats and the glimmer of jewels in the glow of the night-light as her mother came to bid her sweet dreams. For a time she didn't know these things were called luxury; she thought everyone had them. Later, when she learned this wasn't so, it worried her a lot; but there seemed nothing she could do about it; and now that she was old enough to sit in the rear of a limousine in an ivory pointelle sheath with pearls at her ears and throat, she was aware above all that she mustn't deny the pleasure that life had brought to her – that her father had brought to her out of the agony and terror and despair of the camps and the ghettos of Nazi Germany. To deny it would be to betray him; to betray his memory.

The plane had crashed a year ago, almost to this day.

The Lincoln moved on again, and she looked through the windows, watching the crowded pavement. Beyond it the black glass buildings stood row upon row, forming canyons whose sides rose sheer and shut out the grey January sky; a haze of spinning wheel discs traced the traffic flow from street to street as the exhaust gas rose like the smoke of a ritual sacrifice to mammon in this stronghold of commercial enterprise. Though the crowds along the pavement were huddled into their coats against the cold, Lorraine felt a sudden excitement as the thrumming energy of the scene reached her through the smoked glass windows; and she pressed the intercom button.

'Frank, stop where you can, will you?'

Her chauffeur's eyes flicked upwards to look into the mirror, surprised. 'Yes, ma'am,' his voice came through the speaker. He found a slot by the ITT Building, pulling the limousine into the kerbside and getting out quickly; but she was already on the pavement before he could open her door.

'I feel like walking the rest of the way.' She gave him her brilliant smile and watched him react, his strong weathered face relaxing. Stirred by the noise of the street, she suddenly wanted to break down his dutiful formality, and with her special smile she'd succeeded, though not of course to any great degree. Frank Cummins was chauffeuring the head of a fifty-million-dollar company, and even though she was only thirty-one years old and had starred in her last movie only last year and was still used to the relaxed atmosphere of Hollywood, Frank was a man to do his job according to his own rules. His function in life was to drive her through the city – *Yes, ma'am* – and stop when she told him to stop – *Yes,*

9

ma'am. That was the job.

'Meet me at five as usual, Frank.'

'Yes, ma'am. Er . . . I gave the Rolls-Royce a test drive, like you told me.'

'The what?' She was looking up at him against the glare of the winter sky, thinking it would be rather nice to climb back into the limo and tell him to keep on driving, and find a little restaurant in the Village and eat some fettucini and drink some Chianti together and then maybe drive out somewhere and stop the car and after a while persuade this tall and quite good-looking but too circumspect man to relax and talk a little, and unwind, and finally do something about the throbbing in her libido. The idea astonished her, even as she played with it. But she understood. She was unconsciously dreaming of escape.

'The Rolls-Royce,' Frank said. 'You told me to give it a drive and let you know if –'

'Oh. Yes, I remember now. What's it like?' A brand new Rolls would look rather too conspicuous standing outside a little restaurant in the Village . . .

'It's an exceptional piece of machinery, ma'am. I couldn't fault her; she's beautiful.' He added quickly, 'A sound investment, in my opinion.'

Lorraine nodded. 'Okay.' Opening her pocket-book she signed a cheque and ripped it from the stub and gave it to him.

'Fill in the rest, would you? Just buy it.'

He blinked a couple of times and folded the cheque and put it carefully into his wallet. 'Yes, ma'am.' She was trying not to laugh, because it was going to drive them crazy in the accounts department: a *blank* cheque on the loose, with the stub not filled in . . . She watched Frank's smothered surprise, conscious of the power she had, the power of money, of doing impulsive things with it, of blowing a lowly employee's mind just by handing him a scrap of paper that was worth nothing, nothing at all, until her signature had transformed it into a hundred and thirty thousand dollars. That was the price he'd told her.

10

Then suddenly she felt ashamed, because all she'd done was cheapen herself by showing off to her chauffeur. Too late now. 'I know you've checked over the car very carefully, Frank; and of course I value your expert opinion. I imagine a car like that will keep its price for a long time, and prove an economy.'

'That's how I see it, ma'am, yes.'

He touched his cap as she nodded and turned away and joined the rush-hour crowds along the pavement, suddenly indistinguishable from anyone else, a young woman on her way to work – except perhaps for her dark sable coat. She picked up the pace and was carried along by the vitality of this city on its way to another day of concerted endeavour; yet she was conscious of acting out a false role, trying to see herself as the bright, confident tycoon who was doing such a terrific job in this city that she could pick up a brand new Rolls on her way to work like other people would buy a pretzel from a vendor at the corner. But with each step she felt her act wearing thin, and giving place to reality, even a sense of foreboding.

As she reached the doors of the Bank Trust Building and tugged at one of the massive gold handles she was aware of only one thing: it had been a year ago when she had first passed through them as the new head of Floderus Incorporated, her father's company, determined to prove that a young woman with no business acumen but with fair intelligence and fierce devotion could keep it going, and even increase its fortunes. And she had failed.

Judy Pollack, Personnel Manager, sat hunched over her desk with the telephone buried in her arms as if she were trying to hug the person at the other end of the line: perhaps to death.

'Okay. Sure. Right. I have a lot of understanding. But this is the third time I've called and I'd really feel flattered if you could get him out of his meeting, if that's what he's in. And while you're doing it, will you kindly refrain from leaving me stuck with that tape by the Grateful Dead? If they're so

11

grateful, just hook me up to the silence of the grave so I can share their joy.'

She waited two and a half minutes by the big sunburst clock on the wall in the corridor and then dropped the phone like a dead rat. 'You know something,' she told her assistant, 'I think if I called up Suicide Hotline they'd put me on hold.' She swung around on the swivel chair to reach for the in-tray, her bright orange blouse scorching its reflection across the glass partition that gave her office the semblance of privacy; today, feeling the onset of what passed in Judy Pollack for black depression, she'd chosen an emerald skirt to go with the blouse, since a young artist friend had mentioned that green and orange made a natural complement for each other in the visible spectrum. She'd realised it was a mistake the first time she'd caught her reflection in a window of the Union Carbide Building on her way here from the subway, too late to do anything about it.

'Chief's here,' Betty Lou said.

Judy looked up through the glass partition, secretly annoyed that she hadn't been first to see the slim figure coming out of the lift six doors along. Though the glass was intended to give a sense of privacy, Judy Pollack saw things differently; while most people considered they worked in a goldfish bowl because others could look in as they passed, Judy only wanted to look out, so that she could keep track of what went on inside the complex structure of Floderus Incorporated. As Personnel Manager she needed to see people, and know where they were going, and where they were coming back from, and if possible why. This was why she'd asked for an office with a glass partition, even though her status rated solid walls and a door; and why she had chosen this one, right at the intersection of the two most-travelled traffic lanes on the executive floor with a view that included the Chief's corner suite, the lifts, the ladies' room and the doors of the offices harbouring the top-ranking executives from the President down to VP Research. Her job was people; they were also her joy. 'What else is there?' she had once asked Betty Lou. 'The rest of this ball game is

12

just the ball.'

As she watched Lorraine Floderus walking towards her from the lift, she checked the clock on her desk. Frank must have dropped the Chief at the door five minutes late. But Frank had never dropped her off five minutes late, nor even one minute, never in a whole year. Something was up, and this confirmed it.

Betty Lou, quiet and almost subdued in contrast with Judy's bright vitality, watched the head of the company nearing their doorway and caught her breath. 'Will you just look at her, Judy? I'd give half my salary for a face like that.'

'I gotta better deal. I keep the face I already have, and take half *her* salary. You ever been to Las Vegas? We could both have a ball. In fact on two hundred and fifty grand we could have a ball just anywhere.'

'Is that what she earns?'

'And it stops right here,' Judy said sharply. 'Okay?'

'Okay. Sure.'

Judy nodded, satisfied. One of the reasons she'd pulled this quiet, deceptively-competent twenty-five-year-old Katie Gibbs graduate out of the secretarial pool six months ago was that she never passed anything on: the word stopped here.

'Good morning, Chief!' Judy called through the doorway, and noticed it took a moment for Lorraine to turn her head and flash that sensational smile. She'd been distracted, walking with her head down – and that too was something new.

'Hi, Judy!' She waved to them both and passed on towards her office at the end of the corridor. Again Judy noted two things: the slower-than-usual stride, the hint of drooping shoulders that the shimmering sable coat couldn't conceal.

Starting on her in-tray she said conversationally to Betty Lou, 'Do you catch any vibrations this morning?'

'Vibrations?'

'The way Carl Blatt arrived earlier than usual and shut himself straight in his office? The way Barry Corbett forgot

13

to say hello in the lift? The way the Chief looked just now? Maybe it's just me, but I'm sensing vibrations, Betty Lou. Nothing major, but somehow I'm seeing rivers of blood filling the corridors, human tears gushing from every fawcet in the ladies' room, heads rolling with a dull, sickening thud behind closed doors, you know what I'm trying to say?'

'Kind of,' said Betty Lou. But she didn't let it bother her any; Judy always exaggerated things.

'But we won't let ourselves worry about it,' Judy told her bravely. 'It's just the mood I'm in this morning. I knew it was going to be a bad day when I woke up face down on the pavement outside the city morgue.'

Before Lorraine was halfway through the ante-room to her office, Maggie was out of her chair.

'Good morning, Ms Floderus.' She was shuffling a stack of papers. 'We've heard from the Palm Beach convention at last. They want – '

'All right, Maggie. When I buzz.' She didn't even smile, because she hadn't the heart for it. Closing her door firmly, she realised that a lot of the pressure – maybe even *most* of the pressure – she had to deal with every day was produced by Maggie Welford. But weren't secretaries supposed to *reduce* the pressure on the person they worked for? With this one it wasn't like that. How many days were there in a year? Okay, then three hundred and sixty-five times since Lorraine had started work in this office, Maggie had tried to bring things to her attention before she could get to her desk and riffle through the *New York Times,* the *Wall Street Journal* and the still-unread sections of *Forbes, Business Week, Fortune, Barron's, US News and World Report, Harvard Business Review, Beauty Fashion* and the five news letters that covered ninety per cent of what was going on in the perfume and cosmetic world.

This was the ritual, and Maggie knew it. It lasted a strict forty-five minutes, and it was sacrosanct; Lorraine had instituted it within a week of her coming here to head the company, after she'd tried picking up one journal after

14

another at snatched moments during the day. It hadn't worked. This amount of reading had to be done: it was important; it was her homework (which she'd tried to do at home, but that didn't work either); it was also a form of meditation, of settling herself in at the beginning of a long day, of clearing the decks. And if the Chairman and Chief Executive Officer of Floderus Incorporated couldn't have forty-five minutes to herself in her own office, then something was wrong, and something would have to be done about it.

Fire Maggie.

Staring at the closed door, Lorraine felt a shiver pass through her. She'd never fired anybody in her life. 'You'll have to get used to it one day,' Barry Corbett had told her a while ago with his rueful smile. 'Hiring and firing are the two most important facts of life in any business enterprise.'

'Have you ever fired anyone, Barry?' she'd asked him.

'Dozens of times.'

And Barry Corbett was without any question the kindest and most humane man she had ever known. Okay, call him right now. Or, even more cowardly, send him a memo. *Barry: I need you to fire someone for me.*

Out of the question. She was the boss. And Maggie Welford was her personal secretary, so there was only one person in the whole of this company who had the power to fire her.

Lorraine picked up the *Times*, and read the main headline three times before she understood it, because if she ever got used to firing people there was one person in the whole of this company she couldn't do it to, and that was Maggie, who had been here as her father's secretary when he had sat here at this desk, running the company he'd created and expanding its profits year after year until the plane crash.

'I believe I was a help to your father,' the stricken-faced woman with the horn-rimmed glasses and the pile of dull ginger hair had told her, standing in front of this desk a year ago with her eyes still wet with grief, 'and I believe I can be of help to you.'

15

Maybe she had. More help than hindrance: that was on the positive side, wasn't it? More cooperative than infuriating: that was a plus. But whatever she was, Maggie must stay, simply becuse of the fact that she had been here, in this office, when Lorraine had walked in here with her life broken apart and her mind numbed with disbelief that what had happened was impossible, but still had happened. Maggie had been part of all that, and had stood here offering help at a time when Lorraine had thought she was forever beyond it.

Okay, so we forget it and we read this goddamned headline for the fourth time, and it says: *ARMS RACE INTENSIFIED. 'We have to close the gap,' warns Congressman.*

But what you don't realise, boys, is that there are just the two of you sitting there on top of the powder-keg and complaining that one of you has more matches than the other.

By 9.50 she had got through the reading she'd allocated for today, giving herself the extra five minutes she'd lost in getting out of the limo and walking the rest of the way, inspired by the vibrations of this city and playing the role of the successful business magnate who had earned her place along the crowded pavement. In future she'd face reality.

By 9.54 she had dropped six letters beside the blotter for later reading, eleven others into the silk-brocade waste basket, and stacked the rest neatly at her right hand, slitting the first one open with the onyx-handled paper knife and glancing across only the first few lines before she realised that her sense of foreboding as she'd come into the building was absolutely right; and as she read the rest of the letter, slowly now and word by word, she had the image in her mind of an ocean liner steaming at full speed through the dark against the huge mass of an iceberg, with the name *Floderus* across its bows.

16

CHAPTER 2

AT TEN O'CLOCK, when Lorraine was reading the letter a second time, there was a brief knock on the door and Dean Powers looked in.

'Can you give me five minutes, Lorraine?'

She looked up from the letter and for an instant didn't even recognise him, simply because if she'd suddenly seen her reflection in a mirror she wouldn't recognise that either. Then he took another step or two into the office, confident that she could, yes indeed, give him five minutes, just whenever he felt like dropping in.

'No,' she said.

'Uh?' He stopped dead, with the door still open behind him; his handsome, sculpted face was wrinkled in exaggerated confusion. 'Did you say no?'

'Right.' She waited, watching him with steady eyes above the letter from Carl Blatt.

'Oh.' Dean gave a sudden grin, shrugging extravagantly, making a joke of it. 'Wrong time?' He turned and crept to the door, as if his shoes might make the slightest sound on the pile carpet. 'Call me, will you?' he said in a stage whisper. 'It's important.'

She watched him go out, shutting the door with studied care; then she dropped the letter onto the wide ebony-topped desk and pressed the intercom buton.

'Maggie, did you see Dean come through?'

'Why, yes I did, Ms Floderus. He just –'

'Maggie, would you please try to remember that I don't see *anyone* without they check with you first? I want you to

17

tell me who they are, and what they want. Will you *please* try to remember that?'

There was a short silence while Maggie recovered; she always needed a few seconds for this. 'Why, I thought that Mr Powers – you know – wouldn't want to see you unless it was something important. That's why –'

Lorraine closed her eyes to look for strength from within. 'It always has to be something important, Maggie, or they wouldn't want to see me about it: they'd just go to someone else. Now please don't let *anybody at all* get past you into my office.' She looked at the letter again. 'Right now I *do* want to see Mr Blatt, so please ask him if he has a moment.'

'Yes, Ms Floderus.'

Lorraine sagged suddenly, releasing the tension. She'd never spoken like that before to Maggie; she'd always tried to lighten her criticism with a little joke – 'not even if it's Father Christmas, Maggie, he has to wait in line' – something to acknowledge that Maggie wasn't just her secretary, but had been her father's also, and for many years. She certainly hadn't ever refused to talk to Dean Powers – or anyone at all – once they'd got as far as her desk without an appointment. Today she'd found anger, and had turned it on, and for the first time had seen a man like Dean Powers – tall, lean and muscular in his thousand-dollar Dunhill-tailored suit – reduced in two seconds to the size of an ordinary mortal. And all she had said was no.

Maybe she should say it more often.

Carl Blatt came along ten minutes later. He didn't knock.

'Good-morning, Carl.'

'Hi.'

He stood perfectly still in front of her desk for a couple of seconds and then turned away, pacing across the big windows overlooking the Waldorf Astoria, a small man in a green sports jacket a fraction too big for him with a soft wool necktie and soft suede shoes, his eyes too bright behind the steel-framed spectacles, his ruff of hair thinning too early in life – he was not yet thirty-five, despite his position as a senior vice president in the company.

'You want to sit down?' Lorraine asked him.

He swung on her and away again as if it had been a mistake, and paced again from the window to the long floor-to-ceiling bookshelves, his hands restless until he took another little swerve and reached her desk, taking a paper clip from the magnet-top holder and beginning to work on it as he swung away again; whenever Carl Blatt came in here he dropped the remains of the conversation into the waste basket: paper clips bent into the form of question marks, S-bends, Ws, and TV antennae, sometimes by the dozen.

'No,' he said indifferently.

'Okay. I got your letter.'

'Fine.'

'It doesn't tell me much, Carl.' She felt the anger rising again, but this time controlled it, because she knew it was built on fear, and he too would know it.

He stopped pacing and faced her with his eyes bright behind the lenses. 'It says I'm resigning, and that doesn't tell you much?' His voice was high in tone, as always, but now he raised it even higher, putting a lot of studied surprise into it.

'It doesn't say why.'

'Oh.' He pretended he hadn't thought of that. 'And you're interested?'

Lorraine stared. 'I don't understand you, Carl.'

'I believe that.'

'You believe what? That I'm interested, or that I don't understand you?'

Now he was staring her back, and for a time there was a silence in the room; even his hands had stopped moving, with one end of a broken paper clip in each. Then he said very softly: 'I think there's a certain lack of communication between us, Lorraine. Even of a common language. Suppose you tell me what's on your mind, and I'll see if anything comes through to me.'

She got out from behind the huge desk and stood with her arms folded, facing him, feeling better now she was on his level, even an inch or two above him; and now she knew it was going to be easy to stop the anger coming, because this

19

man had come in here in a quiet, unadvertised rage, and it was still going on. One of them would have to keep cool.

'All right, Carl. I'll make it as direct as I can, so you'll know exactly what I'm saying. After a whole year of working together, you suddenly send me a letter of resignation that doesn't even say why you want to go, or even that you feel we might discuss it together. And I think that is an act of deliberate and calculated discourtesy.'

He blinked once, then went on waiting, his small stubby hands working again on the bits of paper clip. But she wasn't going to say any more.

'Oh.' He moved away from her, his eyes everywhere, but never on hers. 'Right, there is a lack of communication, yes. After a whole year of working together, I think you said. But we haven't been doing that. We've been working in the same building, and that's about all.'

She still didn't understand him, but mustn't say so. It was conceivable, horribly conceivable, that she had been in the chief executive office of this company for twelve whole months without actually knowing what was happening around here.

'Please go on,' she said, very low.

He looked up, either surprised or feigning it; with this little man she felt out of her depth, maybe out of her class: he was so engrossed in his rage or bitterness or whatever it was, that he was overlooking important things – that it might be necessary, for instance, for him to talk down to her before she could understand. He was a bright, sharp, city boy, a New York intellectual who maybe spoke –as he'd said – a different language.

'Please go on,' he mimicked, seemingly puzzled. 'Okay. Since you came here we've gone to meetings and called each other and exchanged half a million memos and said "Hi" in the lift, sure. But that wasn't "working together." It was just working in the same company. Under your captaincy we spent two million dollars on a campaign to revitalise the Floderus image domestically and overseas, and the Floderus image has gradually become extinguished in the public mind, domestically and overseas, due to the fact that you fired our very efficient ad agency and hired a bunch of hayseeds who believe we sell our products to the heartland of home-spun America instead of to the sophisticated women at the top of their class in fashion, the professions, the arts and in society. That wasn't "working together" either. It was going a long way to running this company into the ground.'

It seemed a long time to both of them before Lorraine answered; it probably was.

'Go on.'

His hands stopped moving again.

'Jesus Christ,' he said, 'you want it all?'

'I want it all.'

In a moment he said, 'Maybe I will sit down.'

She sensed, as he lowered himself uncertainly onto the ivory calf couch, that in some subtle and totally inadvertent way she had actually knocked him down.

'We'll both sit down,' she said quietly.

'Uh? Sure. But not over there, do you mind?'

'Not over here?'

'Not at your desk. Isn't one of those chairs okay?'

'This one?'

'That one's fine.'

Sitting down, she tried to understand what the hell was going on. Was he using, maybe unconsciously, some kind of psychological trick – now they were sitting in the same suite of furniture, they were closer to a common understanding? Something like that?

'It's lower,' he said, nodding gently.

'Lower?'

'Less dominating.' He dropped the bits of paper clip into the pedestal ashtray and began using his hands to demonstrate, speaking more rapidly now. 'You know what happens when anyone comes into this office, Lorraine? They see your desk, and it's an awful long way off. It's at the end of the oblong, and it's facing the door. It means a long walk, while you sit there at your ease, watching us. So we

21

feel dominated.' His hands flew upwards. 'That's the biggest window, behind your chair, behind your desk. It gets the most light: it faces south. You like the curtains wide open, because why not? There's the sky up there and the daylight coming in, better than those damn vision-polluting tubes in the ceiling out there in the main office. But when you're sitting at your desk the light's behind you, so we can't see your face too well: it's remote, mysterious, masked. At the same time, we're half-blinded as we make our way into the Presence. Capital P. But things are going to get better, aren't they? As soon as you invite us to sit down, we can sink into all this plush upholstery and feel at our ease, right? Wrong. By the time we've done sinking, we're practically on the floor, while you're sitting up there like Washington on the monument, gazing down at us. We feel dominated.'

It's the SMS, Lorraine was thinking with a sudden access to understanding: the small man syndrome. They think *every* chair is higher than theirs, and they suffer. This is all it is.

'And that's okay,' Carl went on in his deliberate sing-song tone, 'if you actually want to dominate. A lot of top executives arrange their offices just this way. The thing is, I believe it wasn't your intention, when you changed the whole décor in here and moved the desk in front of the south window and had the dais built under it and chose this very low and very comfortable suite. And the bottom line is that while you've sat there wishing we'd come and talk to you about things every day, we've all been thinking up excuses not to. Doesn't that sound silly?'

'Yes.'

'Well it isn't.'

'I think you pick up these ideas from your therapist.' She got up and went behind her desk again, angry with him for treating her like this, like an idiot child who couldn't even get the alphabet right. 'I hoped you were going to tell me why you want to quit, instead of this load of –'

'Lorraine,' he cut in gently. 'You don't have to go back up there into the castle, just because you feel defenceless.'

22

Staring at him from behind her desk, she realised she could only see his head and shoulders, and that – yes – she felt easier sitting here, more confident. From here she could talk from a position of strength.

Okay, he was right. But there was another position of strength available to her, one that had never failed to reduce the power-level in a man right down to where she could handle him.

'This is a pretty weird game you want to play, Carl, but I'll go along.' She left her desk again and moved across to the long settee, using her hips under the perfectly-cut sheath dress with a studied grace, as she'd learned to do in front of the cameras. She then began counting his eye-blink rate as she sat down right beside him and gave him that stunning smile. 'Is this where you want me?'

His mouth had come open and for a moment he simply stared at her from behind his glasses; then he got up fast and began pacing like he was training for a marathon.

'Now you're acting like a whore.'

'I'm a *what*?' She stood up too, and just as fast.

'I didn't say you *were* a whore!'

'It was damn close!'

Now they were facing each other again in the sudden charged silence, staring each other down. Then he took a deep breath and shook his head slowly. 'Jesus, I've heard that being fired is a pretty traumatic experience, but it has to be better than resigning!' He went trudging off again, and now he looked genuinely beaten by the whole thing, at a loss to know what he should do next; and for the second time Lorraine allowed a chink of light to play on her mind, and let herself believe that his viewpoint might just be more valid than her own. But there was just one little point she wanted to clear up right now.

'Carl. When a man sits down next to me, I think he's just being friendly. But when I sit down next to a man, I'm acting like a whore. Right?'

He turned at the end of his run and gazed at her for a moment. 'No. It's just than when most women sit down next to a man they're just being – sure – friendly; but when *you* – I mean you *personally* –' he suddenly blew out some breath. 'Lorraine, let me put it this way. You may believe in all modesty that you're no different from most women. I have news for you. If you want to show how friendly you're trying to be, there are six or seven other places you could sit in this office, apart from behind your desk. I mean –' he was getting out of his depth a little – 'with looks and a body like – excuse me, a figure – like yours, there's a new element introduced when – what I'm trying to say is, this is a business office, so couldn't you try dressing the part? Maybe a nice severe two-piece suit that wouldn't – you know – accentuate the overall effect? For everyone's sake. I'm not the only one who –'

'Carl,' she said, and he broke off. 'I'm a woman. So I dress like a woman. And I don't ask you to put on a pretty silk blouse and high heels.'

'That's crazy! You –'

'Not really. You're just imposing double standards, that's all. But you didn't come in here to act like – and I am saying "act like" – a male chauvinist pig. You came to tell me why you want to quit, or at least I hope you did. You must have known I'd ask. So why don't you tell me?'

He began moving again, taking a swerve past her desk to grab some paper clips. 'You know you're almost out of these things?' He began playing with them. 'Everyone is. It's the same whoever I go to see.'

His face was perfectly straight but she knew he was making a joke to break the tension. 'I'll order a whole crate of them, Carl, with your name on.'

He gave a quick sigh. 'I appreciate that. Lorraine, I'm quitting because I don't see any future here for me. Or for any of us. It doesn't really concern me – or anyway, not too much – the fact that you're giving us a tough time by walling yourself up in a castle because you're a woman and you're the boss and you expect a lot of hostility and are maybe getting it. You're having to over-correct, that's all, and we understand that. My main reason for quitting – and if you don't mind, I prefer to call it "leaving" – is the condition of

24

the bottom line. It's flat. It's levelled out. No profits for this year, no progress. You know what it means when that little line stops jumping across the screen of the electro-cardiograph in the hospital and levels out? It means the patient's dead.'

He had said it quietly, but a dull shock went through her and she turned away, going to sit at the far end of the settee. He wasn't telling her anything she didn't know; she'd seen and heard the signs all over the office, in the annual report, in the interim figures and on the sales charts. He was simply the first to have put it into words, and he hadn't bothered to spare her feelings.

Looking up at him across the long bright room she asked steadily: 'Do you have a solution?'

'Sure. I'm getting out.'

She tried not to hate him for that.

'I meant a corporate solution. To save all of us, not just yourself.'

He shrugged casually. 'I'm a research man, Lorraine. I'm not a business consultant.' He went back to concentrate on his paper clips.

'All right, Carl. I apologise for keeping you.' She got up and went to one of the windows, standing with her back to it, facing him. 'And I wish you luck. Better luck than you've had at Floderus.'

It was one of those occasions when you said something so fast that you knew at once that you didn't even think of the words: they were out, and you couldn't take them back. Sometimes they were dangerous, but not now; they were just bitter, and her tone had been raw, echoing in the room.

'Sure,' he said, nodding, and dropped his paper clips onto the desk, going towards the door with that jerky trudge of his, lifting his hand to turn the handle, then dropping it, standing with his head down for a moment. 'A *corporate* solution?'

Lorraine waited, forcing herself to say nothing, while the words tried to break into the silence . . . *I don't want your corporate solutions, Carl. Just get out of here.*

But perhaps he wouldn't have heard her in any case; he

was shifting his feet, watching the carpet, lacing his fingers together and flexing them, lost in his thoughts. The buzzer sounded on her desk and she ignored it; when Carl had come in here she'd put the red light on above her door, and Maggie was ignoring it, as she usually did.

'I could suggest something.' Carl was looking up at her now, his stare steady behind the glasses.

'That I step down.'

'You think that might do some good?'

'It seems the obvious thing to do, doesn't it?'

He shook his head slowly. 'Who'd replace you?'

'Barry Corbett.'

His stare widened. 'Are you serious?'

'He was my father's partner.'

'He also has a drinking problem.'

She felt herself taking the shock again. This too was something she'd begun to suspect, but Carl was the first to have said it out loud.

'Dean Powers, then,' she said unsteadily.

Carl went on staring. 'All Dean can think of right now is just how many of the office girls he can screw.'

Her shoulders touched the window, and she realised she must have physically recoiled from him, from this new attack.

'I don't listen to rumours,' she said, but there was no conviction in her tone, and he would hear that. He was very bright, a very bright little bastard.

'Fine. Fine. Don't listen to what's happening out there, way down below the castle walls.' He didn't say it with any heat; it sounded like a throw-away line. 'But I don't think Dean Powers is quite the guy for the job. It isn't the kind of solution I'd want to come up with anyway. I mean this is your company, the whole damn thing, and it's been shoved on your lap and that's very tough, a very tough bequest on the part of your old man. He must have been crazy. He –'

'*Get out of here.*'

He shrugged. 'Sure. I guess I could have put it another way.' He turned to the door again. 'The only real solution I could suggest would be to create a new fragrance.'

26

The turnaround in his thinking made her dizzy for a while. First he said the company was dead and there was nobody who could set it on its feet again because they were drinking too much and screwing all the office girls, and now he said they should create a new fragrance, which would involve a hell of a lot more in terms of talent and money and effort and planning than putting a show on Broadway.

'I thought you said we were dead.'

'I did.'

'And that the executive force has gone to pieces.'

'Pretty well. And now I'm talking about a resurrection, and putting the pieces together again.'

'By creating a new fragrance. By taking a huge risk.'

He shook his head. 'By throwing out a challenge. Could be the people here have been going to pieces because they saw there wasn't any future. Give them a future they can go for, and things could be a lot different.'

She came away from the window, moving restlessly, not looking at him now, strangely aware that there were things she had to hide from him, and from herself. 'Carl, you're talking about two years' work, and five million dollars. At least. We can't afford to launch a new fragrance. We don't even want one. Picaresque is still selling, after all these years. *Sophistiqué* is still selling. So is *Oriflamme*. So is *Wildfire*.'

'Sure, they're still selling. They're just selling less and less, month after month. Ever since we changed the image. They were good fragrances, still are. Your father knew what he was doing. It doesn't mean you can't go out and do something better. You can break anyone's record if you try.'

She swung towards him. 'What makes you think I want to break my own father's?'

'Nothing. Nothing at all.' He took a step closer. 'I know that you don't. And I think that could be the problem, Lorraine. You're not going to get anywhere with this company till you've banished your father's ghost.'

She felt herself flinching, and caught her breath; Carl's face opened in surprise as he watched her, and his hand came out helplessly.

'I guess that was rather – ' he didn't finish.

'It was to the point, Carl.' She spoke very softly, as if at a graveside. 'That's okay. But I'd like you to go now.'

He gave a little shrug. 'Sure. I'll be in touch.' He tried to shut the door quietly, but even that didn't work out, and the sound made her flinch again, and she realised how raw the wounds still were, after all these months.

It had been, after all, what Katina Mercuris had called a double whammy, the first one starting the moment when the assistant director at the Golden State Studios had come looking for her in the commissariat while she was snatching a salad with Alan Pearson, the film editor. 'Lorraine,' the assistant director had said when he found her table, 'I need to talk to you.' She assumed he meant in private, so she stood up and he put an arm around her as he led her a little distance away and spoke quietly, close to her ear. 'There's been an accident, Lorraine, out at the airport.' She thought immediately of Bruce, her husband; but he didn't have any trip planned; he was at home, working. 'Your folks were flying in,' the assistant director said, 'and there – there was a bad landing.' As he went on talking he drew his arm tighter and tighter around her shoulders, so that when she passed out he managed to stop her falling.

As soon as she came to with the studio doctor splashing her face with cold water, she wanted to go there, to the airport, before she was ready to believe it. She'd known they were flying in; they hadn't seen her for six weeks because they'd been busy in New York and she'd been tied up with the movie, and she'd called them one night in the middle of the end-of-shooting party on the set and asked them if they'd like to see a rough-cut. It had been a surprise for them, because she hadn't told them how soon *Tango Bay* was going to be finished; and she'd realised later, among all the other things she'd been made to realise in a world that was suddenly spinning from under her, that they must have decided to surprise her in their turn by flying in to L.A. without telling her first.

She didn't call Bruce, her husband, to give him the news;

28

it wasn't anything that could be said coherently over a telephone, and he'd want to go with her to the airport; so she stopped off at their white Spanish-style house on Beverly Drive: she'd need, in any case, his arms around her when she told him, because it might make her pass out again. But that hadn't been possible, because instead of finding him in his study, writing his screen-play, she'd found him rolling around in the little palm court by the pool with Teresa Manning, the starlet they'd met two nights before at a dinner party; and the worst thing about it had been the merciless clarity of her memory for detail: she'd seen again, a hundred times, the girl's strapless sandals lying across the bed of petunias where she'd kicked them off in her hurry, and Bruce's expensive space-age watch hanging halfway off his wrist because the clip had come open in all the excitement, and the pale bikini-mark across Teresa's bronzed pelvis where his semen was still trickling because he'd withdrawn when he heard Lorraine's footsteps.

Nothing had seemed real anymore; it was like seeing one film cut by mistake into another, one about a woman rushing home to her husband for comfort in her grief, and another about the seamy side of Tinsel City, for showing on the blue movie circuit. There'd been a crazy kind of dialogue going through what was left of her mind: *Bruce, I hate to interrupt, but my parents have just been killed in a plane crash, so could you wipe that stuff off Teresa and drive to the airport with me?*

Two phrases, out of all the voluminous dialogue that had been spoken since that day, had remained hauntingly vivid in her memory. On the day when she and Bruce had gone to see the divorce attorney, Bruce had said ruefully, 'I'm truly sorry, Lorraine. I guess I got my timing wrong.' And Katina Mercuris, who had given her the only kind of support that could ever have got her through the post-synching sequences of *Tango Bay*, had said, 'After a double whammy like that, I just don't know how you survived.'

Today, staring at the door that Carl Blatt had shut with such a decisive little slam as he'd left her office, it occurred to her that there was still time for her not, finally, to survive.

29

CHAPTER 3

ANGELO BACCARI LOOKED down the length of his eight-inch Santa Ynez Emperadores Panatella with his dark eyes narrowed against the smoke. Through the smoke he watched the woman.

'Where did you find her?' he asked, without taking the cigar from his mouth.

'I didn't find her,' Tony said. 'She just walked in here.'

'Like that?'

'Like that.'

'Didn't she have a coat?'

'Yes,' Tony Marinello said. 'She checked it.'

Angelo fell silent again, watching the girl through the grey-blue tendrils of smoke. She had begun dancing now. Or at least throwing her slight, pale body around, the thin arms and the thinner legs trying to coordinate and achieve some kind of rhythm. She was dancing – if that was what it was – to the rhythm of the trio all right, but her body didn't seem to know where to go next. She was wearing a rag, and that was all; she'd kicked her shoes off. It was a rag, Angelo admitted to himself, made of white wild silk, and cut with such exquisite expertise that she looked more naked in it than had she been naked. It would weigh, that dress, maybe a dozen ounces. He could hide it, probably, in one fist.

The two men sat in the gloom of the corner, where the glow from the rose-red lampshades didn't reach. This particular corner of this particular room (there were other rooms here at the club,) was reserved for Angelo Baccari, and Tony Marinello usually sat with him here during the early hours of the night; from here they could see the small spotlit stage, the trio playing just this side of the curtains, and the entrance door, where members would be coming in every night, or just some nights, who would expect a personal welcome. If they were important, they would receive it from Tony; if they were very important, or perhaps dangerous, Angelo Baccari himself would rise and walk across the centre floor with the jewelled cufflinks flashing at his wrists and his wide shoulders swinging slightly as his tapering legs and tiny feet took him in a gliding motion towards the newcomer, whom he would greet with such massive charm that even the most important, or perhaps the most dangerous, would feel it had been a good decision to come here tonight.

The Lotus Club didn't fall easily within the otherwise well-defined parameters of the New-York-by-night scene. This wasn't Elaine's, where you would find Dick Cavett sitting sometimes at the bar, or Woody Allen, or Gay Talese; at Elaine's, if Jackie Onassis walked in, people would make a point of not seeing her, because that was why some of them were there: to be seen not seeing Jackie. If she were ever to walk into the Lotus Club, the music would stop dead. It was unlikely she would ever walk into the Lotus Club.

Yet it had its own particular *chic*. This wasn't Studio 54, or the Red Parrot, or Le Cirque; nobody came here who could be considered as Art, Hamptons, Rich-Foreigner, Young-Wasp or Old-Money. But the place had an atmosphere that was on the surface what could be called low-key elegant: quiet rich carpeting, beautiful lamps, flock wallpaper and discreet touches of gilt. It was beneath the surface where was to be found – or left alone, as preferred – the particular brand of chic the Lotus Club possessed. It could be called an undertone of discretion. People came here when they didn't want to be 'seen' by the smart-crowd spectator buffs; they didn't want to be introduced to another member unless they asked Angelo to do so; and even then of course 'the Angel' would need first to go to the other party and find out if *they* wanted to be introduced. No names were named at the Lotus; there was no gossip, no scandal. If a member were unable to pay his fees, his name would be removed from the list, and that was all; no one would ask what had happened to him, and if they did, they would not be told.

This degree of discretion would be fitting to the finest clubs in the world – White's, even, of London, or the Savage. What gave the Lotus its special ambience was that many of its members lived their lives so close to unlawfulness that the club had become a kind of refuge, not only for the survivors of minor bank crashes but for congressmen under the threat of investigation and real-estate brokers fleeing from the wilderness they had been trying to pass off as rich mineral land.

The Lotus Club, then, was honest in the pursuit of its intentions, which were to provide a meeting place or a hiding place for those of the world who felt the need to mingle with their kind and find strength in the knowledge that they were not alone. At $3,500 per year the fees were not rapaciously high; the address, on the Upper East Side, was respectable; and the service was quietly efficient. The worse thing anyone could say about the Lotus Club was that it was going broke.

'What's her name?' Angelo asked.

'I don't know,' Tony shrugged.

'She a guest of someone?'

'Could be.'

'She high?'

'Could be.'

Tony Marellino watched the girl more attentively. When the Angel asked questions, there had to be answers, and when Tony said 'Could be,' he meant he'd find out. He was a very good manager, and it wasn't his fault that in the last year or two the membership had been falling off; part of the reason was that quite a lot of the members had been arrested.

'That face,' Angelo said.

'Sure. That face.' Tony, six-foot-three and with his exprize-fighter's muscles still in place, shifted his position in the gilt-and-plush chair so that he could concentrate better. The girl looked small and fragile, with a head that was a fraction too large, so that it gave her the look of a china doll; her skin was alabaster pale, with blue shadows under the jaw and under the arms; her eyes were very big, accentuated by lots of mascara, so that the irises and pupils were half-lost in darkness; but even from this distance the two men could see they were violet: a pale, shimmering violet. She was doing what looked like the Charleston.

'Get George over here,' Angelo said.

Tony came back with the doorman. 'Who is that dancing?' Angelo asked him without looking away from her.

'She said her name was Madlen, Mr Baccari. She didn't have a card.'

'Why did you let her in here?'

'She said she was meeting Senator Williams here, eleven o'clock, Mr Baccari.'

'I see. And who is Senator Williams?'

'I guessed he was a member.'

'You guessed he was a member. I see.' Angelo went on watching the girl, who was now loosening the stringy satin shoulder-straps of her dress as she went on dancing the Charleston, or whatever it was.

'What kind of coat did she check, George?'

'Mink, Mr Baccari. Beautiful.'

'I see. Thank you, that's all.'

When the doorman had left them, Angelo said: 'Tony, go and look at the coat. You're an expert.'

While Tony was gone, the dress of the girl with the violet eyes began slipping lower across her pointed little breasts, and Angelo beckoned to one of the waitresses.

'Yes, Mr Baccari?'

'Just stand here, Yvette. I may need you.'

Over at the long mirrored bar the talk had fallen off and people were turning on their stools to watch the dancer. The trio was playing a bit louder now, maybe thinking they could

33

keep the attention of the members and their guests on the music alone.

Tony came back and said: 'Not mink. It's prime sable. Worth around a hundred thousand dollars.'

'I see,' Angelo said, watching the fragile china doll who was dancing. Her name probably wasn't what the doorman said it was, or what she said it was. Most people carried a card. And there wasn't any member here by the name of Senator Williams, though it was a title impressive enough for a man like George to take for granted. What kind of club was it where the man at the door let in strangers, just because they wore sable and looked exquisite and dropped the name of a senator? It was outrageous.

'Tony,' Angelo said as the white scrap of a dress reached the girl's hips and left her small sharp breasts bobbing under the spotlights, 'I want you to do two things for me. Tell George he's fired, and take Yvette over there and get Lady Godiva behind the curtains. Then I want to talk to her.'

She'd been having such a good time.

'But I like this place!'

'That's nice,' the big man said, 'but it's for members only.' He smelt richly of cigars and cologne. He looked a very strong man. She liked strong men. Sometimes.

'Look,' she said, 'I can dress myself.' The girl was still pulling at the shoulder straps.

'Okay, honey. That's a real pretty dress.'

Madlen got the straps right and began dancing again, though the music had stopped now. She took three steps towards the gap in the curtains and felt a hand on her, but she shook it off and ran onto the little stage, spinning and whirling to a music of her own, watching the lights go swinging across the shadows till they were like a great big carousel; and she sang to them, not with any words, just a kind of crying like the Indians did, no words but a lot of meaning, a lot of soul. Some people had begun clapping.

'*Get her into a cab,*' someone was saying.

'No,' the big man said. She knew his voice now; it was

34

deep and strong, but quiet; she could hear it below the song she was singing, like a bass accompaniment. 'Just get her into my office.'

The carousel went whirling around and around and she whirled with it, weightless, flying on the air with her dress floating up around her like leaping water. She was having an absolutely *fantastic* time.

Then someone was holding her arm again and the man was waving to the people and saying she was great, wasn't she, but she had to go now, and they started laughing, and the music began again while she brought her hand with a loud crack across the man's face, and the music played a lot louder and the laughter was fading out and she was suddenly off the floor, lying in the big man's arms and swaying along as he walked her through the curtains.

'*I can walk, for God's sake!*' She tried to hit him again but he'd got her arms caught. Along a passage with rose-and-gold lamps and into a room with the tall man and the girl shutting the door; then the big man put her down and gave her a little push and she fell into a deep comfortable chair with the breath knocked out of her and the pain starting again, not in her head or her stomach but everywhere, not really in her body at all but everywhere around her, closing in all the time.

'I'm stoned,' she said.

'I know.'

She shut her eyes.

'Who's Senator Williams?' the big man asked her.

'A friend.' Stuffy old bastard she'd met in Washington; he'd tried to make her at a dinner party, well not *at* the dinner party but afterwards in the library, *in the library*, Jesus Christ that was how stuffy the old bastard was.

'Is he a member here, Madlen?'

She opened her eyes. 'How d'you know my name?'

'Mine's Angelo,' he said. He was sitting behind a desk, looking very composed, like a judge. 'This is my club.' He glanced up and away from her, saying quietly, 'We're okay now.'

The tall man and the girl went out.

'I like it here,' she told Angelo. 'It's a great place.'

'Thank you. What made you come in here?'

'I was lost.'

He watched her attentively. He looked a nice man.

'Couldn't find your way home?'

'This is home,' she said. 'I mean, anywhere is. I was having a fantastic time, and now you've spoiled it all and I'm lost again.'

'You're lost again. I see.' He had a calm face, and a faint, kind of accommodating smile behind his deep brown eyes. He looked like a wrestler, but well-dressed. She wasn't stoned. Or not that much. She'd just hit a high, dancing. But if he told her to leave here she'd be lost again. Nobody wanted her, or they wanted her in wrong ways.

'Like me to call your husband, Madlen?'

'No husband.'

'Your folks, then.'

Everything slammed in on her like a sea-wave and she blacked out. Then he was standing over her, holding one of her hands.

'Are you okay?'

'What?' She got him into focus again. 'Yes.'

'I'll have somebody see you home, Madlen.'

'This is home. Let me stay a little.'

They were sitting not far from the corner table reserved for Angelo, but here there was more light. They were sipping champagne. The girl had brought her small gold sandals, but she hadn't put them on.

'I like dancing,' she said.

'You dance very well.'

'I'd like to dance here. I wouldn't want money.'

What she wanted, Angelo thought contemplatively, was to draw attention to herself. The question was, why? It could be an interesting answer; Angelo often found the most uninteresting questions sometimes had interesting answers, if you were listening.

36

'We just have a singer,' he said. Watching her closely in the soft light he thought how exquisite she was, with her pale skin and large eyes and delicate mouth; he would very much like to lay her, but didn't believe there was any chance of that; the kind of woman who'd start taking her clothes off in public wouldn't be interested in sex; or more correctly, that would be her sex act: to be looked at, but not touched. Also, there was that look in her eyes that warned him off, or that non-look, that sudden emptiness that came there when she wasn't talking, and wasn't listening; the first time he'd seen it, he'd shivered; it had been scary. There wasn't any sex in those eyes, or much life; she was something she switched on and off. 'We don't have a dancer,' he said. 'That's for a different kind of place. Younger crowd.'

'What am I doing here?'

'Uh, you kind of wandered in, I guess. Now we're having a nice drink together.' He tried again. 'You live near here?'

'I don't live anywhere.'

'Okay. A lot of us don't. That's why we have clubs. But what's your address?'

'It's not far from here. Can I have some more champagne, Angelus?'

'Angelo. Sure.'

He beckoned a girl over and they started on another bottle of Cristal Roederer Brut, and he asked her what she did in her life and she said she'd done some modelling and 'a few things'. He couldn't place her: she wasn't a hustler or a whore or just a good-time girl – the fantastic time she'd said she was having was just in her mind, just a way of proving to herself she wasn't really lost. Running away from a messy divorce? From home? She didn't look more than twenty-two, could even be a virgin. At this thought, Angelo felt the blood going right to the spot and the muscle begin to move; he'd always had this thing about them, maybe because there weren't too many left.

He ordered a third bottle, because she was holding her liquor too well to answer his questions, and halfway through the third bottle she warmed up suddenly and took off and before he could do anything she was on the table with the bottle in her hand, spinning round and round in tight circles with her rag of a dress flying up around her naked hips and her head thrown back in a peal of laughter that sent the hairs rising on his scalp. One of the girls was hurrying over but couldn't get close enough because the champagne bottle was swinging in a series of lethal arcs as Madlen brought it low and swung it high again and low again, its weight and centrifugal force balancing her own slight weight as she leaned back from it; then it flew from her hand and Angelo caught her as the bottle crashed into a mirror and some of the women screamed and Tony came up at a run, while for an instant Angelo found himself holding the girl like a child, naked from the waist down with the dress caught round her and her legs kicking and twisting as she tried to escape.

By the time they got her outside she was burned out again, and just said that was her car over there, the black Ferrari with the gold bumpers. Tony brought her coat and they got her into it; the night was cold and she was shivering, though mostly with nerves.

'Just tell me the address,' Angelo said as he got behind the thin stitched-leather covered steering-wheel and looked for the button to roll the seat back so that he could get his chin off his knees.

'Keys?' he asked her.

'Where are you taking me?' She was curled up facing him with her shoulders against the other door panel; the sable coat had fallen open and the wisp of a dress was gathered around her thighs; her legs were together and she was barefoot again, having kicked off the small gold sandals when they'd dumped her into the car. She looked like an orphan abandoned on somebody's doorstep, with her large violet eyes watching him with a kind of wonder. He didn't know whether it was all a deliberate act or whether she was some kind of natural innocent that the world had left far, far behind; but he knew at least that if this chick were an orphan she'd done pretty well to land up in a hundred-thousand-dollar sable coat on the doorstep of a hundred-thousand-

38

dollar Ferrari with gold bumpers and pigskin upholstery and brushed nickel fittings.

'I'm taking you home,' he said. 'If you have the keys.'

'They're in there.' She pointed to the padded glove pocket on the central console and he slipped it open.

'You always leave the keys in the car, and the car unlocked, Madlen?'

'Why not?'

'You know,' he said as he looked away from her body and put the keys into the ignition and started the engine, 'you shouldn't go around on your own. There are some funny people in this city.' He was one of them, and he just wanted to get this doll safe home before the nature boy in him broke through the thin skin of social consciousness and drove her straight to the nearest park and ate her all up like a triple-cream fudge-ripple sundæ.

'I can take care of myself,' she said.

'Sure, but you know what I mean.' He glanced down at her as the car surged forward into the traffic, and found himself looking into the barrel of a 9mm Browning Renaissance model with decorative tooling. 'Right,' he said, 'I guess you know what I mean.' His voice had become suddenly gentle, even – he hoped – soothing. He'd stopped thinking about taking her to a park and eating her all up; he was now thinking he might be lucky to get out of this car on his own two feet before this Kewpie doll psychotic blew his brains all over the pigskin upholstery and had to get them scraped off at an all-night car wash.

'I live in Sutton Place,' she said, sliding the gun back under the seat. 'Do you know where that is?'

'Five minutes away. Forgive a personal question, Madlen, but do you have a licence for that piece?'

'Do you have to have licences?'

'I think the Police Department feels more comfortable, yes.' He turned right onto 54th Street and lifted his foot off the throttle again; by the feel of the engine under the long sleek hood it could push this gold-plated barouche right up the side of a building without losing speed if he cared to hit

39

the juice. 'You could probably get a licence,' he said, 'if you could prove you were – say – extremely rich and sometimes threatened by kidnap attempts, that kind of thing.'

'What would you call "extremely"?'

'Uh, well, with a coat like that and a car like this and a Sutton Place address, you know, I'd say that's getting kind of extreme.'

She gave a delicate belch of champagne bubbles. 'I think it'd be less hassle to shoot first and get a licence afterwards, don't you?'

'They might turn down the application.'

She giggled melodiously and then gave him the name of her apartment building, and when he stopped at the entrance to the garage she told him: 'I'll have the attendant call you a cab.'

'That's okay. Tony followed me up here.'

She looked behind and saw a bronze-tone Cadillac standing at the kerbside. 'Oh.' She didn't make a move to get out, so he said: 'We'll wait till the attendant comes.'

'I can park it myself.' Her voice had gone suddenly flat, with an undertone that was deadly serious. 'I didn't behave very well tonight, did I? I want to apologise.' She opened the glove pocket and gave him a card. 'Tell me how much I owe for whatever I broke, when you get the bill. I owe you for something else, too. I was lost, you see. I mean really. It happens sometimes.' Her eyes were set as she gazed at him in the shadows, their brightness catching the light from the street. 'I walked in there because it was a doorway, and I knew there'd be lots of people inside. Thank you for not throwing me out right away. If you had, I would've just gone on driving, into the East River.'

CHAPTER 4

THREE MILES AWAY, northwards along the River, Lorraine Floderus stood at a window of her apartment and looked across the trees of Central Park, a mass of black winter twigs under moonlight.

'Do you like *this* one . . . or *this* one?'

The echo of her father's voice was so clear to her in the silent room that she started, and looked around. But there were just the shadows. After Tilly had cleared the dinner table and taken the two brandy glasses from near the hearth, Lorraine had turned off the lights and let the moon's rays flood in through the windows and silver everything, and leave these shadows.

'This one?' Her father's face, at that time, through her child's eyes, had been possessed of an impishness more suitable to a gnome, or a wizard; the wrinkles ran upwards from his raised, questioning brows almost to the top of his head, for even at his young age then he'd been almost bald; his dark eyes had glittered with mischief as he held up the three little phials. 'Or *this* one?'

She had sniffed at each of them in turn, saying they were all lovely, and asking him were they for her to keep. They were much the same colour, a pale amber that held up to the light in his thin sensitive fingers looked like liquid gold; the phials were of clear glass, and nothing to look at; but each had a coloured ribbon wound around the neck: green, blue and yellow.

'Yes, you can keep them. But first you must tell me which is the *best*.' He had taken the dropper and touched her hand

41

with it, just below the wrist. *This* one?'

She'd wanted to say, again, that they were all lovely, because they were. They smelt like flowers, but different ones. And then, because they wouldn't be hers to keep unless she did what he wanted, she began comparing them, while the wizard took the droppers and touched her with them, making his magic; and it wasn't long before she kept coming back to *this* one, in the phial with the blue ribbon.

'You're sure?'

'Oh, yes! *This* one!'

His smile spread over all his long and pointed face, and she had flung her small arms around him because it was the kindest face she had ever seen in the whole world.

It still was, as she remembered it; and somewhere, in a sealed box at the back of a cupboard, or perhaps high on a shelf in her dressing room – she couldn't remember for the moment – there were dozens of those small colour-coded phials, the first essays from the laboratory he had set up with 'Uncle' Barry.

Looking back on her childhood, over this past year (when it had become desperately necessary to look back and question so many things and try anew to find her place in them), she had realised how much she must have disappointed him. Here he was, bringing the essences of his own creation to touch her with their spell and leave her small room heady with the scent of flowers, and all her young passion was devoted year by year to a different kind of world which didn't in fact exist outside of the movie theatres. She received his gifts in great excitement, partly because they were from him and partly because they were magical in themselves, in their miniature and mysterious bottles; but there it had stopped. She never wanted to know why he made these wonderful fragrances, when you could simply go out to a store and buy them, in bigger bottles. Then, when she was old enough to know that he'd also made those too, she was for a time impressed; but the first time she'd been taken to the Floderus Laboratory and shown around it, all she'd seen were benches and tanks and retorts and what seemed to be miles of tubing, and gone home disillusioned; it was as if all that magic of the secret bottles, lit and made potent by her father's smile in the glow of the night-light by her bed, had suddenly vanished, explained away by workaday chemistry.

Looking back . . . again and again during this year of desolation . . . she had realised how traumatic that day had been for both of them, when her father's shining pride in showing her the very home of his creations had been dashed by her disinterest, and when for her the magic of her childhood had been reduced to the mechanics of an ugly factory. At the time, he was too careful not to show his hurt, and she was too young to understand her own loss of innocence. Later, it would have embarrassed them both to talk about it. But that had been the turning point, when she'd begun to do no more than admire his talent and success and talk about it with great pride among her friends, without any longer being touched by it. The night-light had gone from beside her bed, and she became old enough to kiss her father goodnight downstairs, the men among his dinner guests standing as she left the room; and the last of the little phials, their magic distillations corked tight and never to be opened again, had joined the others in the sealed box, at childhood's end.

'Grief,' Barry Corbett had told her after the memorial service, 'is mostly regret, and especially regret for all those things we didn't do, and didn't understand. Part of grief, too, is what we see as a bad conscience, so we can blame ourselves, and feel better. So blame yourself all you want.' The big car had wound its way through smooth lawns and theatrically-grouped pine trees, carrying her away from the past. 'But they both knew how much you loved them, and that's all that really matters.'

'I should have taken more interest in his work.' She could still remember the ball of soaked Kleenex bunched in her chilled hand, and the swinging motion of the car. 'I should have realised what a beautiful thing he was doing, creating perfume. I should have gone into the company, instead of hamming my way through Hollywood and thinking it was something real.'

'We should all have done a whole lot of things, Lorrie. And we didn't. And that's good, because they wouldn't have wanted us to change our lives and live in the shadow of theirs.'

He'd gone on like that, trying to make it easier for her, possible to bear, with his strong arm around her and the lapel of his black suit-coat sharp under her cheek as she'd lain against him, her eyes shut and the tops of the pines swishing past the lowered windows.

Two days later she'd known what she had to do. Walking with Barry in Central Park under the bare winter trees she'd told him: 'He knew that one day I'd wake up to it all, and want to get involved. When I was old enough, or when . . . something happened to . . . shake me into my senses. That's why he left the company to me, and I'm going to take it over and run it with all the love and all the dedication I should have given it before.'

That had been a year ago, and tonight Barry had said with a heart-stilling directness: 'It was a mistake.'

He'd wanted to talk to her at the office, earlier; but after Carl Blatt's visit she'd been too fearful to risk facing another shock of the same kind. So she'd asked him if they could talk over dinner tonight, at her apartment – with Virginia, of course. He agreed to come, but would leave Ginnie at home and in peace, since this was business. Before leaving the office she'd steeled herself and called Carl Blatt, asking him if he'd consider staying on for a day or two while 'everything got sorted out.' After a long silence on the line he'd said yes, he would.

Across the dinner table, decked out by Tilly in pink and silver with two tall candles burning, she'd asked Barry: 'You mean it was a mistake for me to take over Floderus?'

He reflected, as he always did with an important question, his right hand curled around his glass of bourbon, his eyes lowered and his head on one side. 'A mistake on your father's part, Lorrie. I see why he wanted you to have the company, to keep it in the family – what's left of it. But he was asking too much of you. You'd no training in business management, no experience, no background in office politics – '

'But a fair degree of guts and enthusiasm and determination – ' she broke off, not wanting to hurt him. And anyway she was talking nonsense; her sudden anger was only a cover-up for her sense of failure.

'Oh, right,' he said, 'right,' looking up at her and nodding slowly, 'all of those things, yes. And they're all necessary to the chief executive officer of a substantial company – on top of all those things you didn't have – couldn't have.'

'You helped me, at first. You all did. Helped to train me, gave me what amounted to a crash course in management.'

'Right,' he said, nodding again, 'that's right. And a lot of it got through to you. At the end of this first year, you're not bad, not bad at all.'

'Just,' she said bitterly, 'not good enough.'

He looked down again, and she realised how stupid it was of her to go on driving him into corners like this, goading him to come out with the naked truth when she knew what it was already.

'You know something?' he said in a moment, and lifted the slender glass of Pouilly-Fuissé that he hadn't yet touched. 'That dear Tilly of yours cooked us such a beautiful dinner, and we're not even started on it. Here's to her.'

She drank some wine with him, and watched his hand go back to curl around the glass of bourbon. Wine wasn't his drink; this was the fourth straight shot he'd poured for himself since he'd come here an hour ago. *He has a drinking problem*, Carl had told her earlier today, and now the thought came to her, like a sudden shift in the scenery: *How much has it contributed to the mess the company's in? Has it really been all my doing?*

They fell to small talk before the food got cold: Tilly had produced sautéed scallops, with spinach and saffron sauce, baked in skillets and brought to the table on a pedestal hot-plate, maybe knowing that with Mr Corbett here there'd be

45

a lot of shop talk going on. As they toyed later with the lime sherbet splashed with Kirsch, Lorraine found herself watching the man opposite her, once the beloved 'uncle' and now one of her fellow-adults in an adult world where life was frighteningly real. In the candlelight he looked like a traditional Father Christmas without the hood and whiskers; his face, russet-red and rounded and benevolent, was topped with a mass of curly hair that left a boyishness in his looks, though it was prematurely grey – in the glow of the candle flames, almost silver. She had never, she realised, seen this man angered, or anxious, even very surprised. In surprise, his eyes would show nothing, except perhaps sudden interest, while his brows would be raised and he'd become still, watching, listening, not commenting until he felt he'd heard enough to know what had to be said. It was as if all the surprises in his life had already been faced and dealt with, leaving only the need to study them again in a new light.

Lorraine had never seen him shaken – as she had been today – or heard his voice raised in argument or protest. These things she'd always admired in him, but tonight, when she felt the world had begun spinning faster and faster to fling her across unseen horizons, she knew she must start asking questions, of herself and other people – and they were frightening ones. First: these qualities in Barry Corbett – his unsurprisability, his philosophical acceptance of things, his absence of anger – were they really strengths, or weaknesses? Didn't one need sometimes to be roused, to protest, yell at people to convince them, to sway them, to show them where they were wrong? Wasn't surprise a trigger to action?

And more specifically: in this past year, how much of Barry's own deep grief had led him into a mood of defeat, of not wanting to try any more, now that the company's inspired captaincy was lost to him?

'That was excellent, my dear,' he was saying suddenly, 'and what a good idea to spend the evening here instead of at some noisy restaurant, where one can't really talk!'

'I'm sorry Ginnie couldn't join us,' she smiled, and rang the bell for Tilly to take the things away while they went into the drawing-rom. 'Would you like some brandy?'

'That would be very nice.'

'Pour some for me, Barry.'

'With great pleasure.'

And then, as they sat near the long stone hearth where there were logs glowing, she said: 'Tell me the worst.'

'They're asking for a meeting,' he said after his usual pause. 'Dean, Carl, the others. The board wants you to step down.'

In the silence her memory played a trick, flashing a scene of years ago before her eyes: a small girl with a bandaged hand, climbing to a man's knee for comfort. 'By golly,' he was saying, 'it looks as if you've been in battle, young lady. And it looks as if you won out, because I don't see anyone else around here.' And now the same man sat here, staring into his brandy glass while she absorbed the thought that this time, after her year-long battle, she'd lost. And she couldn't climb on anyone's knee, ever again.

'You, too?' she asked him with her voice as steady as she could make it. 'Do you want me to step down?'

'No.' He added quickly, to allay any false hopes: 'There's no one to take your place.'

She touched his arm. 'But you started this company, with Dad. You worked together for all those years.'

'That's right,' he nodded slowly. 'Too many years, Lorrie. I'm an old man now, for a job like that. It's a fast track out there, and the new people are coming up on the inside, with an awful lot of steam to spare. Mine's running out.'

'But – ' she tried to think how to counter this, how to reassure him, support him; but tonight was a time for reality, for hard truths. Barry was nudging sixty, and he'd been a workaholic for as long as she'd known him. Now he was a burnout, hitting the bottle. Face it.

'You and Dad made Floderus,' she said, 'but I can understand how much you need a rest from it all. What

47

about Dean for CEO, if I stepped down?'

He looked up at her with his head angled wrily. 'Dean's suffering. He got divorced three months ago, and he's still suffering.'

'Divorced?'

'Right.'

'I didn't know.'

He left it, shrugging; and she knew what he'd decided not to say: that any chairman who didn't know that a senior executive had recently got divorced wasn't paying enough attention.

'Carl Blatt?' she asked him.

'Carl is research, not management.' He drained the balloon glass, putting it down beside the hearth. 'There's no one, Lorrie, who can take your father's place. He was the energy of Floderus Inc, the inspiration and the guide, *le grand patron*. He's irreplaceable, at least from within the company.'

She felt herself shiver.

'Go on,' she said.

He swung his head up again to look at her, but failed at the last moment to meet her eyes. 'How shall I say it, Lorrie?'

'There's only one way to say it. You think we should sell out.'

'Right,' he said quietly, 'that's right.'

He had left soon afterwards. There hadn't been time, tonight, to talk about anything so climactic. It would take days, weeks of deliberation and turbulent meetings to reach the final decison on how best, how least painfully, to put Floderus Incoporated on the block.

'Tilly?'

She thought she'd heard a sound, deeper in the apartment, and went to the hallway and then the kitchen, only now remembering that tonight was Friday and that Tilly had left them talking without disturbing them, to take what was left of her night off. The place had that silence about it that told Lorraine she was alone. But what would

48

she have said to Tilly anyway? She could only have asked about her mother, or the pap test she'd taken three days ago, or whether the young man who had dated her three times in the past month was serious about her or simply taking advantage. Lorraine couldn't have said to her: 'Tilly, I've come to the end of the worst year of my whole life, and I don't know what to do, or how to start up again, or where. Can I share my thoughts with you?'

Tilly had her own problems, and would have started worrying over Lorraine's as well.

Coming back to the drawing-room Lorraine passed a telephone and thought of picking it up; this was a time when you called close friends, to say, 'Listen darling, the bottom's just dropped out of everything; can I come over for a drink, or will you come here?' But there was nobody she knew who would understand that she wasn't only going to lose a business company, but also something her father had brought to life and nurtured and set on its feet in his own pround name – and in hers. Friends could only give her sympathy, and she wanted none, deserved none.

But she couldn't stay here in an empty apartment, prey to a sleepless night. She must seek the one refuge open to those who were truly alone: the company of strangers. Tonight New York City had started relaxing, swinging into its weekend spree in the bars and restaurants and nightclubs; it was a city where, surely to God, you'd never have to be really alone.

She lifted the telephone and dialled.

'Is that Frank?' Even as she asked, she caught the time on the rosewood clock by the door. It was past eleven.

'Yes, ma'am.'

'Frank, I've just realised how late it is, I'm sorry.'

'If you'd like me to drive you anywhere, Miss Floderus, I can come round straight away.'

'No, I'll get a taxi, really.'

'On a Friday night? I'd best come round, ma'am.'

Lorraine hesitated. She didn't even know where she wanted to go. Maybe the Village, get lost among the artist crowd and find a café, people to talk to. 'Well, that's very kind of you Frank. I'll wait for you.'

He'd be here in less than ten minutes, but that was long enough to peel off the Victor Costa taffeta gown she'd worn for Barry and slip into jeans and a woollen sweater. She was in the hallway, a soft deerskin bag slung at her shoulder, when Frank was announced over the security phone and a minute later rang the bell. He was in uniform.

The long, smoke-grey Lincoln was waiting at the kerbside with the garage attendant keeping watch over it. Frank closed the rear door and got behind the wheel.

'Where to, ma'am?'

'Greenwich Village. And Frank, don't go past the office. Take Madison.'

'Madison, right.' His blue eyes flicked to the mirror, and she noticed.

'I – I guess I've seen enough of it for this week,' she said lightly.

'Yes, ma'am.'

Along Madison Avenue the lights flowed in a never-ending rainbow from block to block as the evening pleasure-hour traffic carried people to the restaurants and clubs and movie houses; limos slid in towards the lighted marquees, and for a moment the flash of a white shirt and the glow of a long dress passed across the sidewalk into the warm foyers; at the corners chestnut vendors stood flapping their arms and blowing out cloudy breath as passers-by stopped to dive for change and go on their way poking their hands into brown bags, turning to each other and laughing as they burned their fingers.

Lorraine had never felt so desolate.

'Everyone looks so happy tonight,' she said without thinking; the glass division was down and the chauffeur half-turned his head.

'It's Friday,' he smiled.

'Of course. What do you do with your week-ends, Frank?'

'I've got a small cabin, ma'am, up in the hills.'

They waited for the signals at 48th Street, and for a

moment she expected him to make a left, to the office; then she tried to get it out of her mind again. It was Friday, yes . . . Didn't she deserve some time off too?

'That sounds lovely,' she said. 'You take a fishing rod, things like that?'

The signals changed, and the limousine surged effortlessly across the intersection. 'I listen to music, quite a bit,' Frank told her. 'And watch the stars. There's a small telescope there.'

'You always go there alone?'

It wasn't her business; she was just desperate for the sound of another human voice.

'Sometimes I take a girl.'

'For you, that wouldn't be difficult.'

She saw his eyes flick to the mirror and down again. 'I don't know, ma'am.'

The morning's fantasy was back in her mind suddenly, the unreal idea of just driving on with this man, out of the city, out of the crowds, to some green place where there was peace.

She leaned forward, almost without thinking. 'This weekend, Frank, take me.'

CHAPTER 5

JUST BEFORE 9pm Pacific Standard Time, the cabin crew went aboard TWA Flight 204 at Los Angeles International Airport and began setting up the galleys. Donna Shapiro, described in the personnel records as *White Female, age 25, 5' 5", 121 lbs, single, Type A personality, 4 yrs domestic experience*, slung her flight bag off her shoulder and checked her hair in the narrow mirror at the end of the first-class galley.

'Then where is she?'

'Just late, I hope.'

'That's all we wanted.'

Nora Vincent, on this flight working Coach, squeezed past an empty cart and vanished aft as another girl came at a half-run through the jetway, took a left and halted sharply.

'That's the flight deck,' Donna told her.

'Oh.'

'Who are you?'

'Marianne.' She slung her bag and stowed it. 'Are you Donna?'

'That's right.'

'They told me about you.'

'Don't let it phase you. Are you replacing Joan?'

'I guess. I'm newly graduated.' She gave a quick scared grin.

'Terrific,' said Donna with her heart sinking. 'Just do as I do, but don't do it better; it gives me hives. Where's your base, Marianne?'

'New York.'

'Me too. You can't have everything.' She flashed a very white grin and saw the kid relax; then she checked the water and pressure gauges, turned on the bunwarmers and plugged in the tray cart holding ovens. 'Are those in freeze mode?'

'Are they in – oh. Oh, right.' The tall, thin blonde probationer checked the freezers above the ovens. 'Yes. In freeze.'

'Okay. I want you to – ' she broke off as another flight attendant came in from the jetway with two bags and a folding umbrella.

'Where's Joan?' she asked Donna.

'Pregnant.'

'That has to be Rick.'

'Better tell her.'

'Okay,' Donna turned back to Marianne, 'I want you to check the oven cavities, make sure there aren't any quartz rods broken. Then check that we have four serving carts and tops.' She'd seen them already, but she wanted to get the kid busy and take her mind off her first-flight nerves. 'The crew meals are going into the tray cart under Bay number 4, okay?'

'Yes.'

Donna took a couple of seconds off to see how the girl was doing. It looked like she was dancing. 'Done some modelling, Marianne?'

'Three years,' she called over her shoulder as she checked the ovens.

'Not hard enough on the feet for you?' She took the clipboard down and ran her eyes over the menu and wine list, then got out the entrée preference forms. 'Okay, you can take A Zone Right, Marianne. That'll leave me to help the pax as they come aboard in – ' she checked her watch – 'forty-five minutes from now. You get any problems, give them to me.'

'Any I can't handle myself.'

Donna threw the blonde girl an appreciative glance. 'Good for you, champ.'

53

One hour and thirty minutes later, when Flight 204 was heading steadily east at thirty-thousand feet over Oklahoma, Donna slipped one of the menus into her flight bag for Dad; he was a short-order cook at a Krazy Kitchen chain café in Queen's, and his personal dream world was lovingly filed away in the album of flight menus Donna had started for him four years ago. Tonight's edition, she thought, rated a full five stars.

APPETIZER

MELON AND PROSCIUTTO
Wedges of fresh cantaloupe with slices of Prosciutto Ham garnished with a lemon wedge.

TERESA SALAD
Fresh garden vegetables are lightly tossed with lettuce and then
garnished with tomato wedges. Offered with our own creamy Parmesan cheese dressing.

A SELECTION OF OVEN-WARMED BREADS SERVED WITH BUTTER.

ENTRÉE SELECTION

CHICKEN BREAST ZOUAVE

FILET OF FLOUNDER MEUNIÈRE

A boneless breast of chicken roasted then simmered in a lightly flavoured tarragon sauce.

A delicate filet sautéed in butter and enriched with minced herbs.

NEW YORK STRIP SIRLOIN
A choice strip sirloin broiled to perfection and seasoned with Marchand de Vin butter.

FROM OUR DESSERT CART

ICE CREAM FESTIVAL
*French vanilla ice cream with your choice of
strawberry or hot fudge topping, and chopped walnuts.
Or enjoy your favourite cordial over ice cream.*

The wine selected was a California Brut Champagne from
Hanns Kornell Champagne Cellars, St Helena.

There had only been four complaints. Mrs George
Harland had ordered a vegetarian meal before the flight,
and it hadn't gone through; the two youngsters at the rear of
the compartment had seen the movie twice already; Mrs
Adelaide Jones, travelling with her husband, said with a
certain hesitation that the champagne was flat (from which
Donna concluded that Mr Jones didn't have the nerve to tell
her himself, nor the experience to know that the bottle had
been opened immediately before serving); and Commander
Steven Bryce, travelling with a young lady who seemed too
affectionate to be his daughter, maintained that the coffee
was cold (since, Donna had noticed, he'd left it a good ten
minutes before drinking it).

This was par for the course on a full-load flight, and
Marianne, the probationer, stood up well. The only
interesting passengers were the three men in dark suits at
the rear of A Zone Left.

'They look so *sinister*,' Marianne said in a low voice as she
helped Donna stow the last tray cart in the galley.

'Rich,' Donna said, wiping up the remains of a fallen ice
cream. 'Very rich.'

'Well, that's sinister, isn't it?'

'Suspect, at least,' Donna laughed, and went over her
make-up again. 'They're not all of them rich, though. Just
the elderly guy by the window.'

'How do you know?'

'The suit. The crocodile shoes and wallet. The Concord
watch – that's real gold and those are real diamonds – and
the way he treats the other two. The one sitting next to him is
his private secretary, and the one sitting behind is his
bodyguard.'

55

Marianne was watching the group through the gap in the curtain, her soft blue eyes intrigued. 'You've seen them before, then.'

'No. People like him come through once in a while. The executive jet's under repair, or their mothers insist they fly commercial for safety –'

'Their *mothers* . . .'

'People like that have mothers who are never less than ninety. It's a long-lived breed.'

'There's something . . . scary about him. Unreal. I don't like him.'

'He sure likes you, honey.'

Marianne swung her head. 'He's never looked at me.'

'Not while you're looking at him.'

Then there was a slight bump and the seat-belt sign lit up. They each took an aisle and went down it checking the buckles.

It was soon after two o'clock in the morning – six o'clock New York time – when the captain made his destination-approach announcement and the thin, quiet man in the dark suit came along the aisle to speak to Marianne; he was the one Donna had said was the private secretary to Mr Frederick J. Vanderkloot III, sitting by the window.

'Marianne,' the thin man said softly, glancing at her name tab, 'Mr Vanderkloot is spending the week-end on his yacht in the Sound, and he needs some congenial companionship.' As she listened to his slow, persuasive voice, she was aware of his eyes as they watched hers carefully, narrowed against the smoke rising from his cigarette: cool, confident eyes that never left hers as he talked. 'Mr Vanderkloot is a generous host. He realises that it might inconvenience you to change your plans for the week-end at such short notice, and would be happy to offer one thousand dollars by way of compensation.'

It was a moment before Marianne could take it all in; when its meaning struck her, she couldn't think of anything to say – anything *really* appropriate. She swung away from him and went straight to the forward galley, white-faced and

56

furious.

'That *snake* . . .' she told Donna through her teeth. 'How dare he?'

Donna straightened up from checking the catering inventory. 'Did you get goosed or something?' It happened sometimes, at the end of a long flight and a few drinks.

'That dirty old *creep* . . . ' She told Donna what had happened.

'Okay, honey. You don't need the grand?'

'Are you *serious*?' Marianne's eyes were shocked.

'A thousand bucks is pretty serious. Just thought I'd check.' She put an arm around the kid's shoulders for a moment. 'We'll be down in ten minutes. Take the right-side aisle again and I'll see to the rest. Now you can just forget the whole thing, honey, it's part of the job.' Then she went through the curtain and down the left-side aisle, looking at the three men in turn and stopping when she reached the secretary. 'Sir,' she told him with a dead stare, 'I think you have the wrong airline. And if Mr Frederick Vanderkloot III has a few minutes to spare before we land, I suggest you tell him to stick his thousand bucks right up his gold-plated ass.'

The three men made their way through the VIP lounge at Kennedy Airport without stopping; two others met them and went with them to the limousine; a third was already waiting at the baggage claim carousel to see the luggage through. As Frederick Vanderkloot boarded the limousine, one of the men stood back and waved it away, then went into the terminal again to use a telephone.

'He's in, and he wants a woman.'

The voice on the line sounded drowsy. 'He must have slept on the plane.'

'Just fix him up.'

'Right now?'

'Listen to me, asshole. He'll be there in forty minutes, and if she's not there waiting for him it's your hide.' He hung up and went to help the other man at the baggage claim.

As the limousine heeled on its soft springs from 49th Street onto Park Avenue and gathered speed northwards, a four-door Cougar GS sedan went through the signals on the yellow at East 86th Street and turned south, going two blocks at high speed and then swerving into the underground garage on 84th.

Fifteen minutes later, as the sun showed its rim above the dark mass of Long Island, Paulette Duvivier was standing in silhouette against the translucent net curtains of the east window of the Vanderkloot penthouse, after going through two security checks on the ground floor and showing her ID to the man in the entrance lobby of the apartment itself. He was standing at the double doors between the two marble columns across the room from her, not speaking to her, not looking at her. He stood paring his nails.

Paulette took in the details of the room a little apprehensively: she'd been told that Mr Vanderkloot was 'sophisticated' in his preferences. But everything seemed normal enough: a huge double bed with a brocade canopy and gold tassels, a silk-covered Regency couch and several padded chairs to match, lofty curtains, seal-red pile carpet, silk wall panels, a chandelier with brilliant amber drops. She didn't see any whips, chains, boots or strait-jackets around; this place looked real civilised.

In the silence of the room she stood with one knee slightly bent, hands behind her, a lingering bitter taste in her throat from the pill she'd swallowed in haste and without water, a faint burning sensation under her black lace briefs from the antiseptic swab. Looking again at the manservant, she asked hesitantly:

'What do I call him?'

He didn't look at her.

'Mr Vanderkloot.'

She nodded, swallowing. She wished the client would come. And she wished he wouldn't. 'Do everything right for this one,' Falcone had told her, 'and he could even set you up. You know what that means. This guy isn't on welfare.'

She didn't believe Falcone, at least about this client

58

'setting her up'. If was everybody's dream, to get picked out as a permanent; it was what Falcone was always telling them, when he sent them to a difficult client. He'd told Alicia that, and in a couple of hours she was back at the house sobbing her heart out, bruised everywhere. Falcone had slipped her another hundred, to keep her mouth shut.

She shifted her weight onto her other leg. Mostly she was told she could sit down; sometimes she'd get a cup of coffee while she was waiting, or even a glass of champagne. This guy had just told her to stand over there against the window, facing this way. He looked a real cold bastard, wouldn't even look at her, like she was dirt.

A door sounded somewhere in the apartment, and she caught her breath. The man went straight across to an archway on the other side of the room and disappeared. Then one of the double doors came open and the client came in, shutting it behind him. He turned around and stood looking at her, a short, bald-headed guy in a red silk dressing-gown, his square face very smooth, his ears pressed right up close against his head like they weren't hardly there, his mouth in a straight line, his black eyes watching her, not blinking. There was a kind of power in him, in the way he was standing, the way he was holding his shoulders; she could almost feel it, right across the room.

'What's your name?'

'Paulette.' It came out with a kind of jerk.

'In there.' He nodded towards another archway, opposite the one the man had gone through.

She went across to it, and he watched her; a slim body, professional walk; young, and afraid: he'd heard it in her voice. He followed her.

'In here?' she asked him.

'Yes. Strip off.'

He watched her, as he had watched a hundred of them, a thousand of them, baring their bodies for him at his command, their young eyes scared, their voices faltering, their hands fumbling with their clothes as if it were the first time they'd ever undressed.

When she was naked he went to a closet and opened it. 'Put these on.'

She hesitated. 'These?'

'*Put them on*.' He hadn't raised his voice, but she could hear the urgency in it. She did what he told her. That was what she was here for.

He pressed a switch on the wall, and the lighting turned rose-coloured, deepening the shadows; he watched her as the soft light touched across her shoulders while she moved, standing on one leg, now the other; she had a good body; slender, long-limbed, with a flat stomach, the shadows dark between her thighs where the black hair grew thickly, her small breasts hanging as she stooped, their tips pointed and reddened in the rose-coloured light. He could smell her body now as the heat-lamp warmed her skin and brought out its volatile oils; there was a tang to this girl, the hint of smokiness in her perspiration, and it excited him.

'This, now.' He reached again into the closet.

'Jesus,' she whispered, 'I don't know. Look, I –'

'*Do as I tell you*.'

'But honey, I –'

'*Don't call me that*.'

He bent forward and helped her with it. She'd begun shaking, her breath loud in the small room. 'You want me to –'

'Sit there. There.'

'Okay.'

'Squat. Do it naturally, you little bitch. Don't play. Now put your legs over here. You understand what I want you to do?'

'I guess I –'

'*Do you understand?*'

'Yes, sir.' It was hurting now, but she didn't tell him. He'd like that, and make her pull it tighter. But Christ, when she got back to Falcone, she'd really tell him something. And she wasn't coming to this place again.

'I can't,' she told Vanderkloot.

'Yes, you can. Make the effort. Come on.'

60

She closed her eyes, and heard the hissing of silk as he took off his dressing-gown; through the slits in her lids she saw his strong, compact body, covered with dark hair that shone in the warm light. He smelt like an animal.

'*Try. Make an effort.*'

'Sir, I don't think I –'

'It won't hurt you! How can it hurt you? Now come on, you little bitch. *Do it.*'

Then he was persuading her suddenly, by the sheer force of his will; and as they began moving together she shut her eyes tight this time and let everything go, with the warm red light fluttering against her eyelids as his body moved across and across her, until she couldn't do anything but go with him, clinging onto his arms and feeling the hardness of their muscles; this guy must play an awful lot of tennis, or lift weights or something; or maybe it was doing this so often.

'Slower,' he said, 'slower. And don't let them come off.'

'Okay.' She relaxed again, because it hurt if she resisted; and she didn't think about the other thing, what he'd made her do first; it'd be okay afterwards, and she could forget it; right now there was a feeling coming into her she'd never had before; it was like he was starting to push her through a kind of barrier and on to the other side of something; she wasn't very good at analysing her own feelings, and this whole thing was so far out that she didn't even understand it, not really; but the more they went on doing it, the more she was able to relax, until she was giving herself to it, feeling the hard animal body sliding against hers, feeling its weight, feeling its strength as his hands moved over her, guiding her, setting the rhythm. The sweat was running on them both now, under the heat of the lamp, and when she opened her eyes for a moment she saw his dark body was silvered with it; in the rose-coloured light his face was contorted, his lips drawn back from his teeth and his nostrils dilated; he looked like a man climbing a mountain, or running a marathon, drivng himself on and on and on, torturing himself; and after a long time she understood why he'd made her do these things for him. It wasn't the way he liked best: *it was the only*

61

way he could do it.

He came suddenly, pulling one of them off and burying his bright wet face in it while she fell away from him, exhausted, and his sperm kept on coming and coming as she shrank away from it, sickened, not because of what it was but because it was his.

CHAPTER 6

LORRAINE WOKE TO the aroma of toast and bacon cooking, and lay staring at the ceiling, trying to remember where she was. It took a second or two, because it was somewhere she'd never been before, and she was already wondering what the hell she was doing here.

She must have been crazy.

She stared around at the knotty pine walls and ceiling, the rustic furniture, the faded poster of a racing car pinned not quite straight on this side of the bathroom door. Absolutely crazy, the whole thing. She should have been in her apartment in New York, worrying her guts out, calling Barry, calling Carl, calling Dean Powers, getting them out of the shower, off the golf course, in from the tennis court, wherever they were, whatever they were doing.

Panic rushed in, and she called out to Frank. They had to get into the car right away and head back to Manhattan, never mind the speed limit. Frank didn't hear. The door to the main room of the cabin was ajar, and she could hear the sizzling of the frying-pan.

'Frank!'

She got out of the bed, naked, and pulled on her jeans that she'd left hanging over a chair; she was doing the zipper when he came in, standing in the doorway with a slow smile dawning.

'Hungry?' He was holding an omelette knife.

'What? I don't know.' She made an attempt to cover her breasts, then thought how Victorian she was being, then had a flashback memory of Frank Cummins in his uniform,

63

solemnly guiding the company limousine through the Park Avenue traffic with her sitting behind him – stop here, Frank . . . Yes, ma'am – and covered her breasts again, shocked and confused while he went on admiring her with his steady blue eyes, the smile still there.

'Well,' he asked her, 'how many eggs?'

She controlled her impatience. 'Frank, I want you to – ' but she stopped. She wanted him to take her straight back to Manhattan – right? Wrong. It was the last place she wanted to be. She relaxed, taking her hands away from her breasts and putting them on her hips. 'Frank, I went crazy.'

'You did?'

'Absolutely.'

'What was it like?'

She thought about it. 'Unbelievable. I must go and brush my teeth. Two eggs.' She turned at the bathroom door. 'Three.'

They had their breakfast at the rickety table, sitting on the equally rickety school benches on either side, both of them setting to as if they hadn't had a meal in days.

'More toast?' Frank asked.

'Love some. I'm ravenous.'

'It's the air up here.' He went across to the little kitchen with an easy, loping stride in his checkered shirt and jeans, a wide leather belt creaking at his waist.

Lorraine got up. 'Frank, you don't have to wait on me.'

'Certainly I do; you're my guest, young lady.'

She thought about him while he was in the kitchen. It was absolutely right: she'd gone crazy, and it had felt unbelievable. She hadn't even been drinking last night, just some wine and a cognac with Barry; yet, looking back, she realised how desperate she must have been to talk to someone, anyone at all, the nearest person she could ask; because there'd been no hesitation: it had simply sprung right into her mind and she'd said the words before she'd known they were there. *This week-end, Frank, take me.*

They'd stopped to pick up groceries at an all-night store in Peekskill, then headed north again, turning off the highway at Poughkeepsie along Pleasant Valley. The cabin had been cold when they'd arrived, the headlights swinging across the massed green pines and sending a barn owl gliding away, disturbed. Frank had lit a fire, bringing the stuff in from the car while she'd crouched on the Indian carpet in front of the hearth, shivering, lost and embarrassed. From the instant she'd asked him so impulsively to bring her here, there'd been no possibility of changing her mind. You might, if you were crazy enough, tell your chauffeur to take you to his cabin for the week-end; but you couldn't then say no, let's forget it.

They'd bought some wine, a whole case of California Burgundy, and Frank had stuck a poker into the glowing logs and plunged it red-hot into a jug of it, mulling it and adding spices. She didn't remember what time it was when they went to bed; it was night, that was all, a night with firelight on the pine ceiling, the hoot of the owl out there in the frosty starlight, and Frank's strong body locked with hers as he'd made love to her with a kind of lingering hesitation, treating her as if she were a fragile novitiate who might be startled away by too much show of passion.

There'd been no question of passion, anyhow; in his quiet way, Frank had divined her need of him, and knew it wasn't of him particularly; he'd sensed she was in trouble, and her impulsive demands on him had been a plea for help, and he'd been handy. But once the love-making had started, she hadn't let him go; it had been almost three weeks since she'd slept with anyone, when Tom Dyson had flown in from location in Florida for a few days. Maybe it had been as long for Frank; she didn't know; they hadn't talked very much. Once, as they'd lain with his arms around her sometime towards the dawn, she'd heard him laughing quietly.

'What's funny?'

'Nothing's funny, I guess. I was just wondering, what happened?'

'You mean, why am I here?'

'Yes.'

'I don't know, Frank. But I'm glad I am.'

She'd meant it, and he'd understood that, and they'd made love again as the first light of the new day had come creeping in through the window, and the embers in the hearth had creaked to the morning's chill.

'More coffee?' he asked her as he came back with a dish of golden toast.

'Yes. And if we need anything else, I'll go get it next time.'

'It's a deal.' He sat on the bench facing her. 'I must admit I'm not too strong this morning.'

'Something wrong?' She was concerned, because he wasn't smiling now.

'Wrong?' He shrugged. 'Maybe nothing serious. You know, nothing major. I'll get a check-up when we're back in town, but I don't have a lot of faith in their diagnostics.'

'What are your symptoms?' He looked so very fit.

'I guess you could call it a general lassitude.' He was frowning now, reluctant to talk about it. 'Tendency of the legs to buckle when I walk, you know.'

'What d'you think it is, Frank?'

'Well,' he swung his head to look at her, 'maybe it's just that I'm out of practice, but you know we did it *five times* in the night? I mean if that isn't enough to make any guy's legs buckle when he goes to fetch the toast . . .'

He waited till she was laughing before he dropped the act, and laughed with her as she buried her face in her hands, blushing now and unable to stop.

'Oh, Frank . . .'

'A killing pace, young lady, yes indeed.'

'You're making me so ashamed.'

'And so you should be. You're no respecter of age in a man.'

She studied him for a moment. He was handsome, with his very straight blue-eyed gaze and his rugged chin, but that was nothing to do with his age, which – as she knew from the company records – was forty-eight. It was his lack of reserve, his lack of stuffiness, once the game was on, that made him seem so much younger, ready to change, to go out on a limb and not look back. And to laugh about it, mostly to himself. 'You know something, Frank? You're going to have to fight the girls off for another thirty years yet.'

'Sounds awfully tiring.'

She buttered toast for him, and they shared the marmalade pot, using the same knife, laying it on the bare planks of the table, just like she'd done as a kid in camp or in the tree house Dad had built for them. She too, this week-end, had lost a lot of years.

'What did you think, Frank, when I asked you to bring me here?'

'You mean the moment? The very moment?' He looked grave again.

'Yes.'

He frowned reflectively. 'Well now, I hope this doesn't embarrass you, but at the very *moment* you asked me that, I thought the motor had dropped clean out.'

She laughed again with him, and gave up asking him serious questions; with that intuition of his, he knew she hadn't come up here to be serious, and he was going along with that.

After breakfast she helped him wash the dishes; then he showed her round the place, though there wasn't a lot to see: a closet or two where he kept spare rough-country clothes and a few fishing-rods; the battered stereo and a stack of records; the old-fashioned telescope on its brass tripod near the window; the wood pile and water pump and lean-to shelter for the car – the big Lincoln wouldn't even fit into it; he'd left it outside under the trees, and pine needles had gathered along the trim of the windshield during the night.

'I've never known such peace,' she told him as they wandered back from the creek where white water was running.

'What you came her for, I guess.'

She perched on a fallen tree. 'I don't want you to think I – I asked you to bring me here, just because you were – maybe –' she gave up, wishing she hadn't started.

'Available.'

'Yes.'

'Without having to make the effort,' he said thoughtfully, 'of going to look anywhere else.' He broke a twig and nibbled on it.

'Yes. I – I'd meant to go to the Village, and – '

'Just bum around for company.'

She almost flinched, though he'd spoken casually. 'If that's how you want to put it.'

His head swung to meet her gaze. 'How else would you put it?'

She looked away. 'It surprises you.'

'You better believe it. I don't know how rich you are, Lorraine, but I know how beautiful you are, and I guess you must have maybe two or three hundred friends; and when a very rich and very beautiful young woman leaves all her friends behind and goes out looking for just *anyone*, even her chauffeur, there has to be a very big reason.' As she got up from the limb, he said quickly, 'But don't get me wrong. Whatever the reason is, I don't want to know it; it isn't my business. I – '

'I'm at a crossroads, Frank. And I'm scared of the traffic.'

'Sure.'

'I can go two ways. There are people dependent on me, and there's something I want to do, more than anything else in the whole world, which is to – to honour something my father did for me. And if I go on fighting to do it, I can get badly hurt, along with the others. And if I don't, I'm going to get hurt even worse.'

'Okay.' He nodded slowly. 'Okay.'

She swung around and found him watching her, his big frame stilled and his eyes clouded. 'So I needed a break,' she said defensively, 'that's all. I needed someone to . . . I needed just *someone*.'

'And I was there.'

She looked down. 'I'm sorry you feel that way. It wasn't – '

'Oh,' he said, 'listen a minute. It was a privilege.'

'A privilege?'

'I don't mean because you're rich, and everything. Maybe I don't even mean because you're the most beautiful girl I've ever been close to. What I mean is you wanted help, and you wanted it very bad, and you wanted it now, right now – and I was around, and *that* was my privilege. You know? To find yourself with someone, anyone at all, who's really desperate for help, and be able to give it to them, without thinking first . . . that's a pretty good feeling, Lorraine.' He shrugged. 'Not that I want to make too much of it, for God's sake.'

She came up to him and laid her head against his shoulder. 'I thought you were bawling me out, like all the rest of them. After the last year running all those people, or trying to, it's hard for me to believe there are any nice guys left.'

He held her gently. 'Throw in the towel. You put up a good fight. Now you can quit honourably.'

She raised her face. 'How much do you know about it?'

'I'm a shareholder. Went and bought me ten whole shares, a while ago. So I get to see the annual report. And the figures. Seems to me like you're on a losing streak, Lorraine.'

She moved away from him, standing a little distance off, where she couldn't see him, and couldn't be tempted to go back into his arms and feel his strength and long for his help, in whatever way he could give it. 'Okay, I'm on a losing streak. So I'll change it. Monday, I'll go back there and grab a hold of that place and turn it upside down and shake it, and anyone who doesn't want to cling on can drop out. Then we'll see what we can do with what's left.'

Frank watched her, the way she was standing, hands on her hips and shoulders set securely, head lifted, her eyes on the horizon. 'I think you can do it,' he said.

She swung to face him. 'You bet your sweet ass I can do it. And you know what I'm saying, Frank?'

'Well, as I understand it, you're asking me to bet my sweet ass –'

She laughed explosively, coming back to him. 'I'm saying that's what you did for me. I've got my courage back.'

'After just one night? What's it going to be like Monday?'

'You wouldn't believe.'

The rest of the day they went fishing in the creek where the white water ran, and caught three minnows and threw them back; then in the evening they watched the stars come out, and Frank brought the ancient telescope outside and showed her four of the moons of Saturn strung out in a line, and the fuzz of white near Cassiopia that he said was the galaxy in Andromeda; later they lay on the Indian rug in front of the crackling fire and made love, this time with more urgency because their time together was going to be over in a few more hours – with so much urgency, in fact, that they didn't notice it when a spark flew onto the rug and set it smouldering before they knew anything about it.

Sunday they did nothing, and everything, and mostly it make them laugh, and mostly about nothing; they waded in the creek till their feet were so frozen they had to sit by the fire with the dishwashing bowl as a footbath, while Frank recited what he knew of *The Ancient Mariner*. He showed her how to feed crickets with honey on a toothpick, and how to take a motor down and put it together again, while she dozed off in his arms; in the evening they cooked prime spare ribs over a charcoal fire and opened the fourth bottle of Burgundy and lit candles and afterwards sang all they could remember from *Hello Dolly* and *South Pacific*, before the great silence of the night overcame them and they sat outside the cabin with rugs around them, watching the stars and the first pale glow of the moon rising above the pines.

Monday they made the fire safe and locked the cabin and Lorraine sat next to Frank in front of the limousine as they started off, she still in her sweater and jeans and he in his dark blue uniform again; and when they were halfway down the interstate she felt tears trickling on her face and said:

'Frank. There's something you have to know.'

He turned his head, hearing the hollow sound of her voice.

'Such as?'

'You're fired.'

CHAPTER 7

'OKAY,' JUDY POLLACK was saying on the phone, 'but all I'm asking you to do is check on it for me. Nobody knows everything. I bet you don't even know it was Theophilus van Kanal who invented the revolving door. Have to keep up the pace, Henry.'

She hung up and dragged a top drawer open as Betty Lou came in with a stack of memos left over from Friday night, stopping dead as she saw Judy's bright yellow skirt and black-and-yellow ringed sweater.

'You look real sharp,' Betty Lou said, and dumped the memos into the in tray.

'I'm dating a Wasp.' The phone began ringing and she picked it up. 'No. She's not checked in yet. I know. Let's try not to worry, okay?' She hung up and looked at Betty Lou with no attempt to hide the anxiety in her eyes. 'This hasn't happened before, Betty Lou. Ever.'

'Didn't she call in?'

'Not to me. If she'd call anybody, it'd be me. We have a private understanding: nobody in the whole of this emergency ward can get information around so fast or sit on it so tight as Little Miss Yours Sincerely.' She peeled off some gum, not offering it to Betty Lou, who didn't chew. 'What did you do for the week-end?'

'Had a fight with my ex.'

Judy stopped chewing. 'You have an *ex* and you have *fights* with him? Don't you know what having an ex is for? It's for not having fights any more!' She called the Floderus apartment and got the busy tone again. It was almost 10.30

71

by the sunburst clock on the wall and people like Barry and Dean were starting to call Judy's office to ask where the boss was. 'Tell you something,' she said to Betty Lou. 'People who study tea leaves say there's no progress ever made without a crisis. So this company's going to make more progress this week than it's done since it started. Nothing's all bad.'

Then Lorraine Floderus came out of the lift in a black-and-white houndstooth check suit that dazzled even at this distance, and Judy took a deep breath and shut her eyes and counted five and opened them again. 'The boss is in, Betty Lou. Drinks are on me.' She watched Lorraine coming down the corridor with a walk that would have done justice to the runway at a Calvin Klein show, except maybe it was a little too fast, and a little too militant: Lorraine looked like people had better open the doors for her or she'd go right through the woodwork without stopping.

Now where in hell, Judy asked herself, has the boss been for the week-end, to generate this much force?

'Has anyone asked for me, Judy?' Lorraine halted abruptly in the doorway. The flashing smile was there, but with a lot of pent-up energy underneath it.

'Barry, Dean, Sam McNair.' She felt a certain pride in the Chief's asking her; it was tacitly understood that Maggie Welford along there didn't get too many calls, though she was Lorraine's secretary: she made people feel they were trying to call Holy Mary without counting their rosary first.

'No one else?' Lorraine asked.

'No one else, Chief. Good week-end?' She saw Lorraine's eyes go dark for an instant, and the smile falter.

'Yes. I got out of the city. How was yours?'

'I painted a door.'

Lorraine's smile took in Betty Lou and she was on her way again. Maggie tried to intercept her as she went into her office, but Lorraine didn't break her stride.

'I have the airline tickets for Los Angeles, Ms Floderus. You take off from Kennedy at –'

'Thanks, Maggie. Later.' She went into her office and

shut the door and stood looking around the room, trying to see it as Carl Blatt did, as if she were coming in here for an interview. The overall impression was one of lightness, with its theme of pale blue and ivory, the tall windows, the filmy curtains, the bright colours of the books along the floor-to-ceiling shelves, the blue-and-Conté Etruscan prints, the bowl of flowers. But yes, maybe the desk looked rather a long way off: she walked slowly towards it, imagining someone sitting there waiting for her; it made her uncomfortable. And it was too high, on the dais she'd had built; someone sitting there would look, as Carl said, 'dominant'. And yes again, the light from the big south-facing window was too bright, so anyone sitting behind the desk would be shadowed – 'remote, mysterious, masked,' as he'd put it. Damn the man, he was right.

Going across to her desk she made, in the next three seconds, three changes in her life. She left the *New York Times* and the *Wall Street Journal* and the neat array of business periodicals untouched; she pressed the intercom to let Maggie know she was now available; and she asked her to call the décor people and get them over here as soon as they could come.

'Are you ready for me, Ms Floderus, after I've done that?'

'Yes, Maggie.' Then she remembered something else she had to do, and picked up a telephone.

'Judy, Personnel.'

'I forgot to tell you, Judy,' she tried to sound normal. 'Frank's leaving us.'

'Frank Cummins?'

'Yes. He's been offered a better position. In case he needs it, though, I want you to make out an A1 reference for him, with my own personal and unqualified recommendation. And find a replacement.'

'For when?'

'Right away. I – I told him we wouldn't risk his losing a better job by keeping him here too long.'

'It shall be done, Lorraine.'

'Thank you.' She hung up.

A replacement. Not too handsome, next time, or too . . . available. A married man, who wouldn't want to take her away with him for a passionate week-end in the country. A more suitable replacement, an appropriate chess piece for the empty square on the board. That's how Frank had seen it. In the car this morning he hadn't said anything when she'd told him he was fired; he'd just stared at her until he had to look back at the road, while she sat numbly with her head back against the headrest and her eyes shut, waiting for him to answer. But he didn't; she had to listen to the rushing of the big trucks and the fluttering of the slipstream past the outside mirrors.

After a time she opened her eyes and looked at him, but he was just staring straight ahead with his hands motionless on the wheel.

'Frank. For God's sake, will you say something?'

He didn't turn his head. 'Like what?'

'Like – ' she shrugged helplessly – 'like you understand.'

'Sure I understand. It's simple enough. I'm fired.'

'Frank, please . . .'

In half a mile he took an exit ramp and pulled the limousine onto some waste ground at the edge of a building site, and switched off the motor and turned in his seat to gaze at her with his eyes bright. He didn't raise his voice; Frank was always quiet in everything he did – even when he went into a rage.

'When did you know?' he asked her.

'Know what?'

'That you were going to fire me.'

'A while back. After we left the cabin.' She put her hand on his arm, but he didn't move.

'Do I get any reason?'

'Yes.' She left her hand there, and felt the warmth of the body that had lain with hers so protectively and so intimately in the long hours of the night; and in its stillness now, felt its cold. 'For giving me a perfect week-end. For making me feel loved again, and secure, and finally brave enough to go through with what I have to when I get back to my life.' The tears were starting again, as if his hurt were so deep that she needed to cry for him, since he couldn't do it for himself. She opened the glove pocket and found the tissues again, blowing her nose, feeling better, feeling almost angry herself now because he wouldn't understand. 'Frank, you must see it's impossible. You'd have to sit there up front, the trusted and impeccable employee doing his job so diligently, while I'd be there in the back, the aloof and distant tycoon preoccupied with her business worries – ' she gripped his arm now with both her hands, like she had to shake him into understanding – 'For God's sake, don't you see what it'd be like? Be here at the usual time, Frank – yes, ma'am. Stop right here, Frank – yes, ma'am. And we don't even let our hands touch by accident as you open the door for me? We don't let our eyes meet, in case we'd suddenly want to kiss again, and go somewhere and make love again? Don't you see it wouldn't work?'

He didn't look away from her once; it was like he wanted her to see, just from his eyes, how bright his anger was.

'I could forget this week-end,' he said. 'It wouldn't be that easy, but I'd do it.'

In a moment she said: 'Then I couldn't, Frank. I know it's easier for men; they can take a woman and make love to her and the next day get it clean off their mind – '

'I'm not talking about that – '

'But it's a biological fact.'

'I know that. But with you it's different. You weren't just someone I picked up.'

'I wasn't just a good lay for the week-end, right?'

'You know damned well it wasn't like that!'

'Of course I do — *I* picked *you* up. And now I'm going to let you down and it's going to hurt me too, Frank; right now I'm feeling a complete bitch and a damned idiot for letting it happen, can't you realise that?'

'Oh, sure. Right now you feel that way, but in a couple of days it'll be okay again. But I'll still be out of a job.'

'I'll want to make amends, Frank. For my own sake, I'll want to be generous.'

75

The anger brightened in his eyes again. 'For you, that's so easy to do, and it won't cost you anything, at least not anything you'd ever notice.'

'Please, Frank –'

'What's it feel like, Miss Floderus? I'm feeling kind of blue this Friday, so I think I'll call the chauffeur up and spend the week-end with him and then fire him Monday, that'd be a whole lot of fun, and –'

'*Frank* . . . ' She lay her head against his shoulder, wanting to make him stop, but he pushed her away and got out of the car and she watched him walking down the roadway past the big concrete mixer and the line of pickup trucks, his stride purposeful, as if he'd run out of gas and had to reach a service station as soon as he could – or as if he were walking away from someone he never wanted to see again.

That was going to be too easy. All she'd have to do was call Judy, once she was back in the office. The practical terms were already in her mind: $5000 in immediate compensation, plus a solid commitment to find him a job at the same rate, or better. But it would have to be done by someone else – it was for Judy to hire and fire below executive level – and in writing, and with nothing in the agreement about a lost week-end . . . or mulled wine in the firelight . . . or his strong muscular body locked around hers . . .

He'd been gone a long time now, and she couldn't see him down the narrowing perspective of the road. It occurred to her suddenly that he was walking back to the highway, to thumb a ride into the city, rather than go with her. Already she knew him well enough to believe he'd do that, just walk out of the situation and leave her stuck in a building site in the middle of nowhere, taking his pride with him, taking, maybe, his hate.

He must have walked full circle, out of sight, because he was back suddenly, pulling her door open. Startled, she gave a breathless laugh. 'I thought you'd run out on me!'

His face was stony. 'That'd be easy, but I'm not running out on the job.' He snapped open the rear door. 'If you want to go to Manhattan, you'd better sit in the back. It's where you belong.'

There was nothing she could say to him, she knew now, that would do any good. As she sat in the comfort of the rear seat with the cocktail cabinet and the white telephone and the built-in radio reminding her how instantly her life could be provided with helpful facilities, she went over her make-up to remove the traces of her tears, already thinking ahead to the challenges she must meet today, with no help from Carl, who was quitting; nor from Barry, who was on the bottle; nor from Dean, who could think of nothing better to do than chase the girls in the office and create cheap gossip in the ladies' room. She felt the temptation to lean forward and say, 'Frank, let's forget the whole thing. Just turn around and take me back to your little bit of heaven up there and we'll let the rest of the world go by . . .'

She said nothing. She didn't have the right any more; in a strange way this man with his simple tastes and his peace of mind and his own little haven up there in the pinewoods had banished her from his world, sending her back to her own useless existence in the plush rear seat of a company limousine. 'It's where you belong,' he'd just told her.

An hour later, driving down Park Avenue towards her apartment, she wondered if it would be possible, at all possible, to keep Frank on as the company chauffeur. He was a reliable man, able to keep secrets and not give anything away with the slightest sign; nothing would ever be said to anyone; no one would ever know. But no: it wouldn't be possible. Frank wasn't the problem; she was, herself. This snatched, crazy week-end had come to mean far more to her than she'd been able to realise beforehand, because Frank had been a stranger to her then, and she couldn't have imagined how much strength and courage he would give her in those two idyllic days of discovering she was wanted again, and for a brief time loved again; and that was why it would be impossible to keep him on: she'd never be able to treat him simply as an efficient employee, giving him orders and expecting obedience, without letting him see – and letting others suspect – that he meant much more to her than that.

'Excuse me, ma'am.'

She looked up, startled out of her thoughts; she could see his eyes in the driving mirror, but they were looking straight ahead.

'Yes, Frank?'

'You'll be going to the apartment?'

'Yes. Please.'

'Thank you, ma'am.' At the intersection he made a left onto 106th Street, and she took her deerskin bag from the seat beside her. The moment he pulled up outside her apartment she opened the door and got out, before he could do it for her.

'Will that be all, ma'am?' He was standing in front of her on the sidewalk, with people passing by; above the buildings the sky was overcast, not clear with white clouds as she'd seen it above the pines yesterday.

She looked up at him, her eyes narrowed against the light.

'Yes, Frank. That's all. But I want you to know something. I don't think I can save the company. Floderus. Things have gone too far. But I'm back here in this city feeling very different from how I felt before – before the week-end; and I'm going to try. And if I succeed, it's going to be mostly because of you. Because of what you gave me.' She had to look away from him suddenly, because there was nothing in his eyes but the cold, circumspect attention of an employee listening to his boss. If he were trying to break her heart, he was doing a good job. Already the things she'd just told him sounded false in retrospect; and yet they weren't. They'd had to be said, because this was a time for truth. 'I know it's not a very big thing in your life, whether the company survives or goes under; but it's a big thing in mine.' She took a deep breath and hitched the strap of the bag higher across her shoulder. 'About practical matters, Frank, you have to see Judy, in Personnel. I'll give her instructions to offer a settlement, which I hope will be generous enough for you to accept. She'll also be told to find

78

you an excellent position, better than this one, as soon as there's an opening.'

He was silent for so long that she had to look up at him again; and only then did he say quietly: 'There's no offer you can make that I'd accept. And I'll find my own work, in my own way.' He stood back, but she held his arm for a moment; and if any of the passers-by chanced to notice, they would have seen a young and pretty girl in jeans and a sweater reaching up to kiss the cheek of a uniformed chauffeur, before she turned away and hurried under the gold-and-white marquee of the apartment lobby, brushing away tears before the doorman could see them.

That had been an hour ago. The girl in the jeans had vanished, and now there was a young woman in a sharp black-and-white houndstooth suit, cut for elegance and dash for someone on the move, as she went through her morning mail at the huge ebony-topped desk in the power centre of Floderus Incorporated.

Maggie had been in twice with memos and requests for a meeting; Lorraine had dealt with them fast, cutting some of them out and scheduling her day so that she could see the people she wanted to see, and not those who wanted to see her. Then she went back to the one letter that had left her uneasy, and read it again. It was from the Chairman of Century Cosmetics, Frederick Vanderkloot. She had met him once at the Barbizon-Plaza dinner gala thrown by Saks and once at the Hotel Palace-Carlton two weeks ago for the Donatella launching of a new fragrance; she remembered him as a courteous and rather impressive fellow-guest, with an air of contained power that wasn't altogether surprising in the head of a company that last year had turned in a net sales figure of $450 million. She remembered also that on the last occasion he'd been difficult to get away from; but she was used to men paying a lot of attention to her wherever she went; there was also something compelling in his personal brand of charm, as he expressed his admiration for Floderus Incorporated, 'a company not only distinguished, elegant and exclusive in the crowded market-place, but with a chief executive officer so easily capable of personifying feminine beauty, the major theme of the whole cosmetics industry.'

The letter she was reading now, headed with the discreet family crest of the Vanderkloots, was just as courteous, and just as charming as the man had been himself.

I would therefore like to suggest an early meeting between us, not only to afford me the pleasure of your company, but to explore the present structure of the cosmetics field and ask ourselves whether Floderus and Century might not find an opportunity of establishing mutual interests and advantages by a closer rapport.

What made Lorraine uneasy was the veiled suggestion of a merger – a euphemistic word that could mean anything from a genuine joining of forces to an outright takeover. If Century Cosmetics made a good enough offer, it could swallow a small company like Floderus whole. It was tempting to drop the letter from Vanderkloot into the paper shredder and forget all about it; but business ethics required her to answer it. It was tempting also to answer it by just saying no, she didn't consider there was a case for 'exploring the present structure' to seek a 'closer rapport'; but then again, company ethics demanded she pass this letter on to the board.

What made her still more uneasy was a very simple question: had Vanderkloot written to her spontaneously, or had someone at Floderus dropped him a hint that they might be ready to sell out?

The idea of treachery was repugnant to her; but if she discovered that any of her executives had made contact with Century behind her back, she'd force his immediate resignation.

Even if it were Barry Corbett? *You think we should sell out*, she'd told him bitterly after dinner on Friday night. *Right*, he'd answered quietly, *that's right*.

She shook the idea from her mind. Within the company – within every company – there were dangerous undercurrents in time of crisis, and people were driven to do things that were quite out of character; given enough

80

pressure, they'd resort to the most elemental acts of human behaviour; if starving, they'd steal. But Barry had founded this firm with her father, bringing his own money into it; how could he possibly, after all these years, decide to betray it?

Lorraine buzzed for Maggie, the letter in front of her on the desk. There was of course another point of view; Barry, out of loyalty, might see a deal with Century as the best means of saving the company's name, even though control might pass into other hands.

She looked up to see Maggie standing in front of her desk, her eyes hidden as the light flashed obliquely across her glasses, her dried-up ginger hair burning fiercely in contrast with the blue-and-white décor behind her.

'Maggie, I'd like copies of this letter to go to every member of the board, in a sealed envelope.'

'Yes, Ms Floderus.'

'And here's a priority memo to the same people. I'm calling an extraordinary meeting for Thursday, at ten o'clock in the morning.'

It was an hour before she managed to free her mind of the Vanderkloot letter and its implications, by which time she was feeling a degree of neck tension that drove her into her blue-and-gold private bathroom to find an aspirin. The determination in her, inspired by those long hours in the company of poor Frank, was a driving force, and she could feel its potency; but until Thursday, unless the crisis came to a head in the meantime, she'd have nothing tangible to fight against, and she'd be prey to the slow accumulation of adrenalin.

So be it. If she'd ordered the meeting before Thursday it would have looked as if Carl Blatt's resignation, and Barry's talk of selling out, had panicked her into an immediate reaction; even more important, she had three days – and three sleepless nights – in which to prepare herself for battle.

She picked up the office phone and called Carl Blatt. At the tenth ring she was certain he'd quit on her after all, despite his agreeing to stay on until things got sorted out; then his secretary came on the line, a little breathless.

81

'Mr Blatt's office.'

'Is he there?' Lorraine never announced her name; her soft, husky voice was easy to recognise.

'Not right now, Miss Floderus. I believe he's with Mr Corbett.'

'Find him, please, and tell him to call me, wherever he is.'

'Right away.'

Carl took five minutes, by which time Lorraine had begun wondering if the delay were deliberate, to point up his independence as someone who'd officially resigned.

'This is Carl.' He sounded cool, and Lorraine longed suddenly to know what he and Barry had been discussing.

'Carl, I'm calling a meeting for Thursday. There's a memo on its way to you. Will you stay till then?'

As before, there was a silence on the line, and she felt driven to add something in persuasion – 'it's important, and I think you should be there.' But damn him, she wasn't going to coax him into staying; if he wanted to go, he could get his ass out of this building right now.

'You mean this coming Thursday?' he asked her.

'Yes. The 8th.'

'Okay.' She waited for him to soften it a little . . . sure, I'll be there . . . but there was just the silence going on, until she said curtly: 'Thank you.' She hung up.

The ache at the nape of her neck was dulling away now, thanks to the aspirin, not to the thought that whatever Carl and Barry had been discussing would bring her any joy. One wanted to quit; the other wanted to sell out. In a moment of desperation she thought of calling Dean Powers, asking him along here to sound him out: maybe, even though he was so preoccupied with his sexual prowess, she could find an ally in him; but that was doubtful; if she asked him along here at all it would be to say that unless he could put the company's concerns before his own he could follow Carl Blatt into the street.

Try Sam McNair? No. He was too political, too adept at the power game, pretending weakness to gain strength when people were sufficiently disarmed. If Sam joined forces with her it wouldn't be for the company; it would be for Sam. There was no one else she knew well enough; of the three other members of the board, two had joined it within the last twelve months and were concerned only with consolidating their position; one, in any case, was nudging retirement.

She must go it alone.

By lunch-time she had dealt with most of the morning's chores, signing reports, querying statements, dictating mail and directing priority material to the computer room. On her way down to the new Danish buffet in the next block she noticed Dean Powers crossing the lobby with a girl from the typing pool, their hands joined as they approached the revolving doors; and ten minutes later Lorraine saw them again, their heads close together as they talked at a table across from the long smörgåsbord. Not long afterwards, Dean chanced to see Lorraine, and smiled briefly before turning his attention to his companion again; she was young, pretty and dressed more stylishly than most of the typists, in a charcoal-grey batwing sweater and black suedette pants; as a luncheon companion she looked suitable enough for Dean, sitting there in his expensive suit with a lot of white cuff showing, handsome and at ease.

Lorraine bit vigorously into a stick of crisp celery. All right, Dean, this afternoon is going to be show-down time. You know the rules, even if they're not written down anywhere. What you're doing is absolutely okay for Hollywood, with its producers' couches, but absolutely not okay for a first-line Manhattan company with my name on it.

Then by five o'clock she'd forgotten about him, spending most of the afternoon in Records, Accounting and the computer room, taking home a sealed box of papers containing the sales, marketing and advertising history of Floderus Incorporated for the past twelve months; the chief accountant had blanched when she'd asked for them, and had insisted on sending one of his staff to escort her home in a taxi and extracting a solemn promise from her to wait for a similar escort service in the morning.

Climbing into the cramped and sooty cab, she shed a last tear in her mind for Frank, who had been here in the limo to meet her at this hour for the past year. Where was he now, and what was he doing? She had left a sealed envelope for him in Judy's care, for picking up when he checked in for his references and termination pay; in it was a brief message wishing him good luck in the future, and saying that if he ever felt like calling her or looking in at Floderus, she'd be delighted to talk to him again.

'. . . Not so much,' the young accountant-escort was saying in hushed tones, 'that we don't have copies, because we do, of course; it's just that if these papers became *lost*, and fell into the *wrong hands* . . .' He left it to her to imagine the consequences. Of course he was right; the affairs of a company were strictly top secret.

'I'll guard them with my life,' she assured him solemnly.

'We would *much* appreciate it,' he nodded, though his tone was still apprehensive, as if he felt that putting her life on the line wasn't really going far enough.

She'd called Tilly to say that she needn't prepare any dinner for her: she'd raid the fridge when she was hungry enough. Tilly had naturally disregarded most of these instructions and laid the table in the breakfast room, with a Caesar salad and a bottle of chilled Chenin Blanc in the cooler.

'Raiding the fridge, not very nice,' she told Lorraine with a solemn shaking of her dark head. Half-Spanish with Navaho blood, Tilly at thirty still had something of a girl's innocence about her; the black eyes had a light in them that Lorraine had only seen go out a year ago, when she'd brought her to the apartment within a week of the plane crash. Tilly had been a parlour-maid in the Floderus mansion in Connecticut at the time when Lorraine had gone through the heart-breaking business of dismissing the servants and trying to find jobs for them elsewhere, now that the mansion was up for sale and unoccupied. Why she'd chosen this particular girl, Lorraine wasn't sure; perhaps because Tilly had cried for three days alone in her tiny room in the servants' quarters when the accident happened, or because there was a certain grace in her bearing – a blending of Spanish pride and Indian reticence – that was reassuring to be near in a world which at that time had thrown Lorraine headlong into a bewildering future.

'Will you come and look after me?' she'd asked Tilly as the auctioneers came to invade every room with their note-books.

'I would like, ' Tilly had said, her small face still bleak from tears, 'I would like very much.'

Her black eyes were bright again now as she opened the wine, laying the cork beside the glass, turning the slender bottle in the cooler and folding the napkin around it, going across to the door with her slight limp – the legacy of child-hood polio – and turning to smile at Lorraine.

'If anything else, please ring.'

Lorraine dropped the heavy box of papers onto one of the breakfast chairs, pouring herself some wine. 'Bless you, Tilly. You spoil me rotten, do you know that?'

'Is good,' the girl nodded with a quick laugh, and left her.

It was an hour before Lorraine surfaced from the mass of papers that now littered the table, and tried some of the salad, not enjoying it but simply eating, too worried over the figures and the depressing 'bottom line' in the accountants' reports. By midnight Tilly had gone to bed, after telling the security guards on the ground floor that Miss Floderus was expecting no one tonight.

It was just after two o'clock in the morning when the telephone rang and Lorraine, red-eyed and tired beyond even the thought of sleep, picked it up, listening for a moment with her face going pale.

'I'll come right away,' she said.

CHAPTER 8

THE LOTUS CLUB had an all-night licence and around two-thirty in the morning there were usually a few people still at the bar and sitting at the little gilt tables or dragging their feet up and down the miniature dance floor while a pale tired-looking man played the sax for them, thinking of something else.

This morning Angelo was standing at the end of the bar, which was the closest part of the main room to the entrance doors. Tony Marinello, his manager, wasn't with him right now; he was leaning patiently against the wall of the corridor behind the stage and the long plush curtains, watching the door of the ladies' room.

At the long mirrored bar where Angelo was standing, the bartender was saying, 'Then the judge says, this man has to go to prison. Society needs protection against him.'

Two men in tuxedos sat perched on stools, listening to him.

'Who was this?' Angelo asked the bartender.

'Johnny Belfatto. He'd had a little accident with a sawed-off shot gun down at the warehouse, and Lucasi got in the way. I mean, he'd been asking for it, right? And what d'you think Steigman – he was the defence – what d'you think he said to the judge? He didn't say anything!' He rolled his eyes. 'He never did say a goddamned word till he was outside the courthouse. You believe that?'

'What did he say,' asked one of the men listening, 'outside the courthouse?'

'He said, fuck the judge.'

'What good would that do?'

'A judge that old, it wouldn't do any good at all. He wouldn't even notice it.'

Then the doorman came through from the lobby, bringing a woman with him, showing her down the three carpeted steps in the low lighting; and Angelo left the bar and went to meet her, and when she said her name he took her quickly along the side of the room, with the rose-coloured lamps casting a sheen on her white face as she passed underneath them.

'How long has she been in there?'

'Maybe ten minutes, a bit more,' Angelo said, and held the curtain back for her to go through into the corridor. He noticed the perfume she was wearing; like everything else about her it suggested class, the real thing; all she was wearing was a pair of velvet pants with a mohair stole wrapped around her, because she said she'd been on her way to bed when he'd phoned; but she wore it with panache.

'Ten minutes is an awfully long time,' she said anxiously.

'Well,' Angelo said, shrugging his huge shoulders, 'it kind of depends. In a ladies' room, people are different, you know? Tony,' he said as they reached the thin man, 'this is Miss Floderus. She's Madlen's sister. This is Tony Marinello. She still in there?'

'Yes. Hello,' he said to the woman, taking her in with a whistle in his eyes.

Lorraine knocked at he door of the ladies' room and stood listening. She thought she heard a sound, something like a groan, but she couldn't be sure; she was liable to hear things like that tonight, just because she expected them. The two men watched her.

'Why the hell did you let her go in there?' Lorraine asked them, 'after what she said?'

'She said she was thinking of going outside and shooting herself,' Angelo said, pained. 'She keeps a gun in her car, did you know that?'

'She does?'

'So when she went along here, I thought she'd changed

her mind, you know?'

Lorraine rapped at the velvet-covered door again.

'Madlen! It's Lorraine! Are you okay?' She listened again, and this time was sure she heard something like a human voice. She looked quickly up at the big man. 'I want her out of there. Now.'

Angelo went across to the door and hit it with his shoulder and the lock broke with a noise like a gunshot and his momentum carried him inside, and when Lorraine came in after him she saw Madlen on the floor with a plastic pill container lying in the corner and three purple-and-green capsules scattered around it. She bent and shook her sister, calling her name; but she didn't respond.

'Tony,' Angelo said, 'get an ambulance here.'

Ten minutes later Lorraine was sitting on the jump-stool beside the bunk in the ambulance, watching the red flashing of the lamp reflected in the windows along First Avenue while the siren filled the deserted street with its wailing.

'We're on First and 64th,' she heard the paramedic saying on his radio, 'heading for St Catherine's. Vital signs are BP low at 105/65, temperature 97.9, weak pulse at 68 bpm, shallow respiration, skin pale and moist. The capsules we found near her are Seconal 100mg.'

The vehicle heeled on soft springs through ninety degrees at an intersection and Lorraine saw the glow of traffic signals in the smoked rear windows as a distorted voice sounded from the driver's cab.

'OK, 14. If the respiration weakens, get ready to put her on the ambu-bag.'

Five minutes later at 3.44 am the ambulance swerved onto the ramp of the emergency clinic at St Catherine's Park and the howl of its siren died away. Two men in white coats were at the rear doors with a wheeled stretcher as the paramedic swung them open and helped them take the patient out. Lorraine went with them at a half-run as they swung down the ramp and turned at the end of the brightly-lit corridor into the emergency room. Another man was coming at a trot from the far end, shrugging into his coat, a stethoscope bumping against his chest. He took one glance at the girl on the stretcher and shouted to nobody in particular – 'Get Res. Therapy down here, *now*!'

Lorraine kept out of their way as the paramedic showed the doctor the Seconal bottle.

'Was this full?' he asked Lorraine sharply.

'I don't know, I –'

'Who are you?'

'Her sister –'

'Were you with her?'

'No. We found her on the floor –'

'Doesn't *anybody* know how many there were in this bottle?'

He was a young man with a pinched face and hollow eyes, his thin hands darting around as if he were trying to find something to hold onto. Lorraine thought he might have been wakened from sleep, at this hour.

'I don't think anybody knows,' she told him.

'What? Okay. Did you find a note? Did she leave –'

'We didn't see one.' She thought the only way she could help was to be quick with her answers, if she had any; it might also hold off the waves of panic that kept coming into her mind. Madlen had talked about doing this a few times before, but she'd never gone through with it. 'She said –' remembering what the big man had told her – 'she was thinking of going outside and shooting herself. She has a gun.'

The young doctor didn't seem to hear this, or he thought it wasn't important. Two men and a woman in white coats came at a run from the corridor, hooking Madlen up to some tubes and peeling her thin gold cocktail dress down to her waist.

'Okay, Felice, watch her breathing. All the time. Shane, you want to know what we're doing?'

'Yes, sir.' He looked almost a boy, with his wrists sticking out of his white coat cuffs; freckled, ginger-haired and licking his lips, he found a place to stand nearer the bed.

'Okay, she's on the oxygen now, and Felice is watching

89

her chest, watching her breathing. Get me the hammer – no, you can do this, okay, check her reflexes. I'm checking her pupils, and they're pinpoint.' He moved around the equipment, his eyes narrowed in the bright light. 'You know how to do a gag reflex?'

'I'm not –'

'Okay, Mary, you do it.' He reached to a shelf and got a pin and began prodding Madlen's finger pads, then pulled off her shoes and prodded the soles of her feet. 'High pain threshold, Shane. You can make notes if you want.'

Watching them, Lorraine thought, *If she comes out of this, it's going to be different. Everything's going to be different. I'll see to it. Just let her come through.* But if wouldn't be easy. For the first weeks after the plane crash she'd argued with Madlen endlessly, telling her that they needed each other, just until they could take up their lives again; but her sister had changed dramatically since the tragedy; it wasn't just grief: the psychiatrist had told Lorraine that Madlen's natural grief was bringing out all the buried resentment that a younger sibling nurtured in secret during childhood; she was now actually blaming Lorraine for their parents' death, because they'd flown to Los Angeles to see the first rough-cut of the movie she'd just made, and that was where the Floderus executive jet had crashed in flames on landing.

But things would be different now, if only Madlen came through; they'd work out their differences somehow, and live together for a while until Madlen's grief was healed at last.

'Gimme a 7 tracheal tube,' the young doctor was saying, 'and set up the ventilator. Felice, take an X-ray when I've got the tube in – I want to make sure where it is. What's her BP now?'

'109 over 67, Doctor.'

'Take it every five minutes, and call the lab, I want some blood drawn.'

There was a squeal of tyres outside the emergency entrance but nobody looked up. Lorraine was watching her sister's white, drawn face as the people worked on her; Madlen seemed to have shrunk, as if the life were going out of her over the minutes, draining away; a gleam of light showed between her lids, which were not quite closed, but it expressed no more life than a sleeping-eye doll; her tender mouth was drawn back from her teeth as the tube was thrust inwards, and now Lorraine had to look away, feeling an insane urge to pull these people away from Madlen and hold her against her own warm body and bring the life back, willing her to live again and give her another chance to care for her and this time make everything better, for always.

'Okay,' the doctor was ordering, 'set up an IV of D5W. Did you call the lab, Felice?'

'They're on their way down here, Doctor.'

Then someone came in with a rush and Lorraine looked up and saw it was the big man, Angelo, getting his breath, darting a look at the figure on the bed, seeing Lorraine and moving to her – 'She okay? She going to be okay?'

'I don't know.' She listened for the doctor to say over his shoulder, yes, she's going to be okay, but he didn't. He didn't say anything at all.

'I couldn't keep up with the ambulance,' Angelo said, tucking his tie in and smoothing his thick hair back and glancing again at the group of white-coated people around the bed.

'Who are you?' the young doctor asked him as he reached for a chart.

'It happened at my place,' Angelo said. 'She –'

'How many capsules were in the bottle?' the doctor asked him sharply, and waited, his strained eyes fixed on the big man's. 'How many?'

'Jesus, I don't know. She had them with her – we just broke the door down and –'

'Okay. Stand over there and don't get in the way.' He turned as two women came hurrying in. 'Right, I want some blood drawn. I want to know if there's any alcohol in –' he swung to stare at Angelo and Lorraine in turn – 'had she been drinking before she took this stuff?'

91

Lorraine looked at Angelo. He said, 'Yeah. Not much, though.'

'*How* much?'

'Maybe a half-bottle of champagne, while she was with me. I don't know if she'd been drinking before then, but she didn't look like it. She holds it pretty well, and –'

'I don't care whether she can *hold* it,' the doctor said impatiently, and turned away from him. 'All I'm interested in is how much alcohol there is slopping around with the Seconal.' He told the two women who had just come in: 'I also want a barbiturate level test and a drug screen, to see if she took anything else – you'd better write this down – test for blood urea nitrogen, the electrolytes, a complete blood count to check for any infection, and a blood sugar – ' he swung round to Lorraine again – ' does she have diabetes?'

'No. At least, I –'

'Do the test anyway,' he told the technicians.

Lorraine sat with her eyes closed, suddenly aware how terribly isolated Madlen had been since their bereavement: Lorraine *didn't even know if she had diabetes . . .* How many hundreds of other things didn't she know about her, how many thousands of things that might be important, vital for her to know, like what had taken her to the ladies' room of an Upper East Side club to try ending her life?

Things will be different, if only you'll come back to me.

'Put in a Foley,' she heard the doctor ordering, his voice weary, 'and check her urine output.'

'Doc,' the young probationer asked suddenly, 'is this a coma?'

'You bet. This is a coma, and it's a classic. Take a lot of notes, son.'

Then Angelo was moving forwards suddenly, his thick arms held slightly away from his body as if there were something he could do with them, use them for, maybe to hold that little broken doll on the bed there. 'Doc, I want to know something. Is she going to make it?'

Watching him, Lorraine felt sudden compassion for him; he was suffering the helplessness that all big men felt more acutely than others in a situation where their strength wasn't enough.

The doctor glanced at him. 'You say you're her brother?'

'Huh? No. I only saw her twice in my life.'

'She took this stuff at your place, though?'

'Right. I run a club.'

'Okay.' He shrugged, narrow-shouldered in his stained white coat. 'I can't tell you whether she'll make it, yet. We're doing all we can.'

Angelo's big hands fell to his sides, and he nodded, and came away. '*Madre di Jesu*,' Lorraine heard him whispering.

The doctor stood watching the catheter going into the patient's urethra, then checked that the IV was dripping correctly and watched the senior lab technician draw two measures of blood; then he turned to Lorraine.

'But you're her sister, you said?'

'Yes.' She got off the stool they'd given her to sit on.

'Okay. Stay where you are. You need your strength.' He became suddenly human, now that he had time to concern himself with things other than his patient. 'Let me tell you what's happening. We don't know how much Seconal she took, but it was a lot. If she can –'

'Doctor,' someone called from the corner of the room, 'she's stopped breathing. The machine's –'

'Okay,' the doctor said to Lorraine with his hand on her arm, 'it's perfectly okay, we're breathing for her, with the machine, okay? Don't worry.' He called to the technician, 'We'll get a blood gas study in another ten minutes.' He turned back to Lorraine, pinching the bridge of his nose and focusing his eyes again. 'That's the key to this whole thing, the ventilator. The breathing machine. It'll keep her going while she tries to metabolise the drug, and she can do that, if she's in normal health. In a minute I'm going to give you a questionnaire to fill in – what illnesses your sister's had, that sort of thing. It'll help us a lot. What we're going to do now is put a lavage tube into her and try pumping what's left of the Seconal out, and what we can't wash out we're going to bind with charcoal and a few other things, so she can't absorb it any more. Then we'll be looking at the results of all the tests, and by that time we'll know a whole lot more than we do now. Okay?'

'When will that be?' Lorraine asked him.

'A few hours.' He glanced up at the clock with red-rimmed eyes. 'I can't give you a definite time. By morning. Okay? By morning.'

They waited in a small lounge at the end of the corridor from the Intensive Care Unit, where Madlen had now been moved. The black-and-chrome clock on the wall, with its long sweeping second hand, showed a minute after five. Angelo had been pacing a lot, going from wall to wall like a caged bear; when he saw it was getting on Lorraine's nerves he sat down on the end of the burnt-orange settee and tried to talk again.

She had asked him a while back, 'How did you get my phone number, Mr Angelo?'

'She said if anything happened to her, to call it.'

'She didn't say it was her sister's?'

'No. That was all she said, to call the number.'

As if Madlen didn't even want to acknowledge having a sister at all. But if she'd given him her number, it meant there was nobody else to call. No friends, no one who'd be shocked when they heard the news, no one who'd cry.

'You said you'd only seen her twice in your life, Mr Angelo.'

'Sure,' he nodded his large head, watching her mournfully.

'You don't have to stay. I'll be here if she – when she comes out of it.'

He sat straighter. 'Am I bothering you?'

'Of course not.' She didn't know how to say it, that she didn't expect a stranger to hang around a hospital waiting for news. And she didn't know how to ask him the things she should be asking: if he knew why Madlen wanted to do such a thing. She knew already. Madlen was lonely, so

94

desperately lonely that there was only one person she could think of who should be told what she'd done: the sister she hated. But there might be things Angelo could tell her that would help, later, if the jumping light across the screen in there didn't suddenly flatten out. 'I just thought,' she told the big man, 'that you could use some sleep.'

'I'm used to being up nights.' He came over and sat next to her, with the palms of his big hands flat on his knees. 'Okay, I only saw her twice in my life, but you know, when someone comes into your place and has a drink with you and then goes off into the ladies' room and stuffs herself full of Seconal, Jesus, it gets to you. Can't you imagine?'

'I'm sorry, Mr Angelo.' Lorraine put her face in her hands for a moment to blot out the light and his steady, interested gaze. 'I'm not thinking very straight. Of course you're concerned for her.'

'Sure. The name's just Angelo.' She heard his quiet, sorrowful voice in the darkness of her closed eyes, aware of his stale cologne and his heaviness on the cushion beside hers. 'I'm just sorry for the kid,' he said, 'that's all. What made her do it?'

'I don't know her very well.'

'Don't get on?'

Lorraine took her hands away from her face, looking around for her bag and remembering she'd left her apartment in such a rush that she didn't bring it with her. 'Do you have a cigarette?'

'Sure.' He produced a heavy gold case, springing it open.

'Thank you. What did she say, Angelo, while she was having that drink with you?'

He flicked his lighter for her. 'She didn't say anything particular. She asked me about the club, you know. She liked the place, felt at home there, she said. She wanted to dance there for me.'

'To *dance*?'

'Sure. Not for the money. We don't need a dancer. But she's an interesting kid.'

'In what way?' She was trying to learn something about

95

her own sister, from this stranger who was the last person in the world she'd talked to before she'd decided to leave it.

'Well, I've only seen her twice, like I say, but the first time she came into my place she started to strip off on the stage and then broke a hundred-year-old Tiffany mirror with a ten-year-old bottle of Veuve Cliquot, and the second time she went off to the ladies' room and ate up a lot of Seconal. You can't say she isn't an interesting kid.'

A couple of hours ago when she'd seen Madlen flung out on the bathroom floor like that she'd been too shocked to feel heartbreak, but it had started later, when she'd watched them working on her pale, fragile body with their tubes and gauges and needles while she lay there not even aware of them, or of anything; and it was still going on, the heartbreak, making her realise for the second time in her life that it wasn't a feeling that was suddenly over, but something that went on and on.

'Yes,' she told the big man beside her, 'you could say she was an interesting kid. It's just that we lost our parents a year ago, very suddenly; and maybe she took it harder than I did.'

His thick fingers drummed on his knees. 'I see. That's a real shame. Floderus . . . ' he said reflectively, 'are you anything to do with the perfume company?'

'I own it.'

In a moment he said, 'You own it. I see. Sure, there was an airplane crash, isn't that right?'

'Yes.'

'A real shame.' His big moist hand was suddenly on hers; then as if he'd forgotten himself he removed it, and got to his feet, wandering across to the water fountain and bending over it, making little slurping sounds that, absurdly, she began counting: one . . . two . . . three . . . up to nine, until he came away and mopped his face with his handkerchief.

'Floderus,' he said with a gentle smile, 'that's why you smell so nice.'

A little time later Lorraine noticed a creeping of faint light at the edges of the windows, and on the side of the building opposite. It was morning.

96

CHAPTER 9

By 11.15 LORRAINE was in her office, looking pale and exhausted, even though she had slept for almost three hours after getting home from the hospital. The strain of the long night, with its recurring moods of bewilderment, anguish and guilt as she had waited near the intensive care unit at St Catherine's, would need more than a few hours of snatched sleep to be eased away.

As soon as she had reached home from the hospital at a little after seven o'clock she had left a message on Barry Corbett's tape at his home, asking him to cover for her at the office until she could be there; she said simply that there'd been an accident but that all was now well. It wasn't entirely true; when she'd left Madlen, now in the recovery ward, it had been hard to keep her tears back; in the last few hours her sister had changed from a pretty, vital creature to a white-faced, silent survivor from the closeness of death, her eyes watching Lorraine as if she were a stranger, their glowing violet colour faded to the pallor of a dying flower.

'She'll be okay now,' the doctor had said before he had lurched off to find a spare bunk where he could drop into sleep. 'We'll keep her here for two or three days; then you can make whatever arrangements you want; she'll need a lot of reassurance in the next week or two, a lot of love; and you'll be well advised to seek counselling of some kind – if you like, we can give you the names of one or two people who specialise in this kind of case.'

So Madlen was going to live.

It was all Lorraine had been able to think about, since

97

she'd known. Emerging into the pale sunshine of the hospital grounds, she'd thought it was still yesterday, and had to keep looking at her watch before she could orientate; it had felt worse than getting off a long west-east flight. After she'd slept, fitfully and with recurring nightmares, she'd forgotten the company records the accountants had let her bring home last night, and her first phone call from her office had been to tell them to fetch them from her apartment, where Tilly was standing over them like a guard dog.

Two bizarre incidents – that would have seemed perfectly normal at any other time – occurred soon after she arrived at her desk. Maggie informed her that she was to make her flight to the West Coast in exactly two hours' time, and here were the reservations and all necessary information. And a receptionist called to say that the Rolls-Royce had arrived.

Lorraine felt as much like flying to the West Coast as diving out of a window; the way she was feeling right now, she'd just got back from a flight round the globe and had twenty-four hours' jet lag to catch up on. She'd told Maggie to cancel her appointment in Los Angeles, and five minutes later told her to cancel the cancellation; there was an important perfumers' convention at the Hollywood Hyatt Regency, and she ought to be there.

As for the Rolls-Royce, she'd totally forgotten having ordered it; and when she remembered, it brought back her memories of Frank, and her idyllic week-end with him in that other life before last night.

'Maggie, get me George.' As she waited, Lorraine was shocked to realise how the draining away of psychic energy during the night had left her unable to work out the simplest thing. 'George? Listen, we've just bought a Rolls-Royce and it's down there on the street waiting for somebody to look after it.'

'I'll see to it.' George had the warm, gravelly voice of a favourite uncle.

'But what about parking space?'

'Is this an extra vehicle, Miss Floderus, or are you selling one of the others?'

'Yes,' she said, as if she'd thought of it first. 'I'm selling one of the limos.' She knew, at least, the situation with midtown Manhattan's garage-space; it wasn't that it cost a king's ransom every year to rent just one slot, but that you had to wait in line forever just to get it.

'Okay,' George said. 'I'll get the Rolls parked and take a limo along to the dealer.' When he hung up she called Judy Pollack and told her to forget hiring a new chauffeur; she'd drive the Rolls herself, as an economy. Absurdly, having just bought a $100,000 dollar sedan for her personal use, she was pleased with her idea of dispensing with a chauffeur as an 'economy' move; she felt she had done something towards rescuing the entire company from financial ruin.

Then Dean Powers called, asking if he could 'look in for a few minutes,' which might mean anything from a five-minute chat to an hour's conference in depth. Remembering what she'd seen at lunch yesterday at the Danish Buffet, she said she could see him briefly in twenty minutes, and then had Judy pull Dean's résumé from file and send it along. As she began looking through it she felt the tension rising inside her; whatever Dean wanted to talk to her about, it was going to take second place to what *she* wanted to talk about, which was Dean's blatant breach of company discipline.

This was the résumé that Dean had presented to her father almost eight years before, and in it were all the facts she didn't know about him, and should. There hadn't been time in the past twelve months to bone up on everyone's dossier, though she should have made it, she knew that now.

Under the heading of Education there were no startling details, though Dean had shown himself to have tackled his earlier years with success, completing his five-year course in business administration and economics in four years, mastering in science and picking up a bachelor in physical education along the way – both *cum laude*. His activities had been Varsity football, all intramural sports and archery; he'd received a trophy for all-round athletic achievement and had been senior year president of his social fraternity.

This was at Yale.

His personal record at that time was more interesting. *Born 6/5/45* – which made him 38 right now – *Married 1973, wife graduate Chalmers College, Connecticut. Two children. Health excellent, no physical limitations* – which he was now busy trying to prove, thought Lorraine scornfully. *Finances excellent, no debt encumbrances; hobbies: sports (active and spectator), astronomy. Affiliations: Rotary International; Yale Archery Club.*

Somehow Lorraine didn't see the tall, elegantly-dressed Dean Powers with a bow-and-arrow in his arms, but maybe he'd given it up now, since his arms were so fully occupied. Even as she thought this, she realised how bitchy it was, how prejudiced; she was reacting as if the man had divorced *her*, instead of someone else. Or had his wife divorced him? She'd need to ask.

He was five minutes late. As a senior VP that was okay; but she noticed it. She also noticed that he'd let Maggie open the door for him this time instead of just walking in here.

'Hi,' he said, and stood staring for a long moment. 'My God, what happened to you, Lorraine?'

She felt her mouth tighten. All right, she looked like death this morning, but did he have to point it out to her?

'I lost some sleep last night. Sit down, Dean, will you?'

'Sure.' But he didn't take one of the low chairs; he perched on a window-sill, dangling one elegantly-trousered leg and watching her from about the same level. Maybe Carl wasn't the only one who didn't like having to look up at the boss. For the moment there was nothing she could do about it; the décor people had promised to get the work done over the next week-end.

'I wanted to talk to you anyway,' she said evenly, 'and right off the bat I want you to know that you're a grown man and I'm a grown woman and we both have our private lives and susceptibilities, and the only way you're meant to show any responsibility to me is where the company is concerned, and not outside.'

He watched her steadily from his window-sill, looking,

she thought, like an ad for a good suit or even a good pair of horn-rimmed glasses, which he wore with style; but she noticed that the elegantly-dangling leg had started to move very slightly, swinging back and forth.

'The Danish Buffet,' she went on lightly, 'is outside the company, but a lot of our execs go there for lunch; below that level none of our staff go there, simply because they can't afford to; and none of the other execs take employees there because they're aware of the dictates of discipline and its value in keeping up our corporate public image. Do you agree?'

She waited, sitting back at her desk with what she hoped looked like perfect composure, while the ache went on extending along her neck muscles until she wanted to hold her hand there, and close her eyes for a while.

'Agree with what?' His voice was low and precise; whether it was more or less precise than usual she couldn't judge, but any increase in precision would reveal the edge of his anger, if he decided to get angry at all.

'That –' but she couldn't remember exactly how she'd put it to him; all she remembered was that even as she'd been saying it, the words and phrases had sounded stuffy and pedantic. 'That our corporate image is worth protecting.' Christ, why couldn't she just say what she meant, instead of all these fancy phrases? *Dean, I want you to stop playing around in public with the girls in the office, and if you don't, you're fired.*

Not possible. It was never possible in life to say exactly what you meant, unless it was in the middle of a family fight. And even then it could do terrible damge.

'Mind if I smoke, Lorraine?'

'Go right ahead.' She would have joined him, but she'd got through a whole pack last night; and it would have made a little ritual for them to share and she didn't want that.

'What you're trying to say is, I should stop dating the girls in the office. But that's none of your concern.' He blew out a cloud of smoke and clicked his gold lighter shut.

Even in her state of utter fatigue she was aware of

revelation; in his easy way he could say things she'd thought were impossible to say. Very well, they were going to let it all hang out; but as she took the plunge she was surprised at her own tone, at its vehemence. 'Yes, Dean, it is my concern, because this is my company; and when you play around with any girl here who believes in the total myth that to sleep with an executive is the fastest way to the top, you're harming the company, and that means you're harming me. So let me put it this way.' She got up from her desk and took a turn across the end of the room, not looking at him. 'Either you play by the rules, or you're fired.'

This time he didn't make her wait. 'You can't fire me and you should know that. You'd need the board's unanimous decision.'

'Then I'd get it.' She swung to look at him now as the tension became raw anger. 'And if I didn't get it I'd make your life here such a goddamned misery that you'd be only too glad to go.'

He studied the ash on his cigarette, and his leg was no longer moving; but she could hear the anger in his voice, because he couldn't hide it anymore. 'I don't see why you feel so strongly about this, Lorraine. You've only been one year working in an office in this city – less long, probably, than the tea-boy – so I'd better tell you that a typical business corporation in Manhattan isn't exactly a nunnery. As regards what you call the corporate image, this one is probably as good as the next. Maybe better.'

A buzzer sounded in the silence. Maggie. If Maggie came in here, Lorraine decided, without being asked to come in, she'd get fired on the spot. Anyone would. Because this tall, easy-mannered senior vice president was doing something to her that she'd never felt in her life before. Even on the set in Hollywood, when the director and the actors and the crew had been sweating through a long day of foul-ups and camera-jamming and repeated takes, she had always kept her cool; and now she was losing it. All right, she'd had a bad night and she felt as she looked: like death; but that wouldn't make her furious like this; it would leave her almost

102

indifferent to this bastard's veiled insults. So what was getting into her?

An accumulation, perhaps, of resentment against Dean over the weeks since she'd first heard the rumours about him. This was just something that had to come out, and she was letting it come out right now. But she'd have to make a final attempt at showing reason.

'I feel strongly about this, Dean, because your . . . philandering – which isn't what we called it in Hollywood – not only – '

'Fucking around,' he said brutally, 'is what you mean. Right?'

She felt her tension increase another kilowatt. 'Right. Your fucking around is not only harming the company, and through the company, me personally. It's also harming my employees. They're trying their best to do their job, as we all are; being human, they enjoy swapping notes about their lives during the course of the day – hey, Betty's getting married again, isn't that great? And Joan's having a baby – and that sort of thing takes a lot of the grinding drudgery out of their work schedule. But what you're doing, Dean, is filling the ladies' room with unpleasant gossip and bringing an unwanted element into the corporate atmosphere. Worst of all, some of these girls really do believe that to play around with a senior VP is a guarantee of fast promotion. And that's where you're being downright callous.'

She waited to see if he'd react. He didn't. Unwilling to face him while she was on the attack, she watched his reflection in a window at right-angles to where he was perched. He was motionless, and by the set of his head he might have been listening to a suggestion that the company should extend its marketing field to embrace the Philippines. Whether he was really as cool as he looked, inside of him, she couldn't hope to tell; she would only know when he spoke; and she knew intuitively that his quietness and his silences were designed to trap her into saying too much, going too far, to the point where her argument would collapse under its own weight.

103

So she'd finish him off right now. 'I may not have been here longer than the tea-boy, but I know this much. Just as soon as a young female employee has been cajoled into bed with an executive, she's ready to be thrown aside; she becomes an embarrassment, because her shining knight is out after the next girl, the next week. So she's quietly fired. She may be given a promotion first, just for a while, to take the sting out; and she doesn't ever see it as a form of payment for sexual services, which it is. She finds herself trying to do a job she can't handle, because she got it without any merit; so when she's fired she thinks it's because she flunked the job.' She swung to face Dean now. 'You know this. It happens all the time. How many has it been so far, for you? How many of these ignorant little typists have been thrown quietly out of this building because you didn't give a damn for them, even while you were holding their hands across the table at the Danish Buffet? I don't actually want to know, Dean. Because this one's going to be the last.'

The acoustics in this elegant room were designed by experts to soften the sound of telephones, to lend a hush to the human voice and give it the tone of discretion and authority; the hubbub of busy commerce could wash at the doors of the executive suites, but within their hallowed walls the decisions of top management were reached in the quieting atmosphere of pile carpeting and decorative acoustic-tile ceilings. Lorraine was therefore vaguely surprised to hear her voice echoing brassily from wall to wall with the strident ring of a fishwife in the market-place; and for an interminable moment she wished she could put the clock back just five little minutes and start all over, and come up with a dignified, balanced and convincing argument that would have swayed this arrogant subordinate while leaving his ego intact.

Instead, she'd just made an enemy.

So be it.

'Have you finished?' He'd turned his head to look at her.

'Yes.'

'Good.' He swung himself from the window-sill, drew

deeply on his cigarette, blew out a stream of smoke and watched it contemplatively for a moment before moving easily across to the desk and dropping the stub into the ashtray. 'What I came to ask you, Lorraine, was whether you intend selling the company.' He measured the silence. 'Or maybe you don't think that's more important than what we've been discussing.'

Suddenly she hated him. His air of detachment, his easy ridicule, his unerring ability to make her look like a child in a tantrum, all came together in her mind and she hated him; and only faintly did she hear the warning note that was sounding in the background: only a few days ago she'd stood in this same room and hated Carl Blatt for what he, too, was doing to her . . .

'I don't know,' she said coldly, 'what plans I have for the company. I've called a board meeting for Thursday. I'll know by then.'

He nodded reflectively, watching her with no discernible expression in his deep brown eyes. 'The thing is, if you're asking me to quit, that's quite okay; but if Carl's leaving too, as he tells me he is, you'll have quite a few empty offices around by the time you want to sell out. It wouldn't look very good.'

It was designed to goad her, and it did. 'If you'd rather quit than stop preying on the junior typists, don't let anything stop you, Dean. I can fill an empty office soon enough.'

He nodded again. 'Oh, sure. The other thing is, whatever decision you want to make on Thursday, you may need support, from wherever you can get it. Even from me.' He gave a shrug. 'So why don't we wait till then?'

Lorraine was so intent on sifting what he'd said for another implied slight that she couldn't think of a reply; and when she turned around she saw he'd gone quietly out and closed the door.

Chapter 10

'Ladies and Gentlemen, the captain has turned off the "No Smoking" sign. TWA is pleased to offer you a smoking and no smoking zone. We request that you smoke only in the smoking zone as indicated by the sign at the front of the cabin.

'The captain has also turned off the "Fasten Seat Belt" sign. For your safety, passengers are requested to keep their seat belts fastened while seated.'

Donna Shapiro, senior flight attendant in First Class, hooked the mike back against the bulkhead and went into the forward galley, thinking, among a few dozen other things she had to think about at this stage in the flight, that there would come a day, sooner or later, when even the glamour of the uniform, even the romantic attraction of exotic places, even the drama of an airport crowded with high-tailed international jetliners moving slowly towards the runway and its far horizons, wouldn't any longer be enough to compensate for the basic fact that a flight attendant was nothing more than a flying waitress. Despite all the personality screening, the stringent training courses, the inborn and implanted abilities to cope with a crisis and handle human beings and contribute to the safe and efficient operation of huge air carriers, you spent ninety per cent of your time tranquillizing people with food and drink to distract them from the boredom of a long and fatiguing flight.

To know this, you had to do the job first. That was why TWA alone received an average of 10,000 applications a month. It was also why Donna Shapiro, after almost a year looking for work with her brand new degree in civil law, finally dropped into the TWA office in New York and asked for details. One of the first questions on the list was, why did she decide to apply? She said that the TWA office happened to be right across the pavement from the bus stop she'd used on her way to the law college, and she'd seen the posters so many times she'd begun to feel like a flight attendant. Maybe they'd given her the job for being honest.

'One day,' Jinnie Metcalf had told her on their last flight, 'there's going to be a white Anglo-Saxon Protestant in the front aisle seat, with a kind face and nice manners and a loving disposition and 50% shares in General Motors; and he's going to fall for me so hard that I'll just have to carry him bodily out of this cabin and through the terminal and down to the church, and then you can wipe your own jello-stains off the floor, honey chile.'

Jinnie was with her today, trying to make the kid in Aisle 6 stow his skateboard in the locker. Maybe, thought Donna as she mixed the drinks in the aux. bar and began serving them forward to aft in Zone A, there'd be a white Anglo-Saxon Protestant, or a black Eurasian Brahmin for that matter, with only a few little bitty shares in, say, Presto Clothes-Pins, who would fall for her hard enough to carry *her* through the terminal and into a town house in the Village where they could play mahjong to the tune of a zither for the rest of their lives. Or whatever.

They all fantasised this way sometimes; it made the job easier. They knew it was a lot more likely they'd meet some kinky creep like that zillionaire a few days back, Vankloot or some name like that. Up in the clouds, life was just as real as anyplace else.

'Donna.'

'Yes?'

'Do we carry any rice wine?'

'Could be. Try the top bin on the left hand side in the aux. bar. Did you fix the kid?'

'Sure. It's stowed. We made a deal: he gets the captain's

autograph when we land.'

In another twenty minutes the huge airliner had reached its ceiling and was settled on course across the clouds, while Donna and Jinnie worked at the tray carts and in the galley, serving, smiling, remembering names, forgetting them and checking the pax list again, catching a glass before it fell, keeping a distance from the little guy in the aisle seat at the rear because he had restless hands, burning their fingers at the bun-warmers, mopping up liquor from the plastic hardtops, checking the seat belts when the sign went up as they flew through bumps, until the real work began and they started serving lunch: Sautéed Scallops with Spinach and Saffron Sauce, or Roast Leg of Lamb New England, and a choice today of a Blanc de Blancs by Sebastiani or a 1973 Souverain Pinot Noir from Alexander Valley.

And a copy of the menu for Dad.

It was when Donna was clearing the tray from Seat # 9 in Zzone A that Mr Clyde C. McLoone lurched into a passenger in the seat behind him as he came back from the lavatory, cursed under his breath, sat down with a thud and ordered another Bourbon, straight up. Donna had been waiting for this. She leaned over the frail, white-haired lady in the seat behind and said she was sorry. With a wan smile, the lady said it was perfectly all right, and no harm done. But Donna didn't miss the apprehension in her eyes.

'Mr McLoone,' she said with a crisp smile, 'won't you let me offer you something different this time around? We have a really super fruit punch.'

McLoone stared at her rheumily. 'A fruit *what*, for Christ sake?' He was a custom-tailored Texan, overweight and heavy-jowled, thick-skinned and sun-tanned, with – to Donna's personal knowledge – five straight Bourbons already behind his snakeskin belt. 'Look, kid, don't play around, okay? You know what I want. Go get it.' His voice was deliberately loud.

'Sir, flight regulations won't allow me to serve you with an alcoholic beverage at this point in time.' She was speaking close to him, so that the other pax couldn't hear, and took in the slight grey stubble and the large calloused hands; he was a cattle baron, and could probably drive his own herd if he had to; he was used to a rough life in the open, on a ranch where his word was law.

'And what the fuck, young lady, is "this point in time"? Are we flying over a dry state or something?'

'Sir, you appear to have been drinking, that's all.' It was also in flight regulations that she mustn't call him drunk, even if he were stretched out on the floor – which he would be if she kept on plying him with Bourbon.

His small red-rimmed eyes became mean. 'Are you trying to tell me I'm drunk?'

'No, sir. I'm just asking you to lower your voice and try and cooperate. I don't want you to upset the other passengers.' It was in fact too late now to do anything about that; his voice, used to shouting at cowhands across the open range, had already reached every passenger in the forward cabin. It was always at this point that Donna wondered if she'd done the right thing; it was possible that this leather-skinned cowboy could hold his liquor for the rest of the flight, and deplane without incident. But she'd already seen him lurching in the aisle and upsetting the little lady behind him; and if he got out of hand after a few more drinks, it would be her ass. She knew the regulations by heart on this point. *No air carrier shall serve any alcoholic beverage aboard an air carrier aircraft if such person appears to be intoxicated.*

'Okay, dimples, are you going to bring me a drink or aren't you?' He said it more quietly, with a very rough edge to his voice. 'And before you answer that, just let me tell you that if you refuse, you're going to be in one helluva lot of trouble.'

Without looking around, Donna could tell the effect this man was making on the rest of the passengers. This particular problem didn't often arise; but when it did, it caused more anxiety – at 30,000 feet in the confined space of an aircraft cabin – and more unpleasantness than any other type of incident; because there was a kind of unspoken code

109

among normal passengers: they had to share each other's company for these few hours, and despite all the efforts to make them comfortable it was going to be fatiguing, so they would be kind to each other and behave like civilised people. A drunk was the one type of passenger who could destroy that code and set everyone's nerves on edge.

Donna tried again, this time having to speak with her small white teeth close together, since she was working up a really fine anger. 'Sir, I am not going to serve you with any more liquor. If you wish to complain, you may attach your business card to the flight report with a note of your complaint. I'll see it's forwarded to my supervisor. You will then receive a letter of acknowledgment from In-flight Services. In the meantime, let me offer you – '

'Now you just listen to me, you pink-assed sassy little bitch.' His voice was very loud. 'I'm not asking for any goddamn' letter from anybody, I'm asking for a fucking drink, and if you don't bring it to me right now I'm going to fetch it myself – now you better just understand that!'

Donna was suddenly aware of Jinnie beside her. 'Shall I get the captain, Donna?'

'No. Just smile at everyone, like you really mean it.' Then she put her head right close to the grizzled rancher's and began speaking very quietly, so only he could hear. She spoke for longer than a minute, with only a short break; and he listened without interrupting; and then she was moving down the aisle to the aux. bar to mix him a fruit punch – *his* way, with his rumbling chuckle following her like music in her ears.

When she came back with the drink, he raised his glass.

'Here's to you, gal. And I guess I'm going to do something I ain't maybe used to.' He looked around and raised his leather-lunged voice. 'Ladies and gentlemen – I apologise!'

Someone gave a laugh, and others took it up; the kid at the rear began clapping. They were just relieving the tension that had been building up in the cabin, and suddenly the call-lights were popping on as people ordered drinks.

'You *have* to tell me something,' the attractive woman in

110

Aisle 12 said to Donna as she came past. 'What *did* you say to that man?' According to the pax list this was Lorraine Floderus, the movie actress.

'I – well, he was just nice and cooperative, Miss Floderus.'

'Oh, come on, he wasn't nice and cooperative before you talked to him. If it's a secret, I'll keep it.' The stunning smile appeared, and Donna was almost dazzled enough to tell her what had happened; but it wouldn't do. She'd handled the Texan successfully, but TWA wouldn't want anyone to know precisely how.

So she simply said, 'We get to know people, in this job, and I thought I knew the best way to handle the situation. I guess I lucked out – I was right. Can I get you something to drink or anything?'

'Not right now.' She didn't persist about Donna's secret, but tilted the seat back and got her pillow. 'I'm going to catch up some more before we get in.'

'You do that.' Donna pulled the window-blind down for her and doused the lamps, moving on. Miss Floderus had come on board at LAX looking pooped, which was par for the course, she supposed, for a Hollywood actress, the kind of hours they had to work and the kind of parties they went to.

Jinnie was mixing drinks in the forward bar. 'Okay, Donna, come clean. How did you fix Mister Musclebound along there?'

'Tell you later.' She had two more drinks to mix and she never liked talking when she was doing that, because some of the pax were touchy about how you fixed their cocktails. She could use one herself, as a matter of fact; the first time she'd had to handle a noisy drunk in mid-flight she'd made out okay, but thrown up in the lav right afterwards, out of sheer nerves. This time it had only left her shaking a little. Thinking back, she realised she'd taken quite a risk, because the first part of what she'd told the big Texan wasn't likely to soothe him down any.

'Okay, Daddy-o, now it's my turn, and this won't be going into the flight report.' She'd paused for a couple of seconds right here to test his reactions, but he didn't interrupt; so she kept right on, speaking real close against his weather-beaten ear. 'You're acting like a little five-year-old in a tantrum, and you've got me jumping mad, and if I were your size I'd sock you back into that seat so hard your brains'd go clean through the headrest, and then I'd drag your guts out and hang 'em from the luggage rack, are you getting my message, mister?' She was looking right into his mean red eyes, because that's where she'd see the warning first if he decided to get out of his seat and start throwing everything around, including her; in which case Jinnie could get the captain here real fast. But right now this cute cowboy was just staring her right back, with something like surprise dawning.

'But we all of us get those days,' Donna pressed on quietly, right up close, 'when for some reason or another we decide it's a good time to get smashed out of our minds, and I know you don't normally carry on this way. I think that normally you act like what you really are, a successful, important member of the community with the kind of responsibilities that'd turn my hair white just to think about; and I want to remember you as a charming and intelligent mature *man*, who knows how to listen to a girl and get her drift even when he's stacked some fire-water under his belt.' With some trepidation she put a hand on his big shoulder.

'What I want is to go home to my Mom and Dad tonight – I always have some chow with them between flights, see, because they're real nice folks, you'd like them – and tell them who I met today, none other than Clyde C. McLoone, the famous Texan rancher; and tell them he was just about the most gallant gentleman I ever had as a passenger, and I'd sure like to meet him again.'

Then she waited, watching his eyes. Around her she knew everyone in the whole first class section was waiting too, and wondering what in hell she'd been saying to this dude. She knew that somewhere behind her there was Jinnie, halfway to the flight deck in case Clyde C. McLoone decided to take off; but Donna always worked with the idea that the captain

112

should fly the airplane while the flight attendants handled the passengers. This one still didn't move, and Donna kept perfectly still too, because this was the critical moment when things could go one way or the other, and suddenly.

It must have taken a full minute for a change to come into his eyes; the hot bright meanness was leaving them, and there was something like amusement there instead as he pulled her closer and spoke into her ear. 'Missy, that stuff about the gallant Clyde C. McLoone was just a load of steaming bullshit and you know it. But that stuff about what you'd do to me if you was my size . . . holy cow, *that* was the truth, and you spat it out real feisty.' A slow laugh started from deep inside his big hulk. 'So you go and fetch me one of those goddamn' fruit punches, with one finger – just one little finger – of the real thing with it, and I'll give you my word I'll behave myself, like that civilised goddamn' orangoutang you were talking about. Is it a deal?'

Donna straightened up so she could see all of his face, but left her hand on his shoulder for a moment longer; scenes like this always left her shaky, but her relief now was so great that she could feel her eyes swimming. 'It's a deal, Mr McLoone. You'll get a fruit punch and you'll get it your way. And I don't care whether you believe me or not, but I think you're a real nice guy.'

Lorraine woke to a voice over the speakers, too late to hear what it had been saying. The 'No Smoking' and 'Fasten Seat Belt' signs had gone on, and she could feel the massive weight of the jet settling as the power came off. She dropped the pillow onto the empty seat beside her and tilted her own upright; she'd set her watch to New York time when they'd left Los Angeles, and they must be landing soon.

She'd dreamed of her parents again, because today she'd gone closer to them than she had since the crash; she'd never got around to thinking of them as being in New York, at the little cemetery behind St Mark's on Long Island where they'd been buried. In her mind they were always where they'd actually died; and today she had looked from the

113

window as the plane had rolled along the taxi-ing lanes, and seen the ground still darkened near the Federal Express hangars, where the Floderus executive jet had stood burning at the end of its gyrations, a year ago. She'd sometimes forced herself to imagine how it had looked, feeling guilty because she should have been there and by some miracle prevented it, and trying to get rid of her guilt by pretending she'd been there after all, watching the sickening spin of the small twin-jet across the wastes of concrete, and then the dull orange flames and the long dark pall of smoke drawing out to spread across the sunset, casting shadow, while the huge yellow fire trucks poured foam everywhere much too late because the crash had been totally unexpected.

Dan Segrave, the psychiatrist she'd been to see when the ghastly nightmares began soon afterwards, had said it was okay to picture the crash scene if she wanted to, and think of it as the dramatic, blazing end to two beautiful lives, with the column of black smoke growing tall against the sky like a monument; from what she'd told him about them, Dan had said, they would rather have gone that way than lingering in a hospital from a disease that would have diminished them first. He'd also told her that there was another aspect of the tragedy that would continue to leave her disoriented long after the grief was calmed; with the burial of her parents she'd seen her own childhood laid to rest; she was no longer anyone's daughter; she was free now, and independent; and it would take her a long time to learn how to live without the authority figures who had all her life provided her with love, security and spiritual shelter. This too she'd become intuitively aware of as a part of the grief; she'd not only lost her parents; she'd lost her way, and must now make a new direction of her own.

Donna came past along the aisle, checking the seat belts, flashing her crisp white smile. 'We'll be down in fifteen minutes.'

'Thank you.' Lorraine shook off the memory of the dark smudge across the concrete in Los Angeles; she'd faced

114

going there at last, and in a way had said 'Hi' to Mom and Dad on her way through, however tragic the thought. Quite a lot of the people at the convention had made a point of mentioning her father briefly, by way of belated sympathy. 'An amazing man . . . A true talent . . . A man with a flair for elegance . . . Who could hold his own with the greatest names in the field . . . Fabergé, Molinard, Chanel, Givenchy . . . ' Frederick Vanderkloot, the chairman of Century Cosmetics, had been the only one there to talk of her mother first.

'I thought she was the most beautiful woman I had ever seen in my life, and I still think so. And you remind me of her so touchingly, my dear.' The heavy lids had lowered for a moment; then he smiled wistfully. 'She lives on in you. They both do, and always will.'

Lorraine had been moved, and had warmed to him; she'd met him only twice before, and last evening she'd realised she was the only woman in the group that had formed in the centre of the hotel ballroom; Vanderkloot had led her there to meet the others, all of them important figures in the industry; but the aura of real power had been around the short immaculate man with the dark eyes that had glittered so strikingly with interest, amusement, concern as he had escorted her for a little while among the rest of the men. They'd gathered around him, earlier in the evening, drawn, as she knew, by his magnetism, as she had been. It was even in his low, vibrant voice as he spoke to them so softly that they had to move closer to hear him. He'd drawn her aside after the formal banquet, and talked again about her father.

'He always astounded me, Lorraine. Just when everyone else was cutting expenses and concentrating on economy, he'd launch a new fragrance, and with such a fanfare that it wóke us all up again.' He was laughing now, mischievously, admiringly. 'For Wilhelm Floderus, the time was right whenever he decided it was. That is the way of the true pioneer: the man who sees the way ahead and strikes the path himself.' He became wistful again. 'It's my private feeling that he was ready, you know, to launch something

115

new again, for the spring season; he might not have confided in even his own colleagues at that stage, but in some ways he and I were very close, and I could see the signs of a potential new challenge for the rest of us in the industry – a new and unique fragrance from the house of Floderus. He was always dashing off to France as you know; and that was where he looked for his essences, in the old-world flower gardens of the Alpes Maritimes, while the rest of us were concocting things in test tubes in New Jersey . . . If it would interest you, Lorraine, we might discuss it over dinner one evening; as I said in my letter, there could be mutual advantages in a closer rapport between our two companies.'

Yesterday morning she'd dictated a reply to his letter, saying she didn't feel the time was right; but last night she told him to ignore that; she would welcome a meeting in New York. It was his talk of her father that had changed her mind; she hadn't known they'd been so close. There was also a distinct possibility that if she were ever to save Floderus Incorporated from an outright sale, a company like Century Cosmetics, with assets in the hundred-million-dollar range, might prove a big help.

'Hey, remember I get the captain's autograph, okay?'

The boy's voice brought Lorraine back to the present, and she checked her seat belt again. On both trips to the Coast and back she'd managed several hours' sleep, and felt more ready to tackle the problems she'd left in New York. She'd go straight from the airport to the hospital to see Madlen, for a start; she'd called her intern this morning, and was told she could be released 'almost any time now'.

The aircraft's mass was settling lower, and through her window Lorraine could see the perfect curve of the Verazano Bridge. For a moment a feeling of panic came again as she looked down on the city where all her problems lay; and black doubt clouded her thoughts: she would lose Madlen, by not understanding her needs; she would lose Floderus Incorporated, by not understanding how to save it; she would lose, finally, her way in life, before she could make out its direction.

116

If there were any one thing that could get her through the days and months ahead, it would be the knowledge that she wasn't utterly alone. But she didn't have it. She had many good friends, but not the kind who'd be ready to listen to her problems: they had enough of their own, despite their families, their wealth, their apparent security. She had business colleagues, but they too were useless to her, even opposed to everything she was striving to do.

There was no one.

The aircraft settled, banking against the early evening sky. The first of the city's lights were beginning to glow as the day began its dying.

'You don't have any baggage stowed, Miss Floderus, do you?' Donna paused briefly on her way down the aisle.

'No.' She looked up at the clean-cut features with their quick smile and attentive eyes. 'No, I don't.'

'Okay. We'll be in –'

'What did you say your name was?'

'Donna.'

'That's right. Where do you live, Donna? You have a base where –'

'New York City.' It was said with the rueful smile that most New Yorkers shared when they said it.

'This must be an exciting job you have. Rewarding.'

'It's okay. For a time.' She gave a quick shrug and made to pass on.

'Donna.'

The girl stopped and turned. 'Ma'am?'

'If you'd like to work for me, I'd pay double your present salary. Whatever it is.'

Donna's deep brown eyes snapped open a fraction and the professional smile froze; but that was all. She wasn't very surprisable. 'I guess it's not my life style.'

'What isn't?'

'Hollywood.'

Lorraine shook her head. 'I work in New York.' She saw the other flight attendant coming up the aisle, making sure that movable things were stowed under the seats. 'Donna,

117

you're busy now. But here's my card. Give me a call, will you?'

CHAPTER 11

AN HOUR AFTER the Los Angeles flight had landed at
Kennedy, rain followed it in from the mountains of East
Pennsylvania, darkening the pavements of Manhattan for a
while and then, by ten o'clock in the evening, brightening
them again with the reflections of the street lamps and the
neon signs. Taxis became scarce, and soaked raincoats
clustered at the intersections as people walked home from
the theatres and bars and restaurants.

On the fifth floor of his apartment building on the West
Side, behind drawn curtains and with the stereo playing very
softly and the lights turned low, Dean Powers was already
home, and at this moment, asleep.

'Do you date a lot of girls?'

He woke with a pleasant fluttering sensation at the tip of
his erect penis, and when he opened his eyes he was looking
at the mass of dark hair covering his companion's mons
veneris.

'I guess not,' he said, now fully awake and hoping to hell
she hadn't noticed; it wasn't the greatest compliment you
could pay to a girl, falling asleep while she was trying to give
you an orgasm. In case she was going to ask him any more
about his dating habits, he buried his face into her warm
pubic hair. He hadn't realised how exhausted he'd been at
the end of today after meetings with Carl, Barry, Sam, and
half a dozen other people in management; each of them had
his own idea about what Lorraine was going to say at the
meeting tomorrow. They all knew why she'd called it: even
she with her limited experience had caught the vibes along

119

the executive corridors of Floderus Inc. If she didn't feel good and ready to step aside and let somebody else run the show, either they'd vote her out of the chairman's seat or they'd put on their hats and leave.

'Is this nice?' Dolores asked.

'What?' He nuzzled a little harder. 'Terrific.' But *Jesus*, what had things come to? Was he losing interest in *sex*? The idea chilled him, just when he ought to be feeling hot. He was still hard, which was reassuring; and any guy who could fall asleep with the mast still high couldn't be that far gone. Maybe there'd just been too many. Nine girls in the past three months, five of them from the office and starting with Joan Someone, an eighteen-year-old from the typing pool, just ten days after his attorney and called up and said, 'Okay, Dean. It's final.'

Final. It was a word he never wanted to hear spoken again.

Armanda had been standing just outside her bathroom door, looking at him as he'd been taking off his socks; she was in a pale blue nightdress with her fair hair loose and her makeup removed, a line down her cheek where it had lain pressed against a crease in the sheet while she slept. It was a Thursday in January, a year ago, at five minutes before midnight by the digital clock on the table between their beds.

'You want a what?' he'd asked Armanda. The sock fell halfway between him and the linen basket as he threw it, too tired to put any effort into it.

'I want a divorce.'

He couldn't remember when he took the other sock off; maybe an hour later, maybe two. Armanda had been asleep since half past ten, when she'd finally gone to bed after waiting two hours for him, taking the roast out of the oven and putting it back and eventually leaving it cooling in the blue-and-white willow-pattern dish on the table, the wine poured and still in their glasses, the candles burned halfway down and then snuffed out.

It was in the early hours when they finally stopped talking

120

and he took the other sock off and went to sleep on the divan in his study. Most of what they'd said, he assumed, had been said by thousands before them when a marriage began breaking up. Accusations, protestations, recriminations, voices raised, voices lowered, depending on whether there were any kids who might wake to this new and bewildering world that was being so lovingly created for them behind their backs; and somewhere buried in all the splurge of hurt and misery and unleashed emotion was the actual nub of the argument, the psychic charge that had at last become powerful enough to blow away ten years of shared life together.

'I'm not actually certain,' Armanda had said, 'whether you really work late at the office, or spend your time fucking your boss. And I'm – '

'*Lorraine?*'

'I believe that's her name.'

'You're out of your mind!'

'But not certifiable. You're in close proximity and she's a real pin-up.'

'Would you mind not inventing circumstantial evidence, for Christ's sake, before the fact? There *isn't* any fact!'

'Okay. "I swear to God I have not laid my boss." I won't ask who else you have or have not laid while you've been "kept late again". I don't know whether you're working too hard or fucking too hard, and I don't particularly care; the thing is that I'm not enjoying marriage with a husband in permanent absentia. So this is it, Dean. I'm seeing Clive Weinberg in the morning. And I think it's traditional to say that if you're hungry, there's a cold roast downstairs.'

She'd then gone into her bathroom and shut the door and thrown the big frosted-glass Lalique pot of blue and pink cotton balls at the rose-tinted mirror, and then run a faucet as soon as the glass had stopped falling, to let him know she hadn't injured herself and given him an excuse for going in and making everything all better again with a box of Band-aid.

He'd made three solid attempts at getting her to change

121

her mind, because he'd really loved her – and did still. He had Barry, Carl and Sam go see her and confirm that he'd ben working all hours and even some week-ends at the office, because the company was heading fast for a crash and they had to do something to save it. He hadn't asked Lorraine to speak for him too, because he'd only known her for a few months and she wouldn't feel very good admitting she was herself responsible for steering the firm towards the rocks. Armanda had believed them. She'd said she was sorry about the company, but what bothered her a little was that her husband was so concerned about it that he hadn't notice that their marriage was also heading fast for a crash, and that was more important to her personally.

Dean had also, in those bleak and unfriendly meetings with her in the lobbies of impersonal hotels, challenged her to remember if, in the past ten years of their marriage, she had ever come upon a pair of theatre tickets, or a restaurant bill, or a lace handkerchief somewhere in his coat pocket or brief-case or his car; had there been a puzzling phone-call, or the hint of a strange perfume, or a woman's name in his appointment book? Anything? Anything at all? Sure, there'd been a couple of times, both at conventions, when he'd been far from home and lonely, and he'd never seen them again, hell, they were just tarts laid on for the occasion, it happened all the time.

There'd been a moment, sitting with Armanda in the lobby of the Barclay, she with a streaming cold and he with one arm in a sling because of a lift door, when he'd believed he might get her back if he went on trying.

'You're making quite a big effort,' she'd told him, red-eyed and with a Kleenex box on her lap. 'I'm flattered.'

He'd known she meant it; she'd never used sarcasm, preferring the direct blow at the frontal lobes. 'I'm going to go on making it,' he said, and put his hand over hers on top of the Kleenex box, trying to make out if these were tears in her eyes or just the cold. She didn't answer for a long time, and as the seconds went by he grew more and more certain she was going to give him another chance.

But she didn't. 'Dean, it's just that I'm someone who demands a lot of tender loving care. I have to be wanted, all the time. I have to be the one singular super-colossal *need* in a man's life. You used to understand that; then you began forgetting. And I think it's asking too much of you to take me back to where we were. After all, I haven't been getting any younger in the last ten years, any more breathtaking, any more unliveable-without.' She lifted her head and looked straight at him then, and he could see it wasn't tears. She'd shed them all by now. 'It's the breaks, Dean. You win some and you lose some.' Walking away from him a few minutes later, she'd turned once, and he'd seen in her eyes that she was looking back at the stranger he was going to be for the rest of their lives.

And here he was with the ninth girl since then, trying to pretend he was a hell of a dog and this was what freedom meant and now he was going to make up for all the girls he'd never had for the past ten years, with their different eyes and different hair and different ways they had of holding his cock, some of them shy and virginal, some of them stripping off their clothes the moment they got inside the apartment and pulling him onto the carpet, onto the settee, into the bedroom while he tried to believe how fantastic it must have been in ancient Rome with all those orgies; but somehow it wasn't the same in a small apartment in Manhattan where Armanda had never been, and would never come.

'You okay?' the girl was asking him again.

'Sure. Keep on, just like that.' And while her small pink tongue licked the lollipop he felt the beat of his heart skipping again, and held himself very still, waiting for the next time, and feeling it, *ski-bump, ski-bump*, while he held his breath. Sure, you can go on having sex, the heart man had told him three weeks ago, but just don't go in for any marathon stuff. You have any worries? Not really, no, my wife just left me after ten years and the firm I work for is heading for a crash, nothing you could call important.

You're Type A, the man had said, sitting at his desk and making notes, looking at charts, calling his assistant in to ask her about the results from the lab, and you know what that means, it means you'll have to change your life style, slow up, play more golf, let things ride a little. And I want you back in my office in six months. He'd looked at another chart and made another note and said, make that three, okay?

'Gee, you can sure stay hard a long time.'

'Sure.' *Ski-bump, ski-bump.*

Change the life style, yes. But exactly how do you quit a company you've been with for eight years, starting as a marketing junior and working your way up to senior vice-president and really feeling it's like another home; and exactly how do you stay in it and agonise with the rest of them at the board meeting tomorrow while your Type A personality is taking you on a collision course with a brief obituary in the *Wall Street Journal*?

Okay, some kind of decision would have to be reached tomorrow; then he could decide on his own future. Lorraine would have to step aside and become a figure-head president of the company while he or Barry or Sam took over as chairman and chief executive officer. Of if she wouldn't do that, and they couldn't force her, they could propose to sell the company for what they could get in the market after a year in which the sales had gone down steadily to the halfway mark compared with previous years.

Or he'd simply walk out. That would hurt. He'd worked hard for Floderus and he liked it there. It was a small but very select, very elegant model company with a reputation for old-fashioned quality in its product; and it had only one product: perfume; with no ventures into side lines like face-creams or body-lotions or shampoos. The company had class.

And it would hurt Lorraine, of course, if he walked out. She'd had a bad year too, and he'd been easy with her – they all had – when he'd seen her making one mistake after another, taking too much on herself instead of delegating, so scared of looking incompetent that she'd fabricated an image for herself of the late boss's daughter who could offer them all the same expertise and drive and solid business acumen they'd been used to in her father. For a time she'd had them fooled, burying her still-raw grief under a show of energy that had brought them to their feet in admiration. Then they'd come to their senses; she wasn't the most incredibly attractive young company boss in the business; she was just the most incredibly attractive young woman in Manhattan who was right now running a previously successful company into the ground.

He'd been quite sincere when he'd told Lorraine she might need his support at the meeting tomorrow; at the time he'd believed he could give it. But after reflection he'd seen that none of them would be able to give her any support if she refused to hand over the chairmanship. When she looked down that long polished table at ten in the morning, she wouldn't see a friend.

'You wanna work on me too?' he heard Dolores saying.

'I'm sorry.' He nuzzled the warm pubic hair aside and sent the tip of his tongue searching for the hard little clitoris; and as he worked on it he began fantasising that it wasn't Dolores licking and nibbling at his hard, inflamed penis, but his boss; and as he pictured those amethyst eyes and that dazzling smile he came at last, explosively.

The rain swept in gusts across Long Island Sound, the wind whipping it against the furled sails in the harbours and the windows of the waterfront bars. Farther inland, where trees gave shelter, the rain fell more softly across the dark rose garden where Barry Corbett had started cutting blooms for the house: Queen Elizabeth, Fire and Snow, Sterling Silver, Angel Face, Sutter's Gold and a hundred more, their colours conjuring a glow in the half-dark as the rain tried vainly to quench their fire.

More were inside the house, where the curtains were drawn against the night; an arrangement of Tropicanas blazed in a silver bowl on the bar in the living-room, where Barry was pouring a Courvoisier.

'Darling, should you?' Ginnie asked him gently.

'Is this one too many?' He'd stopped pretending he didn't know what she meant.

'It's an important meeting, isn't it, in the morning?' He always had such crippling hangovers on brandy.

'If you remind me of that,' he told her ruefully, 'I'll make it a double.' He brought his drink over to where his wife was sitting, thinking how patient she was with him, wishing perhaps she'd occasionally tell him to straighten up and get a grip on himself – he wasn't always like this. He lifted his balloon glass, half-mockingly. 'Cheers. I don't know how you put up with me.'

'A man who brings me roses can't be all bad.' She'd laid aside the tapestry she was making, and one hand rested on the cushion beside her on the couch, palm upwards; he didn't, probably, actually see it there; he was aware on a much deeper level that she was inviting him to sit with her. It had been happening for more than twenty years: they'd gravitate towards each other when nobody else was in the room. He sat down and took her hand. 'We depended on him too much,' she said, talking about Wilhelm Floderus. 'Everyone did. He was like that. So now we're all feeling lost and incapable without him. He wouldn't respect us for that.'

Ginnie was younger than Barry by ten years, but had matured early, even for a woman, and had long ago lost interest in the night life of the city and the endless parties where people never said anything, or if they did, weren't heard. She was a pretty woman still, her eyes soft and her skin flawless and petal-textured; she had a lot of friends, because she listened to them, and to everyone, especially of course Barry and especially since the children had moved away. Barry was nudging sixty, the last of the crisis ages beyond which a man either resigned himself to old age or picked himself up and found his second wind. The crash had come at a bad time for him. (They'd formed the habit of calling it 'the crash,' instead of 'Willie's death.') Sandra had been as mourned as Wilhelm, but by different people and for different reasons; she had been beautiful, graceful, exotic and totally selfish, though in a way that hurt nobody, not even herself; she was, as a friend had said unkindly, 'Willie's ornament,' a woman who could make an entrance and stop the show and not even notice. Madlen had taken after her quite a bit, where Lorraine had inherited only her dazzling looks – if 'only' was quite the word.

Wilhelm had been the bigger loss to everyone; he'd lived with dynamic energy, creating Floderus Incorporated and gathering people around him who were drawn to his flame; now it was extinguished, and they were in the dark.

'Don't be too hard,' Ginnie said gently, 'on Lorraine tomorrow.'

With slight impatience he told her, 'It's not a question of being hard, or being against her. We've got to save her from herself, and from what she'll do to the company if we leave things as they are. You don't really think I'd be "hard on her" after all she's been through?'

'I didn't mean it that way, darling.'

'God, she's enough on her plate with just Madlen.' He and Ginnie had paid another visit to the hospital last night, to find Madlen sullen and brooding rather than depressed; depression would have been natural enough, but there was something in her close to anger, and it was directed against Lorraine, not so much in what she said but in her silences when Lorraine was mentioned. They left the hospital not knowing whether Madlen was angry at her sister because Loraine had saved her life, or because she'd in some way let Madlen get that far without trying to stop her. The only thing she'd said outright against Lorraine was itself only indirect. 'She had to fly to *Los Angeles*, of all places?'

For them, it was called 'the crash'. For Madlen it was 'Los Angeles'. It was where all their lives had felt the jolt; something had jogged the record player and the needle had jumped, and they'd had to pick up the music as best they could. Before the crash, before Los Angeles, Madlen had been a bright, pretty girl with a lot of her mother's looks and a lot of her father's vitality; she and Lorraine had lunched together, seen plays together, called each other up when there was a party; there'd been signs of belated sibling rivalry, yes, and Madlen had refused ever to compete with Lorraine in any situation where she might not win: she'd dismissed her sister's film career with remarks about 'Tinsel City' and 'Hollywood-Schmollywood', jealous of Lorraine's success but unwilling to audition at the studios and risk rejection.

Maybe this was all it was, Ginnie thought as Barry left her side to throw another log onto the fire, an extension of sibling rivalry rekindled by the trauma of loss and the complicated needs of grief.

'The trouble with people who are irreplaceable,' Barry said with thoughts elsewhere, 'is that they're irreplaceable.' He came back to the couch as a flame caught the new log and brightened the hearth. 'I don't think *any* of us could have kept Floderus going for long with an increasing profitability; we wouldn't have made the mistakes Lorraine did, but we'd have felt the same lack of that man's flair for making a company work, and for creating a perfume and promoting it, and selling it, and delighting the whole of womanhood with it.' He leaned forward. 'Remember the ad for *Ecstase? You'll never have felt quite this way before* . . . And it was true. We used to hear it at parties. There was something we put into *Ecstase* – that *he* put into it – that went deep inside and reached them; and the men noticed. He said to me once, "Remember we're not creating perfume for women, we're creating it for men – for women to wear." That was the Floderus touch: he not only knew how to make fantastic fragrance; he knew what it was for.' He drained his brandy, savouring it for a moment. 'So tomorrow I have to tell Lorraine the truth. We none of us could have kept the company going, any more than she could. All we need to find out is whether we can sell it proudly – for his sake – or whether we'll have to take the highest bid, however low.'

A spark flew from the dry wood in the hearth, and he got up to pick it off the Marrachine rug, whose pattern had been altered randomly over the winters by countless tiny embers, because he didn't like the screen drawn across. Ginnie watched his humped shadow flickering on the ceiling,

128

thinking how much he'd aged since just a year ago; he and
Wilhelm had been more than partners in the firm; they'd
been like brothers; and though Barry had shown his grief
less than others, he'd felt it more deeply.

'I wish I could be there tomorrow,' she told him pensively.

'At the meeting?'

'Yes.'

'It's not going to be a whole lot of fun.'

'I know. That's why I wish I could be there, to help out.
There are so many people going to get hurt; and one of them
is you.'

CHAPTER 12

OUTSIDE ST CATHERINE'S Hospital in midtown Manhattan the wind blew raindrops from the glistening leaves of the trees across the bodywork of the peacock-blue Rolls-Royce Corniche sedan that stood not far from the entrance.

High in the building, where at this late hour the lights burned only at the nurses' stations, Lorraine Floderus sat watching over her sister in a private room. Madlen had been asleep when she'd arrived here an hour ago, and she'd asked the nurse not to wake her. The pillows framed her face in an aura of ghostly white under the glow of the pilot lamps; sleeping, she looked like a child again, the one Lorraine remembered. Sitting upright on the chrome-and-vinyl chair beside the bed she waited, in dread and longing, for Madlen's eyes to open and see her there. When she woke, Lorraine could tell her she would protect her always from this minute on, and love her and comfort her; this she longed to do. But Madlen might not believe her, or care, or even answer her; and this she dreaded.

As a nurse looked in at the doorway Lorraine asked her, 'Is she still under sedation?'

'Oh, no. She's sleeping naturally. But she'll take a while.' Her eyes lingering on Lorraine, she added, 'Excuse me, but didn't I see you in *Tango Bay*, the movie?'

'You might have.'

'Gee . . . You were great. Really.'

'Thank you.' When the girl had gone she closed her eyes, trying to remember when it had been exactly, when she'd made the movie, but the date wasn't significant anymore;

130

she'd made it in another time and another world, when she'd had a mother and a father, and a sister who'd been bright and vital and happy, and a husband who'd been handsome and loving. Yes, I was in *Tango Bay*, and you might have seen me. I'm glad you thought I was great, and it's okay if you tell people, hey, I met Lorraine Floderus today, you know, the movie star? Don't tell them, though, that it's not really as exciting and glamorous as it sounds; it was just the particular movie I happened to be making when the world I knew was blown apart, and I was left with this one, where I'm trying hard to make out.

In the darkness behind her closed eyelids she drifted into a half-sleep, where reality and illusion changed places and changed again, and faces of people she knew floated from the dark into the light, coming and going fitfully: the faces of Frank and Dean and Bruce, her ex-husband, and others she hardly recognised. Frank had called her at the apartment earlier tonight, only minutes after she'd reached home from the airport.

'I just wanted to apologise,' he'd said rather formally. 'You were perfectly right – I couldn't have stayed on as your chauffeur. I didn't know quite how to take it, that's all, because it meant more than – well, anyway, I'm sorry.'

Listening to him with her ears still buzzing from the long flight, she felt disoriented, and crazy ideas came into her mind: of asking Frank to pick her up right away and take her to see Madlen at the hospital; of asking him if he wanted to meet her again later and take her somewhere, so she could feel again the strong warm shelter of his arms; of offering him his job back. But all she said was, 'Whether I was right or wrong, Frank, I didn't have to hurt you like that. I should have done it less brutally.'

'You did it honestly. I wouldn't have wanted it any other way.'

She was listening for any hint in his voice that he wanted to see her again, but there was nothing. 'Frank, I – we're not hiring anyone to replace you. I'm going to drive myself from now on.' Stupidly, she thought it might mean something to him; that he'd in a small way been irreplaceable in her life. But he just laughed lightly.

'Take care with that traffic, then, in the rush hour.'

She sagged suddenly, feeling rejected. That was too bad. She'd seduced him, fired him, and then thought he should be yearning to see her again and overjoyed that she hadn't hired anyone else. She said as lightly as she could, 'They delivered the Rolls-Royce.'

'How d'you like it?'

'I haven't used it yet. Frank . . . ' She was trying to think how to put it.

'Yes?'

'Frank, I – just bought it on a silly impulse. I'm always doing impulsive things.'

'I know.' His voice was muted suddenly, and she bit her lip.

'I wondered – you see, we don't really need a car like that. It's impractical. I'd like you to have it.'

'The Rolls-Royce?'

'Yes. With a car like that, you could start your own limo business.'

There was a moment's silence, in which she began thinking he was going to unbend, and let her atone by at least this much for the hurt she'd given him. But he was laughing quietly again, and it piqued her.

'Have I said something funny?' she asked him.

'No. I guess I'm just laughing at myself, Lorraine; because the first time I see that fabulous automobile around town I'm going to wake up to how dumb I can be, knowing it could've been mine.' Before she could answer he was saying, with no longer any laughter in his voice, 'But I'll give a wave when you go by . . . Have fun, and take care.'

She'd stood with the phone in her hand until the dial tone started again, remembering the firelight, and the scent of the pines in the warmth of the morning sun, and his strong, reassuring embrace in the long sweet hours of the night, while now the echo of his voice grew fainter across the minutes . . . *Have fun . . . and take care . . .*

132

Then his face was gone again, and there was Dean Powers' floating from the dark as she half-waked, half-dreamed, a face as strong as Frank's but in a different way, his dark eyes watching her obliquely as he turned his head a little, as if to listen as carefully as he could while she was saying . . . 'When you play around with any girl here who believes in the total myth that to sleep with an executive is the fastest way to the top, you're harming the company, and that means you're harming me. So let me put it this way. Either you play by the rules, or you're fired.'

Watching her with his handsome head on one side, he'd answered in a tone so much calmer than hers, 'You can't fire me and you should know that. You'd need the board's unanimous decision.'

'Then I'd get it.' She still hadn't been able to control the anger in her voice. 'And if I didn't get it I'd make your life here such a goddamned misery you'd be only too glad to go.'

Listening to herself over again in the half-dream, she was astonished how crudely she'd handled the situation with Dean Powers, how easily she'd let him see how angry he'd made her. But why? Before he'd come into her office she'd made up her mind to treat him coolly, to tell him simply that he had to conform; but there'd been something about the way he'd responded that had set her on fire; maybe his own almost insolent calm, his way of tilting his head and eyeing her slightly from the side like he was studying a human specimen in a laboratory. Did it amount to nothing more than male arrogance, or was there something deeper – much deeper – about his personality that had seemed to present immediate challenge?

Had she been right, about his office liaisons? Who else among the executives would support her in this? No one, certainly. They were men. This was a man's world, and they closed ranks at once in the face of a threat from a woman, especially the boss. *Was this the whole problem – that she was a woman?* Probably. How would a man have handled the company, after her father had died? With more confidence, more force, more authority? Again, probably. She was a

133

woman, and couldn't think their way, or even talk their way. She knew the way they talked in the men's rooms, even at the highest levels of big business: they talked just like the jocks in the locker rooms at college. So what would a man have said to the arrogant, insolent Dean Powers in the privacy of the chief executive's office?

Okay, Dean, I want you to listen to this and I don't want you to interrupt. You're screwing around with the girls here and you're letting everyone know, and that's bad for morale, so you're going to stop. Right now. My balls are bigger than yours and I call the shots here, and if you don't do what I'm telling you to do, you're getting your ass out of this company so goddamned fast it won't even touch the ground. Okay, enough said. And hey, what about a couple of sets on the tennis court tonight, can you make it?

They knew how to talk to each other. They understood a language of their own – the adolescent macho lingo of the sports field and the war games table. And she couldn't speak it; if she tried, it would sound absurd, obscene.

But this was something that all women in business offices were having to contend with. The thing that had preyed on Lorraine's mind, even with Madlen to think about, even during the trip to Los Angeles and the crowded hours of the convention there, was that there seemed something very *personal* in her reaction to Dean's philandering, as if . . . as if . . . And there it always stopped, with the answer still just over the wall, on the other side of understanding.

And now Bruce was here in her half-dreams, at the end of a telephone, his face not very clear because it was a year since she'd seen him except once in the divorce court. *I'm in town, Lorraine,* he'd told her a couple of days ago, *and I thought I'd call you.* He'd stopped right there, waiting to know if she were going to slam the phone down or give him a dignified brush off or show real interest. He was a nice man, actually, and had been a good husband in a lot of ways, treating her as an equal and deferring to her when he'd seen she was serious about something; in fact he would've been pretty well perfect if he could have found somewhere other

134

than the palm court in their own home as the locale for his extra-curricular fucking. *How are you?* she'd asked him on the phone, without sounding frantically interested. He'd said he was fine, and he'd missed her, and wished he hadn't been such a damned fool . . . et cetera. But she really believed he was just hoping to get her into bed again and do all those crazy things they always used to do. *I'm tied up,* she'd told him, *but call me when you're in New York again, and give me a bit more warning.*

Hanging up on him, she'd known perfectly well that the love they'd shared was over – had been over the instant she'd seen him lying there in the sunshine that was coming through the glass while his semen trickled milkily across that strange girl's stomach. The only reason she'd been friendly to him on the phone was that she wanted to see the same thing happen again, but this time with her own heated body lying under his. Bruce had, yes, been extremely good as a lover.

His face floated away again, fading into the dark as she heard herself saying . . . *Maybe next time . . . maybe next time you're in town . . .*

Her eyes came open, and looked straight into Madlen's.

Neither spoke. Lorraine didn't know how long she'd been half-asleep, and didn't want to look at the clock on the wall, in case her sister thought she didn't have much time to spare for her; she had to go so carefully now with Madlen, and try to sense her every mood and her every thought, leading her hand in hand along the difficult path back to health and vitality. It was her fault that Madlen was lying here with the pallor of death still on her young pinched face; during this past year when Lorraine had been driving herself without respite to keep safe the company their father had created, Madlen had withdrawn from her day by day, aware that her voice was no longer heard, aware that the grief she felt was to be worse than unbearable: it must be borne alone.

This is what she saw in her sister's eyes as they looked at each other in the glow of the pilot lamps: an unfathomable loneliness. And something more.

135

'Hello,' Lorraine said softly. 'Was it a good sleep?'

There was no answer; but Madlen didn't look away, or shut her eyes again. In a moment Lorraine left the chair and sat on the bed, cupping her sister's head as she kissed her cold cheek, waiting for Madlen's hand to seek her own, and waiting in vain; she lay propped on the pillows like a life-sized doll, the curly hair clinging damply close to her head, and her white skin cold with sweat. Lorraine straightened up, and looked again into the watchful eyes.

'I came to say it was my fault,' Lorraine told her softly, 'all my fault. I came to tell you that in whatever way I can, I'll try to make up for what I did to you, however long it takes, however much it needs. I'm asking you to give me another chance to prove how much I love you.'

In the silence Lorraine could hear the faint tinkling of metal from somewhere along the corridor, of metal on glass; and the voice of a nurse at the telephone . . . *she's sleeping right now . . . I'll tell her you called . . .* There was no answer from Madlen; she was still watching Lorraine with her large violet-hued eyes, the pupils dilated because of the low lighting in here; for a while Lorraine wondered if Madlen had heard her, or understood; had the effects of the drug left her disoriented?

'Tell me,' Lorraine said in not much more than a whisper, 'that you'll give me another chance.'

There was something unnerving in Madlen's stillness; her pallor, her unblinking stare gave her the look of someone dead. When she answered at last, Lorraine caught her breath.

'Thank you for sending your maid to see me. And for sending the flowers. It was considerate of you.'

Every word brought home to Lorraine the appalling truth she'd already suspected. She'd heard of hate, simply as an expression, the name of an emotion; now she was suddenly faced with it, the real thing, its malevolence filling the room like a chill wind and leaving Lorraine numbed and bewildered, forced in this brief instant to reappraise all that she'd ever believed about herself as a human being.

136

Somebody hated her. Worse even than that, it wasn't just somebody. *It was Madlen.*

Out of the dizzying kaleidoscope of images flashing through Lorraine's mind, a scene leapt into focus, and she was back in the nursery of the big house in Connecticut, acting out one of the bewildering little dramas of early childhood. She was in her bed, one arm in a sling and a whole array of dolls and picture books across the counterpane. Mommy was there, and Nanny, and – Madlen, pale and defiant, the frill of her blue dress singed and her small fingers blackened. Lorraine was aghast as she watched from her bed, knowing that among the many taboos in the nursery was Playing with Matches – which her small sister had obviously been doing. Yet it wasn't, apparently, just a case of mischief or daring. She'd been trying to burn down the swing, under the huge beech tree. Mommy took her out of the house to visit the scene of the crime, and found plenty of evidence: two empty matchboxes, countless burnt match-ends and the charred wood of the swing.

Back in the nursery, where Lorraine had been waiting feverish with impatience, the truth was brought out. Two days before, Lorraine had come flying off the swing and broken her arm; the ensuing drama, with Lorraine lying there on the grass with her face white and tear-stained until the tyres of the doctor's car came shrilling along the driveway, had shocked little Madlen to the point where, sleepless, she had spent the whole night kneeling by her sister's bed to make sure 'the angels didn't take her away'. After what must have been long cogitation, Madlen had decided on implacable revenge against the garden swing that had caused the tragedy . . . a revenge so final that it could never again harm her sister . . .

Lorraine, herself only five years old at the time, had barely understood the implications. Fire was dangerous; matches were forbidden; and Madlen had tried to burn the swing down, defying all authority. Lorraine hadn't clearly understood, as the grown-ups must have done, that her small sister was showing her sympathy and devotion in the

137

most extravagant way she could think of, and had tried to make sure such a terrible thing could never happen again.

Sitting in the hospital room with her now, Loraine looked at her sister and wondered where that much love, that much devotion, had gone in the years between. 'Madlen,' she heard herself saying in quiet desperation, 'don't punish me like this.'

But again there was no answer, and she had to remind herself that although she was here with her sister Madlen, whom she'd known since earliest memory, she was also with a kind of stranger, a patient lying in a hospital bed, with a Social Security number and a progress chart and clinical data filed in the computer room here with hundreds of others; a patient known as having *suicidal tendencies*, a young woman who only days ago had tried to die and had come close to it, *to death*. A kind of stranger, and yet . . . with the same extravagant sense of drama she had shown even as a child of three, she had come near to sending Lorraine, dressed in black and still weeping with shock, to another funeral so soon after the last, where again she must stand at the graveside and ask herself how much she had been to blame.

Why had Lorraine remembered, out of all those other childhood scenes, the incident of the garden swing? Perhaps because there were parallels. In each case Madlen had shown a frightening sense of drama; in each case she'd failed, by only a little, in what she'd been trying to do: just a few more matches . . . and the swing would have taken fire and burned out; just a few more capsules . . . and Madlen's life would have been extinguished.

'You have to remember,' the psychiatrist had told Lorraine just before she'd come in here to see her sister, 'that grief takes many directions; often it'll bring out an underlying emotional pattern – pervasive anxiety, morbid fear, resentment – and express it overtly. Your sister is two years younger than you. Can you remember how you thought of her, when she was born?' He gave an understanding smile, spreading his thin tobacco-stained

138

fingers in the air. 'I know you believe you don't remember very much about your thoughts as an infant of two, but you actually do; it's all there. I mean, did you feel there was someone suddenly in the house who was going to kind of get in your way, make trouble for you, play with *your own* special toys? Or did you feel this was a new and exciting toy in itself, this red-faced creature waving its arms and legs around?'

He'd talked to her for almost half an hour, leaning with his back to the desk, asking if she'd mind if he smoked 'I've had a long day,' he'd said with a weary smile, 'and it's been less than terrific.' On her way to his office, three floors below in the enormous building, she'd glimpsed one of his patients, a young woman backed into a corner of a treatment room while a nurse tried to calm her, a rather pretty girl but with her mouth ringed with black and her arms and legs scarred with needle-marks, her wrists heavily bandaged. The thought had flashed into Lorraine's mind, sickening her: *would Madlen be brought here again, and again, looking like this poor junky?*

'Okay,' the young psychiatrist had said, 'so there was a lot of fondness between you as kids, but there were also these incidents of obvious sibling rivalry, and much later, her failure as an actress off-Broadway while you were succeeding in Hollywood; her inability to find a terrific hunk of husband like yours – ' he gave a wry shrug – 'until he messed up, that is. Things like that were an extension of this natural sibling rivalry; but her jealousy and envy and resentment didn't find overt expression – or even seek it; they weren't too important to her, *until* the sudden and traumatising death of *both* your parents. Then I believe, from the few insights you've given me, that in her grief she had to reach out and grab everything she could use to express it. She had to *blame* someone – so she blamed you; she didn't have any sibling resentments against the pilot of the plane, or the manufacturer of the tyre that burst and caused the crash, but she had them against *you*. So *you* became the focus of all the grief, the irreplaceable loss, the

139

feeling of total abandonment that she was having suddenly to deal with, out of a clear blue sky and with no warning.'

He'd been called away twice to talk to the young failed suicide in the treatment room, each time coming back and going straight to the pack of Marboros on his cluttered desk, to light a cigarette and blow out a slow plume of smoke before he could gather his thoughts again. 'Okay, from what you told me, your parents flew to Los Angeles because you'd asked them to – was it a sneak preview – ?'

'The rough cut – '

'Okay, the rough cut of the movie you'd just finished. So, from your sister's distorted point of view, if you hadn't made the movie, or hadn't asked them to see it, they wouldn't have been killed. And we can see the logic in this: it's absolutely true! But where the irrationality comes in is that Madlen sees it as something to *blame* you for. I mean, it's also absolutely true that if you'd never been born, that crash wouldn't have happened – because then you wouldn't have made the movie and you wouldn't have asked them along to see it, and so forth. And wrapped up in all this there are other things, including the extended sibling rivalry expression of jealousy – it was because you were *successful* in Hollywood that caused your making the movie and hence the plane crash. If you'd – say – gone to Los Angeles to find a job, but didn't succeed, and your parents had flown there to bring you home, a *"failure"*, then there'd have been no jealousy, even no thought of *blame* from Madlen. See how involved it gets?'

The last thing he'd told Lorraine before she'd left his office was that there was a fair degree of hope. 'Okay, she blames you now, but that's really grief. As the grief slowly diminishes – which it has to, however long it takes – the feeling of blame will diminish, and the jealousy, and all the other things. You just have to be patient, monumentally patient, and understanding, and loving, and forgiving . . . and you'll have to do it in the face of her implacable hostility. I don't envy you the task. But it must be done.'

As he'd shown her out of his smoky and cluttered office

140

Lorraine had put the one question she dreaded to ask him.

'Do you . . . think she might try again?'

'That's going to be up to you.'

Madlen lay unmoving against the pillows.

So this is where the world is.

Before, it had been somewhere else: in the ladies' room at the club. The last she'd seen of the world was shell-pink mirrors with small ping-pong-ball-sized bulbs glowing all around them, and a tissue box in reproduction Florentine, and some bottles of perfume standing around the shell-pink bowl; the world had looked cosy, and intimate, and private.

This one was different. Colder-looking, efficient, with people going around in white, with bright smiles and clipboards and rather obvious wrist watches, reminding you that in this place time meant everything; you had time to live or time to die, but you'd better get on with it.

'How're you feeling, Madlen?'

She looked at the bright, white nurse.

'I'm not feeling anything.'

The fixed smile puckered to a look of mock vexation. 'It'll take time, honey. You want to go for a little stroll?'

'No.'

'How about seeing what's on the TV?'

'No.'

'Get you some coffee? You're allowed coffee now, did they tell you?'

'No.'

'Then try to sleep again, sweetheart. You'll wake up feeling a heap better. It always happens.' She straightened the bedclothes and the window curtains and the tray on the trolley, her deft hands flying efficiently around to tidy the world up, a mingled scent of ether and perspiration coming from her. She was worried. The answers she'd been looking for were yes, I'd like to take a stroll and see what's on the TV and have some coffee; and when she hadn't got them it had confused her. It wasn't normal not to want things; it didn't fit into the scheme of things here. 'You know it was a real

141

surprise to meet your sister today. The last time I saw her she was up there on the screen in *Tango Bay*. And she's even *lovelier* in real life. You must be very proud of her.'

'No.'

The nurse gave a little bright smile, touching the back of her head to tighten the hairpins; it was what she always did, Madlen had come to know, when she was confused. As soon as she could she went out, her soft shoes making kissing sounds along the parquet corridor.

Now how can you honestly be *proud* of having a sister who looks so fucking sexy that she can go straight from the producer's couch into a contract? Is that really anything to be proud of?

They all said it, of course, as soon as the name rang a bell. Are you . . . by any chance . . . any relation to *Lorraine* Floderus? You're her *sister*? But my dear, how wonderful!

I am also me. That may not be very wonderful, but I think it counts. A few men think so. Or at least they say so. Brian, and Roberto, and Gaylord, and Daryl. They say they think I'm terrific. They've proved, at least, that I'm worth fucking, so isn't that something? Some kind of identity?

I don't feel like fucking right now. Oh, God, it'd be obscene . . . all that gasping and groping and writhing around and moaning . . . I just couldn't take it.

I can't take anything, as a matter of fact. There isn't any point. I'm lying here in this bed with the smell of ether and perspiration in the room and that's all I'm doing, and I could get up and brush my teeth or go to the john or turn on the TV but what would that do for me, what would it mean? How do people live, when most of their day is spent in doing things like that? And most of their night spent in sleeping? I mean what in Christ does it add up to, when you think about it?

You have to get back your sense of direction.

He'd said.

Do you mind if I smoke? Dragging on his cigarette, like it was the last thing he had in life. And which direction was I going, exactly, when they – when it – when it all – ?

You have to find your courage to go on.

142

His stained fingers shaking so much he dropped ash all over the bedclothes. Courage? To go on brushing my teeth and going to the john and turning on the TV and fucking with Brian and Roberto and the rest of them? You have to be joking.

Or maybe you're right, in a weird kind of way. Maybe it does take courage to get back my sense of direction when I've nowhere to go, and find my courage to go on, when there's nothing to go on doing.

But listen.

She laid her head back, the damp curls against the pillow, and stared into the dark of her eyelids, with her hands clenched into fists under the bedclothes and the hot rushing of tears that wouldn't come, not coming. And made her statement. It was this.

You don't know what it's like. You were trained to be a shrink, mister, and you've read all the big heavy books about how it is to be abnormal and you've sat in the classrooms and the lecture halls and listened to all those bald-headed guys with their beards and their glasses, *eminent in their profession, eminent in their profession*, and you've sat in your office listening to all those weirdos on the couch and you've sat on the bedside of all those freaks with the powder marks still on their heads where they missed and the bandages on their wrists where they didn't go deep enough, *and you've studied their cases, you've studied their cases*, so now you know exactly how it is, don't you, mister, what it feels like to lie here with the smell of ether and sweat in the room with nothing to do and nowhere to go, no courage and no direction, nothing but charts and bright smiles and *drink this* and glances exchanged and heads nodding wisely while *all the time, all the time*, are you listening, it doesn't matter to me, it doesn't mean anything to me, I'm not a part of it all, I can't relate to it or share in it because *nothing, nothing nothing can ever bring them back and let me see them again and love them again and know they're always there, always there when I need them, when I'm frightened, when I'm lost, when I'm in the cold, in the*

143

dark at the far, faraway end of the world where only they can ever find me and bring me back. And now they've gone, and I can't ever find them, or bring them back to me.

So I am lying here in this bed, you see, mister, feeling so cold that I never knew what it was before, though I can't even shiver; feeling so lonely that even if you filled this place with people it wouldn't do any good, because the loneliness is in here with me, not outside; feeling so frightened, of nothing and of everything, of living, of dying, that I can't call for help because there's nothing anyone could do; and feeling so lost, so scared and so depressed that even the tears won't come, because they dried up when I went in there all alone and unscrewed the top and shook them into my hand and shovelled them into my mouth and drank the water and after a minute or two lay down with my cheek on the carpet and my eyes still open for a little bit longer while I thought, and can remember, very clearly, thinking, it's strange to finish up with my face against the floor looking at the john in the cubicle and an imitation pearl earring someone dropped onto the carpet that one day, when I'm, goodbye now, one day someone will find and pick up, when I'm, goodbye now, gone, 'bye now, gone.

So you don't know it all, mister, because what is really happening here in this bright and efficient hospital is that I'm lying here with my hair gradually growing, if I lie here long enough, and the caries attacking the enamel of my teeth, if I lie here long enough, and my fingernails growing, and my toenails, and the urine seeping gradually into my bladder and the catarrh gathering in my sinuses and the blood pulsing uselessly, uselessly through the veins of this body that wouldn't have any meaning if these things weren't going on, uselessly going on, *because what's it all for?*

What's it all for, mister?
What use is it?
Is this all there is?

Then I'd rather be dead.

144

'Can I get you anything?'

'No.'

'Not hungry?'

'No.'

Stand there in the doorway. It's your job.

'You didn't eat your supper. Let me get you some soup.'

'No.'

Stand there and ask questions. It's your job.

'Want to go to sleep, Madlen?'

'No.'

'I think you should doze off, you know. You'll wake up feeling better. I'll get you a Somneril. Just one.'

'No.'

She'd been watching the hands of the clock on the wall. The small one had reached the top, and now the big one got there too, so they were together.

Big deal.

Time going by. Time to do what?

Midnight. In a minute, another day.

I don't think I can take another day. Not like this.

I'd rather be dead. If I were dead, I wouldn't have to think about how awful it was to be dead. But like this, I have to think about how awful it is to be alive. That's the difference.

Another new day, but I can't start up. It's gone. I lost it. I screwed up. I have no courage, no sense of direction. So that's it.

Oh my God, oh Jesus Christ, nothing means anything anymore.

'Are you awake, honey?'

'Yes.'

'How d'you feel?'

'I feel like shit.'

She stood in the doorway touching the back of her hair.

'There's a visitor.'

'Tell them to go away.'

'You don't want to see him?'

'No.'

'It's Mr Baccari again.'

'Who?'

She looked at the card in the dim light.

'Angelo Baccari.'

In the old world there had been an imitation pearl earring on the floor, this side of the cubicle where the john was, lying on the carpet she had her face against.

In this world there was the girl in white standing in the doorway, her head angled down to look at a card she held in her hand. There was a kind of meaning to it. Because of his name.

She pulled herself upright against the pillows, and the nurse hurried to help her, surprised.

'I'd like to see him.'

Then he was standing there, huge in the doorway, and as she looked into the kindness of his smile something broke inside her, and the tears came so fast that they blinded her with their hot salt overflowing.

CHAPTER 13

THERE WEREN'T TOO many people at the Lotus Club tonight, and Tony Marinello noticed this as he took the package from the doorman and made his way between the tables to where Angelo was sitting. It was three o'clock in the morning, but there were usually more people than this around even at this hour.

He ducked beneath the rose-coloured Tiffany chandelier, as he always did, because of his height; he had said to Angelo so many times, just two inches, Angelo, just a couple of inches higher, then I wouldn't have to duck. It would be too expensive, Angelo had told him as many times, didn't he realise how much it would cost them to raise that chandelier even a couple of inches? It weighed half a ton; besides, once you disturb something like that, after such a long time, you never know what might happen; the whole ceiling could come down with it. Tony could maybe take a different route between the tables, so he didn't have to duck under the chandelier; but he didn't want to do that. Angelo called the shots around here; he was the boss; and he had the right to leave the goddamned rose-coloured Tiffany chandelier like it was. But Tony also had the right to go where he wanted among all the tables, because he was the manager; so he'd take the same route he always did, and if he had to duck every time, that was the breaks. It had become a little joke between them, like a lot of things did, and sometimes when Angelo was sitting at his table in the corner and Tony came across to him, he'd say, Tony, one day you're going to crack your skull on that chandelier, you know that? And Tony would say, sure, because that damn thing is a couple of inches too low, Angelo.

They liked their little jokes. They understood each other. It was a good double act they did, had done for seven years now. While Angelo mostly kept to his table, right in the corner where the rose-coloured lamplight barely reached, and watched the customers and thought about them and thought up new ideas to keep them happy, Tony moved around all night, checking the door and the bar and the rooms upstairs every so often to see that everything looked okay. He was a very experienced man. He could identify a non-union hooker by the bounce of her tits, and if one of them came in here to look for customers he'd run her back into the street so fast she'd have to brake at the lights; and if some guy came in here a little bit overdressed, Tony would smell the gun-oil on him and tell him to move his ass.

'Hi, Tony,' a girl at a table said.

'Hi, sweetheart.'

'Where's everybody tonight?'

'I guess it's the rain.'

Or it was a big-game replay or the cab strike or whatever he could think of first. The thing was, this place was taking on echoes. Clubs were a luxury in a recession year, and the membership was down to half.

'From Billy,' he said as he reached Angelo's table and gave him the package. 'Billy Madigan.'

Angelo opened the box and saw they were Santa Ynez Emperadores Panatellas, his known favourite smoke. He dropped the box onto the table. 'Billy's a nice man. He's late with his fees?'

'How did you guess?' Tony dropped his muscular frame into a chair and sat cracking his knuckles for a while, watching the jazz combo on the spotlit stage and wondering how he was going to break the news. The news was going to hurt; and one of the things people didn't realise about Angelo Baccari was that underneath that craggy head and those enormous shoulders there was a heart. It wasn't, maybe, a very big one, compared with, say, a Salvation

148

Army Sally's; and it didn't bleed too easy, where other people were concerned; but it was there; and tonight Tony had to go in and rough it up a little, because he couldn't put it off any longer. The facts were there, and the figures were there, and Angelo had to be told.

'Billy is a nice man, though,' Angelo said. 'Plenty of people don't pay their fees, but they don't send me a box of Santa Ynez.'

'Sure,' Tony said, 'he's a nice man. He knows how to make a gesture. Tomorrow I have to tell him we're going to terminate his membership, and he's going to come over here and look at you through all that beautiful cigar smoke and say how can you do this to me, Angelo?'

Angelo left it at that. Watching the people drinking at the bar, and wondering whether they'd be happier, maybe, with a girl behind the counter, a girl with a really stupendous pair of frontal lobes and a Miss America smile, he decided to put Tony out of his misery, because three or four times in the last hour, since Angelo had got back from the hospital, he'd come drifting across here to sit cracking his knuckles and not saying anything. And the message was very clear.

'So,' Angelo said, taking a panatella from the box and lighting it, 'you did the figures.'

Tony pulled three knuckles in a row with the sound of a muted fusilade. 'Yes, Angelo.'

'And everything's going along fine?'

Tony turned his head slowly to look at his boss, thinking for a moment that Angelo really hadn't been getting the picture over the past six months; then he realised he was just making another of their little jokes. But that took a lot of doing, this time.

'No,' Tony told him. 'We're broke.'

Angelo watched the sax player on the little stage, the way he swung his bright chrome instrument as he played, like he was dancing with it in a dream. It caught the light and reflected it all over the place, and Angelo felt hypnotised by it. All his life he had liked bright lights, even as a small kid, never wanting to go to bed because there the day stopped, in

149

the dark. He had always wanted the day to go on forever, even through the night under the bright lights; maybe that was why he had chosen to run a club, so the day never had to end, so he never had to go to bed, in the dark.

'We're broke,' he said reflectively, 'I see.' He drew carefully on his panatella, preserving the ash. 'That's a real shame.' He brought out the smoke slowly, letting it lie on the air in skeins under the rose-red light.

Tony watched him but said nothing. He knew Angelo well enough to know that he wouldn't blow his top over this, or blame anyone out of hand. But he didn't know him well enough to know what exactly he would do, when the truth finally got to him. The Lotus was Angelo's life.

'What would have to happen,' Angelo asked him after a while, 'for me to keep the club going?'

'You've heard of miracles?' Tony wished Angelo weren't taking it quite so calmly; it meant he was having to find a lot of control. 'We'd have to pay off the bills,' Tony said heavily, 'and we'd have to redecorate the whole place.'

'What's wrong with the place right now?'

It flashed into Tony's mind to say the Tiffany chandelier was a couple of inches too low for a start; but the time for jokes was over. 'There isn't anything wrong with it, Angelo. It's very plush; it has class. But we need twice as many members as we have now, because half of them have dropped out. To bring in new people, you have to have a new place to show them. We would also have to promote it, advertise it, sell it hard, a whole page in the glossies, a half page in the *New Yorker* and *Playboy* and *Esquire* and maybe even *Cosmopolitan*.' He tried to think of all the other things they'd have to do, but his heart wasn't in it. As he looked around in the rose-red light he saw for the first time that when he'd first walked in here seven years ago he'd thought the place was plush, classy, and had gone on thinking so ever since; but tonight he noticed little things he'd never seen before: flakes of gold paint beginning to peel off the wall over the bar; worn patches of carpet in the places where the waitresses turned around at the tables; a dark area on the

150

ceiling near one of the fluted columns, where last year some
rain got through and Angelo had said leave it, don't worry
about it, because even then he'd started to see they'd have to
economise.

'So what would it cost?' Angelo asked him.

'All that?'

'All that.'

'You mean everything? Grand total?'

'Grand total.'

Tony took his time. If he made the figure too low, Angelo
would get an optimistic picture and maybe decide to keep on
going, and that would mean the club would just gather speed
down the slope and crash at the bottom. If he made the
figure too high, Angelo might take it so hard he'd have a
cardiac arrest: it happened to a lot of people when they had
bad news. So he worked out an approximate figure that
would cover everything, plus twenty-five per cent, to cover
the excess you never were prepared for. Then he drew a
breath and said:

'A million bucks.'

The light flashed on the chrome of the saxophone,
sending blue and red and yellow prismatic reflections across
the smoky air. Angelo watched them, drawn to their glitter.

'A million,' he said in a moment. 'I see.'

Tony felt terrible. It had been like he'd stabbed Angelo in
the back. 'That's a – that's kind of a ballpark figure,' he said.
'I mean, you know, doing it without a computer.'

'Sure,' Angelo said, 'sure.' He sat for a long time, not
moving until the sax player pushed out a long sweet note that
gathered all the coloured reflections and poured them into
the silence as the music stopped. 'You didn't ask me,' he said
to Tony, 'about the kid.'

'The kid?'

'Madlen. At the hospital.'

'Oh.' He switched his thought. 'How is she?'

'She'll be okay. She's had a hard time, but she'll be okay
now. She's lonesome, you know? Needs a home,
somewhere she can go to where she feels she's welcome.'

151

Ash fell at last from his cigar, and he took a moment to deal with it, holding the glowing end of the panatella flat against the ashtray to trim it square before he held it to his lips again and drew smoke. 'She likes this place,' he told Tony. 'She feels at home here.'

Tony said, low-key, because Angelo felt paternal about her, 'Sure, she's a nice kid. Just needs a little house-training.'

Angelo said slowly, 'That was just because she was unhappy. She wouldn't do anything wild again. I told her she was welcome any time. As a matter of fact, I did a few figures recently in my head, and I came to about the same conclusion as you did. The kid wanted to know all about the club, and I said we'd have to close unless we could find a million dollars from someplace, and she said that was okay, she'd put a million into it as an investment, so she could feel she really belonged here. We're seeing her attorneys tomorrow. So she's welcome here any time' – he turned his head to look at Tony's expression – 'don't you agree?'

CHAPTER 14

IT WAS THURSDAY.

At five minutes before ten in the morning, the boardroom in the offices of Floderus Incorporated was deserted. Pale sunlight filtered through the windows, touching on the gold letters of the company's seal and the clear glass ashtrays ranged the length of the table. Surfaces shimmered in the early light: the dark mahogany table itself, the high-backed leather-covered chairs, the velum-bound volumes filling the bookshelves at one end of the room. The smell of furniture polish was on the air, left by the cleaners overnight; one of them had dropped a worn yellow duster in a corner near the door.

At three minutes before ten a young woman came in quickly, glancing around her, straightening a chair, picking up the yellow duster and dropping it into a waste basket, and putting her note pad onto the shelf opposite the windows. She was Nadine Keller, secretary to Barry Corbett, vice president. Slight, sharp-eyed and quick-moving, she was here in place of Maggie, secretary to the chairman, who had gone home after lunch yesterday speechless with laryngitis.

By ten o'clock there were four men in the boardroom: Dean Powers, Barry Corbett, Sam McNair, and Joe Fisher. Since the meeting was not yet convened, they couldn't sit down; they stood along the windows, looking out and seeing nothing, preoccupied with their thoughts. By two minutes after ten, three other men had come in: Carl Blatt, Sy Goldman and Charles Fox. These completed the members of the board, with the exception of Lorraine Floderus,

153

chairman. As they moved towards the others already there, two of them made an attempt at conversation, but it died away, and their corporate silence brought to the boardroom the hush of a cathedral.

Barry Corbett, standing by himself below the portrait of Wilhelm Floderus, the founder, felt the weight of coming events already heavy on him. 'Call me,' Virginia had told him when he'd left home this morning, 'just as soon as the meeting's over.' He didn't think it would be long; in his mind there was no question they had to sell out, and rescue what was left of the company's good-will.

At the far end of the room, Carl Blatt was making shapes with a paper-clip, staring out of the windows and already regretting he'd agreed to stay on here until this morning. The only man who could take over the company when they forced Lorraine to step down was Barry Corbett, whose face this morning was pouched with hangover. If anyone here, Carl thought bitterly, was still in his office a week from now, he was an idiot. There weren't many good positions going in town these days with the recession the way it was, and they'd better start looking right now.

Dean Powers, perched on the low windowsill, was studying his elegant Florsheim shoes. Last evening he should have spared some time for thoughts of this morning's critical meeting, but Dolores hadn't let up until he'd said she could stay the night; either she was a nymphomaniac or couldn't get an orgasm, or both; this morning he felt like a jaded carthorse rather than the dynamic marketing-director who should be sitting at the boardroom table very soon now, making his astute and productive contribution to the matter in hand. It occurred to him, with a wry amusement that surprised him, that if he'd spent the night with the chairman of the board instead of an insatiable nymphomaniac from the typing pool, he'd have been more use to the meeting this morning; on the other hand, with a chairman as disturbingly attractive as Lorraine Floderus, he wouldn't have given much time last night for thoughts of her company and the mess it was in. Almost at once his amusement switched to a

154

kind of anger, again surprising him: anger that he'd somehow allowed this *film actress* to screw up the company which he'd supported faithfully for so many years, giving it so much of his devotion that it had cost him his marriage. It was the well-documented 'halo effect': she'd dazzled him with her looks to the extent that he'd been blinded to the shadows behind the light.

Dean lifted his head, and found himself looking at Carl Blatt. 'What was that?'

Carl looked blank. 'I didn't say anything.'

'Oh.'

Silence came again, and Dean looked at the clock on the panelled wall; its bronze hands showed seven minutes past the hour. Where the hell was Lorraine?

Nadine Keller, the only woman here and the only non-member of the board, stood circumspectly near the door, ready to greet the chairman when she came in. Looking at her watch, she stopped the movement halfway; it wasn't for her to point up the fact that the boss was late.

Over by the windows, Sam McNair blew his nose suddenly, and heads turned; distracted from his thoughts, Barry Corbett began pacing the length of the room, finishing up staring at the portrait on the wall, the portrait of the man who had brought them together here in the beginning, and whom they had now come here to betray.

Carl Blatt, who always believed he could display the ultimate cool in any situation, felt the paper-clip break suddenly between his fingers, and looked down at the drop of blood starting where the sharp end had pricked him.

At ten minutes after the hour Nadine Keller moved unobtrusively down the room to where the president was standing, her voice low as she asked him, 'Should I go and see where she is?'

Barry glanced at his watch, pretending he hadn't noticed the chairman was so late. 'Why don't you do that?' he said quietly. Watching Nadine's polished heels as she went out, he thought it was possible that Lorraine had decided to chicken out at the last minute. He would have sympathised,

155

but the rest of them here wouldn't show any mercy: they'd stay here and hammer it out, even with the chairman absent; it wouldn't constitute a formal meeting, but they could still reach their joint decision. And he'd have to add his own vote to theirs. *Et tu, Brute!*

He looked down from the portrait and began pacing the other way, so that he was facing the open doorway when Lorraine Floderus came through and was suddenly among them.

She came in with her steps perfectly measured, her elegant Halston check suit making a distinct statement as she walked to the chair at the end of the table, looking at nobody, her glittering black shoes making the only sound in the room as their heels scuffed the carpet, her face perfectly composed as it caught the light from the windows. It was the kind of entrance she'd been trained to make for the cameras, under the bright lights and the critical gaze of the director; and this morning she did it in one take. She was the head of a fifty-million-dollar company, and they'd better remember that.

Reaching the chair, she paused, looked around, and spoke.

'Thank you for waiting. Two days ago my sister tried to commit suicide and she's just out of intensive care, so it's taken up some of my time. Please be seated, gentlemen.'

Something like a shockwave ran through the room, and it was a moment before the first of them moved, pulling back his chair and sitting down. The rest followed, looking neither at each other nor at Lorraine.

Sam McNair cleared his throat. 'We're sorry to hear about that, Lorraine. We had no idea.'

'Thank you. But my intention isn't to get your sympathy – which I nevertheless appreciate. It's to explain why I'm late this morning – which isn't my habit.'

Sy Goldman, Publicity, made a quick mental review of the sympathetic statement he'd prepared on the subject of what Madam Chairman had done to this company in the past twelve months. Then he dropped it, and started preparing a new one. Madam Chairman hadn't tip-toed in here this morning like a guilty schoolkid; she'd come in here armed to the teeth and had shot down Sam McNair just for trying to show her a little sympathy. They'd all been wrong about this meeting; it wasn't going to be difficult: it was going to be murder.

Nobody spoke again until the meeting was declared open and Nadine Keller sat poised over her note-pad.

'We're here to – ' Dean Powers began, and stopped as Lorraine cut right across him.

'For your information, gentlemen, I know the figures. I've seen the reports – all of them. I've talked to each one of you, as you know, about the present situation with my company. I believe we know where we've been going wrong, technically. Under my leadership we've concentrated too much on the Floderus image, and we've advertised it in the wrong places.' She looked from face to face. 'That was my fault.'

Nobody was looking up. Joe Fisher made a small movement in his chair, and Lorraine waited; but he said nothing.

All around the table, the members of the board were doing what Sy Goldman had just done: dropped their original attitudes and sitting a great deal straighter. At this point, if Lorraine hadn't shown she was out for war, they would have been trying to take some of the sting out for her . . . Well, Lorraine, you don't have to be too hard on yourself. You had grief to bear; you had a nomination for the Oscar instead of a Yale business degree; you were new to the game . . . All that was out now; and there was at least this to be said: she *had* screwed everything up, and she was ready to take the blame.

Lorraine was still waiting for someone to speak; but they were silent. She didn't know whether she'd said anything that would interest them; maybe they'd already made up their minds that whatever she said, they'd either put her out of her office or put the company on the block. As she

157

watched Barry, and Carl, and Dean and the other faces along the table, she longed for one of them to look up at her and give her a hint as to their thoughts. Instead, they were deliberately keeping silent, waiting for her to get in deeper, and drown.

The familiar ache was beginning at the nape of her neck, but she resisted the temptation to put a hand there for a moment to ease it. 'We changed the advertising agency,' she went on crisply, 'and for the worse. That too was my fault. There were a lot of other things we did wrong, some of which were my fault too; and there were the effects of the recession, reduced retail inventories and sluggish conditions in the market-place. I want you to realise, gentlemen, that I'm fully aware of the situation that's brought us here this morning, and aware of most of the things that caused it. And now I'd like to hear from you.'

The silence went on for a long time, until Barry Corbett realised they were giving him, as vice president of the company, the first word. He looked at Lorraine, sitting on his left at the head of the table. 'You've indicated you're here to talk turkey, Lorraine, and won't take kindly to any blandishments. But this isn't one, and that's why I'm going to say it. Your father was the kind of man who could not only create something, but manage it, develop it, make it succeed. He did that with Floderus Incorporated, and now he's gone.' He looked along the table at the set faces there. 'I don't believe *anyone of us here* could have kept this company growing the way he did. And if a company doesn't grow, it can only fail.'

Before Lorraine could answer him, Charles Fox came in with a point on discounts, which he felt were contributory to the general decline in sales; then Sy Goldman followed with his own ideas on the change in direction of advertising during a recession, of the advertising image; then they were all doing their own thing, sometimes addressing Lorraine formally as 'Madam Chairman', sometimes talking across the table to each other until she had to call them to order. She gave them more than half an hour to express what they

158

felt about this 'rudderless ship adrift on stormy seas', as one of them floridly termed it; then she called them to order again and looked directly at Barry, beside her.

'Okay, gentlemen, you've put your views. Now I'd like to hear what you feel is the best solution. Barry?'

They all turned in his direction, but he kept his eyes down, knowing they were bleary from too many brandies last night. 'I haven't changed my mind, Lorraine. I think we should find the highest bidder for the company, and sell it while there's still some of the goodwill left.'

'Thank you,' Lorraine said briefly, though her president's official vote in the boardroom had left her shaken. He hadn't changed his mind. None of them would. 'Dean?'

He didn't even glance up at her.

'Sell,' he said. A couple of days ago when Lorraine had tried to make him leave the company, he'd kept his patience for her sake, believing he'd find some way of supporting her at the meeting today; but in the interim he'd had no inspiration; every time he'd come round to a means of rescuing Floderus and setting it up again, there'd been that mental image suddenly in his mind: the image of a brash young film actress with no experience in management sticking her pretty neck out and exposing them all to this nerve-wracking situation, of humping a dying company off their shoulders and going out there into the job market – in the depth of a recession.

Lorraine kept her eyes on him for a moment, willing him to look at her, to silently acknowlege that he'd not only backed down on his idea of 'supporting' her today, but had done it with one brutal word.

She didn't thank him. 'Carl?'

He spoke immediately in his high, plaintive tones. Most of what Carl Blatt said in his working day was uttered in this voice-pattern that was so special to him; it was meant to indicate that what he was saying was not only correct, but at variance to what most other people were saying, so that he had to explain it and defend it at the same time against the ignorance of his fellow creatures.

159

'By tomorrow night,' he said without looking at Lorraine, 'I'll be out of here. But since you've asked my opinion, I'd say the only way to go would be for you to step aside, take over the presidency and have Dean Powers go in as chairman and chief executive officer.' He paused deliberately. 'If he's willing.'

'That wasn't,' Lorraine told Carl, 'the idea you voiced in my office last week.'

He gave her his blank stare behind the steel-rimmed glasses. 'It's my idea right now.'

Lorraine put a hand to her neck, where the ache was now burning intolerably; then she changed the movement to smooth her hair in place. If there were ever a time to show weakness it wasn't now. Already, forty minutes after she'd come in here with something close to hope in her, she'd cost herself the battle; it had been her strategy to slam into them, cutting out long explanations, recriminations, technical cud-chewing that could have kept them here for hours, and instead tell them that she knew the facts, accepted blame for some of them, and wanted their proposals for a solution. But she'd gone too fast, and tried to hit too hard; she'd made an enemy of every damned one of them, except for poor Barry, who had no real voice anymore. She had demonstrated with absolute perfection that she *still* didn't know the first thing about how to run a meeting, *still* didn't know how to express herself without antagonising the board – and *still* wasn't the person they should choose to lead this company, even if they thought it could be lead anywhere at all.

She'd tried to be tough, forthright and honest. She'd been aggressive, hostile and shrill. These men weren't fools, and they weren't against her for any dubious motives; she'd run their livelihood into the ground; and she was a woman; and that was something they couldn't help in themselves: if she'd managed to keep the company going during the past year, and increase its fortunes even a little, they wouldn't have worried about the sex angle.

'Joe?' she asked the thin, pensive advertising director at

160

the far end of the table.

After a moment he made himself turn and look at her as he said quietly. 'I agree with Barry and Dean.'

The only note of sympathy was struck by Sy Goldman, despite her warning them that sympathy wasn't what she was here for.

'Sure, I'd say you'd make a pretty good president, Lorraine, if you decided to step aside for a while.' His fat pale hands rested on the table in front of him, and his paunch reached as far as its edge as he turned his massive, brooding gaze on Madam Chairman. 'Besides which, I think you've done a pretty good job out there representing the firm. You took out the kind of image we should have tried harder to stay with; our product has elegance, chic, and class.' He looked around the table deliberately, daring the others not to at least give a nod of approval. There was only Barry.

'Thank you, Sy.' Lorraine gave her first faint smile since she'd come in here, but it was only a sign of gratitude. Sy had always been a gentleman. 'Okay, I have all your opinions. I don't need a show of hands; there are five votes for selling the company, and two for my stepping aside to put Dean Powers into the chair. So at this point I have a question, and it's extremely relevant.' She glanced around to make sure they were all paying attention. 'Did anyone here make contact with Frederick Vanderkloot recently, and suggest we might be ready for a takeover?'

They looked away immediately, and as fast as she could she glanced across every face to see if she could catch an expression – of surprise, secrecy, guilt, anything that might tell her that trust had been broken behind her back.

Nobody answered.

'Barry?' She hated asking him, but he could have gone over her head and contacted Vanderkloot for the sake of the company.

'Lorraine, I – ' he gave a hopeless little shrug. 'I'm sorry you had to ask me that one.'

Quickly she murmured – 'It would have been for my sake.' Then she looked across the table. 'Dean?'

161

'No.' He was eyeing her obliquely; head on one side, his tone close to contempt. 'Not quite my style.'

She drew a breath, forcing herself to go on: because one of them here might have betrayed her in this way, for whatever reason – to save the company, to save his job, even to make certain she lost the chairmanship. *And she wanted to know.*

'Carl?'

His eyes grew round. 'Shit, no.'

'Joe?'

'Vanderkloot,' Joe Fisher said, trying to conceal his embarrassment, 'isn't the nicest guy in town, Lorraine.'

'He's extremely powerful. Capable of setting this company on its feet again.'

He said in a flat tone: 'I didn't contact him.'

'Sam?'

'Now see here, Lorraine, it isn't a very nice question.'

'I'm asking it, Sam.'

He looked at her with an expression of open distaste. 'No, it didn't actually occur to me to go behind your back and try selling Floderus down the river, to Frederick Vanderkloot or anyone else.'

She bit her lip. 'Thank you.'

Then there was silence, as if nobody knew what to do next.

Sam McNair took out his handkerchief and blew his nose again, while Joe Fisher got his cigarettes and began passing them around. Dean sat pensively, his chin in one hand, a pale band around his third finger showing where the marriage ring had been, before he'd flown out to Nassau for a lonely week in the sun.

Then Sy Goldman said: 'We haven't heard your own proposal, Madam Chairman, for pulling the company out of trouble.'

Their heads came up in surprise, and Lorraine took a couple of seconds to deal with the humiliating realisation that they hadn't even considered, until Sy had spoken, that the chairman of this company might have something to propose that would interest them. It gave her the eerie feeling that she wasn't there; that she didn't exist.

'Thank you, Sy. I thought you'd never ask.' She took a deep breath. 'What I'm going to do, gentlemen, is call a share-holders' meeting and announce that Floderus is to create a dramatic new fragrance.'

Everyone froze. They were all watching Lorraine, and didn't look away. Ash dropped from Joe's cigarette; a sheet of paper escaped from Nadine's clipboard and she let it stay where it had fallen; Charles Fox was blowing out smoke in a low whistle.

'Oh, Jesus . . .' Dean Powers said softly.

Carl Blatt went on watching Lorraine.

'I'd like your views,' she said.

Dean squinted through his cigarette smoke. 'You'd be committing suicide.'

Suddenly all their eyes were down, and the strained silence drew out, embarrassing them.

'I'm sorry,' Dean said at last, 'that wasn't a very good choice of . . .' he shrugged, letting it die.

Stepping in, Charles Fox said impatiently: 'Lorraine, you're talking about a two-year project. You're talking about two million dollars to create the right fragrance, and two million per annum for advertising.' He blew out smoke.

'And four,' Joe Fisher said, 'maybe five years before the real profits start coming in. I tell you frankly, Lorraine, it's a beautiful concept – and crazy.'

She looked along the table, from side to side, trying to find a friend. Nobody was looking at her. 'Is there any one of you who believes I'd have even a chance?'

Most of them were shaking their heads, reluctant to damn her proposal out loud. Carl Blatt hitched himself around in his chair, so he could watch Lorraine as he spoke.

'Are you serious?'

'Yes.'

'Is this your own idea?'

'No. It was yours.'

Everyone was suddenly looking at Carl.

'I'm not too sure,' he said with his blank stare, 'that it was

163

a very good one. But I'd be ready to go with it.'

Three people spoke at once: Joe, Dean, and Charles.

'Carl, you're crazy –'

'Do you know what's *involved* – ?'

'Where the hell would you raise the money?'

When silence came again Lorraine asked them: 'Is anyone else interested?'

After a long interval, Dean Powers said wearily, 'The ship's going down anyway. You don't have to scuttle it.'

Sy Goldman jumped straight in. 'Now Dean, I don't think you have to put it quite like that.'

'Our situation's perfectly understood,' Barry said with an unaccustomed show of anger, 'without your constant melodramatics.'

Dean looked at both men, surprised. 'I guess I spoke out of turn.'

'Getting to be a habit,' said Joe Fisher with a quick dry laugh, but no one relaxed.

Lorraine waited until there was silence, then said with her tone as cool as she could make it: 'Dean, this meeting is almost over. For the rest of the time we're going to talk about the idea of creating a new fragrance. Since that doesn't interest you, I'd like you to know that you're under no obligation to stay.'

Everyone was suddenly looking hard at the table.

Okay, Carl Blatt was thinking, so this is how far things have gotten: the chairman and chief executive officer is telling the vice president of the company to get his ass out of the boardroom, and in front of everyone else.

Dean Powers hesitated a couple of seconds, then got his long body together and stood up, taking his pack of Bensons and his gold pen and moving towards the door, in the kind of silence where a slight cough would have sounded like a bomb going off.

As he passed Lorraine, she said without looking up: 'Dean, as my project starts going ahead, I'll need to cut staff. I'd like you to be out of your office by tonight.'

He stopped dead. 'I've already started clearing it.' They

could hear the huskiness of anger in his voice, which few of them could ever remember having heard before. 'But I have a question, Lorraine. In the year you've been here, have you found my work satisfactory?' He paused. 'That's assuming you'd know.'

Lorraine stood up so suddenly that her chair rocked back and Barry saved it as he too got to his feet. 'Yes, Dean,' she said as she faced him, 'I'd actually know. A career in motion pictures doesn't necessarily require the wits of a moron. Your work has been very satisfactory indeed. You have the reputation of a first-class executive with a sound understanding of the perfume market. But I need more than that, in my company. I need faith, and loyalty, and cooperation, and it's quite possible that your own career as a marketing director hasn't so far required the values of a human being.'

As they stood facing each other only a few feet apart, Nadine Keller noted fleetingly that the boardroom, with its polished furniture and dignified décor, had suddenly become a shambles. Barry Corbett was still on his feet, having saved the chair from falling, and was watching the two antagonists as if he might need to intervene; Carl was rooted to his chair with his eyes wide; Sy had half risen, reluctant to be sitting down while the chairman was on her feet; and Joe Fisher was standing with his back to the windows with his hands on his hips, trying to believe what he was seeing.

The rush of thoughts going on in the privacy of all their minds was wide-ranging. Nadine Keller was thinking that if this lecherous bastard – who'd tried twice to lay her – said just one word too many, she'd take off a shoe and nail the heel into the back of his neck. Barry Corbett was also ready to defend Lorraine, but his chief reaction was one of deep sorrow that so soon after Wilhelm's death his portrait should be looking down on such disorder in the company he created. Charlie Fox was thinking that Dean really should go right out and tell this gal the score: his work had been more than just satisfactory; in the eight years he'd been with

165

the company he'd worked his ass off for it, which is why Charlie had just voted to put him into the chair.

Carl Blatt was making a paper-clip into a cross.

Dean was talking again, moving a step closer to Lorraine with his shoulders hunched and his eyes narrowed. 'Faith, loyalty and cooperation . . . You said you had all the figures, Lorraine; now I'm going to give you one of the facts. In the past eight years there's been nobody – not even Barry, the co-founder – who's given this company more faith, loyalty and cooperation than I have; and I was so goddamned good at it that when you came along and put us all on the skids I had to spend so much of my life working overtime that it finally cost me my marriage.' He wanted to stop right there, but his anger wouldn't let him. 'And it was a good one. A good marriage. Ten beautiful years. So I don't owe you anything, you understand? Loyalty doesn't come as a handout; it has to be earned; and you don't even know how to begin.'

Lorraine swung away, swung back. 'I'm sorry about your marriage. Are you sure it was nothing to do with the junior typists you can't seem to keep your hands off? I should imagine your wife might – '

'This is *nothing* to do with you – '

'You mentioned it first – remember, the "beautiful marriage" bit? But frankly I don't have time to discuss it either.' She wanted to say something final, something damning; but she couldn't even think straight, because they'd all come in here to try to save Floderus and it was ending up in an undignified brawl. All she could do was face him, trembling, and hope he might say something she could seize on.

'Okay,' Dean said with his own voice shaking, 'we won't talk about my marriage. You did a lot towards breaking it up for me, but you don't have time to discuss it right now; that's okay, I accept that.' His voice had begun rising, and he lowered it, speaking through his teeth as he faced Lorraine. 'But there's one thing I can't accept so easily. The man you've harmed more than any of us, Lorraine, is your own

166

father, the creative genius who –'

'*Don't you dare mention him, Dean, I'm* –'

'*I have the right.* He was my boss. He was my friend, and I honour his memory. With his brilliance, his flair, and his towering talent for doing things right, he created this company. But he also had a daughter, who threw it all away.'

He was moving towards the door when she broke, and found herself shaking helplessly in Barry Corbett's arms.

'Oh my God, how could he do that to me . . . How could he –'

'It's okay, Lorrie.' He held her tight, trying to stop the terrible shaking of her body. 'He's gone now . . . He's –'

'Oh God, how could he do that . . . ' Tears were springing, scalding her face. 'How could he say things like –'

'Don't worry, sweetheart. He didn't mean them. He's gone now . . . he's gone.'

CHAPTER 15

DONNA SHAPIRO GOT out of the lift at the twentieth floor of the Bank Trust Building and stood there listening to the doors closing behind her as she wondered which way she should go. All she could see to her left were the doors of offices, some with a glass wall and others more private-looking. To her right was a big open space with cubicles, quite a long way off. The place was silent, but for the humming of the light tubes everywhere.

She was in what looked like the reception room, though there was nobody at the big limed-oak desk. It was just ten o'clock, the time when Lorraine Floderus said she'd be here to meet her tonight. Maybe she'd forgotten. The janitor had just said to go on up.

The smells were different here: carpet fibre, wood panelling, copy machine fluids, different from the smells Donna was used to at work: cooking fumes, cigarette smoke, jet-engine exhaust gas. Her ears were still singing from the last two flights, which she'd made practically non-stop, New York-Los Angeles-New York, piling up bonus time so she could take a full six days' leave. Every time she'd landed in New York since last Wednesday – the day she'd met Lorraine Floderus on the flight back from L.A. – she had looked at the business card her passenger had given her, and a couple of times had picked up a phone and dialled the number and then hung up before anyone answered. A film star was a film star, and from what you read about them in *People* and on the front page of the *Enquirer* when you were going through the checkout, the Hollywood crowd wasn't the most reliable breed of citizen, and even though the card said that Lorraine Floderus was the chairman of a perfume company, she could still be one of those frenetic tinsel-city freaks under the skin. But the temptation to make contact again with *this* one – maybe just to *look* at her for a few minutes – had gotten the better of Donna; and this morning, when she'd stepped off the LAX-JFK flight with her bag across her shoulder and six days of leave opening out in front of her, she'd called Floderus Incorporated – and got quite a surprise.

'Who is it calling, please?'

'Donna Shapiro.'

'Donna . . . who?'

'Shapiro.'

'I'm sorry, the chairman is in a meeting right now. May I say what it's about?'

Oh boy, she'd thought, have I heard *this* before . . .

'She gave me her card, and asked me to call her the next time I was in New York.'

'She did? How do you spell your last name, please?'

She spelt it. Jesus, it was an easy enough name, wasn't it?

'Shapiro. Just a minute.' The voice was back in ten seconds flat. 'Oh, Miss *Shapiro* . . . of course! Please excuse me – I'll interrupt the meeting right away for you.'

Then there was that famous husky voice on the line suddenly, and Donna had wanted to laugh. Seat-belt Sally flies into li'l ole New York still covered in left-over food and with her feet in blisters, calls up the chairman of the company that makes *Picaresque* and gets her pulled right out of a meeting . . . Well, sure, it happens all the time.

Delighted to hear from her, Lorraine Floderus had said. What was she doing tonight? Her own time was fully booked until then, but she'd like Donna to see the office and then they could take in a late supper somewhere, if she'd like that.

Donna had almost said no, she was booked up herself tonight; because ten o'clock was a pretty weird time to conduct a job interview – if that was still what the chairman

169

of Floderus Incorporated had in mind. But that husky voice had sounded so friendly, and so persuasive, with an undertone of . . . Donna hadn't quite been able to name it; was it . . . urgency? That couldn't be it, yet she'd thought it was close.

So she'd said, sure, ten o'clock tonight. And here she was. Why? Why, exactly?

If you'd like to work for me, I'd pay you double your present salary. Whatever it is.

Well, sure, gee, yes. If she really meant it. But there was something else to this crazy business. Donna didn't think she really did mean it, in any case. So you're flying in to the Apple from making another movie and you suddenly need a flying waitress to work for you in your perfume company at double the money, whatever it is? That was crazy, Hollywood-crazy. No, it was this gal's *dazzle* that had brought her to this deserted building in the middle of Manhattan tonight; and more than just her dazzle, than just that terrific whoever-you-are-I-love-you smile. Donna had sensed other things, deeper things, underneath it; a kind of vibration; a held-in tension; and something else, even deeper, even stronger, way down there where Lorraine Floderus really lived. And whatever it was, it had something to do with that tone of . . . urgency Donna had detected today over the telephone. Okay, then, maybe not exactly urgency, but close.

That was why, exactly, she was standing here tonight, not knowing where to go next. She wanted to tune in. After the long flights and the frantic rush to put on the service and get it cleared away in time, after the endless smiling and the need for superhuman patience and the night-stops drugged with fatigue and jet-lag, after all the routine and the repetition and the monotony, she wanted to tune in to another kind of life for a while, if it looked interesting. But not just any kind of life: the one that Lorraine Floderus was living; because of that vibration she'd sensed in her, and that undertone to the husky voice, that hinted of something intriguingly, even frighteningly, real.

170

A slight sound came, and Donna turned, going along the corridor to the huge open space where the cubicles were, deserted under the rows of light grilles. As she moved closer she saw a figure standing there, almost in the middle; and though it was half turned away from Donna, she recognised it as Lorraine Floderus. Slight, motionless, and seemingly lifeless, she was standing in the central aisle between two rows of cubicles, her head lifted a little as she gazed at something – or nothing? – deep in thought.

Donna stopped moving, wondering if she should call out or wait till she was seen. It was a little eerie, coming here to find this young woman standing utterly alone in the middle of a deserted office floor and looking more like a beautiful statue than someone human, while out there beyond the dark windows the night-life of the city glittered and grated around her, unseen and unheard.

Suddenly she moved, turning and taking a pace and looking around her – and seeing Donna.

'Who's that?'

Donna took a breath and went forwards, her shoes silent across the carpeting. 'I'm Donna Shapiro, Miss Floderus.'

The beautiful face remained blank for a moment, then the smile came, lighting it. 'Donna . . . of course.' She offered her slim hand, studying the deep brown eyes and the auburn hair and the clear-cut features of the girl she had last seen on the flight from Los Angeles. 'I hadn't forgotten our appointment; I came here specially to meet you.' The smile became rueful as she glanced around. 'I was just communing with a few of my ghosts . . .'

Donna's face blanked out. 'Oh, really?'

Lorraine laughed gently. 'Don't worry, you won't be seeing them; they were real people, and now they've gone, that's all.'

'Oh.' Donna stood there in her crisp blue tunic and skirt, her feet neatly together, her eyes a little wary.

'We had a meeting,' Lorraine told her, 'last Thursday. It was . . . rather eventful. Three of my executive staff walked out.'

171

Sam McNair. Portly, circumspect, ultra-conservative in his black suit, blowing his nose while he was talking. 'Lorraine, I believe it was a mistake, a grave mistake, to let Dean Powers go like that. He was the best man we had. And frankly, I'm going to move along myself; I don't believe I can be of much use to you here anymore.'

Charlie Fox. Slightly rumpled, contemplative, shaking the change in his pocket with the sound of distant alarm bells. 'It's not that you went right out and provoked Dean that way . . . or it's partly that, okay. But if you're going to go in front of the shareholders with this idea of launching a new fragrance, I'd prefer not to be there. I hope you'll understand.'

And Dean himself. A man with no mercy, and no manners, walking out of the boardroom to leave her shaking in Barry's arms, no longer the chairman and chief executive officer of Floderus Incorporated but the little girl who'd climbed on 'Uncle' Barry's knee when there were tears to shed and he was the nearest haven.

Ghosts, now. Dean had left the same day, Thursday, without another word to her. Sam had left on Friday, saying that he'd be 'in touch with events' from time to time. Charlie Fox came in on Saturday morning to clear out his office, after working late into Friday night to wind up his affairs. On Sunday Lorraine had thought so often, during the long day's ending to the week, of Frank, and his homely cabin in the woods upstate; but it had been impossible to call him; that was over now. She had spent her time going over and over Thursday's climactic meeting, knowing where she had gone wrong – appallingly wrong – and trying to find any chance, any hope of righting some of it. By the day's end she'd known there was no chance, no hope; by her own clumsy handling, her own lack of understanding of corporate lore and protocol, she had lost the main strength of her executive staff, and at a time when she needed it most.

The worst had been the scene with Barry Corbett, in the privacy of her office late Thursday night, the door locked against the intrusion of the cleaners as they started their

172

work. As he had sat there, leaning forward with his face cupped in his hands, elbows on knees, she had listened to his quiet voice with its tone of final despair. 'I'm going to tell you something, Lorrie, that nobody else has ever known; not even Virginia. In the years I was with this company, I picked up one or two insights into the business of selling a product; I learned enough of the market, and its problems to do a reasonable job, and do some kind of justice to your father's faith in me. I didn't let him down. When I was fresh out of Harvard with a pocketful of money my own father left me, I happened to be there when Willie needed some to start his business. I also had a few connections, and I'd completed a course in business administration. But that was all it was, Lorrie. I finished up his right hand man: but *anyone* could have done the same, anyone with the few advantages I had.'

Lorraine hadn't interrupted. Watching him objectively, without his eyes on her, she could admit to herself what she'd always known since she'd walked into this building as the new chief of Floderus: Barry was an old man now, an old man of only fifty-eight, nudging seventy. And she knew another thing: it must have happened to him the day Wilhelm had died; from that time, on, Barry had aged precipitously, outrunning the calendar. She hadn't realised, on the day of the memorial service when Barry had held her weeping in his arms, that his own grief was deeper even than hers, and his loss more shattering.

'All the time he was here with us,' Barry went on quietly, 'he lent me the abilities I thought were my own; with his inspiration I did things I couldn't do, after he'd gone. So there you have it, Lorrie. From now on, I've nothing to offer you.' He raised his head at last to look at her. 'If you mean to keep this company running somehow, you'll need people around you with great courage, great strength, and the kind of inspiration we all of us had in the past. I can't give you those things. I'm hoping with all my heart that you'll come around to the only way open to you: cut your losses, sell out, and start again somewhere else. If you don't do that; if you

173

decide to keep going as best you can, you'll have to replace me, and let me go home.' Then his face was in his hands again, and his voice so low she barely caught the words. 'You'll have no problem finding someone better than me to take over . . . no problem at all . . .'

On Sunday Lorraine had called him at his home, but Virginia had answered, and said he was resting. It had been in Lorraine's mind to go over and see them both, and with Ginnie's help try to nurse him back to some kind of faith in himself; but as she'd put the phone down she had realised she was doing no more than go through the motions of trying to save his pride. He was beyond that now.

'Gee,' she heard someone saying, 'that's tough.' It was a moment before she remembered where she was.

'Tough?' she asked Donna.

'Why, sure. Three executives walking out on you.'

'Oh. Yes, in a way.'

'You mean you're probably better off without them?'

Lorraine stared at her. 'My God, are you always this intuitive, Donna?'

'Is that what I'm being?' She looked genuinely surprised.

'Either that, or downright telepathic.' Lorraine hadn't even been aware of the thought in her own head, before this bright little Brooklyn girl had picked it out, in an instant of revelation. Lorraine *would* be better off without those people. In the crudest but the most accurate terms, they were a lame dog, a bastard, and a quitter. 'I didn't make any mistake about you, Donna. I'm a bit intuitive myself.' She took her arm. 'Come on, I'll give you a quick tour of the place and then we'll hole up in a little bistro around the corner and do some talking. How long do you have?'

'As long as it takes. I have six days' leave – will that be long enough?'

'I guess!' She took Donna through the main offices, pausing only for a moment in Barry's, Dean's and Charlie's, suddenly unnerved by the sight of their empty desks, their favourite water colours gone from the wall, reminding her of what Dean had said in the heat of their encounter a week

174

ago: *You'll have quite a few empty offices around, by the time you want to sell out. It wouldn't look very good.* Maybe she'd be better off without them, yes; but until she could find replacements these empty rooms would be a haunting reminder of her loneliness among the executive suites.

'Miss Floderus,' Donna began as they went into the big corner office, 'can I ask – '

'Call me Lorraine.'

'Oh. Gee. Okay. Can I ask you something?'

'It has to be interesting,' Lorraine said with a soft laugh, surprised at her sudden rise in spirits. She realised that she'd been alone with her thoughts since Friday evening, with no one she could talk to, no one who'd understand.

'Is this your office, Lorraine?'

'Yes. Is that your question?'

'No. But it's so beautiful.'

'Thank you.' It looked a little different, even to her own eyes; the décor people had kept their promise, and now the big ivory-white desk was lower, with its dais gone, and against the west windows, leaving the white pigskin suite opposite the door. This way, as Carl had pointed out, her visitors would feel more comfortable, less dominated. 'Sit down,' she told Donna. 'Would you like a drink?'

'Not right now.' She sat down in the chair opposite Lorraine, thinking she could use a drink to calm her nerves, but maybe it wouldn't look right, at a job interview. She hadn't submitted herself to one since she'd walked into the offices of Transworld Airlines four years ago, and this evening she was on strange territory; the floor didn't sway up and down, and instead of vinyl and aluminium there was solid and opulent furniture; but that wasn't all. Instead of talking to the personnel manager during working hours she was face to face with her potential boss at ten-thirty at night among a lot of deserted offices, after being told, in passing, that three of her executive staff had just walked out.

'What's your question, Donna?'

'Uh? Oh. Well, I guess I need to know what made you think I could do a job for you. I mean, without seeing a

175

résumé or anything.' She swallowed, and was instantly annoyed with herself for letting her nerves show.

Lorraine got up and went over to a long ivory-white cabinet in the corner of the room, walking with that incredible grace that Donna had watched on the big screen so many times.

'I think we can both use a drink,' Lorraine said. 'What would you like?'

'Oh. Do you have B and B?'

'I think so.' She swung open the cabinet, and Donna kicked herself again. That bar had *everything*. 'Actually, Donna, I've already seen your résumé, on the flight from Los Angeles.'

'You have?'

'I'm talking about the way you handled that drunk.'

'Oh. You have some drunks for me to handle?'

'Not quite,' Lorraine laughed softly, 'just people.' She brought the drinks across. 'Difficult people. They're worse, in a way. Some time or other a drunk sobers up, but people can stay difficult. Cheers.'

Donna lifted her glass. 'Cheers.'

'How old are you, Donna?'

'Twenty-five.'

'Born in New York?'

Donna drew the zipper along the top of her bag. 'I brought a résumé, Miss Flod – Lorraine.'

'I don't want to see it. It wouldn't change my mind.'

'Oh. Well – ' She held the folded sheet of paper uncertainly.

'Maybe I should,' Lorraine told her quickly, 'since you brought it along.'

'Okay.' Donna passed her the résumé, and Lorraine talked as she glanced over it. 'You've never left New York?'

'Just every flight, I guess.'

Lorraine smiled. 'But you've never lived anywhere else?'

'There's somewhere else?'

'Good question. And you have a degree in law.'

'Uh-huh. But I never practised. For every ten new law

176

graduates, there's at least one opening.'

'It's still a pretty useful asset. What's the IAPA?'

'International Airline Passengers' Association.'

'They gave you an award. What for?'

'We had a flight ditch.'

'A plane went down?'

'Uh-huh.'

'What happened to the passengers?'

'We got them out.'

'I see.'

Donna noticed her sudden change of expression. 'Were you in a crash some time, Lorraine?'

'What? No. My father. And my mother.'

From what she saw in Lorraine's eyes, Donna didn't need to ask what had happened. 'Gee, I'm sorry.'

'Thank you. It was a year ago.' She handed the résumé back. 'My father created this company. Since he died, things have . . . gone downhill.' She took a sip at her drink.

'It happens,' Donna said. 'Some people are indispensable.'

'Yes. And yet . . . ' She got up suddenly, walking slowly to the windows and back, her arms folded as if she needed to enclose herself while she thought this through. 'Yet he was my father. I'm of his blood. Don't you think it's possible there's enough of him in me, enough of his creative talent and his energy and his brilliant flair for doing things right, to give me a chance of success?'

Donna was standing up now, surprised at the tone of quiet desperation in Lorraine's voice. 'I . . . I guess I . . . '

'It wasn't really a question, Donna. How could you possibly answer? You don't know me. I'm just thinking aloud.'

'Then I'm listening.'

Lorraine turned quickly from her pacing. 'Are you?'

'Sure.'

'You don't think I'm talking nonsense?'

'I guess you don't often do that.'

Lorraine gazed at her for a moment, caught by this young

stranger's readiness to believe in her. It was what she needed most of all, and would have to find, if she was ever going to go on. Another's faith. 'I didn't mean to get into this until later,' she told Donna, 'but when you mentioned the plane crash, it suddenly got me going. If – '

'I'm sorry about that – '

'I think I'm glad. I want you to hear this right now, after all. Then you can decide what you want to do.' She began pacing again. 'This company belongs to me, Donna. My father left it to me. In the past year I've – I've come close to ruining it, through inexperience, and impulsiveness, and I suppose the sheer size of the job I had to do. As I told you, three of my staff have walked out. But don't you think, Donna, that anyone can do anything, if they try hard enough? I want to turn this whole situation around, more than anything in the whole world; it's what I dream about; it's what I live for; it's what I *have* to do. So don't you think if I went on trying, if I gave it *everything* I've got, if I let *nothing* stop me, I could win out? Don't you think that just sometimes it's possible to do the impossible?'

As she gazed at Lorraine, Donna recognised instantly what she was hearing: a cry for help; and her memory flashed back to the paraplegic boy in the rear seat of the aisle, his leg trapped by the buckled pannelling and one withered arm waving, his voice lost in the cries of the other passengers as they crowded to the exits. The water was already waist-deep, and Donna would have to half-swim against the tide of living bodies to reach the rear seat before the plane began sinking. It would be impossible; but after a while, after a lot of confusion and noise and a sense of absolute *refusal* to leave him there, she was wallowing in the open sea, keeping the boy's head above water until they could haul him into the life-raft, still fully conscious though not speaking, just watching her with his huge eyes as they hauled her aboard after him.

The scene vanished. 'Yes,' she told Lorraine, 'we can do the impossible, if that's what we want to do.'

Lorraine stared at her for a moment, then came and took

178

both Donna's hands in her own. 'My God, I knew I was right about you . . . I knew I was damn' *right!*'

It was after three but Donna gave a knock and walked right into the shabby, over-furnished fifth-floor apartment, knowing that Dad didn't get in from his evening shift at the Krazy Kitchen until around this hour, and Mom always waited up for him.

'What's that, honey?'

Donna gave her mother a kiss first and then the elegant gold box with its crimson sash and bow.

'For you. Dad late again?'

'He'll be here.'

'They work him too hard, Mom, at that place.'

Her mother was holding the gold box to the light. 'He has a job, honey. There's so many that don't. *This* should be for *me*?'

'Open it up.' Donna dropped her bag onto a chair and fixed her hair in the damp-mottled mirror over the mantelpiece. 'It's a present from my new boss.'

'Your *new* – ?'

'I'm leaving the airline.'

'You're leaving *TWA*?' Ready for bad news, with the recession worse every week, she began tearing the gold paper off the package, unconsciously hurrying, in case there were anything in here that could work some kind of magic, and stave off trouble. 'You're not *fired*, are you, honey?'

'Nope.' She stood with her back to the inadequate electric heater, watching her mother's eyes as she came to the huge 5-ounce flacon of *Picaresque* inside the box. On a thought, she went to her bag and pulled out the first-class flight menu, dropping it onto the table. 'I guess this is the last one Dad's going to get. Now it's going to be your turn, Mom.'

'But Donna . . . what kind of job will you have now?' Quickly she added – 'This is beautiful, just beautiful . . .'

'It's a perfume company. Floderus. And you know who my boss is? *Lorraine* Floderus.'

Her mother stared at her, bright brown eyes under a cloud

of red hair. 'The movie star?'

'Yes.'

'And she makes perfume?'

'Yes.'

'But you had such a good job with the airline, honey. Why – this is just so *beautiful,* so *expensive* – why are you giving up such a good job with the airline, to work for a *perfume* company?'

Donna took a deep breath and let it out again. 'I guess I went crazy, Mom. Clean out of my mind crazy.'

CHAPTER 16

THE NEXT MORNING at five minutes to ten o'clock, Lorraine was in her office, alone. At this precise moment she was sitting behind her desk doing absolutely nothing. Anyone looking in at the door would have said she was sitting perfectly still; from that distance they wouldn't notice the infinitesimal vibration running through her body. She was acutely aware of it herself; it felt as if she'd been plugged in to a power-house, and instead of lighting up or spinning around she was just vibrating. Everything in the large, elegant office was doing the same thing; she knew that if she reached out to touch one of the telephones or the black onyx pen-holder or the perfume-flacon paperweight, she'd feel their vibration; she felt that if she brought anything metal together, her jade-handled paper-knife, say, and the silver-framed calendar, they'd make a spark; she was actually thinking, absurdly, that if anyone came in here with a can of lighter-fuel right now she'd have to yell at them to take it right on out again before they blew the place up.

She wished Donna were here; even though she and Donna had talked into the wee hours last night at the Café St Cloud on 57th Street, it hadn't been long enough to give her the complete picture on what was happening inside Floderus Incorporated. Today, Donna would have done more than learn the history of the company; she would have been present at history in the making, if things took the right direction. But she was probably still in bed; Lorraine had told her to take all the time she needed to get rid of the accumulated jet-lag of the last series of boomerang flights to

181

the west coast, and report for duty when she felt she was ready. Besides which, a total stranger – even with her title as Executive Aide to the Chairman – at a critical meeting like this would constrain the others; they were coming here to give total expression to their hopes and their fears and their inventive faculties, and they'd want to do it in private.

Yet some of the vibration going on in Lorraine at this moment was due to that feisty, fearless and adventurous young woman she'd seen into a cab at three o'clock this morning. That one phrase had sounded a chord deep inside Lorraine that was still thrumming. *Yes, we can do the impossible, if that's what we want to do.* In the way that life seemed to order things, Donna had arrived at precisely the right psychological moment. Lorraine's courage had been beaten down to a new low, after the shock of Madlen's deliberate brush with death, the disastrous board meeting and its repercussions, and Dean Powers' brutal condemnation of her failure as head of Floderus; and the hours she'd spent last night in Donna's company had revitalised her. Without this, she doubted she could have contributed anything constructive to this morning's meeting; as it was, she sat here feeling what a matador must feel, waiting in the arena for the entry of the bull: scared, tensed, but resolved.

At exactly ten o'clock Nadine Keller – taking over from Maggie, who was still away with laryngitis – buzzed Lorraine to announce Joe Fisher; a moment later he came in quickly, as if he might be tempted to turn around and duck right out again if he didn't keep up his pace. This was Lorraine's impression, and it wasn't far off the mark.

Joe Fisher was one of those men whose unlimited capacity for worry kept him lean as a rake. At forty-two he had the vulnerable looks of a younger man; his sandy, wedge-shaped face and faraway eyes gave him an appeal to matronly women, despite the obvious fact that he could run faster than they could. He had married the wrong woman twice; both had believed from his pensive brow and his clouded eyes that he was a poet, only to discover that he was simply worried; both had divorced him for neglecting them,

182

and he had survived the ruptures far better than he would have survived a continuing relationship with either.

At twenty-three Joe was a junior copywriter for a small firm in New Jersey that had a total of seven accounts, all of them in household cleaners. At thirty-two he was copy supervisor to an agency specialising in fast food ads, and his series of deft images for the Bun on the Run franchise chain attracted attention from the major industries. By thirty-nine he was associate creative director of Jefferson-Hall, specialising in auto accounts and coming up with the classic multicoloured 3-D-style double-page pull-outs with the cars looking like exotic space vehicles sliding right out of the star-filled sky to your own carriage drive. Two years ago he joined Floderus Incorporated as advertising director of marketing, and was thus here during Lorraine's disastrous switch to the new ad agency and the new 'popular' image.

Today, he thought as he came into her office at a half-run, they were going to do something about that new ad agency and that new image. Today they were going to do a whole lot of things, and his major worry was over what they would turn out to be.

'Joe,' the chairman said brightly, 'come on in.'

'Hi,' he said, and looked around quickly. Seeing that they were alone didn't calm him; Lorraine was looking particularly slinky this morning in a sheer white knit, and it disturbed him; she ought to wear more . . . to be more . . . but no: she ought to be *less*.

'Cigarette?' Lorraine asked him.

'Thanks.'

'Scared?'

'Hell, no.'

'So am I.' Her smile was brilliant.

Joe dragged smoke into his lungs, got an instant picture of X-ray cancer cells and blew it out again. *Gonna quit tomorrow, and this time I mean it.*

'Sit down, Joe.'

'I'm okay.' He wandered about, feeling trapped. 'You look totally gorgeous today.'

183

'Thank you.'

'Actually, it's no help.'

Lorraine laughed outright, releasing some of the tension, some of the vibration in her. Joe Fisher was one of the few people around her she could feel easy with; they recognised, she thought, each other's vulnerability.

Sy Goldman came in next, with Nadine opening the door for him; as Barry Corbett's secretary, she displayed exemplary manners: she escorted Sy Goldman in here because he was a valuable member of the company and also a true gentleman, who knew how to break a lunch date with the expertise of a diplomat and how to compliment a pretty girl without pinching her ass.

'Mr Goldman,' Nadine said crisply.

Lorraine came forward a little to greet him. Sy had been with the company six years, had loved her father like a brother, and posessed a degree of obstinacy in decision-making that had reduced the business of many a board meeting to a stale-mate, until it was seen that if any progress were to be made at all it would have to begin by the admission that Sy was right – again.

'Good-morning, Sy.' Lorraine offered her hand.

'Madam chairman,' he said softly, bowing over it with the gallantry of a portly potentate and bringing a whiff of Black Tie cologne and shoe polish. 'You're looking charming today, which is going to be the last time I shall say anything even remotely acceptable until lunch, since we have serious business to do.' He leavened it with a soft Hitchcock chuckle.

'You bet,' Lorraine smiled gamely.

Sy left her immediately, as if he were a guest in a presentation line at the White House with others behind him. 'Joe,' he said benevolently, 'you're looking as nervous as a cat on moving day.'

'I work at it,' Joe said with his flickering smile.

Then Carl Blatt was here, wandering in as soon as Nadine had buzzed to announce him; though he held the same executive status as Sy Goldman, he would have wondered what in hell Nadine was doing if she tried to escort him in

184

here; and not because he was short and at first glance unimpressive in his casual tweed jacket and brogues but because this whole floor of the building was his accepted territory, and he liked wandering in and out of the various offices at will, twiddling his paper-clips and perching on desks as he delivered himself of what was on his mind, which was always a very great deal.

'Hi, Lorraine.' His amiable blink was about the closest Carl Blatt ever got to a smile.

'Hi, Carl.'

'Gee whiz,' he said as he looked around, 'there's been a few changes.'

'Which you wouldn't know anything about,' Lorraine said in a private undertone.

He raised his brows and rolled his eyes behind their steel-rimmed glasses, going over to her desk and veering away again.

'It's okay to perch, Carl. This meeting's informal.'

He veered back to her desk without breaking his pace, and perched there with his paper-clip, blinking across at the other two men. 'Hi, guys.'

'Coffee?' Lorraine asked them. 'You know where it is.'

Nobody went over to the elegant percolator; they were probably going to spend their whole day here on regular doses of caffeine, and all they could do about it was at least hold off for as long as they could.

Lorraine buzzed Nadine in the outer office. 'Strictly no calls from here on, okay?' She hesitated, then added: 'Unless it's my sister, Madlen.' Lifting her finger from the button she felt a sudden lurch of the heart. Nothing would make Madlen call her, but she couldn't risk being wrong.

There was a silence in the room, while everyone looked at each other, waiting for Lorraine to kick off; seeing she was preoccupied, Carl Blatt said to no one:
'So what do we do?'

'We take it from here,' Sy said, and dug his plump hands in his pockets.

Lorraine came back to the present. 'Okay, gentlemen. I didn't ask Nathan to join us today. Maybe later.' Nathan

185

Franzheim was the chief accountant. 'But I asked him to give me a ballpark figure for a new fragrance, just for the sake of interest.'

'And he went straight into cardiac arrest,' Sy Goldman said with a hoarse chuckle.

Lorraine took a breath. 'He gave me the rough figures. Two million dollars to develop and make the fragrance, plus two million dollars for the initial promotion over an eighteen-month period.'

'Now *I'm* going into cardiac arrest,' Sy said, and this time he didn't chuckle.

'We could cut corners,' Joe said, 'big ones. Sell the plant and buy from IFF or Dupont.'

'No way,' Carl told him. 'We're here to find out how to jack up the Floderus image, and we can't do that by lining up with everyone else at IFF or Dupont.'

Joe swung his head. 'IFF make stuff mostly for Estée Lauder, and Dupont make *Opium*. That's slumming it?'

'I think I know what Carl's talking about,' Lorraine cut in. 'We've always made our own fragrances, and if we sell the plant now and have to compete for something special from the big suppliers, we'll be down-graded in the trade, and that's important. We want to go out for absolute exclusivity, as we've always done.'

'Right,' Carl said, watching her with a new interest; he didn't realise she knew so much about the industry, after only a year's experience. 'We go for a spectacular – but understated.'

'Now I've heard everything,' Joe Fisher said, worried by the trend of the discussion. 'How the hell would we understate a spectacular?'

'Beat the drum softly,' Carl told him with a round-eyed stare.

'Word of mouth?' Sy asked him.

'Right. Discreet parties. Exclusive little shows revealing work-in-progress. Trips to Paris for selected buyers. Teaser ads in the trades: the word is getting around that Floderus is going for something very, *very* special this time.'

'On only two million dollars?'

'That's why we'd keep it exclusive.'

'The impression,' Sy asked him, 'would be that we could afford to make a much louder noise, but don't want to?'

'Beat the drum softly,' Carl said again, 'but they'll know it's a big drum.' He looked at Joe Fisher now; they needed to get his interest, his enthusiasm. Joe would be doing the ad campaign, and it would have to be effective. 'Not like the thing you did for the auto industry,' he said, 'more like your message for Courvoisier: the respect due to ancient skills, hallowed traditions.'

'The ultimate chic,' Sy put in. *'Class.'*

Lorraine turned her head. Carl had got Sy's interest, and was leading him away from his doubts about the cost involved.

'Exactly,' Carl said. If they could get Sy started, Joe would soon follow; they had mutual respect for each other's work.

Joe crushed out his cigarette and ambled across to the coffee percolator, suddenly needing caffeine. Carl slid off the desk and followed him, by way of encouragement. Lorraine filled the silence, to keep the ball rolling.

'We'd get the essence from Grasse. I'd fly there myself.'

'Fragonard?' Sy asked her.

'No, Farrier. They're smaller, and more exclusive.'

'But the cost. It's crazy.'

'Mr Goldman,' Carl said in his sing-song tone, 'let me remind you of Freeman Dyson's classic words. "For the idea which does not at first glance seem crazy, there is no hope."'

Suddenly they were all standing around the percolator, with Sy handing Lorraine her first cup of coffee and Joe gazing at the ceiling with his poetic eyes and waiting for the onset of tachycardia the caffeine would surely give him, and Carl loosening his necktie and wishing they had Dean Powers here to lend his special air of authority to the meeting.

This was at 10.15.

At 11.35 the air conditioner was having trouble dealing with the cigarette smoke and the percolator had been refilled twice and there were used plastic cups piling up in

187

the waste bin. Joe Fisher was lying on his back on the floor trying to ease his lower back pain and Sy Goldman was sunk deep in one of the armchairs and Carl Blatt was walking up and down with the peculiar gait he had, lifting his feet as if he were in long grass, while Lorraine was sitting in a yoga position on the settee.

'That's hardly what I'd call a profile,' Joe was saying to the ceiling.

'Okay, so what is the profile?' That was Carl.

They'd finished circling around now, and had started brain-storming.

'What do you see, Lorraine?' Sy asked her.

'Exclusivity.'

'Chic?'

'No. Class.'

'Well sure, but – '

'You know, today's class. More fun. More free-wheeling.'

'But what is the *market*?' Sy persisted.

'The sophisticate,' Joe said to the ceiling, and moved his spine an inch to the left.

'Well sure,' Sy said impatiently in his slightly hoarse voice, 'but what kind of sophisticate? What age group?'

'What's our *intention*?' Carl Blatt cut in suddenly. 'What do we want to *express*?'

'You know,' Lorraine said with her slim hands weaving the air, 'what I feel about this is that if we can create the right fragrance – the most exotic and dramatic and *devastating* – it'll find its own market.'

Oh, Jesus, thought Joe.

In the sudden silence Lorraine knew at once that she'd said something so stupid that they didn't know how to cover it. So she did it for herself. 'All right, boys, I'm an ex-film actress, remember?'

'Never to be forgotten,' Sy offered, then caught the unintended *double entendre* and looked up to heaven. 'I mean you were *memorable*,' he said, and they all laughed.

'First the market,' Carl said, 'then the product. The

message has to be This is for You. First we have to know who You is.'

'Are,' said Joe, and they laughed again. They were starting to relax and enjoy themselves, and Lorraine heard the new note in the air; she'd heard it so many times in Hollywood, when people had arrived on the set at six in the morning from the winter streets with their eyes still sleepy and their cold hands fumbling on the gear and the actors' lips reluctant to come to life, and then had gradually started to thaw out and find the rhythm and enjoy themselves. That was when the real work started.

'All right,' Joe said. 'We're creating this one for the sophisticated woman. What's her age?'

'Nobody,' Sy Goldman said, 'knows what the word means until they're twenty-five.'

'And until they're twenty-five,' Carl nodded, 'they won't have the money for this one. I see a hundred and fifty bucks an ounce.'

'That's the ballpark,' Joe nodded his head against the carpet. 'So we hit for the sophisticated woman between twenty-five and – ?'

'There's no upper limit.' Sy. 'They range from the *jeune marriée* to the *grande dame.*'

'Yes.' Lorraine, with emphasis.

'Okay,' Carl said, breaking his paper-clip. 'So now we can work on the profile.'

'Easy.' Joe, on the floor. 'There are only five thousand essences to choose from.'

'We're in no hurry,' Sy told him. 'Guerlain created *Mitsouko* in 1921 and it's still selling today. We want to make this one to last.'

'Someone make a start,' Lorraine said, and poured some more coffee for herself and dumped it into the bin before she could drink it. Today she needed her nerves.

'Well, my God,' Joe said. 'I mean are we thinking of single floral, or bouquet, or spice, citrus, woodsy – '

'Oriental,' Carl said with conviction, and got himself a new paper-clip.

189

'But modern.' Sy Goldman. '*Mit* sparkle. Extremely individual. Personal. Unique.'

'Sultry?'

'No.'

'But erotic,' Joe persisted. 'I mean, the sophisticated woman still goes to bed, doesn't she?'

'Chypre,' Carl said and began walking around in the deep grass again.

'Too heavy. Too clinging.' Sy rolled a little in the armchair, unhappy about this. 'Unless we use a touch of citrus. Otherwise –'

'Look,' Joe said, 'we're being too specific, aren't we? What we want is the *profile*. The perfumer does the rest.'

'Then you tell us,' Carl said.

'Okay. A brilliant top note, with an immediate effect the instant it touches the skin. Citronella, say. We're in her bedroom right now, her boudoir, okay? The night is young and she's stepping out with someone important, and maybe doubting herself a little – are those lines starting or is it just the mirror? – and maybe wondering why he didn't call her earlier to confirm what time he'd pick her up; and *then*, as she starts dabbing the Floderus XYZ – we need a name soon, to give it recognition in our minds – as she starts dabbing it behind her ears she catches this brilliant top note, instantly, and suddenly all the doubts evaporate and she knows he'll be right on time, you know what I mean? It's what the top note's for, no one else but the wearer, right?' He rolled over cautiously on the floor and sat up, bracing his back against Sy Goldman's chair. 'Then we need the perfect middle note as the fragrance reacts and blends with her body heat and her skin chemistry – a note of authority, of *reassurance*, as the brilliant top note fades and gives way to this underlying *resonance*. She's feeling great now; she's loving herself.'

Joe was gazing into the middle distance now, lost in his imagery. Nobody interrupted: he was working. 'Then she's out of the boudoir and into his limousine, and *now* the base note's coming through with the whole orchestra, right?

She's aware of the impression she's making on this guy as the inside of the limo takes on this totally captivating atmosphere of elegance, and exclusivity, and *class*, like the slow wink of diamonds in the shadows as they catch a glimmer of light you didn't know was even there . . . like the muted tones of violins across a moonlit lawn . . . and as he takes her hand in his . . . you know what I'm saying? *This* we have to give her, and I don't care a fuck how long it takes – excuse me, Lorraine.' He led the laughter, pleased with himself.

When it died down, Sy said, 'I'll go with that. Brilliance, resonance, and class. Okay. We can do that.'

'We have the best nose in town,' Carl nodded.

'Should I have asked Elliot along?' Lorraine wanted to know.

'He doesn't know what the hell's happening,' Joe told her, 'outside the lab. We can go see him there, when we're ready.'

Elliot Dietrich was the Floderus perfumer, known in the trade as 'the nose', on whom the whole fate of the new fragrance – and probably the company itself – would ultimately depend. He was the key creative figure in each new venture, comparable with the director of a film or the choreographer of a new ballet; and when he was formally asked to begin work on creating the classic, unique formula they were demanding of him, the moment would compare with the time when the cameras began turning for the first take, or the *corps de ballet* moved into their first untried steps across the rehearsal stage.

'What we should always try to make people see,' Sy Goldman told them from the depth of his luxurious chair, 'and by "people" I mean ourselves, as well as the women who wear our creations, is that the effectiveness of a fragrance is very real, very real indeed. I don't believe anyone out there realises how physically and spiritually evocative any kind of scent really is. We might not feel much of an appetite in the morning, but oh boy, when we smell that toast and coffee, the gastric juices flow; the smell of a dressing-room backstage can pull an actress right out of a coma. And this gal Joe's talking about – he's not kidding; if

191

her date's important and she hasn't just been given that sudden lift of the spirits by a brilliant perfume, she can lose the evening, and maybe a new marriage or a top job or a bigger contract, just because she's passing on her doubts about herself.' He shrugged his ample shoulders, making his jowls quiver slightly. 'Okay, you know this as well as I do, but it doesn't do any harm to remind ourselves.'

'What you're really doing,' Carl told him, 'is starting to think of the slogan.'

'What else is there to think of?'

Around one o'clock Lorraine asked them if they'd like to break for lunch, but nobody wanted to move. There was the feeling in all of them that if they suddenly dropped everything and exposed themselves to the distraction of the mid-day rush-hour streets they'd never quite get back to their present mood. What they had really been doing all morning, as Lorraine knew, was not so much to do with the creation of the new fragrance as with a general, unspoken, but vitally important question. Could they, the survivors of that bitter and climactic boardroom meeting last week, find in themselves the strength, readiness and courage to go on from here and turn near-disaster into ultimate triumph? And the answer was already in the making. Since ten o'clock there hadn't been any fights, or even disagreements; there hadn't been any repercussion of last Thursday; they were even, each one of them, putting on their best behaviour: Sy had agreed with almost every proposal put forward, instead of showing that monumental obstinacy of his that occasionally brought an entire project to a halt; Carl had curbed that tone of his that tended to tell people that only he knew the score; and Joe had put his paranoia and his hypochondria on the back burner and let his mind run freely and creatively.

Barry Corbett, Dean Powers, Sam McNair and Charlie Fox had gone, and until they could be replaced there were only these three left to keep things going; and Lorraine suddenly realised something that touched her so deeply that as she looked around at them her eyes were moist. She had

192

friends. Real ones.

'So nobody's hungry?' she asked them.

'Are you serious?' Joe said, scandalised. 'We're starving! We just don't want to go out.'

'We like it here,' Sy chuckled from the depths of his chair.

Lorraine called up Nadine. 'Have someone go across to Gourmet de Paris, would you? I'd like lunch for four, something like smoked salmon, cold Poulet de Bresse if they have it, Salade Niçoise or a Caesar, and something nice for dessert, like Peach Melba or Poire Hélène or some tubs of Hagendas ice-cream – rum-raisin. As soon as you can fix it, Nadine. What? No, there's plenty of champagne on ice in the bar here. Thanks.'

By three o'clock Joe Fisher was lying flat on the pile carpet again and Sy was stretched out on the settee with a Garcia corona and Carl was trotting up and down with his feet lifting and falling like a puppet's.

'Of course,' he was saying, 'we're probably going to get the name from whatever slogan Sy comes up with eventually, and that could be quite a way down the road; but we need something we can live with, in the meantime –'

'And maybe even stay with,' Joe said, 'if we hit it right.'

'Sure, and maybe even stay with. So what about – well, I dunno – *Aphrodite?*'

Sy heaved himself to sit upright, dropping two inches of light grey ash across Joe's feet. 'Too matronly,' he said, but he sounded excited. He knew, as they all did, that if they could put an actual name to this new dream of theirs it would fix it in time and space, and give it reality. The entity they were trying to create wouldn't be vague anymore, or amorphous; it would suddenly become alive.

'Aphrodite wasn't a matron,' Carl said, sing-song and defensive. 'She was just a regular goddess.'

'Of love, no less,' Joe said.

'If anyone here,' Sy told them, 'seriously thinks we're going to fall for the *first* one we think of, he's not paying attention. Though we could come back to it, after the next few hundred.'

193

Listening to Sy doing his best to mollify Carl, of all people, made Lorraine realise that they were all here to make a success of the day, even though they might have to move a few mountains around.

'*Moi*,' Joe tried from the floor.

'Who?'

'Ma?'

'*Moi*,' he said, louder. 'Me. It's short, personal, has a hint of privacy.'

'Some people would pronounce it "moy",' Carl said.

'Jesus, we're selling this to people like that?'

'Okay,' Sy said through a cloud of cigar smoke. '*Tantalus.*'

They thought about it. Then the ball started rolling.

'Well . . .'

'I dunno. I –'

'*Temptress.*'

'Too cheap. Too *National Observer*. How about *Flamme*?'

'*Oriflamme*?'

'*Feu*. Huh?'

'*Wildfire*?'

'*Kiss-Kiss*,' from Lorraine, huskily and with her stunning smile.

'Will somebody turn the heating off?' Joe asked and they broke out laughing.

'Okay – *Electra*?'

'It's a Buick!'

'*Caprice.*'

'It's a Ford!'

The ball kept rolling. They tried associating and they tried quantum leaps into other themes; they tried *Incense, Arabesque, Piquant, Euphoria, Thrall, Jadu, Fatale . . .*

They tried gems: *Diamenté, Topaz, Solitaire*.

They tried the occult: *Voodoo, Scarab, Succuba*.

Paris again: *Coquette, Esprit, Elysée*.

Sy finished his cigar and heaved his big frame out of his chair and took the butt across to an ashtray, and Carl poured himself another full cup of espresso because he could drink a hundred of these without even dropping a paper-clip, and Joe rolled over and over on the floor until he was by the door with his feet on the wall to filter the blood from his legs through the spleen, like it said you had to do in the book.

Lorraine watched them, willing them to find a name they could relate to, not just a name for the perfume they were going to create, but also for the whole venture, for the renaissance of Floderus Incorporated – and her father's lifework. She tried to think of one herself, her mind circling over the many they'd already tried, in case it were worth going back and taking a second look; but small and inconsequential thoughts were getting in the way: if Sy didn't take off some weight he'd have problems; she ought to call Maggie and ask how she was feeling; there was too much sunshine coming through the west windows: should she order filmy curtains to tone it down? And there were all these trays around on the floor and the coffee table, and an upturned magnum of Dom Perignon in the ice bucket. She buzzed for Nadine.

'Have one of the girls come in and clear things away, would you?'

When the débris was gone, Sy lit a fresh cigar and said, '*Lyrique*.'

'It's too . . . I dunno.'

'*Fatale*.' From Carl.

'*Femme Fatale?*'

'It's okay,' Sy said, 'but . . .'

Joe said from the floor: '*Siren Song*.'

Carl shook his head. 'It's too . . .'

There was a silence.

'Too what?' Joe asked him.

'Huh? I dunno, it's just . . .'

'It's just beautiful,' Lorraine said, and they all looked at her.

'It's what?'

'I love it.'

Joe swung himself cautiously around and took his feet off

the wall and leaned against it instead, looking from one to another. '*Siren . . . Song . . .* ' He said, drawing it out seductively.

Silence again. Lorraine was smiling at him all the time.

'It doesn't have . . . ' Carl said at last.

Joe didn't give him any more time. 'It has what we need. Everything we need. Alliteration. Allure. A sexy sibilance, like brushing your hand over satin.' He watched them in turn.

Reluctantly Sy said, 'Okay, Joe, but will everyone know about those gals who used to lure the mariners off course?'

'High school kids won't,' Joe said. 'We don't happen to be creating this for high school kids.'

Silence again, but Carl had stopped prancing up and down in his deep grass and was standing perfectly still, looking down at Joe with his eyes very round behind their steel-rimmed glasses. 'I like "song". It's very evocative.'

'Right. Song of life. Song of joy.'

'It's affirmative. And there's excitement. Mystery. Yes, I agree.'

Sy dropped ash from his corona. 'Sure. A voice calling over the great distances – '

'A *woman's* voice,' Joe nodded, his wedge-shaped face lit up with excitement, 'calling to a man.'

'Jesus,' Carl said and began walking around the carpet with a sudden burst of energy. 'You know what I think?'

'Yes,' Joe said. 'You think I am a fucking genius. Excuse me, Lorraine.'

She went over to him, her smile radiant. 'You're excused, Joe. Because that's exactly what you are.' She took both his hands in hers. 'Thank you. Thank you for *Siren Song.*'

He let her pull him to his feet, and as he gazed in close-up into those shimmering azure eyes and saw the joy in them he seemed to hear, from faraway across the moonlit waters, the voice of a woman, the sound of his siren song.

'Any time, Lorraine,' he said dreamily, and kissed her full on the lips.

196

They broke up the meeting just before six, with instructions from Lorraine to meet her again at the Four Seasons at eight, where she would try to regale them with the most splendid dinner in town, in thanks and in celebration.

Sy was the last to leave, and stood for a moment in the doorway of Lorraine's office. 'It's been a great day, Madam Chairman. We did a whole lot more than just name the baby; we found out we could go on from where we left off, and work together for a really big success. You know this. You felt it. Right?'

'Yes, Sy. Yes, I did.'

'From here on out, we're invulnerable. Right?' His warm smile made pouches of his face.

'Right.' She waited, watching his eyes. It wasn't like Sy to make a speech.

'So this is the best possible time,' he said in his soft resonant tones, 'to offer you a thought that's very practical, and I believe very valuable.' He looked away a little, lifting his grey brows as he chose his words carefully. 'To make *Siren Song* a really big success, and put this company back on its feet for all time, we'll need the best people in the industry to help us. The very best. One of them is Dean Powers.'

Lorraine stiffened instantly, and he put his hand on her arm, looking into her eyes again. 'No one could have been a worse bastard to you than he was, last Thursday. And no one can bring more effectiveness as a marketing expert to our new project. I will even say that without him we might easily fail, and that with him we can certainly succeed.'

Under his large hand he could feel the trembling in Lorraine's arm, and knew what was tiding through her mind as she thought of Dean Powers: revulsion, enmity, contempt. But he'd known he must tell her; his loyalty alone had made it a duty.

'Somehow,' he said, 'you've got to get him back.'

197

CHAPTER 17

MADLEN STOOD IN the middle of the room, staring at her reflection in the tall gold mirrors behind the dressing-table.

Another strange world. But a lot better than that world of stark white rooms at the hospital, smelling of ether and perspiration. This was a different kind of world altogether. It was her bedroom; and out there through that door was the sitting-room; and there was a small kitchen. Angelo called it 'the guest suite'. It was hers, he had said, for as long as she wanted it. He knew, he had said two days ago when he'd shown her around it, that it wasn't anything like her apartment must look in Sutton Place, but it was the best he could do. He'd get it done over for her if she liked, she just had to say. He wanted it to be nice for her, whenever she felt like staying here.

She wasn't ever going to leave.

In the mirrors she looked like Baby Doll, in her short flimsy nightdress, and with her pale flawless skin, and her big violet-coloured eyes, staring at herself. Behind her and all around her, the room was beautiful, in a way. The bed was enormous, a kind of cloud of diaphanous white frills spilling through the bars of the brass bedstead, with a canopy of white lace half enclosing it, and long satin ribbons hanging down like streamers, and a thousand little bows tied everywhere, like moths alighting. Everything else in the room was either white or gold, with a brocaded chaise-longue and two fluffy chairs and the white lacquered dressing-table, and in the middle of the ceiling a lamp like a birdcage of white wicker and a cluster of tiny bulbs that gave

198

the kind of glow you saw on snow in winter. A lot of the things didn't match, but she could see Angelo's touch here: he'd had no education but had learned – or maybe taught himself, against odds – to be lavish, extravagant, and generous.

'I was going to try again,' she'd told him in his car on the way here from the hospital. He'd sent one of the girls here – Yvette, with the black curls and tiny waist – to Sutton Place with instructions to pack a suitcase with things she'd need; in the car he'd been rather endearing, sitting there at the wheel like a large puzzled bear when she told him she didn't want him to take her home; she wanted to go straight to a hotel somewhere, it didn't matter where; it just had to be somewhere she hadn't seen before, so she could leave the past behind. He'd driven her straight to his club, and shown her the guest suite. 'I want you to know, Angelo, what happened. Then I'm going to forget it. I was going to try again, but it was only in the back of my mind; I only knew it when I saw you standing there in the doorway at the hospital, with the roses in your hand. I knew two things, right then, you see: I knew I'd been going to try killing myself again, and now I didn't have to.'

'Well gee,' he'd said in the car, 'I'm real glad I showed up.'

He was very amusing. She knew a lot about people, what was in their minds. Angelo didn't understand her. He was treating her with kid gloves, like a giant in the forest who'd had a fairy land on his palm; he was keeping his hand perfectly still, not wanting to crush her by accident; at the same time he was a little uneasy, thinking maybe she wasn't actually there, but he was just going crazy. Maybe it was because she'd said she'd put a million dollars into his club because she liked the place; not many people had made an offer like that, she supposed.

Yet she knew it wasn't only the money that was making him kind to her. The night when she'd come in here and smashed the mirror and everything, he'd been very patient, and taken her home. Oh sure, he'd been hoping to lay her; in her Ferrari he'd looked down at her sometimes like she was

199

an ice cream sundæ he'd like to lick all over; but the kindness had still been there underneath, and that was different from the way all the other guys behaved when they wanted to lick her all over. There was something in Angelo she needed, and needed so bad that she'd gone right out and slapped a hefty price-tag on it, a million, no less; and that had been because she'd been scared he wouldn't want her to come here to the club anymore; she didn't want to go along the corridor to the girls' room and get the pills out, every time he said she had to go. She didn't want to die, every time he threw her out of here.

It hadn't occurred to her to go to stay with Barry Corbett, when she left the hospital. Barry had been her 'uncle' all along, and would have taken her in – Jesus, that sounded so melodramatic, like she was a fucking little orphan of the . . . oh yes, sweet Jesus, oh yes, I understand . . . it's actually what I am – Barry would have taken her in at his home in Connecticut, and Virginia would have fussed over her like an aunt. But that would have brought it all back to her, because Barry had been there at the funeral, and she only had to see him in her mind to see the casket and the quiet, strained-looking people and the hideous flowers (hideous because *they* were still *alive*).

Baby Doll, in the mirror. Are you going to come alive again, and be like the flowers? *Isn't it too soon?* Would they understand? Would they say, okay, it's time now, you can think about us again without wanting to be with us?

It had been a week since she'd left the hospital, and she hadn't tried again. Did that mean anything? Or would she suddenly have that feeling come on that would make her look for a knife or a bottle of barbies and do it, try it again, that feeling of not caring anymore, not wanting life to go on happening all the time theirs had stopped?

It wasn't a pleasant feeling. It was like dying. People didn't understand. Lorraine thought she'd done it just to show spite, or to scare her. It wasn't like that. But she was glad it had scared Lorraine. *Madlen, don't punish me like this. Tell me you'll give me another chance.*

No way.

It had been Lorraine's voice over the telephone that had started the screaming in her head. The call from Los Angeles hadn't come at a very good time. Madlen had auditioned three times that week for some off-Broadway shows they were putting together; and the third time she thought she'd got it made. It was only a small part, but if they gave it to her she could talk about it to people, and give Mom and Dad free tickets, and do a simply fantastic job on the stage for them, and hear them applauding. Especially Dad. Mom would sit there looking totally fabulous and appropriately amused, but Dad would go wild and carry them both off to Sardi's and order champagne and get all his friends over from the other tables and tell them he'd just seen his daughter in her new show, his eyes glittering with pride and his smile lighting up the whole damn place. The word from the coast was that Lorraine's movie was already a hit even in the rough cut; that was okay; she didn't begrudge Lorraine her success, even though it kept pouring into her hands whatever she did; but the off-Broadway show would be at least *something*, at least a start, at least so many things . . . the Floderus girls? Oh yes, they're both of them actresses . . . one's in the movies and the other's on the stage . . . There would be, at least, the glow.

Then she was holding a phone and hearing Lorraine saying Mom and Dad were dead, so they wouldn't be coming to see her in the off-Broadway show anyway.

Of course she hadn't said it quite like that. It had just felt like that. 'Maddy, darling . . . ' in a voice she hadn't recognised, partly because Lorraine hadn't called her that since high school, so what was the big deal coming up? 'I've got something bad to tell you . . . ' in a voice that kept fading in and out, but in a way that didn't have anything to do with the telephone; and a kind of snuffling, like Lorraine had a terrible cold. 'There's something that you and I have got to face up to . . . and I want you to know I'll be with you all the time . . . we'll go through this together . . . '

The feeling had started then, as Madlen had stood with

201

the phone in her hand, gripping it a little harder now as she realised something was very wrong. 'Their plane . . . ' and there'd been a silence so long that Madlen had thought her sister had hung up, though there hadn't been a click or anything . . . 'Crashed . . . '

Crashed, crashed, crashed, and then the screaming had started inside her head and gone on and on and on while somewhere in the world outside she could still hear her sister's voice saying, *Maddy, Maddy darling, please say something, are you still there, Maddy, are you still there?*

But what do you want me to say, Lorrie darling? Your new movie's such a success that you had to fetch them over there to see it even before it was finished, and the plane crashed and they're dead, so what exactly do you want me to say, Lorrie darling? That I wish you were dead too? Sure, I could say that. I could say that.

Baby Doll in the mirror, in your short little nightie. It's time to forget all that. You haven't tried it again for a whole week, and there's this nice place to stay in, and there's Angelo, who'll do anything you want, and his friend Tony, who'll do anything Angelo tells him. You should start feeling better about things now, start feeling what it's like to come alive again.

It was warm in here. She could feel the pulsing of the blood in her body. In the tall gold mirrors she looked pretty, and delicate, with shadows in her cheeks because she'd lost weight during the last few days; but the shadows made her look even prettier, with her soft mouth and violet eyes and her light wavy hair falling across her brow the way Marilyn Monroe used to wear it.

She smiled into the mirror. It felt strange. Nobody had seen her smile for a long time, not even Angelo; she smiled into the mirror deliberately, like a show girl, like a whore, for nothing, for no one but herself. She had a pretty smile. She let it stay there along her mouth, knowing it was something that had started to come alive, even though she was doing it deliberately, for nothing, just to feel it there, a touch of new life as she lifted her nightie inch by inch, higher and higher against her thighs and her waist and finally her small ivory-pale breasts. So it was still there, her body. She hadn't thought about it for such a long, long time. It looked pretty. There were faint blue veins making a kind of tracery under the skin, and the hair between her legs made a sudden cloud of shadow, like a puff of smoke. Her belly was flat, and above it her ribs were brushed in with the softness of light and shade, leading upwards to her breats; they were small, almost childlike; but when she touched the nipples they grew hard at once, glowing dark pink in the mirror. She went up to the dressing-table and raised one leg, resting her foot on the edge of the white lacquered surface, so that with her elbow on her knee, her hand fell comfortably against the smoky hair between her legs; then she began using her fingers, separately, one by one, parting the hair and feeling the softness of the lips, parting the lips and feeling the slipperiness coming to them already, as if she . . . *because* she was coming alive again, almost alive again with a kind of slow fire beginning to lick through her body, burning wherever it touched as her fingers kept moving, and now only one of them, the long one in the middle of her small alabaster-coloured hand; she let it delve into the rose-red slippery heat until it found the little promontory, the clitoris, the penis she would have had here if she'd been a boy. The feeling came at once, startling her; she'd thought of her body as something still dead, still sprawled on the floor of the girls' room with the lost earring; but now the slow fire that had been moving through it burst into flame right here where her finger slid and fondled, its tip circling the small tumescent nodule, round and round, slowly round and round while she watched herself in the mirror, the shining red flower of her cleft as it expanded under her hand's teasing, releasing its liquids until the sound of licking, sucking, kissing came into the quietness of the room as she lifted her eyes and watched their reflection in the gold glass, closing their lids until she saw her face in the shadowy frieze of her eyelashes, a curl of honey-coloured hair falling across the wide milky brow, the smile still lying along her

203

mouth but now changing, becoming tensed with her lips drawn back as her hand moved faster and the heat down there went tiding through the rest of her body, flowing everywhere, burning in her face as her breath came faster, keeping time with her hand until she let it move as if on its own, as if it were someone else's playing there, fretting and pulling in a frenzy now, maddening her as she squeezed her eyes shut and there was only the world of feeling, sliding and touching and burning and throbbing quicker and quicker and quicker until *oh – oh – oh –* and her body burst into rainbows, into the coloured fires she remembered now, remembered now as she cried out and half-toppled against the dressing-table, saving herself and letting her head go down until it rested against her knee and the tears came, not surprising her, warm against her skin.

The peacock-blue Rolls-Royce slipped southwards along Fifth Avenue towards the Lotus Club. Lorraine was alone at the wheel, going through the signals on the yellow as often as she could and watching the mirror for any police car. There was no real need, she kept telling herself, to hurry like this; it was early evening and the business day was over and nothing could be signed: Paul Lacognato, their attorney, had assured her of that; but there was an undeniable sense of urgency in her, and until she could talk this whole thing over with Madlen she wouldn't be at peace.

'You realise,' Paul had said in his flat, articulate tones, 'that I'm committing a gross breach of ethics in bringing this to your notice. Your sister is my client, just as you are, and she has every right to expect my absolute secrecy.' Then he'd shrugged, becoming suddenly human. 'She also has every right to expect me to keep her out of trouble if I can. In my role as attorney and adviser to the whole family, in the past, I think I can keep a good conscience in this present situation.'

He had got down to the facts immediately. Madlen had instructed him to draw up an agreement in which it was declared that of her own free will she was to invest the sum of one million dollars in the establishment known as the Lotus Club, on 53rd Street, Manhattan, at the current rate of interest. He had striven to persuade Madlen to wait until he'd visited the place and made some discreet enquiries, but she had been 'rather peremptory' and had told him that if he preferred not to draw up the necessary documents for her, she would have to change her attorney.

'I wasn't too surprised at her vehemence; I believe she realises she's embarking on something pretty rash, and is therefore defensive about it. I'm also aware how deeply she was traumatised by your parents' tragic end, which may have left her to a slight degree – ' he had shrugged again – 'irrational.' His long pallid face had been turned to look directly at Lorraine. 'Would you agree?'

'She tried to kill herself, a week ago.'

He had been shocked. Within the next hour he had put the facts, the options and the dangers on the table for her. He was certain that if he tried again to dissuade Madlen from this venture she would only harden, and take her custom to another attorney – perhaps to Mr Baccari's. She had a perfect right to invest her money in whatever way she chose: there was no question here of mental incapacity, simply of a seeming hastiness to commit one-fifth of her present assets to a questionable venture. He had made his enquiries, in any case, and had learned that though the Lotus Club had never, as far as he could ascertain, attracted the attention of the police for any reason, several of its members were of dubious reputation and the owner himself had been acquitted by a Las Vegas court on a charge of the improper and unlawful operation of a gambling casino five years ago, the court's decision having resulted from a technicality involving inadmissable evidence. From his preliminary meeting with Mr Baccari and his attorney, Paul Lacognato had formed the impression that they were gentlemen 'not to be taken at face value'.

'All in all,' he had told Lorraine uneasily, 'there is in fact only one option available to us – indeed, to you. It is for you alone to talk to your sister and do your utmost to dissuade

205

her from what I believe to be a grave folly, with possibly disastrous consequences – once this fellow Baccari has seen how ready Madlen is to pour money into his business, he could well fleece her of the rest.'

The blue Corniche convertible heeled softly on its suspension onto 53rd Street, bringing a faint whimper from its tyres. Lorraine had called Madlen's apartment in Sutton Place several times a day for the past week, until she'd learned from the maid that she was staying at the Lotus Club as the guest of its owner. God alone knew whether she'd be able to see Madlen tonight, or even whether they'd allow her into the club at all. Baccari had seemed a friendly enough man last week at the hospital, even keeping vigil with her in the desolate waiting-room; she was pretty certain she could persuade him to let her into the club and talk with him – unless Madlen told him to refuse. For a million dollars, and the promise of four million more for the prospecting, he would do exactly what Madlen told him.

At another time Lorraine would have made this journey with a lot more confidence and determination, but tonight she was sick at heart. The question of the million dollars was unimportant compared with the fear that Madlen would never accept her in her life again; at the hospital and over the telephone Lorraine had begged her to come and stay with her for a time, until she felt herself again and out of her own danger. *Do you think she might try again?* Lorraine had asked the psychiatrist. He'd been plain with her: *That's going to be up to you.* But if Madlen could choose to find her own strange haven at this club, with people 'not to be taken at their face value,' what was her future going to be? Lorraine would have no place in it.

At the back of her mind was another sickening dilemma. Yesterday when she'd realised that Carl and Joe and Sy had decided to rally round her and help save the company if they could, she had felt a sense of relief and hope for the first time since she'd realised how far she had brought Floderus towards ruin; yet even at that moment, Sy had crushed her again with his talk of Dean Powers; and this morning Carl had confirmed Sy's thinking. 'This is going to make you sore as hell, Lorraine; but there's one guy in this whole town I want to work with on *Siren Song*, and that's Dean. I know how you feel about him, but one day you'll have to show you're the boss, so why not start right now?'

She hadn't understood, until Carl had spelt it out for her: 'As a company boss, you have to do more than tell other people what to do; you have to tell yourself what to do, and sometimes it isn't easy. In this case you have to try and see what *really* happened in the boardroom last Thursday. It seemed that Dean went out deliberately to hurt you where he knew it would hurt most, to show you up in front of us all, to make what amounted to a public announcement that you'd failed your father. Okay, he was actually doing that, and if you don't think I wanted to hit him for doing it, you're dead wrong. But you'd just done something to him that was equally devastating – and to his male pride. You not only fired your right hand man, but you did it in the boardroom, with his colleagues listening in. I mean there are some things, Lorraine, that *no* chairman of *any* company must let himself do, in *whatever* situation; and that's one of them and you did it.'

'But he had no right to –'

'Lorraine, please.' Carl had stared at her with his wide intelligent eyes. 'This isn't a discussion. We can have a discussion later if you want, but right now I'm trying to do you a service; as one of the team who's going out to make *Siren Song*, I owe you my thinking on this, and I want to give it to you and then walk away and let you think about it, if you want to. Okay? Okay, here's the punch line. What you're going to do now, if you want to act like a real live company boss, is to try and see Dean's point of view, the way I just gave it to you, try and realise you hit him below the belt and he simply hit back – as I would, as any guy would – and forget what he did to you. Get it out of your mind. Review his case, look at his record, stand way back and try to see him for what in fact he is: potentially our greatest ally, our most effective colleague, and possibly the key to saving this company and taking it back to where it belongs – on top of the heap. Okay? It seems impossible, right? Maybe it is. It's up to you.'

'But I –' and she'd stopped. This wasn't a discussion, and she'd go with that; she had respect for Carl. He'd turned away, loping off with his peculiar puppet's gait, then turning again. 'Get him back, if you can. Not for his sake, not for yours. Do it for us. And your father.'

That had been this morning, and for the rest of the day she'd refused even to think about it. Carl was right: it seemed impossible. The very idea of going to Dean Powers with an apology, even of speaking to him on the phone, made her sick and enraged. And even if she could bring herself to do it, there was no guarantee he'd agree to return; he could simply listen to what she had to say and then put the phone down, adding insult to injury. She had her pride, too.

Why did people always speak of 'male pride'? Didn't a female have the need to feel proud of herself, of being a woman?

Of being the woman who'd brought her own father's company almost to ruin . . . ? *Touché*. Scant room for pride there.

Though she'd refused to think about it until now, her thoughts had circled it all day, as if trying to find a way in. There wasn't one – nor was there a way out. Even during the recession, an executive of Dean's calibre wouldn't need to leave his present job and join a failing company. Even if she hired someone half as good, it would take months before he found his way around the Floderus structure, with its markets covering half the civilised world. At the very outset of the new project, it would be madness to bring in a stranger who'd need to be carried with them through the critical period of planning and setting out the guidelines for the creation of *Siren Song*. It could easily be that if she tried to hire an unknown, Carl and Sy and Joe would simply walk out on her; they would have given her the chance of saving Floderus, and she'd have refused it.

Dean . . . Madlen . . . Madlen . . . Dean . . .

208

Her thoughts circled.

The one hopeful moment of the day was when Frederick Vanderkloot had phoned informally to invite her for dinner, reminding her of her promise made in Los Angeles: that she would get in touch with him when she was back in New York. She was flattered, and had suggested tomorrow night. He was the head of a towering international corporation, and just now she felt the need to expose herself to the aura of his power, his success, his ability to glance over the records of her diminutive company and see precisely where Century Cosmetics could step in, if he chose, and raise it from its present condition of jeopardy to the solid terrain of success. If she were ready to listen to him, she might, tomorrow evening, do more towards the creation and launching of *Siren Song* than even Carl could do, or Sy, or Joe. It could be a critical turning point.

It could even give her the means of leaving Dean Powers just where he was, out of her life.

As the phantom-quiet convertible slowed to a stop outside the Lotus Club her thoughts returned to Madlen, and she sat at the wheel for minutes after she'd parked the car, steeling herself, preparing her arguments, plucking up what was left of her courage. Then she got out and walked across the tarmac and along to the huge entrance doors between the carriage lamps.

209

CHAPTER 18

UNBELIEVABLY, LORRAINE WAS in the club for exactly ten minutes.

At first there'd been a resurgence of hope that her day was going, after all, to end better than it had begun. It was not.

The doorman had admitted her straight away when he looked at her card and she told him she was Miss Floderus' sister; then a slim, sultry hostess took her through the main room to where Angelo Baccari and his manager were sitting at one of the tables. They both stood as she reached them, and the big man offered her a drink; it was all very civil. When she told them she was here to see Madlen, Angelo escorted her between the tables and through a softly-lighted corridor to a room at the end, making small talk on the way. She sensed that either he realised that if he asked her what she wanted to talk about to Madlen, she wouldn't tell him; or he felt that to refuse to let her see her own sister might look suspicious. There was no doubt in Lorraine's mind that he knew one thing perfectly well: that the moment she learned of the proposed million-dollar investment in his club, she could be expected to fight hard to prevent it.

'And how has your day been?' he enquired politely as they walked together along the corridor.

'I've known better, Mr Baccari.'

'Life tends to go up and down for us, doesn't it? Like the stock market.'

By the tone of her answer he certainly knew now why she was here tonight: she'd somehow got wind of Madlen's proposed investment. At the hospital last week, Lorraine

210

had thought him rather endearing; his concern for Madlen, considering she was a stranger and had chosen his own private club for her suicide attempt, had touched Lorraine deeply at a time when Madlen seemed to have nobody to protect her but a sister she despised. But now, as Angelo led her past the soft-shaded wall lamps to the end of the passage, Lorraine had the picture: this man was interested in Madlen not only as an exquisitely beautiful young woman but a young woman with a brand-new Ferrari and an apartment on Sutton Place – and unbalanced enough to be conned into whatever project he wanted to sell her.

On Angelo's quiet knock, Lorraine heard her sister's voice calling for him to go in; as he opened the door and stood back for Lorraine, Madlen was sitting at a small electric organ at the end of the room; and in the instant before she looked up, Lorraine took in the environment: worn Chinese rugs across a parquet floor, gilt lamps and baroque furnishings, a fireplace flickering with the flames of an artificial log, and a big framed print on the wall, of a Titian nude. Lorraine's immediate impression was that of a room in a Hollywood back lot, representing a high-class brothel.

Then Madlen was looking up from the keyboard of the organ, staring at her. Lorraine took another step forward, and stopped, repelled by her sister's icy regard. Angelo himself seemed at a loss.

'I – er . . .' He shrugged and fell silent. Maybe he'd half-expected the sisters to embrace, but was now aware of the situation. Madlen went on staring at Lorraine for a moment longer, then deliberately turned to look at Angelo.

'I used to play the piano a bit,' she said easily, 'but I've never tried an organ. Is it very different?' She glanced down at the keyboard again, and played a soft chord. Watching her, Lorraine felt tears trying to come; she closed her eyes, refusing them. If Madlen was hoping to break her heart, she'd succeeded, as she'd done so often before; but Lorraine was here to talk business if she could, and for that she must keep her head.

211

'I . . . ' Angelo began uncertainly, looking at neither of them, 'I really can't say. I bought that thing in an antique sale – can never resist a bargain.'

Lorraine was prey to a chilling thought: that she didn't exist, that there were only these two other people here in the room, talking about the difference between an organ and a piano, oblivious to her. She almost turned and went out, but had the horrible feeling that they wouldn't notice if she did; she'd be like a ghost, fading through the panels of the door. Perhaps as a natural reflex to horror, a kind of anger suddenly took its place, and the spell was broken.

'Madlen.' She took three steps towards the organ, and this time held her sister's attention. 'I want to talk to you, and I want to do it alone.' Her voice was shaking, and she heard it, but could do nothing about it.

Madlen looked like a Dresden figure sitting there at the keyboard in her jewel-blue diaphanous dressing-gown and with her hair loose over her shoulders; she would have made an exquisite picture, but for the cold hostility in her eyes.

'Don't go, Angelo,' she said without looking at him. 'He's a friend of mine,' she told Lorraine coolly. 'He's also my very generous host. But in any case I don't want to talk to you, and if you'd called me first I could have saved you the journey.'

Lorraine took another step towards her sister, but again halted; in the silence, with both of them watching her, she felt like an intruder, a penitent asking for their charity; only the vestige of courtesy left in Madlen was stopping her from actually telling Lorraine to get out.

Lorraine took a breath. 'We both have the same attorney, Madlen. He has a new assistant, and she made a mistake: she called me, instead of you, since we have the same last name. She asked me to go along to sign the documents; I naturally asked which documents; she said for the investment in Mr Baccari's club. She mentioned the sum: one million dollars. She – '

'You're lying!' Madlen was on her feet. 'That bastard Paul Lacognato told you about it!'

'It doesn't make much difference how I found out.' As she went on talking, she was aware that Angelo Baccari was using the antique brass telephone at the end of the quilted bar. 'I'm here to ask you to see reason,' she told her sister. 'Get advice on this, at least, and think it over before –'

'It's entirely my own affair!'

'I agree. But right now you're – you're not altogether responsible for what you do. If this –'

'*What are you saying*?' Madlen was staring at her with hate in her eyes.

'You're still recovering from – severe trauma. You left the hospital only a week ago, and already you're –'

'Are you calling me a head-case, for Christ's sake?'

'I'm just saying that . . . attempted suicide . . . indicates a certain degree of – disorientation.' She took another step towards Madlen. 'Look, I – I know that for some reason you hate me. I don't know what I did, but – but it's suddenly become a fact of life, and I've got to live with it. But I still want to help you, Madlen, in any way you'll let me; and this crazy idea of throwing a million dollars into a place like –' She left it, shrugging.

The room was very quiet.

'A place like – ?' Angelo said softly.

Lorraine turned to face him. 'An all-night club of doubtful repute that's so deep in debt that without my sister's help it'll go broke.'

His expression didn't change; he had the eyes of a poker player. 'Your sources of information are unreliable in the extreme, but I don't mind that. However, you're invading my privacy, and I mind that very much. I'll have someone see you off the premises.'

Madlen put out her hand suddenly. 'Not till I've said this, Angelo.' She turned an icy look on Lorraine. 'You're not getting the message, are you? We grew up together, Lorraine, but that's over, and I'm a big girl now. I'm liberated, free and independent after all those years of playing second fiddle to my loving sister. And I'm going to stay that way. You can't possess me anymore, under the

213

guise of wanting to "help" me; and you can't "advise" me about what I should do with my money, even though you'd like me to invest it in the company that Dad entrusted to you, which is now on the rocks, from what I've heard.'

Lorraine felt herself flinch invisibly. She'd no idea that Madlen was taking the slightest interest in Floderus Incorporated, let alone knew its present position. She said nothing; there was nothing she could say, because Madlen had delivered a perfect *touché*.

'So when will you get the message, Lorraine? I don't want your "protection" anymore, or your "help" or your sisterly "advice". I don't want to live with you until I'm "fully recovered," as you put it; I don't want to share anything in your life. All I want from you is that you keep right out of my way. Beginning now.'

There was a movement in the mirror behind the bar, and Lorraine caught it; the tall man she'd seen here before – Angelo Baccari's manager or whoever he was – had come quietly into the room, to stand watching. Angelo must have called him just now on the antique brass phone. As she went on staring at her sister, she could see that beneath Madlen's show of icy contempt she was trembling, and that in her eyes there was more than hate and hostility. Lorraine had grown up with her, yes, and had seen her in all kinds of moods, from childish tantrums to tenderness and love; and now there was this something in her eyes that Lorraine saw quite clearly, though a precise name for it wouldn't come to her mind; she knew only that beyond the hate and contempt and hostility, Madlen was lost, still, in a region where she was her own deadliest enemy.

And this was the worst of all. Madlen was casting out the one person in the world who loved her, and could help her, and save her; and deep down, she knew it.

Even after what Madlen had just said to her, and in front of a stranger, Lorraine felt tears trying to come again. 'Maddy, please listen to me, please . . . '

'*Don't call me that!*' She drew her small shoulders back and stood very straight, as if to show she was what she'd said, a 'big girl now'. 'I told you, that's all over.'

The silence drew out until Angelo said: 'Tony, I'd like you to see the visitor out.'

As the tall man moved towards Lorraine she stood her ground and tried desperately for the last time to get through to her sister. 'Madlen, please call me. When you feel more – a little better about me, please call, and we'll –'

'Get out.'

Lorraine was still staring at her as the tall man came over and took her arm; she tried to free herself, but his grip was too strong, and he led her to the door with an ease that left her ashamed at her own weakness. At some time, as he took her along the corridor without a word, she heard the door behind them close.

A police helicopter-view of the itinerary followed by the peacock-blue Rolls-Royce after it left the Lotus Club on 53rd Street would have seen that it was totally random. Inside the next half-hour the sleek polished convertible headed south and west, but not with any seeming sense of direction; it meandered through intersections, sometimes doubling back on its own tracks, once entering a one-way street and making a U-turn and heading south again, and west again, as if the driver didn't know where to go. And this was absolutely true.

Lorraine was just driving, and letting the traffic flow take her with it; it was as if, having lost her sense of personal direction, she was willing for life to carry her along for a while until she could find herself again. She had planned to eat at home tonight, but after the scene at the Lotus Club she couldn't face the evening alone, nursing the wounds that Madlen had left on her spirit; nor could she think of anyone who might want to share the next few hours with her; in this whole glittering city whose streets were now filling with the traffic of people pleasure-seeking, celebrating, visiting, dining and partying, she could think of nobody she knew well enough to spend her own evening with, outside of her business associates.

215

So she drifted, alone and disconsolate, isolated in the beautiful car that caused heads to turn wherever it went as the lights of the city flowed across its gleaming body-work.

Slowing to turn at an intersection she saw a man standing on the sidewalk, waving – *and she knew at once it was Frank* . . . When she'd offered him the Rolls for his own, he'd turned it down, *but I'll give you a wave when you go by* . . . She made three quick turns and came past the same place, but the man who'd been waving was gone. Had he really been there, and had he really been waving, and had it really been Frank?

She went on driving, and people turned their heads.

Look! Isn't that . . . ?

It's Lorraine Floderus!

Oh wow . . .

And Lorraine Floderus, her make-up still stained by the tears she had finally shed as she'd left the club and walked to the parking lot, took another left, and another right, and another green light, letting the bright-lit streets take her where they would while she sat at the wheel thinking of nothing, too hurt, too ashamed and too humiliated by her failure to do anything in those few minutes at the club except to show weakness and admit failure. The tall muscular guy had led her out of the place as if she were an undesirable who'd wandered in from the street.

Broadway, now, with its tawdry neon signs and porn shops and cheap jewellery stores.

Broadway and 31st. The sleek convertible glided onwards, its white-walled tyres crushing beer cans and plastic cups and pretzel bags into the gutter.

Times Square, and west again towards Eighth Avenue, the car slowing and then halting for the lights, bringing Lorraine at last to the place that had been waiting to receive her all evening; because it is when we feel most alone, and lost, and without direction, that the personal star we were born under is seen to light the way.

Hajime Shibasaki sat at his small cluttered desk, working on his accounts. Five students had failed to pay their dues this month, and owed him money.

'*Sensei?*'

'*Hai?*'

'Someone to see you.'

The student stepped aside and showed in the most beautiful Occidental woman Mr Shibasaki had ever seen. She stared down at him, looking uncertain.

'Can I help, please?' he asked her.

'I – I'd like you to teach me karate.'

'Oh? Sit, please.' He was polite but puzzled. 'How you come here?'

'I was waiting at the intersection for the lights to change, and saw two girls leaving here, in kimonos. Then I saw your sign.' She seemed almost as puzzled as he was, by her own actions.

'Oh. Why you want to learn karate?'

'To – I'm not sure. To be stronger.'

'Ah. Karate make strong. But take long time. Very long time.' He offered her a charming smile, his head on one side. 'You have bad husband? He beat you up?'

'No, it's nothing like that.' Her own smile was there now, and she was speaking more easily, as if she'd found a friend. 'But I suppose it's self-defence I'm thinking of, yes, in case – in case a man tries to push me around. I'd like to know how to handle a situation like that.'

'Ah. Good. But take four years, then black belt, very strong.'

'Oh. But I –'

'Want sooner.' His smile was mischievous. 'Want now, yes? American way of life.' He reached for a scrap of paper and a ball-point. 'Okay. Understand.' He wrote quickly. 'I teach Shotokan Karate. Very good. Very effective. But take long time. You want Sadie.' He passed her the scrap of paper. 'Her name, okay? Sadie Kaminski. Here, look. She just around the corner.' He got up quickly and beckoned her through the doorway and into the parking lot at the rear. 'You go there, turn left, into next car park. Look for sign:

217

Karate. Like mine. Yes?'

'Sadie will teach me karate?'

'Yes.' He was laughing softly now. 'She teach all kind. She teach many kind. What you call grab bag – right?' Then he became serious, though his smile was still there. 'But she good. She very good. I have much respect, understand? Tell her you come from me. From Hajime.'

Sadie Kaminski was in the doorway of the long corrugated-iron shed that was her workplace, looking into the night sky as she sometimes did. She had been born on a farm in Kansas, and had grown up under the vast cloudscapes that had leaned from horizon to horizon across the prairies of her childhood, so that from time to time she needed to rest her eyes on the patch of sky she could see from her doorway here, and remember how big the world had been.

Now she looked down suddenly.

'Get that thing outa here!'

The long Rolls-Royce convertible bowed slightly on its springs, halting with its bumper against the row of garbage bins against the fence. Sadie watched the woman climbing out, a real number, right out of a glossy magazine.

'You wanna get towed, friend?' Everybody thought they could park here, just because it was right around the corner from the blue movie house. 'Saks is out on Fifth Avenue, okay?'

Lorraine looked at her as she came across the uneven patch of dirt, the thin heels of her Guccis sinking in. Sadie was still standing in the doorway of the big shed, a short, chunky woman of maybe twenty-five dressed in a soiled white kimono and pants, her mouse-brown hair sticking out from her head in spikes and her snub nose bent at an angle. Around her waist was a linen belt that looked as if it had once been black, but was now worn white and stringy. From the shed behind her there was the sudden sound of thumping, interspersed with a series of shouts.

It was at this point that Lorraine felt suddenly that she didn't really need Sadie Kaminski or what she had going on

218

inside of her corrugated-iron shed; but the moment passed.

'Are you Miss Kaminski?' She offered the scrap of paper.

'Sadie Kaminski. Right. What's this?'

'The Japanese gentleman sent me here. Is it – Jimmy?'

'Uh?' The woman frowned up at her. 'Oh. Hajime. Yeah. Look, I don't have no parkin' space to rent, okay? I get a lot of enquiries. So d'you mind – '

'He said you'd teach me karate.'

Sadie looked at the cashmere coat with its silver fox collar, then across at the peacock-blue Rolls-Royce, then at Lorraine's face. 'He said *what*?'

'Don't you teach karate? Self-defence?'

'Uh? Sure. That's what *you* want to learn?'

'I think – yes. Yes, I do.'

Sadie was looking up at her now with a lot of interest. 'You're sure about that? Because frankly, this isn't quite your kind of scene. Things kinda get a little rough around here sometimes, you know what I mean?'

Lorraine felt herself stiffen. 'I'm not looking for ballet lessons.'

'A good thing. You won't get any around this place. C'mon inside.'

She led Lorraine along to a little office, like the one Jimmy – Hajimmy? – had been sitting in, except that this one was much less tidy; the desk was hidden under a mass of paperwork; the threadbare carpet was covered in sandals, cardboard boxes and cleaning materials; and the walls were hung with awards, photographs of karate students and oriental calenders. A mangy, bitten-eared black cat was humped on the top of a rusty filing-cabinet, watching Lorraine through the slits of its eyes.

'That's Tiger,' Sadie said. 'Don't try and stroke him. He hates this place but he ain't got no other place to go. Sit down – drop that stuff on the floor. What's your name?'

'Lorraine.' She dropped the soiled kimono onto the carpet and sat down on the rickety bamboo chair.

'Lorraine who?'

'Floderus.'

'Rings a bell. What job d'you do?'

'I'm a secretary.'

'Uh-huh. So what kinda car does your *boss* drive? How old are you?'

'Twenty-eight.'

Sadie waited until a resounding shout had died away in the gym outside her office. 'Okay, Lorraine, tell me what the hell a gal like you is doing in a place like this.'

Lorraine felt impatience again; she hadn't come here to go through third-degree. 'I believe I told you already.'

Sadie sat farther back in her sagging chair and shook her head. 'No, you didn't. And you don't *have* to, if you don't want. But it'd help me to know whether I can really do anything for you, and if so, what.'

'I want to learn karate.'

'Just suddenly, just like that. And instead of going through the yellow pages to find somewhere on the Upper East Side, you drive downtown through the pimp an' porn district to a dump like this. I like it here; it's my dump; but it ain't you, let's face it. I'm goin' to give you one more chance, an' then if you don't feel like tellin' me what you're doin' here, that's quite okay, but I don't think I'd be able to help you.'

She watched Lorraine with a pair of steady, intelligent brown eyes from under her scarecrow hair, while a series of heavy thuds shook the thin three-ply partition behind her, followed by a blood-curdling yell.

Lorraine watched the woman back, again thinking it had been a very good question: what the hell *was* she doing in a dump like this? It smelt of furniture-polish, old shoes and sweat; it sounded like a bear pit at the zoo, and if the rest of the place was anything like this woman's office, those men out there must be wading through years of accumulated garbage. She got up. 'Maybe you're right. I'll go home and check the yellow pages.' She picked up her python-skin bag. 'It was kind of you to consider my request.' She managed a tight smile.

Sadie sat there watching her, not making a move.

220

'Siddown, Lorraine.' She waited, as if it had been an order.

'I'm sorry. I have to go now.' As icy as she could manage.

'Then don't go,' Sadie said levelly, 'without at least cussin' me out. At least ask me who the hell am I to question what you're doin' here. At least *react*.' She went on watching Lorraine.

And this was the last straw. Lorraine had been thrown out of the Lotus Club and now she was being virtually thrown out of this filthy dump. It wasn't going to be her evening. She went to the door and turned, remembering some of the language of the Hollywood studios.

'Sadie,' she said, 'you really are full of shit.'

She turned to go out, but the woman got to her feet and came around her desk so fast that Lorraine flinched, wondering how she could protect herself. Then Sadie was taking her hand and pumping it up and down, a smile on her battered-looking face so radiant that she became a different person.

'Okay,' she said delightedly, '*O – kay!*' She led Lorraine back to the rickety chair and pushed her down. 'Now we've started talkin' to each other. We got *communication!*' She went behind the cluttered desk again and dropped into her chair. 'So now I know what you're doin' here, Lorraine. Some guy tried to push you around, right? And he succeeded. And afterwards you wished you could have smashed his nose right through the back of his skull and walked away – but you didn't know how. Right?'

Lorraine let out a long breath, releasing the enormous tension that had been building in her since her humiliation at the club.

'*Right.*' She looked at Sadie with a kind of awe. 'But how did you know?'

'Because you treated him the way you just treated me, honey. You let me give you all that bullshit and all you could do was walk out on me.' She shook her head slowly. 'But that ain't no real answer. You need some training, and I'm going to give it to you, with a glad heart and a bill for ninety-

221

eight bucks a month plus the cost of membership and the uniform. Now let's go out there and you'll see the kind of work we do.' She came around her desk again and took Lorraine into the huge main room, where a dozen men and women in white kimonos were milling around; and the first thing Lorraine noticed was that the polished wood floor was as shining and immaculate as the dance floor of the Waldorf Astoria. 'I teach karate here,' Sadie was saying, 'but it's my own kind, a mixture of Chinese Kenpo, Japanese Shotokan – like Hajime teaches over there – Chinese boxing, Kung-fu, Ju-jitsu, Aikido, Tiger Claw, Ninja, and a few techniques outa the unarmed-combat handbook of the good old United States Marines. Thing is, it works. It really *works*.'

As Lorraine stood watching, she realised that nobody had stopped what they were doing to look at her; that was unusual: she was used to stopping the conversation dead when she walked into a room. Here it was different – and refreshing. Two enormous blacks were sparring across in the far corner; a couple of girls were practising what looked like throws on a thick padded mat; and the rest of them were gathered around a short thick-chested man wearing a black belt.

'Hey, Jim!' Sadie called to one of the blacks. 'Not that way! You're not using the leverage. Get down *low* and then swing up, get me?'

The two had stopped work at once, and gave Sadie a quick bow; then the one called Jim went into the technique again, spinning around and trying to floor his opponent. It didn't work.

'Swing *up*,' Sadie called. 'Start the swing from right down low, so you – wait a minute.' She gave the same little bow as she walked onto the polished pine floor and went across to the two blacks, motioning one of them aside and crouching suddenly, facing the other. 'Okay, Jim, it goes like this – and watch how I use the *momentum* to give me the *leverage*. And Billy, I want you to resist. Whatever you do, *don't* let me throw you. Now come at me.'

The huge black moved in with a grab for Sadie's arm, then Lorraine saw a fast milling of limbs and he was hitting the

222

mat and Sadie was standing with her hands on her hips watching him as he got up.

'See, Joe? Did you see the *leverage*?' She came over to Lorraine and took her arm, leading her to the group around the man with the black belt. 'Some of these boys are professional bodyguards, see. We got one or two security men, couple o' private eyes, couple of cops. We run a kids' class in the mornings, four years old upwards; we show them how to look after themselves on the street, how to avoid getting kidnapped, molested, you name it – and you wouldn't believe, Lorraine, you simply would not believe how much self-confidence you can put into a kid four years old, an' how much energy you can get out of him – or her, it makes no difference except that the girls are more ruthless once they know what to do. I had a woman in my office a couple o' months back, cryin' her heart out, one of her kids got snatched an' raped an' left for dead, she's still in the hospital and God knows how she'll ever learn to relate with a man for the rest of her life. But the point is, this woman's three other kids come here for instruction, an' any creep lookin' to make a grab at them on the street is goin' to finish up with his balls in a sling an' his knees in splints an' that's *before* they fetch the cops along to take him away. Hey, Jeff,' she called to the man with the belt, 'where's Cindy tonight?'

The big man turned, the sweat pouring off him, and gave that quick little bow that Lorraine had noticed before. 'She took sick, *Sensei*.'

'She call in?'

'Oh, sure.'

'Okay, Jeff.'

'*Os!*'

Sadie led Lorraine back to the office, talking on the way. 'Cindy's the woman with the four kids – she takes lessons herself. You'll meet her, if you sign on. Okay, this whole place is the *dojo*, means training place; and this outfit we wear is the *gi*, spelt g – i; an' you'll be calling me *Sensei*, means teacher in Japanese; you've seen the way we bow to each other, that's just a gesture of courtesy an' most of all

223

respect for each other, see, an' we really mean it; there's a lot of camaraderie around here. Most of the guys here behave themselves, an' when they don't, they either learn or get thrown out. When they first sign up I always get police clearance on them – y' know, a clean sheet, never been arrested for anythin', because, see, this stuff we teach them here is *lethal* an' we don't want it to get in the wrong hands, like handin' someone a loaded gun.'

Another voice cut in as she reached the office. 'Oh, *fuck*, I'm never going to get this *right* – '

Sadie turned her head. 'Kathy, you know the rules. Get off the floor, ten minutes!' She took Lorraine into the office. 'Don't allow no swearin', an' that's the punishment for most things here – a specific amount of time off the floor, which really *bugs* them, it's like bein' thrown outa the party while everyone else is havin' fun, an' besides, they feel a sense of shame, an' that's important.' She plucked a printed card from the mess on the table. 'Okay, Lorraine, here's my number. Go away an' think it over an' if you're still interested then you can just call me. I guess it's quite a drive to here from wherever you live, so remember the yellow pages – there'll be plenty of places closer.' She put out her square, calloused hand. 'But it was good talkin' to you.'

As Lorraine looked into the intelligent mud-brown eyes she could see only one thing, and that was the short, confident figure of Sadie standing over there by the mat with her hands on her hips as she watched that six-foot, two-hundred-pound black picking himself up from the floor. But it wasn't really the black she was seeing; it was the tall guy at the Lotus Club. And it wasn't, of course, really Sadie.

'I don't need to call you,' she said.

'That's perfectly okay.' Sadie waved an easy-going hand. 'Have a nice evenin' anyway.'

'I mean I'd like to sign on right now.'

Sadie frowned. 'Tonight? You think you know what you're doin'?'

'I'm damned sure I know what I'm doing, *Sensei*.'

CHAPTER 19

THE DINING-ROOM was Empire, its green marble wall panels framed in gold, the fireplace set in polished bronze, the heavy curtains hanging in scalloped folds and tied with gold tassels; two enormous lamps, their opaque parchment shades emblazoned with the Napoleonic crest, threw soft light upwards and below, casting shadows along the ceiling mouldings and the bronze appliqués of the consoles on each side of the fireplace. A gold-framed original in oils, of Napoleon in full uniform astride a caparisoned charger at the gates of Paris, dominated the wall opposite. The whole décor expressed what it had probably been intended to: style, invincibility, and uncountable wealth.

Frederick Vanderkloot III, in black tie, ushered Lorraine to the table, where two of the servants awaited them with the massive gilt-and-brocade chairs drawn back; catching a glimpse of herself in a wall mirror, Lorraine wondered if she should have chosen something less exotic to wear tonight; in a room so sombre she moved like a flame in the Diane Von Furstenburg ball gown of amethyst silk woven with silver and covered with moonstone brilliants; but at least her hair was up, and tamed by a silver headband. She had changed three times this evening before the final decision, first choosing black chiffon with a rope of pearls, since the object of this meeting was to discuss business, however informally; then she remembered the aura of virility she'd sensed on her previous encounters with his man: he would perhaps prefer to see her in something more feminine; then she chose – and rejected – a soft, clinging rose chiffon with a capulet of live

225

sweetheart roses for her hair: *much* too romantic and *jejeune*. She felt that a compromise was in order; as a businessman he'd see too much decoration as inappropriate – she was herself the chairman and chief executive officer of her company; yet as a man – even of his age – he'd certainly expect his guest to express her femininity. And there was one important advantage on her side: there would be no other woman present tonight to vie with her.

'We have mutual friends, of course,' Frederick Vanderkloot had told her, 'in the cosmetic world, and I'll certainly invite a few, if you feel daunted by the idea of spending an entire evening alone in the company of an elederly gentleman; but I thought we might find more to say to each other if we're not interrupted.'

She had agreed, of course; she disliked dinner parties, however small and 'intimate', where you seemed to leave with the feeling there hadn't really been enough time to talk to anybody. She had caught the hint of something in his tone that had warned her to present herself on her terms – which was to say, alone – but it hadn't worried her for more than a moment; he was, after all, a man of immense corporate power, and capable of befriending Floderus Incorporated to her company's unlimited good; and with other guests present the evening would be wasted on gossip, small-talk and pleasantries, which wasn't their objective.

The objective – *her* objective – was to see if this man could help her save Floderus, either by contributing to the cost of creating and launching *Siren Song*, or by supporting the company in any one of a hundred ways open to him, short of an actual take over. And he might, just incidentally, know of a first-class marketing director who'd be willing to replace Dean Powers, if Frederick gave him the nod . . .

'I'm so glad,' he told her when they were seated, 'that we decided not to ask anyone else tonight. I would have found the competition from the other males so very irksome.'

She matched his smile and tone. 'You wouldn't have even noticed it, Frederick. And neither would I.'

'So charming . . . ' He lifted his glass of champagne, his

eyes glinting in the candlelight.

This scene, she mused, was so different from last night's that she was reminded of a film director deliberately cutting for contrast. She'd gone as far as the Rolls in the car park, after signing the membership form in Sadie's little office, and then turned back on an impulse to ask what Sadie was doing after her karate class was over. They'd ended up in a pizza place around the corner, sharing a cracked plastic table and devouring a whole round of pie between them and washing it down with espresso, while Lorraine had listened to Sadie's flat, staccato voice describing her childhood, the repeated battering from her drunken father, the endless bullying from her older brothers, and finally her discovery that 'when the worm turns, everything changes'. They'd talked above the noise as the customers came and went – 'a lot of 'em are tarts, see, gettin' up off their backs to take a bite' – and a fat man with his face shining with sweat under a soiled chef's hat came around repeatedly with a fly-swat because the air-conditioning had broken down.

Tonight she surveyed the table with an admiration so open that Frederick saw it and became the attentive host. 'The porcelain is of course Royal Doulton . . . I found it at the auction of Princess de Designy's estate last year; the crystal is Rosenthal's Bavarian, hand-cut in Paris, a gift from Lord Cavenagh of Gavenny after a horse I sold him won the Thousand Guineas. And this –' he lifted a fork – ' is Golden Baroque from Gorham, with the silver and gold intertwined by their specialist craftsmen; it was a Christmas present from the chairman of International Pharmaceutical Laboratories; friends are so generous, don't you find? They save one the chore of having to *buy* things.'

Lorraine sat smiling as he chatted on, amused by his monologue as she admired the silver candlesticks, the wine goblets with their gold brocade bands, the gold handworked caviar dish with its cut crystal liner, the massed heads of orchids arranged at the table's centre on a bed of heraldic fern . . . 'A little hobby of mine, the orchids; I have the seeds flown from a monastery in Thailand . . .'

227

As the small-talk continued, the servants came and went, the *somelier* murmuring in her ear discreetly as he poured the wine for each course . . . 'Cristal Roederer Brut, Madame . . . ' for the shrimp tempura; 'Stolichnaya vodka, Madame, unless of course Madame wishes to stay with the champagne . . . ' as the Beluga caviar was served; 'Château Yquem, 1961, Madame . . . ' for the duck foie gras in a natural sauce; 'Vin de la Vallée du Rhône, Madame, from the Château Grillet, 1975 . . . ' as they savoured the Maine lobster salad with hearts of palm, going on to the New England scallops St Jacques with truffles; 'Château Lafite Rothschild, Madame, 1959 . . . ' with the roasted leg of milk-fed lamb, as the four servants moved around the table with the expertise of a *corps de ballet*, removing and bringing new dishes, changing the goblets and the napkins with each course, the candlelight shimmering on the gold and silver, the perfect harmony of the chef's presentations delighting Lorraine's palate as she listened to her host's mischievous stories of what he called 'great moments in the boardroom' as he deftly brought the conversation around to business over the sorbet with passion fruit, *petit fours* and Egyptian coffee.

They took their liqueurs in the drawing-room, where soft shaded lights and the flames in the fireplace cast a glow across the silks and brocades of the furnishings. While Frederick drank cognac, Lorraine chose a *crème de menthe* for the sake of its lightness; she felt she'd already done too much justice to the wines, and they were really meant to talk business tonight; and yet . . . in the company of this man with his superlative flair for entertaining, she found it difficult to call to mind the phrases she'd rehearsed so carefully in her office earlier today – 'I've no need to tell you my company's fortunes are at a low ebb; that kind of news gets around . . . ' And as a follow-up – 'I remember your telling me the other day in Los Angeles that you felt we might find a mutual interest in the fragrance and cosmetics field; as a matter of fact, I've been thinking about it quite a lot in the meantime . . . ' And finally – 'I must tell you that by

228

nature I'm fiercely independent, and that's the way Floderus is going to go on; but if you feel we could work together in combining some of our market outlets, or in cooperating overseas where my company is still lacking experience . . . '

But after the exquisite food and the heady wines, and in the glow of the firelight as she watched Frederick's compact figure gesturing to express a point in the conversation, his strong, chiselled face turned sometimes to her, sometimes lifted to watch the ceiling as he drew the exact phrase he needed from the air, Lorraine knew how stilted – how *rehearsed*, which in fact they were – those careful overtures of hers would sound, compared with his own delivery of smoothly-marshalled arguments. She'd do better, perhaps, to go head-on at him, like putting a hunter at a fence: 'Frederick, my company's on the rocks, as I'm sure you know. But we're going to create a new fragrance, win or lose; and I want you to invest in it. We'll need five million.'

But she felt herself blushing at the thought. He was so urbane, subtle, clever; to make an approach like that would make her sound like a schoolgirl desperate for her first date. What she would *really* like to do this evening was to forget – no, simply postpone – the urgent business of saving her company, and just revel in all this luxury, in this beautiful room with its priceless works of art; to bask in the aura shimmering almost visibly around this man – the aura of total success, of impregnable security, of awesome power.

Deep in her thoughts, she looked up to find him watching her, his dark, hooded eyes catching the reflections from the fire. 'Are you enjoying the evening, my dear?'

His soft tones broke the spell for her, and she became herself again, instead of a company chairman here to talk business. 'Enormously,' she said, and turned to rest one slender bare arm along the back of the couch. 'I could have imagined the kind of place you lived in, Frederick, before I came here.'

'And what kind of place is it?' he smiled mischievously.

She sipped her drink. 'Oh, luxurious . . . splendid . . .

229

and so very, *very* expensive . . . '

'Ah.' He gave her all his attention. 'You like that.'

'The expensive part? Oh, yes. I always have.'

'It does have a certain appeal, doesn't it?'

'Just how much are you worth, Frederick?' She'd spoken quite without thinking.

'Any man who knows what he's worth,' he answered with a smile, 'can't be worth very much.'

She wouldn't let him get away with that one. 'Fifty million? A hundred?'

He inclined his head. 'My assets world-wide are modest, but not *that* modest . . . '

They both laughed, and he stood up to pour himself more cognac. She wondered perhaps if she'd suddenly come on too brash, too direct. He was so damned sophisticated. 'It suites you, Frederick. You carry it well.'

'I'm glad you think so.' He remained standing, looking down at her contemplatively with the balloon glass in his short, square hand. 'You're not unused to affluence yourself, my dear Lorraine.'

'I suppose it's a question of degree, like most things.'

'Of course. And the difference doesn't really matter, does it? But tell me more about your company, if you'd care to. As you know, I admired your father tremendously, and the company he created and left in your hands is a gem of its kind; not large, not conglomerate, not mass-market. The name of Floderus has chic, elegance, and distinction. That's why I'm interested. If I were to take it over, it would be – ' he looked for the word.

'A jewel in your crown?'

'Well, now, that sounds – '

'But I'm not interested in a take-over, Frederick.' She found herself coming out of her mood of after-dinner euphoria, and coming out fast.

'Oh, really? Then I got it wrong, in Los Angeles. The word is that you're ready to sell.'

'No.' She was on her feet suddenly, facing him. 'The word is that I'm ready to fight as hard as I have to, and save the company. In whatever way I can.'

His heavy lids were lowered for an instant. 'I see,' he said quietly. His dark eyes were watching her again, and she was aware of something different in his gaze, in his voice; a vibration, almost tangible, was in the air, and she tensed to it. 'Your father, too,' he went on, 'had a fighting spirit, yes. And he was prepared – like you – to go to greater lengths, and consider unusual means, to further his interests. A great man.' He tilted his glass. 'I'm going to tell you frankly, Lorraine – and why don't we sit down? – that my advisers have been urging me to make an offer for your company. Its fortunes, as you say, have deteriorated, and it's ripe – forgive the time-honoured expression – for the picking.'

Facing him again on the crimson brocade couch, she felt her back straighten. 'I must tell you again, Frederick. I'm not going to sell.'

He tilted his head an inch. 'My advisers meant, of course, that Century Cosmetics should take over Floderus Incorporated whether you personally were willing or not.'

Lorraine's mouth tightened, and she put her liqueur onto the small lacquered table beside her. 'By making a bid my shareholders couldn't refuse?'

'Life, my dear Lorraine, is very real out there in the corridors of Manhattan. Your experience is limited, of course; you were obliged to take over —'

'My experience was learned in Hollywood,' she said with a bitterness that surprised her, 'where dog also eats dog. I'd fight *any* attempt to buy out Floderus.' Watching him now, she saw him as the man he was, underneath the charming and attentive host; the fumes of the wine were clearing from her head, and she found herself sitting opposite a tycoon of the classic breed: a man old in years but still strong, ruthless, and merciless in his greed for even more power, more wealth, more victories in the bloodied halls of the market-place.

'I applaud your courage,' he said softly. 'You would have no hope of winning your fight, not a chance; but at least you'd earn our admiration.' He put his brandy glass beside

231

hers on the little table, and leaned towards her. 'But before this conversation goes off in the wrong direction, my dear, let me assure you that I told my advisers that nothing in this world would ever persuade me to take over your company by force. I would fight on *your* side, and against allcomers, if you found yourself in danger.'

'Is that true?'

'But of course.'

Her relief was so immediate that she felt tears stinging her eyes. She'd misjudged him totally, and felt ashamed.

'You're very generous,' she said.

'You make it so easy for me, Lorraine. You are young, vulnerable, and – just incidentally – the most beautiful woman I have ever met in all my life. And tonight you chose to wear your own *Picaresque* . . . a light, exquisite floral with an exotic after-note of – is it sandalwood? Tell me I'm right.'

'Yes,' she smiled, nodding. 'I imagine you always are.'

'Oh, I've made a few mistakes. But not, I hope, in inviting you here tonight.' His short, perfectly-manicured hand was suddenly resting on her knee. 'I assumed you wouldn't be going on to anywhere else, as late as this.'

As close to her as he was, he caught no reaction; this, he knew, was because his meaning hadn't got through to her yet; though she'd had her training in life in 'dog-eat-dog' Hollywood as she called it, she was still an ingenous innocent under the skin. What had happened, then, when the producers had shown her the couch? Had she struggled, like a girl out of a Victorian melodrama? Hadn't she learned *anything* there?

'Anywhere else?' She watched him, seeming confused. This, too, left him unsurprised: he'd deliberately led her to think he was ready to force a take-over, then shown himself as a white knight riding by her side, a gallant protector; and now, while the tears of relief were still in her eyes, he was making his bid. 'No,' she shook her head, 'I'll be going straight on home.' She glanced at the ormolu clock over the mantel-piece. 'And you're right – it's late, and I hadn't realised.'

'For us,' he said softly, 'the night is young.' He hated to use such B-picture terms, but they were the ones she'd understand. He couldn't, after all, put it to her directly. During the day, the thought that she'd be here with him tonight, and alone, had obtruded on his work; he wouldn't have believed, after the hundreds – by now it must be thousands – of women who'd passed through his bed, that his libido could have gotten so inflamed as this, and by a little film star; but there was something about Lorraine Floderus, an essence to her, an emanation, that tonight had aroused him almost unbearably as they'd sat together at the table busy with their small talk while he'd watched that devastating smile, the slender neck, the flawless texture of her arms silvered with down, and the line of her exquisite body under the clinging silk of her dress. It had been embarrassing for him to play the attentive and gracious host, while his erection had forced itself upwards under his trousers.

As he watched her now, his hand actually feeling the heat of her young body under it, he felt he'd reach immediate orgasm the instant they kissed; the very thought of stripping her naked, later, and showing her how he wanted things to be, was threatening to bring him to a climax even before they touched.

'I don't understand,' she said hesitantly.

'You'll be staying the night, of course.' Even his tone was unsteady. In Romania last year they'd told him at the clinic that with a man of his constitution, the rejuvenation shots would be effective; but he hadn't imagined he could sit here tonight feeling the heat of a young stallion raging through him . . . or was it just *this* woman, of all women, who was goading him on, tantalising him to the point of exquisite torture, simply by sitting close to him, her sea-blue eyes lit with innocence, the tender line of her mouth confused, her body scent rising in the warmth and driving him mad . . .

'Staying the night?' she said, surprised. 'No, Frederick.'

'There isn't any *question*.'

'I'm sorry.' She was standing up suddenly, her slim body

233

curved inwards, away from him. 'I didn't realise – '

'*How old are you, for God's sake?*' He was on his feet, holding her bare arms, their touch electrifying him.

'Frederick, I – I must go now.' She tried to pull away.

'No. I want you more than any woman I've ever known. I'm – no longer a boy, Lorraine, but believe me, I won't disappoint you.' She went on struggling, but he pulled her against him, thrusting his pelvis forward so that she could feel his hardness. Rational thought was overwhelmed now; everything of the moment conspired to assault his senses: the fumes of the cognac rising from the glass on the table, the rich primitive tang of the logs flaming in the hearth, the scent of this exquisite female body, the warmth of her skin, the movement of her struggling, her excitement, her fear . . . her fear of him, of his strength, of his power, of his total dominance as he thrust his hardness against her, hot and vibrant and straining against the thin silk of her dress, the small, delicate briefs that girls like this always wore, and the warm skin beneath, with the pubic hair flattened under the force of his thrusting as now, already, it was too late and he was coming . . . coming against the body of this glorious creature before he could even meet her flesh to flesh . . . coming with an explosive release he hadn't felt for years, thrusting against her, thrusting with every pulse along his raging phallus – and then suddenly the absence of her, and the sting of her hand as it came against his face, the glimpse of her bright furious eyes as she tugged herself clear of him and span away, leaving him powerless for this moment, crouched over the ecstasy she'd brought to him, his eyes clenched, his hands going down to grasp himself and force out the last fierce pulsations that he had to have, while in the fires of his mind he saw her under him, her smile ravishing, her mouth enclosing him as the seed spurted there against the sweet glistening softness of her tongue . . . Lorraine . . . Lorraine . . . Lorraine . . .

Then as he brought his head up at last he saw her standing by the door, white-faced and with her hands spread out as if she wanted to wash them.

'I didn't know,' her strained tones came. 'I thought you were too old. I'm sorry.'

'*Too old?*' It was a cry of a beast in pain. '*Too old?*' He stood there crouched still, powerless to go after her, the rapture dying and the rage coming into him. 'Lorraine, come back . . . come back!' But she didn't move. 'Lorraine, if I can't have you, I'll have your company . . . I'll take it and I'll smash it, you hear? So you'd better call me, when you realise –' but she was pulling the door open, flitting through and slamming it after her as his voice rose to a pitch of raw fury – '*You'd better call me, Lorraine . . . or you're finished, you hear me, you're finished . . .*'

CHAPTER 20

'SAME AGAIN, Mr Powers?'

'Yes.'

'Coming right up.'

The bartender reached for the shaker and the gin, looking up as the door opened and someone else came in from the rain; tyres hissed along the street outside, the lights shimmering in the puddles.

Dean Powers got out his pack of Winstons again and stuck one of them between his lips and flicked his gold lighter and snapped it shut again and put the cigarette back into the pack unlit, watching Benny with the shaker, waiting for the martini, needing it, his fourth this evening; then he found the pack of Winstons in his hand again and slipped one out and put it between his lips and got his lighter and lit up, streaming out a plume of smoke and saying, 'So why do I smoke these things, when they're bad for me?'

'Sir?'

'What?' Dean looked up at the bartender.

'Did you say something?'

Jesus, he'd said it out loud. Wasn't that a sign you were ready for the funny farm or something? 'Sure. I said I'm going to quit these things tomorrow.'

'That's right,' Benny said with his gleaming gold grin, 'that's always the best time to do anything, ain't it the truth?' He put the martini down in front of the customer.

Dean picked it up right away and started on it. No, talking to yourself was just a sign you were lonely. And this evening, depressed. And scared. Admit it.

236

Ski-bump . . . ski-bump . . . ski-bump . . . He could hear his heart beating in his head, in his chest, in his arms, everywhere. Okay, at least it was still beating.

Scared, sure. Out of work. That was always the most scary thing there was.

And mad as hell at that bitch.

Don't even think about her.

'Hi, Dean.'

A fat guy with a squint took the stool next to him.

'Hi.' Dean didn't know his name.

'Come here every evening, then?'

'What? Sometimes.' He managed a gusty laugh. 'I mean every evening, sometimes, sure.'

Where else, after all, could he go? There was nowhere he hadn't been in this fucking town since the day he'd stepped out of Floderus onto the sidewalk and kept on going, at first rudderless and enraged, then to the nearest travel office – *I don't care, just anywhere, you name it, the Carribean, Mexico City, what the hell's the difference, I've got three months' severance pay and if I haven't earned a couple of weeks in the sun who the hell has, and that isn't a question, it's a fucking statement* – then back to his apartment, suddenly scared, to put a bunch of résumés together for the mail, then twenty or thirty, then fifty, duplicating them from a master copy and thumping some of the stamps on sideways and upside-down *because the thing was to get them out right now, and then take that trip before he started work in the next job, first things first, get our priorities right* – then finally across to Third Avenue to see Charterhouse Associates, the people who took on executives from the fifty-thousand-a-year level upwards and tried to find them another position and mostly succeeded except when there was a recession in full swing, like now.

'You've sent out fifty résumés, Mr Powers. That's fine, but you know there's at least a couple of hundred firms in this field in New York City – not all of them in the fragrance business, but requiring similar executive skills. So why not send out another fifty tomorrow? And keep on going. Have

237

you had any offers?'

'No.'

'Interviews?'

'Four.'

'Okay, well that's a start. You only left Floderus Incorporated eight days ago, isn't that right?'

Don't you know how long eight days are?

'And you don't have to hurry,' Clifford Marks had told him, sitting comfortably behind his desk, *comfortable and secure in his job*, 'because you have three months' severance pay, right? And from this résumé, my goodness, you have all the credentials we need for a really remunerative post. And if we have to take a little more time, in view of the recession conditions, you have your unemployment insurance when the three months run out, so – oh, yes, it's for ten thousand dollars per annum, you should have increased that, perhaps. Ten thousand doesn't get you far these days, does it?' With a smooth, knowledgeable laugh, meaning that in, say, four months from now he could be riding past the bus stop in his cab and not even notice or even remember the tall guy with the glasses standing there with the mud from the taxi's tyres over his shoes. *You get paranoiac, you get very paranoiac, when you've just lost your job; the shrinks will tell you that; there's one thing worse even than enforced sexual deprivation, even than hunger, and that's rejection. Quite apart from the money, ha, ha!*

'I see your ex-wife doesn't contribute to the children's school fees or anything else, is that correct?''

Oh, absolutely. Let's get everything correct.

Scared to hell, *ski-bump, ski-bump*.

'We'll call you just as soon as something *really* worthwhile shows up on the computer, Mr Powys – '

'Powers.'

'I'm sorry, of course, Mr Powers.'

Then back to the apartment to get another fifty résumés out, thumbing the yellow pages, the *New York City Business Referendum* and the *Wall Street Journal* and *Forbes* and *Fortune* and Business Week and anything he could get his hands on in the magazine racks.

Then back to the bars.

Back to this one. The Crock o' Gold, right downstairs from his apartment, downstairs and around the corner, very convenient, very convenient indeed, a place to relax in.

He drained the martini and went over the imaginary scene he'd been running through his mind day after day, like you run an old movie through the video, the scene in the boardroom eight days ago when instead of just walking out on that *bitch* he'd stood his ground and told her she didn't know her company law but for her information she couldn't fire him without going to the board first in a formal meeting; the scene where Barry and Carl and the others had told her he was right, and she just had one option left if she didn't want to sell – she'd have to step aside and put Dean in the chair as chief executive officer. A great scene, but it had been looking less great the more he played it, because it wouldn't have worked out anyway – he wouldn't have stayed on at Floderus even if that *bitch* had gone down on her god-damned knees and sucked his – hey, wait a minute, so *that's* where your mind is, you'd better have another quick martini to straighten you out. You're shot, Dean baby, you know that? Eight days on the street and you're washed up.

Just a phase.

'Benny.'

'Mr Powers?'

Dean pushed the glass across the counter.

Where was he? Oh, yes. That *bitch*.

She was standing in front of him.

He was sitting halfway around on the stool and as he looked up he saw the girl in the gold-coloured raincoat with the scarlet-lined hood and thought *oh wow!* and then she pulled the hood back and shook out her ash-blonde hair and looked at him with her sky-blue eyes and he recognised her and felt his scrotum shrinking: shock, rage, disbelief, whatever.

'There you go, sir.'

239

Benny dropped the cherry in and Dean turned slowly to face the bar and said, very carefully, 'Thanks, Benny.' Then he just went on sitting there until he felt he could trust the steadiness of his hand to lift his drink and take a critical and appreciative sip.

What the hell was she doing here?

Ski-bump, ski-bump.

Lorraine waited a few seconds and then said: 'Benny, when you have a moment.'

'Yes, miss?'

'I'd like a Tio Pepe. Straight up.'

'Sure.' His gold grin shone suddenly. 'Comin' up, Miss Floderus. Liked your movie.'

'Thank you.'

Sitting hunched on the stool, Dean closed his eyes for a minute, dramatising the whole thing so he could understand what was going on: here was the martini-sodden bum licking his wounds after getting fired from the job, and here was his ex-boss slumming it in a down-town bar and getting the famous-face routine from the bartender the moment he looked at her. Not a pretty scene. A pretty girl, or pretty, anyway, for a *bitch*, but not a pretty scene. No, sir.

He opened his eyes again, on a different thought. Little Miss Famous-Face wasn't in such terribly good shape herself tonight; she'd just finished running a fifty-million-dollar company into skid row and any time at all she'd be out of a job herself. He liked that scene better.

'Tio Pepe,' Benny said, placing the glass on the napkin.

Lorraine dropped a ten on the counter.

'My tab,' Dean said, and got off his stool.

'Yes, sir.'

Lorraine put the bill back in her slim gold-coloured bag.

'Thank you, Dean. I appreciate that.'

'It's just a drink, dammit.'

'No. I think it's more than that.' She perched on the stool next to his, and he sat down again. She raised her sherry, and for a moment he decided to ignore it, pretend he hadn't seen the gesture; but she was sitting there looking so damned

240

civilised, so damned cultivated, beautifully dressed and groomed and smiling, the glass poised perfectly in her hand, that he decided to pick up his own drink and tilt it without actually looking at her.

'Cheers.'

'Cheers, Dean.' She left the smile there, hoping he wouldn't notice how forced it was, how desperate. Inside the Ferragamo raincoat her whole body was shaking, as if she'd come in here from a snowstorm instead of the rain. Dean wouldn't look at her, and she couldn't look at him directly because at any instant he might turn his head; so she watched him in the mirror behind the bar – and hardly recognised him. Here was the smooth, elegant, arrogant vice president of Floderus Incorporated perched on the stool with his shoulders slightly rounded, the shadow of stubble on his chin, his necktie a little askew, and his dark brown eyes bloodshot behind the executive-styled Pierre Cardin glasses. And she was shocked. Was *this* what happened to them only a week after they got fired?

She untied the belt of her raincoat and opened it, shaking the water-drops off. 'I almost got drenched, just walking from the parking lot.'

Dean turned his head, and met the full force of Lorraine Floderus' sexuality: the shimmering smile, the light-blue gaze, the slender body sheathed in a clinging camelhair sweater, the line she made with its studied angles as she leaned slightly, hand on hip, her elbow holding back the folds of the raincoat so that her body was opened to him, its warm female scent in the air between them and making its delicate contact.

'You got what?' he asked.

'Drenched.'

'Oh.' He took a breath, looking away. 'How did you find me?'

She tensed. This was the first hurdle: how to admit she'd come here looking for him; because it would put him immediately in a position of power, and at his first taunt she'd want to slap his face and walk right out of here – and

241

somehow have to control herself and not do it.

'Nadine couldn't get you on the phone all day.' She'd got his answering service every time. 'Then I tried myself, on the off-chance, late this evening. Your – a woman answered, and said you might be down here.' Each word like a mine in a minefield, set to explode – 'woman', not 'girl', with its undertone of calumny, a kept woman, a woman of easy virtue. But of course it had been a rather breathless little-girl voice on the telephone, a voice from the junior typists' pool; didn't this mature-looking hunk of a man ever go to bed with someone his own age? And why wasn't the pretty little thing down here with him now – had they had a row, or would the bartender want to see her birth certificate? And why, dear God, was Lorraine Floderus, of all people, so concerned? He could go to bed with a wart-hog for all she cared.

'So now that you've found me,' Dean was saying, 'what can I do for you?' He was sitting straighter now, and facing her.

He too, she noticed, was choosing words with explosive under-tones, as if he were setting her up to tread on his own minefield. *Now that you've found me* – after all the effort you've been making . . . *What can I do for you?* What scrap can I throw you that'll make you go away again and leave me in peace?

So he wasn't going to make it easy for her; he was going to be a bastard, just like he'd always been a bastard; nothing had changed. 'We're going – ' and she stopped dead. It was too soon yet. 'We've been wondering how you were getting along.'

'We?' He lifted one eyebrow.

Oh, yes, he had the best position, all right.

'Carl, Sy and the rest of us,' she said casually.

'There are so many left?'

She felt her lips compress. 'Enough to keep going, yes. Only three ran out on us.' She corrected that immediately. 'Though Barry didn't exactly run out – I could see his point of view. He'd put such a lot of himself into the company, for so many – '

242

'He wasn't the only one.'

Their eyes held, contempt in his, anger in hers.

'I know.'

'We all gave a lot to the company. I gave eight years. Nobody "ran out" on you, Lorraine. We just felt it was time to cut our losses.'

She looked down. Driving here tonight through the pouring rain she'd rehearsed what was going to happen, just like she'd seen the directors in Hollywood rehearsing each new scene. Dean would be a bastard, right; but that didn't have to make any difference. She wasn't going to this bar to have a blazing row with him; she was going there to talk him into coming back to Floderus; so she'd have to take everything he said, and not let it rile her; she'd have to turn her cheek, again and again, and hang in there, and keep her pride and her temper and her control. Or there was no point going there at all.

But now she was here, facing him. And it wasn't going to be so easy.

'I'm not blaming anyone, Dean.'

'No?'

'I – quite understand why you left. It was – '

'Pretty obvious, even to you.' He tossed back the rest of his drink and slid the glass across the counter.

There'd been a moment, when she'd seen how beaten he looked, slack and red-eyed and defeated, when she could have felt pity for him, even a twinge of conscience; but now he was sitting perfectly upright on the stool and looking down at her, down *on* her, his eyes hard and his tone biting; and all she could feel towards him now was a defensive anger. He'd said enough to her, hadn't he, in the boardroom, enough to break her heart, break her spirit?

'Dean,' she said, her anger only just under control, 'I know what I did. You think I don't? I took over the company because I had to, because it was what my father wanted. I wasn't experienced, I wasn't prepared, I wasn't qualified. So I did what I could, and I failed, and it caused a lot of people a lot of pain, including myself – most of all myself,

Dean, though you can't believe that, because you're hurting too much, and I understand. But for God's sake, I don't need any more from you. I've had enough. You want me to suffer? You want me to hurt? Then leave it to me, because I can do a better job even than you.'

He looked away from her. 'Benny?'

'Comin' up, Mr Powers.'

Lorraine took her glass and sipped at it, not tasting anything, sitting perfectly still on the high stool, one hand nonchalantly on her hip while the shaking went on inside, the hurt, the anger, the realisation that she shouldn't have come here tonight, because all she was going to get from this bastard was his own hurt and his own anger, blow for blow.

When was she going to stop making mistakes? To save the company she'd gone to see Vanderkloot last night, only to suffer humiliation and disgust. To save the company she'd come here tonight, and was faced with humiliation of a different kind, and enmity, and hate. *When was she going to get it right?* The way she felt now, she wanted to go back to the office on Monday and call Joe and Sy and Carl in to see her and tell them how it was going to be: *I'm going to create a new fragrance and make a turnaround and put the company back on its feet, but I am not going to do it with Dean Powers in the building, so if you're not prepared to go on without him you'll just have to resign.*

Would *that* be right? Or would that be just one more disastrous mistake? If so, when would they end? Only when her own life ended?

A picture of Madlen flashed into her mind; Madlen lying on the floor in that place with the empty container near her hand. At this moment, she could understand how Madlen had felt that night, and her heart went out to her, as it so often did. But that was no way to go. You had to fight.

Dean was speaking, and she didn't catch it.

'I'm sorry?'

'So why did you come here tonight?'

'To see you.'

'I know. But why?'

244

The edge had gone from his tone; maybe she'd managed to convince him she could do a better job of flaying herself alive than he could. She took a breath.

'We're creating a new fragrance. We –'

'That's crazy – I told you before.'

Keep going. 'We're going to make a turnaround, Carl, Joe, Sy and the rest of the staff who want to stay.' She watched him with the light of battle suddenly in her eyes, and Dean noticed the change. 'We're going to confound everyone, Dean. We're going to fight the good fight, turn defeat into victory, you can choose which cliché you like best, but that's what we're going to do.' She paused deliberately. 'And we'd like you to join us.'

'No way!'

'Just like that?'

'Just like that.'

'Without giving it a second's thought?'

'You imagine I haven't done any thinking? I'm out of a job. Don't you think it didn't cross my mind to call you and suggest we try again?'

'You did?' She felt sudden hope.

'You bet I did! You've never been out of work, Lorraine, have you? Your Dad saw to that. When you sell up, what'll you get out of the company? Ten million? Twenty? And that's out of a *failure*. But being out of work, in the middle of a recession, is different. It does things to you. It even had me being crazy enough to *consider* calling you and telling you I'd come back providing it was on my own terms. But that was just the first panic, you know? The grasping at straws. It passed.' He picked up his new drink and tilted it, cynically. 'Good luck, Lorraine. I hope you make it. Me, I'm not quite ready to join the suicide squad.' He drank.

Lorraine waited, trying to keep a hold on the hope she'd felt a minute ago. 'Dean, give it some more of your thought. You're – relaxed right now, and not in a mood to –'

'Smashed, no less. It eases the pain.' He was raising his voice, and she saw Benny look across from the end of the bar.

'This just isn't the time,' Lorraine persisted. 'Give me a call tomorrow. We could have lunch.'

'Tomorrow is Saturday,' he said, his speech slurred now. 'And I have an airplane to catch. It's going to take me all the way to the golden beaches of the Bahamas, where the gals are all gorgeous and don't try to con a guy into going back into a half-assed wreck of a company that was doing fine till the late boss's daughter took over and thought she could –'

Lorraine's hand cracked across his face and then she was walking away, not hurrying, but walking very steadily towards the doors and the street and the rain.

It was an hour before she reached her apartment, because she'd felt so angry when she left the bar that she'd driven halfway to Sadie Kaminski's *dojo* before she remembered there were no karate classes on Friday evenings. By eight o'clock she was over on the Upper East Side again, taking a right off Madison and slowing towards the apartment block.

A man was standing at the entrance ramp of the underground garage, and as Lorraine turned the blue Rolls-Royce across the sidewalk he stepped in front of the car, holding one hand up. The usual thoughts flew into her mind: keep the windows up and the doors locked, call the police on the car telephone, but if the man tries to smash the windshield or anything, what then – try running him down?

As she braked sharply he lowered his hand and came around to the driver's side, stooping to look in at her – a tall man in a soaked raincoat with the collar up, his wet hair hanging in locks across his forehead.

'Lorraine?' she heard faintly through the window-glass. She did a mental double-take and rolled the window down halfway.

'Oh, for God's sake. What do you want?'

'I want to talk.'

'We just did that, Dean. Now go home.'

He stood gazing down at her while the steady rain fell on him, aslant in the wind. 'I think it's important we should talk,' he said. 'Important to you.'

His speech sounded sober enough, and he wasn't swaying or anything. And it was Friday – Tilly's night off. Otherwise she certainly wouldn't bring anyone looking like this into the apartment.

'Where do you want to talk, Dean?'

'Your place is fine.'

'All right. But you'd better take the lift from the garage; the doorman would never let you in, looking like that.'

'How long is it since the divorce?'

'That's none of your goddamned business.' Dean sat hunched on the settee, his hands around a cup of steaming coffee. His hair was a mess; Lorraine had shown him the nearest bathroom so he could towel off the rain; he'd taken his soaked shoes off, and his socks were leaving dark patches on the carpet.

'It's none of my goddamned business,' Lorraine said, 'I agree. But you –'

'I don't want to talk about it.'

'I know. But you should. You'll have to talk about it some time, Dean, before you can start healing.'

'What makes you think I haven't talked to anyone?'

'Because I know the kind of – ' she left it right there because he'd lifted his head to look at her and she knew that if they started fighting again the evening would be lost. In the bar he'd been bitter, contemptuous, keen to hurt her again if he could. For some reason he'd changed his mood – maybe a good slap in the face wasn't all bad. But they weren't making up or anything; he was just miserable now, and wary; he'd come halfway to meet her – all the way, actually, from the West Side – but that didn't mean they were friends; they never would be. It just meant there was a truce; a temporary cease-fire. 'Okay,' she finished, 'it's none of my business. Forget it.'

'Your business is Floderus Incorporated, what's left of it. And for the sake of those other people there I decided I should make an effort and tell you there isn't a chance in hell of you pulling that company out again. I want to save more

247

pain, and more losses, for everyone concerned.'

She leaned against the end of the fireplace, her arm along the lapis lazuli stonework, not conscious of striking a pose but perhaps doing it without thinking; she felt relaxed here, or almost; this wasn't a crowded West Side bar, but her own territory, and not his. 'That's terribly noble of you, Dean. I'm deeply touched.'

He shrugged. 'Take it that way if you want to. But I know the facts, and the figures.'

'So do Carl, and Sy, and Joe. And they're not idiots.'

He took another swig at his coffee. It was his fourth cup, and he sounded perfectly sober now. 'They're showing you their loyalty, that's all.'

'That's all? I think it's quite a lot.'

He shook his head impatiently. 'Lorraine, all the loyalty in the world won't change the facts and the figures.'

'Not by itself, no. But it's a help, Dean, to feel there's someone around who thinks I can still make it. Without that kind of faith, I can't.'

'You can't anyway. Period.'

Without raising her voice she said, 'If that's what you came to tell me, I'm not interested. As soon as you've had enough coffee, I'd like you to go.'

He drained his cup and put it carefully on the tray and stood up. 'At least it was a good old college try.' She watched him looking around for his shoes. 'Where the hell did you put –'

'Oh for Christ's sake, Dean, start behaving like an adult. You didn't come here just to tell me I don't have a chance – I listened to all that bullshit at the board meeting, and you know it. You came here to say something else.'

'I did?'

'Yes.' She took a long shot. 'You're interested in *Siren Song*.'

He looked blank. 'In what?'

'It's the new fragrance we're creating.'

'The new . . . oh, yeah. You told me, didn't you?' With weary despair he said, 'I think *Swan Song* might be a better name.'

'That was cheap.'

He nodded, surprising her. 'I guess it was. So where are you going to get the money?'

'The bank.'

'Don't show them the figures.'

'I'm interested in the future, not the past. This is America, Dean, and it hasn't changed. Anybody can still do anything they want, if they try.'

'Don't try and sell me the American Dream. That went out with *Over the Rainbow*.'

'Oh really? What about Bessie Carr?'

He looked blank again. 'Who's she?'

'Her father died when she was only twenty-two, and left a company that rebuilt diesel parts. She hadn't even graduated from college, but she got a Nashville banker to put up $420,000 to buy out stock holdings, because he said it was a damned good company and also because she talked him into the ground. Last year her revenues doubled, to $8 million. She's still only twenty-nine.'

'Okay, she –'

'Or take Stephanie Blake.' She didn't care if Dean realised she'd been keeping her courage up by reading success stories in the magazines. They were true, and she wanted him to hear them. 'She couldn't find any reasonably-priced, high-quality clothes for her infant daughter; so she got going with her sewing-machine. The word got out when she sold a few extra clothes to her friends. That was only eight years ago, but last year's sales of the Stephanie Blake labels topped $8 million. Or try Connie Weitz. She was a hat-check girl in a TV series, after dropping out of high school; she's now chairman of Weitz Laboratories and her sales last year were $74 million in cosmetics and hair products. The American Dream isn't dead yet, Dean. It's got the kick of a mule. And I'm in there kicking.'

She left the hearth and went over and poured him some more coffee, while he watched her thoughtfully. 'I don't know whether you're being admirable,' he said, 'or stupid.'

249

'I couldn't care less what you think, Dean. You like facts and figures, and I just gave you a few.'

Looking down, he said: 'You're not going to like me for telling you this, but –'

'It'll be nothing new.'

'I guess I walked into that one. The thing is, those gals just might have something you don't. Business acumen. A flair for management.'

Tears of anger were stinging her eyes as she faced him. 'What I don't have, I can work at getting. I've got the other things, haven't I? Guts, ambition – ' she was holding her arms, crouched over herself as if she were fighting to hold on to whatever she had while this bastard tried to take it away from her. 'I – I'm not just – just *nothing*, damn you! I'm not old, I – I'm not ugly, I can do a good public relations job in the field, you know that. The only thing I'm ashamed of is trying to get you to come back to the company – I must have been out of my mind. If you ever step into that building I'll have you thrown right out again on your neck.'

'I wouldn't be seen dead in the place.'

'*Dean, why do you hate me so much?*'

'I don't. I think you're magnificent.'

She stared at him. 'You think I'm *what*?'

Then he was holding her and his mouth was against her own and she wasn't even resisting, because everything had gone very still as she slipped into this astonishing dream where they were kissing and his body was hard against hers and all she could think about was how tall he was and how damnably good-looking and how damnably expert as his strong hands slid gently upwards under her sweater and burned on her bare skin while in her groin there came a rushing of heat so strong that it almost frightened her, and she tried to pull away from him – 'Dean, this isn't the answer to –'

'There's nothing to say, Lorraine.' In spite of the strength she could feel in him his hands were so gentle, and she closed her eyes again and let the dream go on and on, letting him do what he wanted, giving herself to the longing for this until

250

she was helping him, tugging her skirt down and stepping out of it, her hands working on him now, tearing at the buttons of his shirt and then the waistband of his pants as his tongue came thrusting into her mouth and she began moaning uncontrollably, her head moving from side to side as her briefs came down across her thighs, her senses rioting as conscious awareness slipped away and she was lying suddenly across the settee without knowing how she got there, with Dean's body half naked against her and his penis hard in her hand as she guided it lower across her body hair and into the creaming lips where every sensation was now concentrated in one burning need to feel the horn of the male there; and then he was inside her and she half cried out as she arched herself instinctively and began moving with him as he thrust and withdrew, thrust and withdrew, so slowly that she hooked her hands against his back, clawing at the skin, quicker and quicker until he moved in time with her, setting the rhythm she wanted as she lay under him with his sweat starting to trickle on her skin, mingling with her own and bringing the raw male scent of his roused body into the air, exciting her now beyond reason as she moaned with an animal's soft keening, bringing song to the dance; but he was still too slow . . . too slow . . . and she began clawing at him again, pulling him into her faster and faster, deeper and deeper until the first of the liquid fire was pouring into her loins and spreading and flickering and then suddenly exploding as she cried out with her whole body arching in a spasm that for an instant brought everything to a stop, because to go on would be unbearable; then it came again, bringing another cry from her, and again, and again, as her body leapt and fell away and leapt again, rising to meet its lover and pulling him down and forcing him upwards and harder against her while the fires ran, ebbing and flowing, flooding her with their unquenchable heat, until it was over and she could bear no more . . . *stop*, she heard herself saying, *stop* . . . her breath against his face as she hollowed her body away from him and felt him sliding out of her, bringing a last sobbing cry as the heat blazed for the last time

251

and burned out, leaving her motionless, exhausted, as he grasped her hand urgently and brought it to his penis, so that she understood, and enclosed it, her fingers slipping against the fluids from her own body as she stroked him, faster and faster until he called her name and she felt his climax coming and the soft rain of his seed against her body as she pulled and stoked with her fingers, bringing it out of him until the spasms died away and they lay quietly, the mingled scents of their bodies raw on the air, like the smoke of dying fires.

CHAPTER 21

ON MONDAY MORNING Judy Pollack, Personnel, took a quick look at her réflection in the big glass window as she came into her office and crossed to the desk.

'There's something wrong. Betty Lou.'

'What like?'

'With this outfit.' She studied the reflection of the beige mesh blouson and drawstring pants.

'I think the black and yellow stripe suited you better.' said Betty Lou as she dumped the late Friday batch of memos into Judy's tray.

'The what? Oh, that. That was when I was dating my Wasp. It's over now. You know he came to see me with a rolled umbrella and rubbers on, when it hadn't even started to rain? And did I tell you he spent the whole of Sunday afternoon showing me around a maritime history museum, because his father's an admiral? Did you know that when a timber-built man o' war fires a salvo from all nine guns on one side, the whole ship tilts at an angle of fifteen degrees from the recoil? I wrote it down somewhere, because I was sure you wouldn't believe it. But there *is* something *terribly* wrong with this outfit, Betty Lou. It's the colour, right? Beige isn't too much of a turn-on. And the blouse rolls over too much at the waist; and that *draw*string . . . Don't tell me, I've got it. All it lacks is a quick-firing rifle slung at the shoulder and an ammunition belt; this must be the closest thing to special combat fatigues the US Army quarter-master general ever put on issue.'

'I think it looks very nice,' said Betty Lou.

253

'Shit, you go for soldiers?'

She turned away from her reflection and sat down at her desk with an impact that rocked the chair, and inside of the next half-hour went through the entire batch of memos, arranging them on the desk and playing her own brand of patience to get them into a pattern of priority, then making a dozen telephone calls and taking a dozen more, giving each caller exactly sixty seconds to say what they had to before she cut them off, sometimes in mid-sentence. 'If they can't get it over with inside of one minute, Betty Lou, it's going to take 'em fifteen; it's somebody's law.'

'I don't know how you do it, Judy.'

'Do what?'

'Handle everything so fast.'

'It's easy, once you're into Zen. Like when you're nailing Jello to a tree – so long as you keep on hammering, the Jello takes care of itself.' She looked up through the big window as a man came out of the lift and went into an office two doors along the corridor. 'Oh for God's sake, I've started hallucinating . . .'

Betty Lou looked up from her typewriter. 'What are you seeing?'

'Dean Powers.'

'But he resigned, didn't he?'

Judy looked at her. 'I guess you could put it that way. What actually happened, that Thursday when you were away on the wisdom tooth deal, was that Mr Powers came out of the boardroom at an illegal fifty-six miles per hour with a chair around his neck. Now he's just gone into his office like nothing had happened: brief-case, *Wall Street Journal* and everything. And nobody even told me to sign him in again.' She picked up the phone and dialled the Chairman's number.

'That's right, Judy.' Lorraine slit open the next envelope marked private. 'I'm sorry there wasn't time to tell you before. He's back with us today, so what you need to do is just restore the *status quo* in your records.'

'I'll be delighted,' Judy said on the line.

'I knew you would be. We all are. And Judy, Donna Shapiro will be coming in this morning to sign up as my personal aide – you remember I told you about her?'

'Sure, Lorraine. I have all the details.'

'As soon as you're through with her, I want her to take some stuff down to the laboratory; it's urgent; then later today you can introduce her to the rest of the management; I know that everyone's going to like her as much as I do.'

In a moment she hung up and went across to the coffee percolator, pouring the first of the three cups she allowed herself during the morning. The muscles at the back of her thighs had stiffened up after her first workout at Sadie's *dojo* yesterday, and there was an almost pleasant ache in her hands, from fingers to wrists. 'I'm going to start you on one or two of the Tiger Claw techniques right away,' Sadie had told her, 'so you'll need to strengthen your hands, and don't worry, you won't be punching into sand-bins or anything. What you do is take a newspaper apart and work with a sheet at a time; hold a corner and slowly crumple the rest of it into a tight ball, okay? And keep a tennis ball around, giving it a good squeeze now and then. The newspaper trick is better than those fancy gadgets with springs, because you work your fingers and wrists a whole lot harder.'

But the fancy gadgets, Lorraine had discovered, probably had one advantage; she'd noticed black palm-prints on the ivory telephone in her bathroom – where these secret rites were performed – from the newsprint she'd been crumpling. There was another problem: the sudden appearance of balls of newspaper in the waste-baskets; it wouldn't always be possible to drop them into the kitchen garbage-chute without Tilly seeing. But she felt instinctively that Sadie – that was to say *Sensei* – was right about not telling people she'd started training in karate; on the one hand they'd be tempted to laugh about her doing something so outlandish; and on the other hand she was already learning that karate was a very personal kind of world, which you entered with a certain sense of modesty, even humility. 'I dunno if I can

255

explain it,' Sadie had told her, 'but you'll be drawing into your body, and your mind, a kind of energy, a kind of *force*, that's going to become valuable to you, an' maybe even one day save your life. So keep it to yourself. Nurture it, an' let it grow. I wouldn't say a thing like this to some of these jocks, because they wouldn't know what the hell I was talkin' about; but I'm telling *you*, because this is the way it's goin' to happen with you personally.'

Lorraine had expected practising at home would be something of a chore; but she was already finding a certain excitement in the ritual, and in the need to hide her new *gi* with its white belt at the back of the clothes closet where Tilly wouldn't easily discover it.

Stirring her first coffee of the day, Lorraine could also feel the lingering aftermath of her lovemaking with Dean – with *Dean Powers*, of all people . . . He'd stayed the whole night, and by the next day she was sore, exhausted, afloat in post-orgasmic euphoria, and bewildered.

'But I hated you, Dean. I really hated you.'

'It showed.'

They'd slept until noon, and Tilly had brought them breakfast for lunch, greeting Dean with well-trained lack of surprise.

'But I don't understand,' Lorraine told him. 'I should have slapped your face again and thrown you back into the rain, the moment you kissed me.'

'White man work powerful magic.'

'I've just realised, I don't think I've ever seen you smile at me. Not like this.'

'You weren't terribly encouraging, before.'

'But for God's sake, Dean, what's different?'

'We fucked all night.'

He was exasperating. 'But why did I *let* you?'

'You didn't. You wanted to. More coffee?'

'I did? Yes.'

He stood over her. 'Yes you did, or yes you want some more coffee?' He was similing his slow, dark-eyed smile again, and looking terribly attractive, she thought. He was also, she realised, talking sense.

'More coffee,' she nodded. She'd wanted to spend the night with him ever since she'd walked into the offices of Floderus Incorporated and remembered Dean Powers as just one of Daddy's colleagues, at the same time realising he was now, and very suddenly, one of her own. She remembered thinking of him as handsome, elegant, aloof and intelligent – not exactly the kind of man who turned her on; but in any case she'd known he was married, so any idea of sex with him was out. Then proximity had started to work, and she'd begun wondering what he'd be like in bed; but it was just fantasising; he was still married. Then she'd seen he was dating the girls from the typing pool, one after another; and *then* the jealousy had started, and the tension, so that he only had to come into her office to send her into instant rage. Oh God, those prim, school-marm lectures . . . *None of the other executives take employees to the Danish Buffet, because they're aware of the dictates of discipline and its value in keeping up our corporate public image . . .*

Had Dean known then, as he obviously knew now, what she'd really been trying to say? *If you want to cheat on your wife, don't do it with those adolescent little typists, do it with me . . .*

'Cream?' he asked her.

'What? No.' She studied him in the noonday light from the windows, realising how different he looked from that arrogant, well-tailored vice president who'd been the bane of her existence at the office; it wasn't just that he looked relaxed in the borrowed guest-robe, his dark hair still tousled and his smile coming easily; some of the difference in him was in her own eyes. She didn't hate him anymore.

He was watching her, his eyes contemplative.

'Dean,' she asked him, 'did you hate me too?'

'We don't need to go into all that.' He was looking very serious now. 'You did a lot of things wrong with the company, and instead of trying to understand why, I just showed contempt, which didn't help. There was also – ' he looked down for a moment – 'an awful lot of sexual tension

257

building up, because of the way you look, and the way you walk, and the way you are: and this made it tough for me, and for you too. I had absolutely no respect for you, but I wanted to jump straight into bed with you every time we met. So something had to bust, and it did, in the board-room.' He looked up at her again, with a rueful smile. 'Life's pretty simple when you work it out.'

'You're a very honest man, Dean.'

'I have my good points too.'

When they were helping each other to the coarse-cut Oxford marmalade, Lorraine asked him, 'And what about Miranda?'

'Who?'

'Your wife.'

'Armanda.'

'Sorry. I only met her once. She seemed a very lovely person.'

'She was. Still is, I imagine. And I don't want to talk about her.'

'Do you still love her?'

'Lorraine, I just said . . .'

She touched his hand, but he drew it away. 'I didn't know till a couple of weeks ago about the divorce Dean; but I happen to know what it does to people. I'd just like to help, by listening.'

His lean face was tensed now. 'You weren't listening, in the boardroom?'

'Yes, Dean.' She remembered what he'd said, almost word for word. *When you came along and put us all on the skids I had to spend so much of my life working overtime that it finally cost me my marriage. And it was a good one. Ten beautiful years. And you did a lot towards breaking it up for me.* But it hadn't gotten through to her then, because the other thing he'd said had hurt so cruelly – that she'd thrown away all her father had worked for. Now the revelation he'd made about his marriage came back to her, with the ease that memory has of recapturing time past. And with it came the guilt. She tried again. 'You said it was my fault. I'd like to think you'll go back to her, that's all.'

'Your guilt feelings are your own affair.'

'You know the score, don't you . . .'

'It's the only way to keep track of the game.'

The mood had changed dramatically from the warmth of new-found friendship to the old reserve and distrust; she'd made a mistake again, by bringing his marriage into the conversation; she'd been so anxious to make amends that she didn't stop to think that the very last subject you should bring up after a passionate night in bed was a divorce.

'I shouldn't have mentioned it, Dean.'

'Right.'

He was unyielding, even unforgiving. But Lorraine remembered what Donna Shapiro had told her when they'd talked half the night in the Café St Cloud, after she'd shown her around the office. Lorraine had mentioned Dean Powers, and the traumatic scene in the boardroom. 'Have you seen much of your own ex-husband, Lorraine?' Donna had asked her.

'No.'

'Then you may not know what it does to them. On the airlines, you get a lot of people opening up to you, especially on the long night hauls; you're a stranger, and neutral, and they know you won't pass anything on. With women, divorce mostly means heartbreak, a sense of desolation, that kind of thing – it's the heart that's involved. With men, when they're the one to be rejected, it's the ego, and it goes right into super-shock; they're an instant marital-disaster victim, bleeding profusely from their self-esteem. They're so humiliated by the rejection they can't even talk about it. Some of them run to a shrink. Some start drinking. Some go into sport-screwing, and they'll take on anything that moves. Some go straight into impotence: if they think it's all they have for a woman and she rejects it by divorce, it just folds up. But all of them are fazed in one way or another, and so touchy it's like trying to mend a fuse with the power still on, when you try and help them. I know I've done it.'

Lorraine had reflected, some time in the night when Dean

had slept for a while, that she probably couldn't have gone to face him in the bar, hating him as she did, if it hadn't been for Donna's observations. They'd given her understanding.

Even now, she was able to feel that the man having breakfast with her wasn't, maybe, so unyielding or unforgiving as he seemed; he was just a blown fuse with the power still on.

So she changed the subject completely.

'What time's your plane?'

He looked up. 'My what?'

'You're flying to the Bahamas, remember? To lie on the beach with all those gorgeous girls.'

He said nothing for a moment, but went on stirring his coffee, his dark eyes brooding. Then he said quietly, 'If you still think I can help out, at the office, maybe I'll show up there on Monday.'

Lorraine took a slow breath. 'So we weren't just – ' she shrugged.

'Just what?'

'Fucking all night.'

He considered this. 'Did you think that was all it was about?'

His expression was so serious that she had to smile – could *afford* to smile now there was the hope of Dean's coming back. 'There wasn't much time to think it was about anything else, was there?'

His face relaxed. 'I guess we kept pretty busy.'

'So what changed your mind?'

He considered again. 'There's absolutely no question, Lorraine, that you should sell your company, and right now, while you can still hope for a half-decent price. But the message I was getting last night in the bar was that you don't intend to do that. Period. So if you're going to be crazy enough to try lifting that whole damn building off the ground single-handed, you'll need all the help you can get.'

Then the phone was ringing, and her mind flew back from its reveries. She took her cup of coffee across to the desk.

'Will you take a call from Mr Blatt?' Nadine's voice came on the line.

'Yes.'

The line clicked. 'Lorraine? Somebody told me Dean Powers was back.'

'That's right, Carl. He is.'

There came a pause. 'Did you go ask him?'

'Yes.'

Another pause, while she pictured Carl blinking solemnly behind his steel-rimmed spectacles. 'That took an awful lot of doing,' he said.

'Yes, it did.''

'Well, congratulations. It's great news.'

'Thank you.'

The peacock-blue Rolls-Royce slipped quietly through the Lincoln Tunnel and entered New Jersey along Interstate 495, with Donna Shapiro at the wheel.

'Take the Rolls,' Lorraine and told her, 'and see what you think of it.'

'Oh, sure,' Donna had said, like it was routine. On her first day at work she was having to adjust to the new job, and not finding it easy. The whole 20th floor of the building, which was occupied by Floderus Incorporated, had seemed galvanised by something: phones ringing, doors opening and closing, the lift spilling people out and sucking them back in. 'Is it always like this?' she'd asked Judy Pollack, the sharp little personnel chief in the glass office; but Judy, with a phone at each ear, had only time for a bright smile – 'Don't let it worry you, Donna; it's probably just a bomb scare.'

And Lorraine herself had been so different this morning; a week ago Donna had got out of the lift and found her standing alone in the deserted offices, 'communing with ghosts,' as Lorraine had told her ruefully; but an hour ago she'd found it difficult to get near her new boss, and when she finally made the sacrosanct corner office she was in there only three minutes.

'Donna,' the famous, flashing smile came, dazzling her, 'I

261

can't tell you how happy I am you decided to join us. Right now everything's happening at once, and I can't even take you around to introduce you – but we'll do it later today.' She'd handed Donna a worn black briefcase. 'This has to go right away to our laboratory in Jersey City, and I'm not just using you as a delivery-boy; the material in here is top secret, and I don't want you to let it out of your sight.' Further instructions followed; she was to hand it personally to Elliot Dietrich, the perfumer at the laboratory, and introduce herself as Lorraine's personal aide; if Elliot had enough time, he'd show her around the place: she'd find it fascinating. Lorraine would put a call through to Jersey City and inform them that Donna was coming.

The briefcase was on the rich leather seat beside her, and despite her experience in one of the most responsible jobs in the world, she felt almost afraid the briefcase would suddenly fly out of the window of its own accord. Top secret? She'd heard about industrial espionage. A top secret perfume, not yet on the market? Wow!

She grabbed the black-and-gold telephone and dialled, turning the big car south along the Hudson.

'Mom, is that you?'

'Donna?'

'Right. You okay?'

'Sure I'm okay.' Mom's voice was wary; she still didn't think Donna should have quit that very good job with the airline. 'Where are you?'

'Give you two guesses, Mom.'

'Well I suppose you must be at the office.'

'Wrong.'

'Look, Donna, how should I know where you are?'

'Right – you shouldn't. I'm driving a brand-new Rolls-Royce convertible alongside the Hudson River.'

'A Rolls-Royce?' Mom sounded worried, and Donna gave a little gurgling laugh to herself. It couldn't be decent, surely, for an honest working girl to be driving a car like that . . .

'Nothing to it, Mom, you can pick 'em up anywhere for

just a hundred and thirty thousand bucks.'

'Oh, my God . . .'

Donna laughed again, taking the car smoothly away from the traffic lights. 'Just thought I'd call you, Mom. I got myself a real good job, so don't worry. And twice the pay, remember?'

She said goodbye and hung up, luxuriating in the look and the feel and the rich-leather smell of this incredible automobile with its burred walnut pannelling, its discreet black and gold instrument arrays, the sensitivity of the controls as she took a curve in the road, braked lightly for a slower vehicle and then accelerated past it with a surge of latent power.

Maybe she wouldn't get to be a delivery-boy every day in this job, but she was already enjoying the idea of working alongside a famous film actress who'd revealed herself the other night as a real person, with her self-doubts and her determination to save the company, and with her readiness to trust a complete stranger with her intimate hopes and fears. The airline had been a great experience, sure: good pay, lots of travel, meeting people, a uniform that rated respect from everyone; but what had she actually been doing with her life? What did she do when she'd shepherded a bunch of passengers from Kennedy to LA? She shepherded another bunch from LA to Kennedy. And then she did it again. Just what kind of work Lorraine Floderus had for her, she didn't know. There'd been a few changes, Judy Pollack had mentioned, in the past week. Lorraine's previous secretary, Maggie someone, had been given the golden handshake after long and faithful service, and Nadine Keller, the pale, cool, rather unsmiling girl in the beautifully-cut two-piece suit, had taken over in her place. And the tall guy with the brooding looks – Dean Powers, the 'blown fuse' they'd talked about the other night – had apparently returned to his job, which seemed to explain the rush of activity in the building this morning.

Thinking it over as she drove south alongside the river, Donna suspected she'd gotten herself hired not to do any specific job, but to soldier along with Lorraine in the fight to save her company; and that was okay; she'd soldier with a gal like that, however tough things got. There was a *rapport* between them that Lorraine had seemed to sense the first time they'd met on that flight from LA, and that Donna herself was just beginning to understand. She was trusted, totally, even on her first day at work. Take the Rolls, sure. And take this stuff, it's top secret. And Donna knew enough about herself to be quite certain that Lorraine was instinctively right: her trust would never be abused.

Everything about the day was therefore perfect, and as she took the Rolls smoothly alongside a park across from the river, she delighted in the wash of the bare branches past the windshield, and the sound of children playing that came through the open window; and a moment later – as sometimes happens when life seems at its smoothest – she saw the little kid in the red pullover balanced daringly on a rail of the bridge over the water; and saw him fall.

CHAPTER 22

'Look, I'm okay now, really.'

'We'd just like to take your blood-pressure again.' The nurse gave a winning smile and eased Donna's bare arm out of the blanket, wrapping the cuff around and slipping the stethoscope on. 'You want some more of that soup, honey?'

'No thanks. Did they get my stuff?'

'I can't hear you with this thing on. Hold it a minute.'

'Jeeze,' Donna said to no one. They'd already kept her here almost an hour, getting her circulation going again. They'd done a good job and the soup had been terrific but she wasn't going to sit here in a goddamned blanket forever; she had a mission to do. The briefcase was right beside her. One of the cops had driven the Rolls here while she rode in the ambulance with the kid; but she'd grabbed that briefcase out of the car before she let them pull her wet clothes off and wrap her in the blanket.

'You're okay, honey,' the young nurse said, and took the cuff off her arm.

'You bet your sweet ass I'm okay. Now I want to get out of here. How long are they –' then the girl came in with a brown paper bag and took out a box of panty-hose and a white sweater and pale blue jeans and some sneakers.

'Will they do?' she asked Donna.

'We'll have to see.' She pulled off the warm blanket.

'Try them on.'

'Thanks.' The clothes fitted fine, provided she left the laces of the sneakers loose. 'How's the kid now?'

'He'll be okay,' the older nurse said. 'Right now he's a bit

265

miserable – he really had a *lot* of water in him – but he's fully conscious and getting his colour back.' She gave Donna a look of admiration. 'I guess he was pretty lucky.'

'I guess.' She'd hit the brakes the minute she saw him go off the rail, making a white splash. Then she was out of the car and dragging her shoes off before she ran flat out and put her palms together and hit the water cleanly; the kid was thrashing around and the others up on the birdge were yelling their heads off and then she didn't hear anything more because she was too busy to listen; and it was only when she'd got the kid to the bank and there were hands grabbing him that she realised how *cold, cold, cold* that water was, chilling her through to the bone. A guy was handling the kid pretty expertly, pumping a lot of water out of him and checking his pulse and respiration – Donna had called out to him was he a paramedic and he'd said yes, and he sure looked like it; by the time the ambulance came the kid – his name was Joey, one of his friends said – was trying to stand up on his own; but he was blue with cold and shivering dreadfully.

The traffic was all snarled up because she'd just left the Rolls in the roadway, and that had brought the cops on the scene. The one that drove the Rolls to the hospital took her name and address and asked how it had happened; then he went off to sit with the kid till he could talk; the last Donna had seen of Joey he wasn't blue anymore but a deathly, translucent white as the delayed shock set in; she'd pulled people out of the water before and she knew the signs.

'You look cute in those,' the nurse said as she stood up in the new togs.

'Thanks.' She took the briefcase and her bag from the younger girl, and went out to the main desk to pay for the treatment.

'It's on the house,' the woman behind the desk told her.
'It is?'
'We don't see as you should pay for what you did. You feeling okay now?'
'Sure. Can I see the kid on my way out?'

'I'll call through.'

Donna found Joey in the intensive care unit hooked up to a saline drip and a bottle of glucose. He looked up at her with enormous olive-black eyes.

'How're you doing, Joey?'

He went on watching her for a moment. 'I'm fine.' He had the light voice of a five-year-old. 'Are you the lady that saved me?'

'I guess.'

'I could'a been drowned, in there, couldn't I? They said.'

'Not really. Could've shrunk a bit, maybe. It's time you learned to swim, Joey. Don't let this bother you any. You start in on some swimming lessons, okay? It's a whole lot of fun.'

'I could'a been drowned.' It was all he could think about right now; his huge glistening eyes never left her face.

'Well just don't try it again, that's all. You learn to swim like a fish, before you go climbing around bridges.' She cupped his thin dark face in her hand; he felt like a little corpse, and for the first time she realised that, yes, he could have stayed in that water just a minute too long, and not be here; a shiver of fright shook her: she might not have been there herself, or seen him fall. 'You take care, Joey. It was real nice knowing you, even though we got a little wet.'

He went on watching her, his eyes wide and intent.

'You wanna be my Mom?'

'Uh, your Mom? You don't have one, Joey?'

'I had one, but she died.'

'Oh. You have a Dad, though?'

'Yeah. He's on his way to see me. They called him.'

'Okay. Well, one day he might find you another Mom. That happens a lot.'

'Okay.'

'Take care, Joey.'

She left him quickly, before that intense young gaze of his could hold her too long, and make her worry too much about his need of her in his life, his need of any woman to fill the emptiness.

267

'There she is right now,' she heard someone say as she went through the lobby to the doors.

'This is the lady?'

'Yes.'

The man was standing between Donna and the big glass doors, and as she stopped he stared into her eyes for a long moment and then put his arms around her, and laid his cheek against hers while she wondered what in hell was – oh, sure; this was Joey's father. So she just let him hold her, his cologne heavy on the hair, his slight stubble pricking her cheek, until she felt his tears itching on her skin, and the trembling along his arms as they held her so tightly that she found it hard to breathe. Then he released her, and pulled out a folded white handkerchief and solemnly dabbed her cheek, and then his own, his dark olive eyes – so very like Joey's – smiling through the last of his tears.

'I embarrass you,' he said, his voice unsteady. He was a small man, neat, narrow-shouldered in a well-cut suit, his hair greying at the temples.

'That's okay,' Donna smiled quickly. 'He's fine now, good as new.'

'I know. They tell me.' His gaze had the same shadowed intensity as little Joey's.

'You'd better go see him,' she said, and turned to leave.

'Wait. Please.' She stopped again. 'What is your name?'

'Donna.'

'Donna.' He nodded, as if listening to a note of music. 'You save my son for me.' He was trying to smile, but the tears were threatening to take over. 'He is still here in the world.' His arms were spread out, trying to help him explain. 'He is still . . . around. My son Joey.'

Donna nodded quickly, wanting to get out of here and push on with her mission; but she didn't like to leave the poor guy just standing here trying to thank her. 'Sure,' she told him, 'he's still around, and waiting to see you. You just go on up and –'

'Donna,' he said, reaching for his wallet. 'Here is my card. Take it, please. Keep it.' He was steadier now, and his eyes had something almost like authority in them. 'When you need anything, Donna, you will tell me. Whatever it is. You will call me. Whatever you wish us to do for you, we will do it. Do you understand?'

'Uh, sure.' She looked at the elegantly embossed card. *Aldo Vinicari. Italia Import-Export.* 'Okay, Mr Vinicari. I need anything, I'll call you. Right?'

'Yes. Always remember, you have a friend.' He took her hand and squeezed it gently, then turned away toward the lifts.

Donna went through the big swing doors with the plastic bag of wet clothes and the briefcase. On her way across the car park she looked again at Aldo Vinicari's card, then dropped it into a litter bin and got into the Rolls.

'Okay,' Dean Powers said. 'We'll give it the good old college try.'

Joe Fisher shook his head. 'No. We succeed.'

'Well, sure. We can't do that without trying.'

'No, Dean,' Joe said. Everyone in the room was listening carefully: Lorraine, Sy Goldman, Carl Blatt, Donna. 'What we want you to know is that we are going to make *Siren Song* a five-star, all-time spectacular. We're not setting out just to try. There's a difference, Dean; there's a different kind of chemistry, right down at the cell level.'

Dean considered this, then shrugged. 'Okay. We're going out to win. Okay.' He tried not to sound like he was speaking to a child, Donna noted, but didn't succeed.

Donna was sitting at the far end of the long calf-hide settee and listening to everything intently. Back in Manhattan from New Jersey by lunch time, she had dropped off her wet clothes at a cleaner's and changed into a trim tunic and skirt before reporting back to work. Nadine Keller had told her she was wanted immediately in the chairman's office to sit in at a meeting. Donna had told nobody what had happened this morning; she felt a bit guilty at letting them keep her at the hospital so long in the company's time.

'Dean Powers left us, as you know,' Lorraine had briefed

269

her before the others came in, 'but I persuaded him to come back. This meeting is really to let him know he's welcome, to outline our plans for the new fragrance, and get his views and hopefully his support.'

So Donna was listening intently, getting her first impressions of Sy Goldman, Carl Blatt, Joe Fisher and the brooding, intelligent Dean Powers. She was also getting further impressions of Lorraine Floderus in her capacity of chairman; and what was coming through very strongly was that Lorraine seemed technically not much more than a figurehead, but spiritually the inspiration and lodestar and common-or-garden household glue that was holding this company together. And finally, Donna was inevitably picking up on the rarified wavelengths of glances, body-language and calculated silences that told her things about the relationships here: and one in particular. They all of them suspected that Lorraine and Dean Powers had not only patched up their differences; they'd done it in bed.

But then, Donna mused, it was hard to think of Dean Powers doing anything at all except in bed. Despite his donnish air and his executive spectacles and conservative tailoring, he wore an aura of sexual attraction that would peel the paint off the walls if he stood too close.

'I think we're agreed,' he was saying now, 'that this whole project depends on the Nose.'

'Right.' Joe Fisher.

'On all of us,' Sy Goldman nodded heavily, 'but especially on Elliot Dietrich.' He turned briefly to Donna. 'You met him, I believe?'

'Yes.'

Sy gave an avuncular smile. 'I hope you treated him like royalty.'

'Well, I –'

Sy dismissed it with a wave of his plump hand. 'He's our key man for the project. I'm sure he found you enchanting.'

Thinking back, Donna could only remember a little man with a grey face in a white linen coat covered in what looked like gravy stains. He'd taken the briefcase from her, glanced

270

at the typed sheets, tucked them into his coat, asked if she'd like a cup of tea, and then wandered vaguely back into his laboratory like a hamster going back into its box.

'Do you think,' Joe Fisher asked nobody in particular, 'he has enough essences down there at the lab, for the new fragrance?'

'I'm not interested,' Lorraine told him, 'whether he has or not. This one is for Jacques Farrier.' She looked around.

'No question,' Joe said, and sank onto the floor in a full lotus posture.

Sy spread his hands out. 'He's so terribly expensive.'

Carl Blatt blinked at him. 'We're making a terribly expensive creation. That sow's ear thing doesn't actually work out in practice, you know.'

Lorraine turned her head. 'Dean?'

He looked up and their eyes met, and Donna caught the instant and knew the others were right. 'I think,' he said, looking away to a window, 'we should at least ask what Farrier has, and what's his price.'

'Okay,' Lorraine nodded. One of Dean's strengths was his ability to compromise without seeming to give ground. 'I'll fly to the Riviera tomorrow.'

Soon after three o'clock, when Donna was coming away from the meeting, Judy Pollack stopped her in the corridor. 'There's some flowers come for you, Donna.'

'For me? Where are they?'

'In the reception lobby.' She took Donna along there without saying another word. The reception desk seemed to have entirely disappeared behind the six-foot-high arrangement that dominated the middle of the room, a softly-burning fire of colour in a huge gilded basket.

'For God's sake . . .' Donna said.

'Your first day on the job,' Judy told her in an awed tone, 'you get a thousand bucks' worth of orchids. I mean, who can complain?'

Donna looked at the card inside the little gold envelope. *To Donna. Thank you. From Joey.*

271

'You ever get tired of your boy friend,' she heard Judy saying, 'you'll let me know, won't you? I mean immediately.'

Donna laughed as she slipped the card into a pocket of her tunic. 'I doubt if you'd be interested, Judy. He's just five years old.' *Pink Flamingo*, the name tag read, *from Brazil*. They were exquisite, and there must be at least a hundred crowded stems.

'He's just five years old,' Judy nodded, determined to stay on top of the situation. 'So I'll wait around a little. In fact I'll wait around a *lot*.'

Other people were stopping short as they came and went from the lifts, gathering around the immense arrangement and gazing at the blooms in delight, like people gathered around a fire. At first Donna had thought how ostentatious this was, a monument to extravagant bad taste; but she too became caught up in their overwhelming beauty.

'Are they for Lorraine?' someone asked.

'Nope,' Judy said. 'They are for my little friend here.' She wished to be associated immediately with the recipient of the entire annual production of an orchid farm.

Donna was looking embarrassed now. 'Judy, what on earth will we do with them?'

'We could build a few nests, I guess.'

The reception room was filling up with people.

'Oh, how simply glorious!'

'But I never *saw* such . . .'

'Is it somebody's birthday?'

'Right,' Judy nodded, 'and she's a hundred and fifty today. Count 'em.'

Donna was wondering how Mr Aldo Vinicari had found out where she worked. The secretary at the hospital desk had been given a copy of the police report, where Donna had been asked to state her place of employment; so maybe he'd asked to look at it; or maybe Mr Aldo Vinicari was the kind of man to find out whatever he wanted, if it interested him enough.

'If we stood them nearer the wall,' she told Judy quietly,

272

'would they be in the way?'

'You don't want to take them home? I'd get you a doggie truck.'

'Of course not. I'd like them to stay here, where people can see them. But don't tell anyone they were for me.'

'Okay,' Judy said with her eyes wide. 'I'll tell 'em they were for me. Okay?'

Lorraine got home later than usual, around seven o'clock.

'You did not have a good day?' Tilly wanted to know at once.

'Days vary, Tilly.' She forced a smile. 'I hope yours was better.'

During the afternoon she had felt an increasing hope for the future growing inside her; there was still the sinister shadow of Frederick Vanderkloot in the background, but there'd been no telephone call from him as yet, and maybe he'd changed his mind; even a man like that must have a sense of shame. What had made the day so promising was of course Dean's reaction to their plans for *Siren Song*. 'I think you're all crazy. You don't know the size of what you're taking on. But if you did know, I don't believe it would change your minds. That's why I'm going to stay with it.'

Lorraine went straight to the telphone in the living room, as she always did when she came home from the office, and dialled the Lotus Club.

'May I speak to Madlen Floderus, please?'

'Just a minute.' Then the same voice came again. 'I'm sorry, she just stepped out. Can I take a message?'

'Yes. Tell her Lorraine called.' She lowered the phone, and in the wall mirror saw Tilly leaving the room; she always stayed, in case Madlen came on the line. Tilly knew what it would mean to her. Lorraine didn't know the girl at the Lotus Club switchboard, but she was someone with consideration, never failing to ring the changes on the reason why Madlen couldn't come to the phone: *She just stepped out. . . She's not in the building right now . . . I don't get an answer, so I guess she's not there . . . I'm sorry, will*

273

you try again later? She was simply following the instructions, Lorraine knew. Madlen had said if her sister called, she didn't want to talk to her.

But Lorraine never failed to make the attempt. 'Your sister is playing a game with you,' Dr Fischer had told her a couple of days ago when she'd called him in desperation, 'but you have to take it seriously, because it's a serious game, and if Madlen loses, she's going to lose her will to go on, and that's what we have to avoid at all costs. Every time she refused to come to the phone, she wins again; but if you stopped calling her, she'd start losing. Am I making some sort of sense?' Lorraine saw in her mind the pale narrow face of the expert on the human mind, his tired eyes squinting through the cigarette smoke, his stained fingers gripping the phone. 'Madlen has a tremendous need of you, of your concern, of your love for her; that's why you have to call her, and try to see her, and by those means reassure her. At the same time, she has to develop her new sense of independence, just as you've been having to do since you lost your parents – especially your father. This is what Madlen is doing when she refuses to come to the phone: she's winning a little more independence, and building up her new identity. As I told you before at the hospital, you have to be patient with her, and never give up. In time, you'll make it; but it won't happen tomorow.'

Lorraine had needed to think over what Dr Fischer had told her, when this afternoon she'd had the call from Paul Hennessey, the manager of New York State, and gone to see him after she'd left the office. The Floderus family had banked there since Wilhelm had first opened an account with a hundred dollars, long before the present manager's time; but Paul Hennessey had known the family for seven years, and this afternoon had taken Lorraine into his office and closed the door and told his staff he didn't want any calls.

Greying head on one side, tinted glasses covering his eyes with shadow, long, sensitive fingers playing endlessly with a gold pencil, he had told her: 'I want to talk to you about your

274

sister. In doing so, I'll be discussing the account of another client, for which I could be fired and even sued. I want you to respect the risk I'm taking, and protect me. Any information I give you now must never be passed on as having come from me.'

He had talked for minutes on end before Lorraine had interrupted. 'I know that you don't see much of Madlen these days, which is why I feel I must tell you about what she's doing, out of loyalty to you both. She's spending a great deal of money, Lorraine. I mean apart from the "investment" of a million dollars in the club. She's not spending it on anything worth while – not even luxuries like clothes, cars, jewelry, things of a certain value that could be redeemed.' He glanced down at the papers on his desk. 'She's spending it on frivolous things, parties, extravagant gifts, cases of champagne, cigars, caviar, for people she hardly knows. A recent wing-ding at the club where she's staying cost her seventeen thousand dollars, for instance. And it's going on; I see the figures on her account every day, because I ask for them.' He slipped the papers into a folder and into his desk. 'She's in a vortex, Lorraine, spinning faster and faster, financially. And even a sum like five million dollars won't last for long if it's used like this. It's already only four, as you know, and still going down. I fear for her, and I fear for you, because I know that once she's ruined herself, you'll have to take over the burden.'

'There's no way,' Lorraine had asked him, 'you can . . . freeze the account? On some pretext?'

'No way.'

'Have you asked her to see you?'

'Yes. She wasn't interested.'

'There's *nothing* you can do?'

'Nothing. If anyone can do anything, it's of course yourself. That's why I had to tell you what was going on. God help me,' he'd said with a rueful smile, 'if she ever finds out . . .'

No, Tilly, she thought as she poured herself a glass of chilled Tio Pepe, I didn't have a very good day.

But after showering and putting on fresh make-up and slipping into a wild-silk kaftan from Tadashi, she felt a little more hopeful. Dean Powers was back at work, and tomorrow she'd take the first definite step in the creation of *Siren Song*, by going to see Jacques Farrier in France and asking him to unlock just a few of the myriad secrets of his perfumery. And if she went on playing this mad, dangerous game with Madlen, which she must lose and go on losing in order to win, she would at last see her restored to the charming, intelligent and affectionate young sister she had known before.

Sitting alone at the table, she felt it was a shame not to share this exquisite *Canard à l'orange* that Tilly had cooked for her; she ought to have called Dean Powers to see if he wanted to join her; but on second thoughts it might have been difficult to persuade him to leave, afterwards. Not that she hadn't enjoyed that one torrid night with him – in fact she was aware of a pleasant tingling in her blood at the memory – but she didn't want him to feel she was so freely available as a convenient lay, among all the other lays who were expected to help him forget the pain of his divorce.

'You would like some coffee, Miss Lorraine?'

'Please Tilly. But not too strong.' She had so many things on her mind these days that if she woke in the night she'd go over them all in circles to the point of exhaustion.

She would have, in any case, only another half-hour of peace this evening, though she was unaware of it. She was looking through the brochures she'd pulled from file this afternoon, detailing the operations of La Parfumerie Farrier de Grasse, when the phone call came. She took it herself.

'Yes?'

'My dear Lorraine . . . I hope you are well.' She recognised the suave, resonant tone immediately, and felt the blood leaving her face. This was the call she'd dreaded so much that she'd tried to believe it would never come. Desperate for time in which to think, she asked: 'Who is that?'

'Frederick Vanderkloot. I told you to call me, if you remember.'

Her stomach was turning to acid as the memory of him came flooding back. 'Frederick, I . . . I have nothing to say to you. Nothing at all.'

There was a pause. Heart hammering, she waited for his reply, feeling that despite what this man was, it would be discourteous to simply hang up.

'You remember,' the tone was now softly menacing, 'I offered you a choice, Lorraine. You, or your company.'

She closed her eyes, feeling nausea; at some time she must have hung up, but the next thing she knew she was in the nearest bathroom, slamming the door just in time, not wanting Tilly to hear her convulsions as the fear and disgust reached her stomach with the impact of an emetic.

Dean Powers answered his phone almost right away, half an hour later. 'Hello?'

'Dean?'

'Yes.'

'This is Lorraine.' The fumes from the brandy rose on the air from the glass in front of her as she stared through the film of curtains to the city's lights. 'Dean, can I see you?'

'Tonight?' He sounded surprised.

'I – I don't mean . . . There's something important come up, to do with the company. I don't think we have a chance, after all.'

CHAPTER 23

PARIS, 4.05 pm LOCAL TIME. Outside temperature 67 degrees Fahrenheit, a light drizzle falling.

The Air France Concorde nosed its way through the big-jet traffic to its own private arrival and departure lounge, its shape in the lowering light like a great swan's, its heat baffles only just beginning to cool from the friction of its thousand-mile-per-hour trajectory across the Atlantic, ten miles high.

Through the small windows along the narrow, cigar-shaped cabin, the sky had been a dark indigo. 'It's just that we're at the edge of the stratosphere,' the flight attendant had told a passenger, 'there's not much air left for the light to reflect.'

Inside the Concorde lounge, a flow of movement as the passengers came through: furs, pearls, Savile Row suits, a pop star in designer jeans, a black world athlete in a stream-lined track suit, the glint of gold watches and diamond rings, the flash of cameras. Among them Lorraine, catching the eye in a Regina Porter linen dress with a swirl of black and white spiral stripes, no jewelry, nothing to distract.

Incredible, of course, that she was here at all.

Dean had come over right away last night, to pour himself an immediate bourbon on the rocks before he turned and faced her.

'So what's happened?'

She hadn't meant to tell him – or anyone at all – about her evening with Frederick Vanderkloot; it would be humiliating. But she had to tell Dean Powers now.

'Century Cosmetics is gunning for us.'

278

Dean frowned. 'Friendly suitor or black knight?'

'It's an odd way of putting it,' Lorraine said bitterly.

'I mean is it a friendly approach, or a hostile –'

'I know the parlance; it's just that he began as a friendly suitor, but –'

'He?'

'Frederick Vanderkloot.'

'You've heard from him?'

'Not officially. I would have been bound to tell you. It was unofficial. I had dinner with him, last week.' The saliva was gathering in her mouth as she remembered those last few minutes of their meeting, his short, immaculately dressed figure crouched over its animal abandonment as his libido lost control.

Dean was watching her steadily, forgetting the drink in his hand. 'I can't imagine why Century should want to take over your company, at this stage anyway. You mean this is a personal caprice of Vanderkloot's?' The cosmetic tycoon's whims were well known throughout Wall Street.

'Yes,' Lorraine said.

Dean was still puzzled. 'Did he give a reason?'

'Yes.' She turned away from him so that he couldn't see her face. 'He wants me, Dean. And if he can't have me, he wants my company.

Dean stared at her. 'Jesus Christ . . .' he said very low.

'He told me I must call him, with my decision. When I didn't, he called me. Half an hour ago.'

'What did he say, exactly?'

She swung around to face him now. 'Word for word? You want me to humiliate myself by telling you –'

'No.' His one strong word cut her short. 'I just have to know the facts, or I can't help you.'

She slumped suddenly. 'I'm sorry, Dean. Yes, of course you have to know the –' Then the tears came, and as she closed her eyes she felt his arms around her, enclosing her gently as he stroked her hair; and she was half-aware how strange this was, and how welcome; during all her struggles and her bouts of despair since her divorce from Bruce, she'd

279

missed the comfort of a man's strong arms around her.

She opened her eyes and stood back from him. 'I needed that, so much.'

He looked embarrassed. 'We all need someone,' he shrugged, 'sometimes.'

'Yes.'

He picked up his drink again. 'Vanderkloot could take Floderus easily, like a toad with a fly. You know that.'

'Yes. I know it.'

'If he wanted it badly enough, he'd simply make an offer the shareholders couldn't refuse. And there's nothing we can do about it, Lorraine,'

'I – I imagine not.' So this was it. Dean Powers, who knew the corporate world inside out, knew also that they hadn't a chance; it was just like she'd told him on the phone, and now he'd confirmed it.

'I mean,' he said, trapped and angry, 'he's just got to pick up a phone. You know?'

'Yes.' She remembered the figures from Century's last annual report. Net sales: two and a half *billion* dollars. Against her own company's fifty million. Yes, a toad with a fly. And even Dean Powers was helpless to do anything about it. Watching him as he went across to the bar and poured himself another drink, dropping the ice cubes into the glass and reaching for the bourbon with slow, studied movements, Lorraine could almost feel the smouldering frustration that must be filling his mind; she was watching a strong man defeated, yet his helplessness didn't diminish him; it made him seem more human, more reachable.

'Dean,' she asked him wretchedly, 'will you tell the others? Carl, and the others?' They'd have to know why the project for *Siren Song* was finished before it had really begun. 'I don't want to tell them myself.'

'What?' He swung around, his thoughts focusing. 'Tell the others? Sure. I'll tell them we're going to fight that bastard, every inch of the way.'

'For God's sake, how?'

'I don't know. But we're going to do it.'

280

He'd left her soon afterwards, saying she must get a good night's sleep before her trip tomorrow; and in the morning he'd driven her to the airport himself, seeing her onto the plane. The last thing he'd said to her was, 'Get him right out of your mind. I'll do the rest. *Bon voyage!*'

She'd been astonished to find this new aspect of his personality: high courage; she'd never seen him in a situation where he'd been tested before; he'd seemed no more than a restless, over-virile male brooding most of the time about his divorce, but now she saw something of a real man coming through, gentle with her last night when she'd needed comfort, and reassuring this morning when he'd seen her aboard the plane.

But . . . fight a man like Vanderkloot?

'*Ma'mselle Floderus, s'il vous plaît?*'

Lorraine turned as the uniformed attendant approached. '*Oui, c'est moi.*'

'*Il y a un message pour vous, ma'mselle.*'

'*Merci.*'

She opened the little blue envelope. *Please call me. Dean.*

In spite of the new-found strength his support in the last few days had given her, she felt a sudden leap of anxiety; it had become a habit with her for quite a while now: the sound of a telephone, the look of an unfamiliar envelope among her mail would fill her with foreboding. She made her way through the throng to the phone booths, only two of which were vacant.

The call went through almost immediately.

'One moment, please, Miss Floderus.' Then Dean came on the line. 'How was the flight?'

'Perfect.' But she knew he hadn't called to ask her about that.

'What's the weather like in Paris?'

She heard his voice echoing over the satellite circuit, like her own. 'Dean, what's happened?'

There was a short pause. 'We just received a letter of resignation from Elliot Dietrich.'

So she hadn't been wrong. This was bad news, almost the

281

worst she could think of. Elliot was one of the few – the very few – 'noses' in the American perfume industry, as indispensable as the master vintner to a winery.

In a moment she said: 'We can't win, can we?'

'I wondered if he'd given you any warning, Lorraine.'

'No. Not by a word.' Elliot, the brilliant, talented perfumer who kept to his laboratory with the devotion of a mother to a nursery, had seemed a part of Floderus Incorporated as integral as a cornerstone to a building. He was hardly ever seen in the offices in Manhattan, and at the last Christmas party he'd crept into a corner of the room and remained there, sipping Perrier water. Yet already Lorraine could understand this way of ending his relationship with the company; it seemed like a stab in the back, but it was just that he was so desperately inhibited that he couldn't face an actual confrontation, person to person. But that didn't explain his *reason*. 'Why is he quitting, Dean?'

'He's found what he calls a better position.' It was the traditional excuse for someone who looked like being fired anyway; but Elliot had no fear of that.

'You think that's true?' Lorraine asked.

After reflection he said, 'What he's probably saying is that the rate this company's been going downhill, almost any position would be better.' Lorraine was silent. 'I'm sorry, I didn't mean –'

'That's all right. It's a logical enough reason. But why so suddenly?'

She heard the shrug in Dean's voice. 'People get fired suddenly in this town, so maybe it's not unfair to quit suddenly.'

'Can you talk to him?'

'His letter ends, *Due to personal and other valid reasons, my decision is irrevocable, and I should prefer to avoid painful discussions.*'

Lorraine watched three small French boys going past the phone booths, dressed as sailors, with bright red pom-poms on their round white hats. How wonderful it would be, just

282

for a while, to be a child again, with no worries, no fears for the future . . . 'All right,' she told Dean at last. 'I'll call Jacques Farrier right away to tell him I'm not coming; then I'll get the next flight back.'

'If that's what you want to do.'

'No, Dean, it isn't. But –'

'Then don't do it.' But he didn't sound defiant, as he had last night; just weary.

'You know the score,' she told him. 'Without Elliot, we can't create the new fragrance. There are maybe three other perfumers in the whole of America with his kind of talent, and even if they were willing to join a company that's . . . going through a bad time . . . they'd ask a price we couldn't possibly afford. Am I right?'

'Absolutely right. I would like,' he said slowly, 'to take that stinking little creep to the top of the Empire State and drop him over the side.'

'You'd only get arrested, Dean, for cruelty to creeps.' She'd tried to make it sound amusing, and entirely failed. 'There's someone waiting for this phone, and I've got to call Farrier. I'll let you know which flight I'm coming back on. Okay?'

There was quite a long silence, while she listened to her echoing, *okay . . ?* Then Dean said: 'Lorraine, why don't you take a break, now you're over there? You've had your nose to the job for too long, and God knows this is a good time to get away from it. Spend a few days in Paris, see a few shows, eat a lot of that gorgeous *haute cuisine*. I'll hold the fort, don't worry.'

Miserably she said, 'I'm never much good at having fun on my own.'

'Then go down and see Farrier anyway; he'll give you a good time. Have you ever seen his operation?'

'His what?'

Dean's slow laughter came, and she wondered at his tremendous ability to take punishment and come up smiling. 'I don't mean his appendectomy scar . . . I mean his perfumerie.'

283

'Oh. No, I've never been there.'

'Then don't change your plans. Your flight leaves Paris in an hour, and you'll be on the Côte d'Azur in time for dinner. Just imagine – snails, frogs' legs – '

'How disgusting!' She managed a light laugh herself, and suddenly wished he were there with her, to share the delights of Paris and the Mediterranean and forget for a few days that the company was now in its death throes. 'Dean . . .'

'Yes?'

'Nothing.' It would be impossible for him to leave the office, at this of all times, and join her here. And their pleasure would be forced, and calculated – and shared every minute with the dark shadows of Vanderkloot and Elliot Dietrich. 'All right,' she told him, 'I'll go and see Farrier, just as arranged.'

'It'll be a good experience for you.'

'Yes.'

Then their talking just petered out as they tried to cheer each other up with bright goodbyes, and Lorraine hung up and apologised to the chic Parisienne who was waiting impatiently for the telephone.

L'Aeroport Nice-Côte d'Azur, 7.14 pm, outside temperature a balmy 70 degrees Fahrenheit under clear skies, with the moon's ivory rim breaking the dark velvet foothills of the Alpes Maritimes and flooding them with saffron light, as Air France Flight 204 lowered its wings across Cap Ferrat and settled into its approach path towards the illuminated runways of the airport.

Nothing on the message board for Floderus. For Lorraine it seemed almost like a reprieve; nothing worse – if that were conceivable – had happened in New York during her short flight from Paris to the coast.

And Monsieur Jacques Farrier had come personally to the airport to meet her, a short, neat figure standing with his feet together as she approached, the lights enhancing his mane of silver hair and his clipped military moustache and

284

shading the strong cheekbones and the alert, appraising eyes under their heavy brows. Lorraine noticed the tiny emblem of the *Croix de Guerre* on his left lapel. 'My dear Mademoiselle Floderus, such an honour to meet you at last!' The grey eyes softened as he regarded her face for a long moment. 'And such a pleasure . . .' He turned to chivvy his porter away to the baggage claim, and entertained her with small talk until the man was back with her two Gucci cases. 'There has been another jewel robbery at the Prince de Valigny's villa, can you imagine? The third time this year, and it is only spring! It is so *boring*! But the mimosa forests are in bloom now along the coast, and I shall show you them tomorrow. Madame Farrier is just back from Tangier, and will be so delighted to meet you; but she is a little fatigued after her journey, so we shall dine, you and I, in the little village of Le Rouret, on our way to Grasse. You do not wish a chaperone, I hope?' This with a gallant laugh.

'Perhaps I should, M'sieur Farrier,' Lorraine turned the compliment, delighting him.

'Ah, *hélas* . . . those days are over for me; besides, after thirty-four years together, I have discovered I am in love with my wife!'

He led her across the car park, where the frieze of palm trees softened the brilliant chain of lights along the Promenade des Anglais. The moon was well above the mountains as their Citroen DS took them along Route Nationale 85, higher and higher among the dark standing pines to the ancient village in the hills.

'This restaurant is not smart,' Jacques Farrier told Lorraine, 'but it is . . . ' He kissed his fingers. 'You shall see!'

During the meal he talked endlessly, with charm and considerable knowledge about the food they were enjoying – 'The chef here is a master, and has his own secrets; he is also *le patron*, of course. He cooks only on wood, the specially-selected oak from the region of Solonge – where he knows it will not be green – and sometimes he uses vine branches, which give a more piquant smoke.' He stopped

285

once, over the hors d'oeuvres, to enquire solicitously, 'I am not boring you, *chère* Mad'moiselle? You also must be fatigued by your long journey.'

'No, I'm fine. It's fascinating – please tell me more.' But Lorraine knew how preoccupied she must seem; she couldn't free her mind of the thought that if it hadn't been for Dean's message she'd be sitting here with a vivacity to match her host's, relishing the idea that tomorrow she would discuss with him the essences for *Siren Song*. Without Elliot Dietrich any work on the project would be like assembling an orchestra without a conductor.

'Very well,' Farrier nodded, 'I shall tell you more. But if I should talk too much, you will please kick my foot beneath the table, yes? You like the *jambon*? He suspends it in cotton nets until the moisture evaporates, leaving a rich flavour; though a little of the moisture remains in the fibres to enhance the rather ancient overtones – of course you would put it differently, my English is atrocious!'

Sometimes *le patron* himself came to visit them in his white smock and *toque blanche*, regarding the table with great severity and retiring again without a word. 'If something is wrong,' Farrier explained to Lorraine, 'he expects me to complain. If all seems well, in his opinion, and I still complain, he expects me to understand if he throws me out on the street! You like the *confit de canard*? It is Landaise, of course.'

Feeling as she did, Lorraine was content to let him go on; it relieved her of the need to keep the conversation going.

As she sat with her gloomy thoughts in the candlelight, she didn't realise that Jacques Farrier, a man whose understanding of people was as sharp as his understanding of food, was in fact giving his exquisite but solemn young guest a verbal *tour gastronomique* in the hope of keeping her amused, despite the obvious fact that she had something very depressing on her mind. An *affaire d'amour*, of course. Or was it to do with her visit here? Would she tomorrow choose the most expensive essences, and then tell him she didn't have the money? He'd heard rumours in Paris that

286

Floderus et Cie was not doing at all well since the great Willi had died so tragically. Perhaps it was just that – a lingering grief over a father she must have loved deeply.

'We have fruit,' the chef told them eventually, standing over them, 'and we have ice cream.' His tone told them that this kind of thing was strictly for tourists or the insane. 'And we have cheese . . . ' Whereupon their waiter produced a vast board of a dozen or so varieties and waited with his cheese-knife poised expectantly.

'I would suggest the Roblechon,' Farrier bent close to Lorraine's ear, 'so that we can stay a while with this very attractive Côte du Rhône – what do you think? Of course,' he shrugged, 'there is the ice cream . . . ' His tone implied that if *le patron* caught them ordering *that*, they'd both find themselves out in the street.

By the time they were sipping their cognac and espresso, some of Lorraine's spirits were restored; with such a meal and with her host's efforts to please her it was impossible to feel dejected; but she knew that nothing had changed. Dean had persuaded her to come here to this ancient littoral and try to put her problems behind her; but her thoughts were still half the world away in New York City.

At midnight, from the Farrier's beautiful *fin de siècle* villa in the town of Grasse, she called the familiar number, and received the familiar reply.

'I'm sorry,' the girl at the Lotus Club told her, 'she's not here right now. May I give her a message?'

'Just tell her I called, from France.'

CHAPTER 24

FRANÇOIS FARRIER WAS a young man of passion. He was also a young man of passions, plural. His first had been for ladders, when at five years of age he had found one leaning against his parents' house, left by a tiler during the lunchhour. Climbing to the top, François was astounded at the new world opening before him. From the topmost rung he could look around and see the entire village, which he had never done before, with people tiny along the distant streets and the white clouds seeming to drift right over his head; and when he climbed onto the actual roof he found a big gap where the tiles were to be renewed, and looked down into an attic, which he knew could only be reached, normally, by the stairs inside the house. The implication of this struck him like a blinding light. The world was *not* as it had always seemed! *You could get into an attic without going inside the house at all!* It was like when he stood on his head and looked at the ceiling as if it were the floor; it was a different world.

His discovery of the magic of ladders brought him close, in the next year or two, to breaking his neck, to severe scoldings for looking into people's upstairs windows, and to police arrest for attempted cat-burglary.

His next passion, at age fourteen, was for flying, after his uncle took him to see an air display at Mandelieu, near Cannes. A month later he took off on his bicycle, which was now fitted with wings made from bedsheets and bamboo, gathering speed down a grassy slope and actually becoming airborne for almost half a minute, stampeding a herd of cows and crashing into a greenhouse with a noise that

288

brought the *sapeurs-pompiers* to the scene before anyone had even made an alarm call.

Two years later he discovered women. Not content with simple dalliance, he took on half a dozen at once, to be subsequently horsewhipped by an irate father, beaten up by an irate brother, and driven daily into the confessional box by an irate priest, where at least the penitent found temporary refuge from the irate young women he had variously wronged.

At twenty, following his military service (during which he conceived a passion for tanks and drove one through the cookhouse at lunch-time), he visited his other uncle – Jacques – at the Parfumerie de Grasse at harvesting time, and had wandered into the huge shed where girls stood ankle deep in jasmine blooms. Their heavy, exotic scent, evocative of all the summers there had ever been, filled his receptive spirit with a headiness that left him reeling, as if – he later put it – he had swallowed a Beethoven symphony. Perfume in all its aspects became his first lasting passion, and within the year he was working for his uncle as an apprentice, to become, only six years later, a *parfumeur* in his own right, and Jacques Farrier's consuming pride.

Six months ago, a new passion had seized the spirit of the now twenty-seven-year-old François, without of course displacing his devotion to perfume. Halfway through an American movie he fell in love with New York, typified by the usual night shots of Manhattan. Having spent his life among the ancient walls of Grasse, where perfume had first been made in the sixteenth century under the patronage of the Medicis, he was assailed by the overpowering contrast presented by the glittering scenes of the New World's most fashionable city, with its towers of light, its crystal walls and its fleets of opulent limousines. Within a few days his bedroom under the eaves of the *parfumerie* was papered with blown-up photographs taken from brochures seized from a dozen travel agencies along the streets of nearby Cannes, featuring the Statue of Liberty, the Empire State Building, Kennedy Airport and the Hudson River. At the

289

moment of waking each morning, François enacted the fantasy that he was viewing these fabulous scenes from the deck of the *Queen Elizabeth II*, which had just borne him through the night across the Atlantic Ocean. A week later he enrolled at the Institut Berlitz in the Rue d'Antibes, Cannes, for a crash course in English, demanding emphasis on the American accent, which for a Frenchman was close to impossible because of the 'r'.

Today his uncle Jacques ushered a visitor into the laboratory where François was busy at work, the young man turned, stared, and dropped approximately a thousand francs' worth of tuberose essence in its glass phial onto the floor, during the turbulent onset of his new and immediate passion: Lorraine Floderus.

The same evening, the charming visitor from the New World was invited to dine exclusively with Monsieur and Madame Farrier in a salon more beautiful than Lorraine had ever seen, not because the décor and furnishings were priceless – though indeed they were – but because of the impeccable attention to the Italian Renaissance period and style, with its marbles and mosaics, its frescoes, inlays, silks and coloured glass, and its softly-glowing, multi-hued chandeliers.

Young François would not be joining them; for his own good reasons Jacques Farrier had despatched him on a spurious errand to prepare for a shipment of ambergris due in Cannes harbour on the morrow. Lorraine was rather thankful for this; the young man had obviously fallen for her the instant she'd entered his laboratory this afternoon, and she didn't want him mooning at her in the candlelight. He was certainly good-looking, with his smouldering, deep-set eyes and his shock of dark hair; but tonight she was more in the mood to shed private tears than flirt.

All day long she'd been filled with a sense of beauty, wonder and nostalgia as Jacques Farrier had performed the duties of host, companion, guide and potential salesman among the fields surrounding the city's ancient ramparts under the soft Mediterranean skies.

'The jasmine here is the finest in the world, as you know; there is no other to touch it; we shall begin harvesting in July.' They had walked among rose gardens, some of them shielded from the Mistral wind by bastions of tall cypresses. 'It is a mild winter, as usual, and we shall cut the blooms in a few months' time; it must be done only at dawn of each day, while the dew is on the petals and before the sun's warmth reaches them. Last year we took almost four hundred thousand kilos, most of them from the gardens you can see around here.' They had climbed into the odd-looking Cirtoen DS again, with its soft suspension and froglike bodywork, to drive into the hills and reach higher ground, where the groves of dark green orange trees covered the hillsides as in a mediaeval tapestry.

'We employ a hundred girls here in this grove alone, to keep pace with the work. They seem like birds, you know, in their black and white dresses, moving among the trees and chattering all the time in their raucous *patois*. But now I am being a poor man's poet.' He took her arm gently. 'Your father was here, you know, two years ago, here with me among the trees. "Why is it," he asked me, "that I don't come here and live in Paradise, instead of the madhouse they call New York? It is that I hear the tune of a different drummer; it is the only explanation." He was a splendid man, your father, one of the few men I know who managed to attain the dreams he reached for without losing the love of others – a difficult feat, you know. And now you are here in his place; and one day my nephew François will be showing you round, and perhaps you will talk of me for a moment. Life goes on.'

In the afternoon, after lunch at a tiny auberge under a canopy of leaves, he had shown her around the factory, where in a few months' time, he told her, the floor would be covered in a deep carpet of flowers poured from the huge baskets in the drying rooms, to be sorted and stacked in flat boxes to await processing. Then they visited the laboratories, their walls lined with amber-coloured phials,

291

where white-coated chemists worked at the essay benches and the enormous copper distillation tanks. 'The process was invented by the Arabs,' Farrier told Lorraine, 'centuries ago after they invaded the coast here.' Most of the time he seemed to talk like a guide book, either because the processing phase of the operation was less romantic to him than the harvesting out there in the sunshine, or because he was aware of Lorraine's preoccupation: not once had she questioned him about specific essences or absolutes, or given him any idea of what she was here to buy.

And it was impossible for her to explain. *La Parfumerie Farrier* had international connections and dealt with some of the most substantial fragrance houses in the world. Its *patron* was obviously a man of discretion, but Lorraine couldn't tell him that she'd be delighted to place an order for certain essences, but unfortunately her company was about to be seized by Century Cosmetics and in any case her chief perfumer had just walked out. The best she could do was to give a token explanation during the evening, as she sat with him and the gentle, rather wistful Madame Farrier, who spoke little English but listened carefully.

'Creating a new fragrance,' Lorraine told them, 'isn't something you undertake without a lot of thought, and a lot of planning. This trip is to give me an insight into your production, and an idea of what you can offer us. Otherwise, of course, I would have brought my perfumer along.'

'I had wondered about that,' Farrier nodded.

'I expect so.' She toyed with her escallope de veau for appearances' sake. This morning she'd believed that among the scented fields of Provence and in the gentle companionship of this charming man she could forget all that was going on in New York, as Dean had persuaded her; but the reverse had happened. She'd planned this visit on the wave of optimism and enthusiasm that Carl and Joe and Sy had created between them, and on the promise of support from Dean Powers; and all day she had believed more and more that she was letting them down. Instead of getting Dean on the phone right now to tell him that Farrier had exactly the essences and absolutes they needed for *Siren Song*, and at the right price, she was going back empty-handed, after simply taking time off in these beautiful surroundings while they remained in New York facing defeat. She felt useless, helpless, and disloyal. 'Since my father died,' she told Jacques Farrier, 'the company's been through the inevitable period of adjustment. As soon as we're through that, I'll be out here again to ask you what you can reserve for us.'

'Of course, Mademoiselle, I understand perfectly.' Which he did not. His wife had told him last night, before they had gone to sleep, 'Jacques, there is something wrong. For one thing she didn't bring her perfumer; and for another thing she's *distraite*, as I'm sure you've noticed.' He had, but he was glad, as always, of Giselle's sensitive insights; she never talked very much, which made people think she didn't think very much either; this, and her rare gift for listening mostly to what was carefully left unsaid, had contributed to the success of the Parfumerie Farrier over the last thirty years.

She was listening now, and even saying something. 'We also understand,' she told Lorraine sweetly, 'that the financing of a new fragrance is also a big undertaking. Money, unlike orange blossom, doesn't come off trees . . .' she glanced at Jacques fleetingly.

Of course, he thought at once. The obvious hadn't occurred to him. Up to a year ago, Floderus et Cie had been a successful company, however small, and Willi had never needed to consider the cost of the essences he wanted; they were to be the best, and he could afford them. But now things were probably different. The bank had said no. Or offered only enough for a deal with a house producing synthetics. Again he caught a glance from Giselle as the conversation proceeded. They had decided that this evening they would attempt something very difficult, perhaps impossible. But now the way seemed easier.

'The quality of our production,' he told Lorraine as he

293

poured some more Pouilly-Fuissé into her tall-stemmed glass, 'is such that we can maintain our prices. I believe that is well known. We do not bargain. We do not have to.'

With a trace of bitterness Lorraine said, 'I'm happy for you. It's the seal of success.'

He inclined his head. 'That is true. But you know, *chère* Lorraine – if you'll allow the intimacy – these fields where we walked today were the birth-place of your father's great *parfums*: *Picaresque* . . . *Nocturne* . . . *Giselle* – in honour of my lovely wife here – *Clair de Lune* . . . And that counts with us, you see. I am a businessman, yet also I have a heart.' He studied his wine for a moment. 'If we have the essences you are looking for, but you feel they are too expensive . . . you must tell me.' His luminous grey eyes moved upwards from the wine to her face.

'That's – a generous thought,' Lorraine had to say, but didn't know how to go on. If their problem were only money . . .

'You would not find us uncooperative,' Jacques told her gently, 'particularly if you felt of the same mind, and were able to cooperate with us, in return.' He left it there, to await a signal from Giselle to go on.

'I'll tell my directors,' Lorraine said, dodging the issue. 'They'll want to thank you for making things easier for us.'

Jacques caught a glance from his wife and pressed on, with a persuasive smile – 'But you must also tell them that it's not one-sided, *chère* Lorraine. We would like you to do something for us.' He paused, but she envinced no interest; nothing seemed capable of bringing her out of her mood of *tristesse*. 'You have met my nephew, François. He is our *parfumeur*. He was at once attracted to you, as you noticed; but that must happen to you a dozen times a day, and we need not discuss it.' He leaned forward a sapphire cufflink sparking inside the sleeve of his velvet smoking-jacket. 'Now, François is a good young man. Impetuous, yes, romantic, susceptible . . . all those things that a young Frenchman should be, at least up to the age of thirty. For some time now he has wanted quite desperately to go to New

294

York, to find work as a *parfumeur* if he can. He has no father; his mother is not dependent on him; I am his closest adviser; we took him on as an apprentice, and now he is our *chef*. We think it would be good for him to go to New York. He needs an outlet for his energies, for his talents; and the experience would be invaluable for him. Obviously, it would be extremely difficult for him to find work in his very rare profession; we know that. But in case you would be willing to help us in this, let me tell you something, Lorraine, and listen very carefully.' He waited until she was gazing at him with her whole attention. 'That young man,' he said with an intensity in his eyes that she didn't miss, 'is already one of the truly great *parfumeurs* in the world.'

Lorraine went on staring at him. Something didn't seem to be getting through to her; her day-long mood of despair couldn't switch in a flash to something different.

Jacques Farrier wasn't smiling. 'I would not joke with you, Lorraine. I would not try to deceive you. François, despite his youth, is a great *parfumeur*. You know what I am saying? *C'est un Maître.*'

'Yes,' Lorraine heard herself answering in a strangely hushed voice. 'A master perfumer. And – and he wants to work in New York?'

'If you could possibly recommend him to someone, yes.' Then he half-rose from his chair and he saw her tears begin glistening in the candlelight as she sat with her head bowed and her shoulders shaking. 'But my dear child . . . what is wrong? Have I said something to distress you?'

CHAPTER 25

'Do it again. Okay, this is your problem. Watch.'

'I don't turn fast enough?'

'Your turn's okay, though its' goin' to get faster. But you're not using your *body*. Look.'

'I don't understand, *Sensei*.'

'Okay. You will.' Sadie Kaminski stood away from the man-sized dummy with her hands to her sides. 'This is what you're doin', Lorraine. You're only using your arm to hit with. You should use your whole body. Like this.' She became instant movement, and the edge of her hand struck the dummy beside the neck, stopping short.

Lorraine, her white *gi* already showing the signs of hard workouts, stood watching in frustration. '*Sensei*, could you do it slowly?'

'Sure. And this time I'll break the stick, so you can see the power's gettin' there.' The dummy was made of lumber and coil springs and foam rubber, and after long use by Sadie's students the only resemblance it had to a man was its height and the four limbs; but the target points were renewed with red adhesive tape almost daily. Lorraine's target point now was the side of the neck, and Sadie had replaced the short round stick – broken by the last student – with a new one. As Lorraine watched, the stumpy figure in the patched *gi* and shredded black belt came to slow life again; then, as her hand struck the stick, it broke. 'See what I mean? Even when you do it real slow, you still carry the power there. But the thing is, you didn't just see my arm come down from the swing, you saw my whole *body* bring it down, the shoulder,

296

the hip and the knee pullin' the arm down, see? You can do that with your punches already – I've seen you. Now do it with your sword-hand.' She turned fractionally as a big man in a ripped *gi* came up, bowing to her.

'*Sensei*, can you –'

'You know the rules, Chuck. You don't ever interrupt me when I'm coachin' someone. Get off the floor, five minutes.'

'But shit, I –'

'*Ten* minutes. You know the rule about swearin'.' She turned back and replaced the broken stick and told Lorraine: 'Okay, go!'

Lorraine went over in her mind what Sadie had told her and swung down with her sword-hand strike, feeling the stick bend and then clutching her hand, nursing it.

'Okay. You won't hurt your hand if you break the stick, see. That's because you didn't go *through* it. Now, you moved okay that time; you used your body; but you didn't *go* for it. You *thought* about what you were doin'. You just have to *do* it.' Her mud-brown, intelligent eyes stared into Lorraine's with a kind of force, as if she were projecting the thoughts in her mind along an invisible beam; Lorraine had sensed this before, and had asked Cindy, a woman student, about it. 'That's her *ki*, honey. She's kind of – well focusing her spirit, her inner force. You'll develop it, too, one day.' Lorraine watched it now, feeling awed. 'Okay,' Sadie told her, 'now listen, this time you're going to *do* it. You're really goin' to *go* at it, see. That isn't a stick you have to break, it's this guy's neck, and if you *don't* break it, he's goin' to come at you, and there won't be a chance in hell for you because this is Central Park and it's midnight and there is *nobody* else around, an' if you don't do somethin' *right now* he's goin' to get you on the ground an' there'll be nothin' to do but pray, and that's never stopped a rapist yet.' Her eyes grew dark as they stared into Lorraine's. '*Now go for it!*'

And the stick broke.

'And the funny thing is,' nodded Sadie, 'you never knew it was happening, right? You didn't seem to move, but the thing broke. That way it don't hurt your hand; that way it

297

don't even take much energy. Now we'll go over there and you can start throwin' Joe around the mat.'

As they crossed the polished floor of the *dojo*, with the warm air smelling of floor-wax and punchbag-leather and human sweat, and with the tin roof vibrating from a chorus of *kiai*'s from a group of green-belts, Lorraine for the first time felt a sense of belonging here – not only to the place itself and the people but to what they were doing, to the ritual and the dedication and the ancient wisdom of the Orient. Her hand throbbing from its impact on the stick and her mind throbbing with a strange and secret knowledge, she said: '*Sensei*, how much of that force was mine?'

'Huh?'

'The force that broke the stick?'

Sadie glanced at her and away again. 'Boy, you're learnin' things real fast. Okay, some of it was mine, but only a little bit. You saw it in my eyes and you used it – an' that's okay too. It was your hand, wasn't it? I never touched that thing.'

'So what are you saying, *Sensei*?'

One of the blacks came up, his hand running with blood; and this time Sadie returned the bow. 'What's up, Beaver?'

'Permission to bandage, *Sensei*?'

'Sure, you know where the stuff is.' As he bowed and went off, she said quietly to Lorraine: 'Some o' these huge guys are like children, y' know? They think if they don't draw blood they ain't gettin' their money's-worth, and when they get hurt they want me to know about it, like I'm their mom and they're showin' me somethin' they're proud of.' She halted at the edge of the mats. 'So what am I sayin'? I'm sayin' that it's okay to use a bit of my force to help you do a technique. It can work for real, too – you're up against a mugger and you have to react, and it don't make any different if some of the force you use is simply because my image comes into your mind. He's still goin' down, right? And one day, you won't have to think of me anymore. You'll have your own force, Lorraine, and then God help anyone who gets in your way.'

The cable said, *Arrive New York Saturday April 24 1900 hours Air France Flt 287 François*, and Lorraine was there to meet him, getting to Kennedy only just in time because the cable had come as a complete surprise: she hadn't expected him to reach New York for weeks. Watching his dark head as he leaned over the immigration officer and tried to understand what was being said, Lorraine hoped to God he wasn't saying he'd come here to work, or they'd want to see his permit. François turned once with an arrogant swing of his head to look across the faces of the people waiting, recognised Lorraine and gave a radiant smile, blowing her kisses; then he went back to the frustrating business of crossing this roped-off little area that was the frontier of the United States of America; she could hear him raising his voice, which certainly wasn't going to get him through any faster.

She wished Dean were here with her, to share this important moment. If Jacques Farrier were right, here was the young man who had the power to give them *Siren Song*, and turn the fortunes of Floderus Incorporated. Dean had had to fly to New Orleans an hour before Lorraine had landed from Paris two days ago, to put out a fire – a major complaint from a distributor that a 100-flacon consignment of *Picaresque* in the 2-oz size had reached them insecurely stoppered. It wouldn't normally need a vice president to make a personal visit, but this distributor had already been complaining that sales were falling short because of irregular advertising. But Dean should be back today – Saturday – at any hour, and would call her the moment he arrived.

'Lorraine!' The tall young Frenchman was dropping his flight bag and opening his arms, and without thinking she simply moved to him and let him enfold her, feeling a rush of electricity through her whole body. His mouth was on hers, and she had to extricate herself as gracefully as she could.

'François . . . this is *not* Paris. But I'm glad to see you.' On their way to the baggage claim she asked him, 'How on earth did you get a visa so soon? And did you have the necessary shots?'

He refused to answer her in French; he was in a new country; this was his new language. And above everything, this was New York! 'My uncle pull the strings for me; he knows people; we have also a doctor who is – commodious?'

'Accommodating. You mean he just signed the certificate? For God's sake, you'd better not tell anyone else, François. And you've no work permit yet – you're here strictly as a tourist, remember. When you start work in the lab, you'll simply be keeping your hand in doing a little research.'

'Keeping my hand . . .?' He looked down at her with a golden light in his deep-set eyes.

'Practising. And you must watch for your baggage, or it'll keep on circling.'

'Baggage?' He went on gazing down at her. *'Mon dieu,'* he said softly, *'comme tu es exquise, Lorraine!'*

'Thank you,' she said sharply, 'but I have *not* given you permission to *tu-toi* me.' It wasn't that she objected to his using the familiar – reserved strictly for relations and close friends – but she had to get him out of the airport somehow. She'd forgotten how devastating these Latins could be; this one just had to gaze at her and a distinct commotion began in her erogenous zones.

'Une Rolls,' he exclaimed in the car park, *'sensationelle!'* All the way into the city he kept up a barrage of questions, though not the usual ones: he knew every tall building by name and recited them to Lorraine. At intervals he swivelled around in his seat and leaned half against the door panel, watching her; she wished she hadn't been wearing this short, flimsy little *crêpe de chine* cocktail dress when she'd had the cable to say he was arriving; under this man's eyes she felt totally naked.

'François, you'll fall out if that door opens. And I want you to tell me the names of all the other buildings.'

'I embarrass you?' he asked, straightening to face the front again.

'Yes.'

300

'It makes you look even more *exquise*.'

She didn't make a left onto 44th Street when they reached Manhattan, but kept on going north; she'd intended originally to drive him straight to the Algonquin, where she'd managed to get a room for him at short notice; but the idea of being alone with him in a hotel room even for five minutes was out of the question now; she'd feel safer in her apartment, on familiar ground, with Tilly within call. But it wasn't entirely François' fault; the heat emanating from his libido felt very pleasant.

This was why, an hour later, she was spread out on one of the twin beds in the rose guest suite, her eyes closed, her little *crêpe de chine* cocktail dress on the floor and her head completely devoid of rational thought while François, his lean body tanned by Mediterranean summers and his dark hair falling over his face, caressed her with his fingers and his tongue so lightly that it felt like the brushing of small flames across her skin, firing her blood wherever they touched. And she remembered Rodriguez, in the hotel in Majorca, his white waiter's monkey-jacket hooked over the chair in the moonlight streaming through the window, his black hair shining and his eyes smouldering in the shadows of his incredibly handsome face; and Salvatore, in that small high room on the Italian Riviera, undressing her with an exquisite and maddening slowness, garment by garment, sliding her gold sandals off as if even her feet were precious to him, baring her shoulders as if he were unveiling a priceless sculpting, at last drawing her briefs down and diving there like a bird, his mouth alighting with such softness that she had begun crying quietly with relief as all her adolescent fears of brutal assault melted away, and she gave herself to her first time of loving with an abandon that brought forth from the young Italian poems of delight. *I am your mandolin, carissima, and you are my song* . . .

'My God,' Lorraine's friend Marcia had told her afterwards on the plane home, 'you were lucky. My first time was with an all-American Jock who came at me like out of the locker-room and went straight for the home run.'

301

These Latins were so different. Beguiling, fickle, capricious, unfaithful; but for a few hours, gods from the court of Eros with the power to make a woman feel there had never been a woman on earth before.

'François . . .' Lorraine murmured, 'what time is it?'

'It does not matter.'

Her blood singing, her sweat mingling with his and the odour of their bodies bitter-sweet on the air, she closed her eyes again, ready to believe him. It seemed they had been lying here for hours, and he'd not even entered her yet; true to his culture, François believed it was his business as a lover to drive her mad with pleasure, leading her to the tell-tale sounds of iminent orgasm and then leading her away again, tantalising, tormenting, until her nails were digging into his back and her teeth were biting in his ear, reminding him in the primitive but articulate language of lovers that she'd draw blood if he dared to stop.

When the telephone rang it was François who leaned over and answered it, with the practiced unconcern of a man used to answering telephones at the wrongest possible moment.

'*Allo?*'

'Is Miss Floderous there?'

'*Non. Elle n'est pas là. Je regrette.*'

Lorraine tried to grab the phone before he hung up, but wasn't quick enough. She'd recognised Dean's voice. 'François, you *sotte!*'

Whereupon he entered her immediately, with one long smooth thrust, knowing very well that if he didn't, the interruption would break the spell and leave them both unsatisfied. *Impensible!*

Then Lorraine's nails were digging deep, breaking the skin in her rage at his impudence and in her desperation that nothing must stop them now as the heat burst in her pelvis and sent fire roaring through her body for seconds on end, and then again, while she called out his name in the tumult, and then again as she leapt under him, arching her loins and lifting him and letting him fall and feeling him deeper and deeper inside her body until his breath gusted out and he

302

went into a new rhythm, faster and faster, riding her like a dolphin in a wind-whipped sea with its waves rising and falling under them both while the telephone began ringing and ringing and this time François ignored it and rolled over and lay supine while Lorraine listened for a while to the ringing sound and at first ignored it, as he had, and then slowly surfaced from the depths of liquid fire and thought about it, and finally drew a long shuddering breath as the real world swung back into focus and she leaned across the slack and naked body beside her and took the phone off the hook and said:

'Yes?'

There was a pause. 'Lorraine?'

'Yes. Is that you, Dean?'

'It is.'

Guilt flooded over her. 'He thought I'd gone out.'

'Who did?' Dean's tone was careful, polite.

'What? François. That's why he said I wasn't here. I just brought him back from the airport.' She wasn't sure she was telling him things in the right order; her body was still deep in its warm scented bath of liquid sunset, while her mind was trying to reason things out; and it was confusing. There was a cool silence from the other end of the line, so she said, 'How did it go, Dean, in New Orleans?'

'Satisfactorily.'

'Oh. With – with you there, it was bound to. When did you get back?'

'Five minutes ago.'

It was like putting questions into a computer. 'Oh. You must be tired.' The lean, tanned god from the court of Eros had started snoring gently, and she poked him in the ribs in case Dean heard.

'No. I thought you might care for me to come over.'

'I'd love to see you, Dean, but – can I call you back when I've got things straight? François has never been to the States before and like most foreigners he's totally disoriented; but I was lucky enough to get him a room at the Algonquin. Would you like to meet us there a little later?'

303

She listened to her voice going on and on, for much too long, but she couldn't seem to stop. 'Right now I'm trying to make him understand that since he doesn't have a work permit he'll be in real trouble if anyone finds out. He's totally lost at the moment, and –'

'I'm sure you'll make him feel thoroughly at home. I'll call you tomorrow.'

'But Dean, I –' I what? Quick! But nothing came.

'Yes?'

'I'd really love to see you.'

'We'll arrange it some time, when you're less busy. Good night.'

'Dean, don't –'

Click.

She slumped against the pillows.

'Who is this Dean?' asked François grumpily.

'Oh, shut up.' Ignoring his look of surprise she set about getting her feelings in order. Dean knew, of course. It had been in her voice: the lingering glow, the not-quite-conscious-again-yet, mingled with the awakening of concern and guilt. It was perfectly okay for François to be here – an important visitor from overseas with the usual need of help with the formalities while she entertained him to dinner; but there had been only *one* thing she could possibly have said to Dean that would have sounded right. *You're back? Oh, terrific! Come right on over!* But even if she could have gotten her tone right, it wouldn't have worked out. If Dean had come over, he'd have taken one look at this sultry and satiated young satyr and gone straight home again.

The feeling of overwhelming guilt bothered Lorraine, and she stayed where she was for a while, her shoulders deep in the pink satin pillows and a manicured nail between her teeth. It took her a while to think it out but when she was finished she knew she was right. She had no reason to feel *sexual* guilt; she'd only spent one night with Dean Powers and it hadn't led them to any oaths of fidelity; he'd probably provided well for himself in New Orleans while he was

304

there. It was that she should have been able to meet him right away when he got back; they'd both been away from New York on important business and there was a great deal to talk about; also she wanted to thank him for supporting her so wonderfully when she was in Paris; it was as if he'd had a hunch about things, because if he hadn't persuaded her to go down to Grasse as originally planned she'd never have discovered François – not François the satiated satyr lying here beside her but François, the *maître parfumeur*.

As his warm fingers began stroking her naked thigh she brought her hand down across his wrist in a none too gentle chop.

'*Merde, alors!*' He drew his hand away sharply.

'François,' she told him, 'you have just used my body like Yehudi Menuhin uses a Stradivarius, and I won't forget it for a long time.' She ruffled his hair, but he was careful not to put his hand on her thigh again. 'But you're in the United States of America on serious business, and I am your employer, so this is the first and last time.'

'*Pas possible! C'est –*'

'It's not only possible, it's sure-fire certain. Now I'm taking you to your hotel.'

At the Algonquin she refused even to see that his room looked satisfactory. At the Algonquin the rooms were always satisfactory, and if they didn't seem so, your demands were eccentric.

'I shall walk all night through New York!' he told her, consoling himself. 'I shall go to the top of the Empire States Building, and walk through Central Park and see a play on Broadway! I shall –'

'François,' Lorraine stopped him short. 'The Empire *State* Building – with no "s" – is closed at this time; Central Park is crowded with colourful citizens snorting cocaine and brandishing flick-knives and waiting for visiting foreigners to take their exercise there; and on Broadway the curtains are coming down in half an hour, after which I wouldn't recommend walking in the streets unaccompanied.' She had the mischievous idea of sending him in a taxi to Sadie's *dojo*

305

with an introduction, then dismissed it. 'You've heard of mugging? It's real. You're not ready for New York yet. I suggest you have a leisurely dinner here – the food's homely but nourishing – and grab an early night before the jet lag sets in.'

His expressive shoulders sagging, he gazed into her eyes beseechingly. 'When shall I see you again, Lorraine?'

'On Monday. In the laboratory.' She lifted her hand for him to kiss it. '*Bonsoir, maître.*'

It was nine o'clock when Lorraine got back to her apartment, and on her way there in the Rolls she invented a dozen good excuses for calling Dean and persuading him to meet her, then realised they were all patently spurious. And by now, knowing Dean Powers, he'd be selecting the most attractive of his city-wide harem – though she must try not to think of him that way anymore. Dean was still going through the agonies of his own divorce – from a wife he said he'd loved – and he'd been under new pressures since then, fired from his job, then reinstated and then faced with the challenge of getting Floderus back onto its feet, under the looming threat from Frederick Vanderkloot and the sudden loss of their perfumer, the key man in the project for *Siren Song*.

For the first time Lorraine was thinking of him with her heart, and as she went into her apartment she felt sick with remorse at letting him down tonight.

She rang for Tilly. That was the arrangement. Lorraine's life style wasn't exactly debauched or licentious, but as an attractive young woman she needed her privacy, especially in her own home; and she'd let Tilly know that she wasn't looking for a servant who was expected to wait on her every minute, haunting her from room to room in the huge apartment; unless there was an important message or delivery, Tilly would be left to enjoy her own privacy in the kitchen of r two-roomed suite, until Lorraine rang for her. Nor would she express much interest in the fact that during the evening one of the beds in the rose guest suite appeared to have been struck by a tornado.

'Tilly, how've you been?' Lorraine asked her; they hadn't seen each other since morning, when Lorraine had gone along to work at the office with no one around to disturb her.

'Very well, Miss Lorraine. Your day was good, also?' Her dark Spanish eyes were noting things, particularly Lorraine's attempt to seem cheerful.

'I haven't counted the score yet, Tilly, so I don't know whether I won or lost. But I skipped lunch; have you got any cold chicken in the fridge?'

Tilly had prawns in aspic, a gelatine of beef, some breast of New England duck, and some brisling. Lorraine went for a leg of duck with some Russian salad. 'I'll have it in my study. Did Mr Powers call?'

'No.'

'If he does, I'm definitely in.'

As Tilly left her, Lorraine braced herself for the humiliation of the nightly call to the Lotus Club, and went across to the telephone; but it was ringing before she reached it, and she felt a leap of hope.

'Hello?'

'Is that Miss Lorraine Floderus?'

'Who is it speaking?'

'Angelo Baccari.'

'Oh. I was just going to call, to ask – '

'Miss Floderus, is your sister there?'

'No, of course – no. Why?'

'She said she'd be back to join me and some friends of mine for dinner here, an hour ago.' His voice was heavy. 'I thought she might have gone to see you. I've tried several other places.'

Lorraine drew a deep breath to steady herself. 'I see. When did she leave the club?'

'Some time this afternoon.'

'Was she – depressed?'

'I wouldn't say that. But you know – we'll be glad when she gets back here, or shows up somewhere.' He paused, and Lorraine found herself staring across the room at the tall

307

French clock, its gilt hands marking off the minutes with a ponderous exactitude, reminding her that life could never go back, must always go on, and that every measured second was a point of no return. Angelo's voice came again. 'If you see anything of Madlen, will you call me?'

'Yes. Yes, of course. And please let me know if – when she gets back.'

When Tilly returned in fifteen minutes to say the dinner tray was waiting in the study, Lorraine was on the telephone, calling every number where someone might know Madlen's whereabouts: half a dozen of their mutual friends, some of whom had been at college with them, and the only boy-friends Madlen had ever been around with: Brian Chetwood, Roberto Madrid, Gaylord Klein, Daryl Hudson. 'Tilly, I don't have time to eat anything right now. Just leave it there, covered over.'

Seeing Lorraine's pale face and the feverish movements of her hands as she went through the phone directory, Tilly asked anxiously, 'Is there trouble, Miss Lorraine?'

'I don't know.' If she explained that Miss Madlen had gone off on her own somewhere and was overdue, Tilly would worry herself sick. 'I don't know yet, Tilly. I've got to find out.'

That was at 9.23.

CHAPTER 26

AT 11.45 LORRAINE called Dean.

He didn't answer.

By one o'clock in the morning she had thought of three other people to call, and called them; and she had criss-crossed the city and visited five or six people who hadn't been answering their phone since she'd first begun calling them from her apartment; two of them didn't answer the door; one – a blond boy, half-naked and stoned out of his mind – gave a wild laugh and slammed the door in her face; and Roberto Madrid was furious with her for waking him when he had to be on the stage for an audition at six in the morning – 'and you mean that freak is still around? I'd've thought they'd have put her in the funny farm by now, for Christ's sake!'

She had also called the Lotus Club five times, knowing that if Madlen returned there they wouldn't be able to let her know. Madlen hadn't returned. She had also called the police, and was invited to go along to Precinct 18 and report a missing person. She had done that, and stated on the form that her sister had suicidal tendencies. The dead-pan, silver-haired sergeant had got through to One, Police Plaza and posted an all-points bulletin effective immediately.

'We'd like you to keep in touch with us, ma'am.'

'Of course.'

She had called Donna Shapiro, whose training in crisis situations would have helped talk Lorraine down from her now feverish anxiety; but the phone went on ringing. This fine spring week-end, a lot of people had got out of the city.

309

At five minutes past one the peacock-blue Rolls Royce was standing at the kerbside in Rockefeller Plaza with the motor running and a patrol car swerving in behind it.

'You can't park there, ma'am.'

Halfway to the telephone box Lorraine stopped. 'I need to make a call, officer. It's an emergency.'

'Anything we can do?'

'My sister's missing.'

'You should report it.'

'I just did. Please let me get to that phone, officer.'

Noting her white, strained face, he said, 'Go ahead. Not too long, okay?' His driver switched on the rotating lights. 'Know who she is, Al?'

'Sure. Lorraine Floderus. I need her autograph for my kid.'

'She looks real upset.' In this job you tended to under-estimate situations, and Al had formed the habit of thinking in headlines. SISTER OF FILM ACTRESS MISSING. He watched the slender figure crouched over the telephone, as a man with a jerky walk and shaky hands came around the corner and saw her and turned in her direction and saw the patrol car and went right on past with his head turned the other way.

'It's late,' Dean said on the phone.

'I know. But I need help.'

'Won't it keep till tomorrow?' His tone was cool, impassive.

'It could be too late by then.' If she told him Madlen was missing he wouldn't think it very urgent; he'd met Madlen a couple of times at company parties before the plane crash, but that was all; you couldn't expect people to agonise about someone they hardly knew. 'Dean,' Lorraine said slowly, 'if I mean anything, please let me talk to you.' There was only this one man in the whole of this city who could lend her his quiet strength. It wouldn't find Madlen, but it would steady her up and let her think straight and maybe hit on some new ideas where here sister might be.

'You'd better come on over,' Dean said.

His apartment was over on the West Side and it took Lorraine almost twenty minutes to reach there, and all she could think about on the way was the dark water of the river with a pale face upturned among the floating débris, and an empty pill bottle rolling across the floor out of reach of the flung-out lifeless hand, and a deep gash of crimson across the delicate blue-veined wrist with the slowing heart pumping the life-blood away.

As she took the lift to the fifth floor of the apartment block she could hardly stand; it was seventeen hours since she'd eaten anything, and her nerves had been burning up the little nourishment she'd taken at breakfast time.

Dean opened his door and stood there observing her coolly for a moment; then his eyes changed and he reached out quickly to help her as she went through the doorway with her legs trying to buckle; then she saw Madlen standing there and she stood swaying for a couple of seconds and would have hit the floor if Dean hadn't caught her.

Madlen leaned back against the end of the settee, looking like a stylised baby-doll painting on the top of a chocolate box, her pale child's body enveloped in one of Dean's royal-blue bathrobes, her small feet naked, her delicate cheekbones shadowed by the light of the big Chinese lantern which alone burned in the room, her violet eyes glowing softly with a strange expression that Dean couldn't interpret. Was it a kind of triumph?

'She does this,' Madlen said with a tone of bored contempt. 'She ignores me for weeks and then suddenly decides to get frantic if she doesn't know where I am.'

Dean said nothing. Barefoot and in his bathrobe, his body was still tingling from Madlen's attentions; but his mind had now been shocked into alertness by the way Lorraine looked as she took another sip of the cognac, half-sitting and half-lying in the low easy chair. A pang of remorse came into him when he thought how he'd held Lorraine off on the phone; but he'd assumed she'd spent all evening with that goddamned Frenchman.

311

The fumes of the cognac drifted through Lorraine's lungs, warming her. She was looking at neither Madlen nor Dean; half an hour ago she'd been frantic to reach here; now she just wanted to go, as soon as she could stand up; go home and sleep. There was no pale face upturned among the floating débris of the East River, no empty bottle rolling across the floor. That was all that mattered.

'It was kind of you,' she said to Dean very quietly and without looking at him, 'to let me come.'

'You said it was urgent,' he shrugged.

'It was. Or I thought it was. Actually, there's no difference.' She finished the cognac and tried to stand up, but felt much too weak. Dean came across and offered a hand, but she shook her head. 'I haven't had any food since this morning. Since yesterday morning. I'm sorry. I'll go as soon as I can.'

'Can you take a raw egg?'

'Yes. Anything.'

Above the whirr of the beater from the kitchen Madlen said with a soft little stage laugh, 'You know, you're really rather embarrassing. I mean, Dean and I were in bed together when you called.'

Lorraine looked across the room at her for a moment, then down again. There was the same expression in her sister's eyes that she'd seen before at the Lotus Club, expressing a mood behind a mood, and hard to fathom. But Lorraine knew, and knew without any question, that Madlen's studied contempt was only one of her masks; behind the other there was something else. It seemed to Lorraine that she was close, headily close to breaking through and finding her sister as she really was: scared, grieving, desolate, hoping against hope for rescue; but the distance between being close and breaking through was frightening: she'd never make the journey, however fast she ran.

'I'm sorry I disturbed you,' she said formally. Somehow she had to stop herself getting up and lurching across the room and taking that frail little thing in her arms and never

312

letting go until their tears were spent and they could start over, after all this time, and put this year of anguish behind them forever. But it wasn't possible. If she touched her sister, she'd slap her face. That was part of the game.

'*She's playing a game with you, Dr Fischer had said, and you mustn't ever stop. It's the only way she can relate to you, because she needs your total concern. She's got to go on winning, and if you give up, she'll lose. And then she'll do it again, and maybe succeed next time.*'

Okay, Madlen. I won't give up. It's your turn.

'We'd been in bed for ages,' Madlen said with another little stage laugh as Dean came back from the kitchen, 'and then you had to call. You were lucky, you know. People aren't awfully keen on taking phone calls in the middle of fucking.'

Dean looked away as he handed Lorraine the tumbler. 'It's just egg and a shot of Worcester, okay?'

'Thank you.' She took a breath and swallowed it whole before she could gag.

'You look pretty far gone,' Madlen said lightly, and smiled to Dean. He didn't return it. What kind of game were these two playing, for God's sake?

'I was just worried about you,' Lorraine said. 'I'll be okay in a minute. But will you call Angelo? He sounded as worried as I was.'

'Oh, he knows I'm not just adrift.'

Lorraine closed her eyes for a moment. *It's not going to be easy*, Dr Fischer had said. Right. 'Then that's fine,' she said. 'And I'm glad you met Dean again. He's a . . . good person.'

'Probably doesn't care for unsolicited testimonials,' Madlen said casually, 'but we know you mean well. Actually, he saved my life the other day.'

Lorraine jerked her head up. 'When?' She glanced across at Dean, but he was looking mystified.

'When you were in Europe,' Madlen said with a shrug of her bare shoulder. 'I got a bit depressed – you know how one does, sometimes. So I went along to your office; when they

313

said you'd gone to France I felt – you know – kind of abandoned. Not the first time. Then Dean asked if he could be of help, so I said he could take me to dinner. I think if he hadn't, I would have driven the Ferrari into the river. I'm glad he saved me from that; I know how guilty you'd have felt when you came back.'

Lorraine put the empty tumbler carefully onto the coffee table and managed to get onto her feet. 'Yes,' she said, 'I would have felt very guilty.' It was obvious what had happened. The first night she'd been in Grasse she'd told the girl at the Lotus Club she was calling from France. The next day Madlen had gone along to the office to 'see' her, knowing she wasn't there, so that she could later say she'd been 'abandoned'. Innocently, Dean had offered to cheer her up by taking her out to dinner; whether they'd gone on to his apartment was immaterial. Tonight, piqued by Lorraine's being 'too busy' with François to see him, Dean had called Madlen at the club, by way of retaliating. But neither he nor Madlen could have known that Lorraine's need of him would bring her here too.

It was all so petty and so obvious, but sex was more than just copulation; it was used as a defence, as a weapon, as a direct means of expressing any one of a thousand emotional statements from simple love to complicated rage; it too was a game, and the rules were well understood.

Madlen gave a stage yawn. 'My goodness, it's late. I didn't realise.'

'I'm going now,' Lorraine said wearily. She glanced at Dean, trying to read his feelings. He looked withdrawn, brooding, and that was all; it wasn't an uncommon mood. 'But I need to use your phone,' she told him.

He looked up. 'Go ahead.' He wished to hell he knew what was going on. A few hours ago he'd landed from New Orleans eager to see Lorraine for the first time in days, give her a *soigné* little dinner somewhere quiet where they could talk, and maybe go to her place, or his, for the night. Now he was sitting here listening to these two playing some crazy game, and one of them was calling the police.

314

'Yes,' Lorraine was saying into the phone, 'I made the report earlier tonight. You can take the name off the missing persons' list. Madlen Deidre Floderus. I'm sorry? She – she went to see a friend of hers, without saying where she was going; she's perfectly safe now. Thank you.'

Watching her strained face, Dean found himself admiring her for keeping this obviously harrowing situation in her life to herself; the only time he'd ever heard her mention Madlen was at the board meeting when he'd resigned. *Two days ago my sister tried to commit suicide and she's just out of intensive care, so it's taken up some of my time.* Lorraine had never talked about her since. She was obviously sick with concern about her, yet Madlen was treating her like a piece of dirt. Last Tuesday when he'd taken Madlen to dinner, he'd had to put up quite a struggle when she'd suggested they make a night of it; with a girl like her it had needed a whole lot of will power to refuse, but he'd held out, and finally taken her back to the club where she said she lived, leaving her at the door with a goodnight kiss. And the simple reason was that there'd been something about that wild night he'd spent with Lorraine that had lingered on, and the only couple of times he'd dialled a girl-friend's number since then, he'd put the phone down before she'd answered.

Even tonight it hadn't occurred to him to call Madlen; when he'd understood what was happening at Lorraine's place he'd just sat with a double bourbon cursing the perfidy of all womankind, and then started wondering if he should call Christine (with those incredible legs) or maybe Dolores (who was getting over her problems and only wanted it a couple of times a night). Then his phone had rung and he was suddenly listening to that soft, husky little voice – like Lorraine's, but less striking – and saying sure, he'd like to see her again, should he call for her at the club? It occurred to him that he was acting like a kid, because he didn't really feel like sex tonight anyway; it was just to get even with that goddamned Frenchman who'd apparently taken Lorraine by storm the minute he'd landed in New York. But after another couple of bourbons he thought okay, so he was

315

acting like a kid, too bad. Somewhere in his mind was the recognition of how deeply he'd been hurt, but he'd lost attention in a haze of alcohol; wives came and went in a man's life, right? Girls came and went. Whole lot of fun.

Lorraine was putting the phone down and getting her bag.

'Thank you, Dean.' She took a hesitant step towards her sister and stopped short with a visible effort. 'Goodnight, Madlen. Take care.'

'I always do.'

Dean went out with Lorraine to get the lift, and they stood in awkward silence listening to the faint hum of the machinery. When the doors opened he said, 'You feel okay now?'

'Yes.'

'Okay to drive?'

'Yes.' Walking into the lift she turned and looked at him. 'Take care of her, Dean. She's – she needs people, and you'd be good for her.' Then she looked down as the doors came together.

CHAPTER 27

THE SCENE, DONNA thought, reminded her of a church. The young Frenchman moved like a priest around the small laboratory, pausing at a desk to study papers, lifting his dark head to look along the higher shelves, moving on again to examine the massive array of bottles and phials and beakers, speaking not a word, looking at nobody, absorbed in his appraisal with an almost holy detachment from everything else, as if he were meditating, communing with higher spirits.

The others felt it too: Dean, Lorraine, Sy Goldman, Joe Fisher, Carl and Donna; they'd started wandering around the place when they'd all come in here half an hour ago, and then one by one they had become aware of François Farrier's mood of total concentration; and now Sy was buried deep in the ancient and stained armchair – the sole item of furnishing that was out of place here among all the clinical equipment – while Joe sat on the floor in the full lotus position watching the Frenchman with a creeping sense of awe. (Ten minutes ago Joe had lit a cigarette to help him cope with his excitement, and caught a swing of Farrier's head that sent him to the nearest porcelain sink, fast, to crush it out.) Carl Blatt was perched like a tennis umpire on one of the high stools that were ranged along the higher shelves, watching Farrier at a slow blink-rate of five a minute behind his granny spectacles and occasionally turning to look at Dean, then Lorraine, to catch their vibes. Dean was looking particularly brooding this morning, and Lorraine unusually withdrawn.

317

Now Farrier took his seat at the organ, the large circular unit of shelves that stood higher than his head when he was standing up, each shelf bearing fifty or sixty identical and labelled phials, most of them containing liquid ranging from colourless to deep amber. Putting his long manicured hands on the lowest shelf, Farrier gave the organ a turn and sat watching the rows of phials swing past him, slowly and smoothly on the unit's ball-bearings.

'*Fantastique*.'

His one word, after the long silence, sent a soft little shock through the laboratory, and Joe's jaw actually dropped; it was as if a priest had uttered the word of God.

These Americans, thought François Farrier. They refuse to move anywhere; if they can make a machine to do things for them, they make it. Even drive-in banks. Drive-in movies. And this fantastic *rondelle* where all you had to do was sit and bring everything to you. But it was going to work, he could see that. He was going to have an incredible time with this space-age toy of theirs.

'You Americans . . .' he said, turning to look at them with a strange, almost affectionate smile. Then he turned back and became lost again.

And what the hell, Carl Blatt thought, did *that* mean?

Donna stole away to the rest room and came back, hitching herself on the edge of a lab table opposite where Dean and Lorraine were sitting on two of the metal-framed chairs. They puzzled her. A while back when Lorraine was in France, Dean had talked to her in the cafeteria over a sandwich, saying what an incredible job Lorraine had done over there in finding a new perfumer; he'd explained to Donna how important the 'nose' was to a perfume company. 'I guess,' Dean had said, 'that in the hierarchy pecking order he comes right next to the chairman. He's an artist. He's not necessarily qualified scientifically, though he'll have done some training in chemistry. He works with four or five thousand essences and solvents and catalysts and oils and bases and fragrances, working out permutations for months on end just to get one particular perfume that no one's ever

318

smelled before. He's got to have knowledge of the materials he's using, and also he's got to be inventive, imaginative – I guess artistic is really the word, like I said: he's an artist. And he's also got to know women, and understand them, right down deep.' Dean had given his low, reflective smile. 'That's a whole lot to understand.'

Donna had heard about Elliot Dietrich's quitting them without warning, and realised what Dean was talking about when he said Lorraine had pretty well saved the future of Floderus by finding François Farrier – 'If he's as good as he's cracked up to be. We'll find out soon enough.'

And now they were finding out, or beginning to. But Dean hadn't spoken to Lorraine once since they'd all trooped in here, or even glanced at her; and Lorraine was very much aware of it. So what had happened? Donna wished she knew; she had a deep liking and admiration for her vulnerable but courageous young boss, and a growing idea that Dean Powers was more than just a handsome, experienced businessman trying to outgrow a divorce. She didn't like to see them this way, estranged. If they were going to work together on this new and apparently critical project for *Siren Song*, they'd have to be friends.

Friends. . . In the rapt silence of the laboratory, Donna's mind swung back to the strange little event of last Friday. Maybe not so strange, when she considered it, but pretty unusual. She'd been coming out of the building onto the street when a short guy in a business suit had stopped her. 'Excuse me – it's Donna, isn't it?' A lined, poker face, greying hair, gold rings, silk handkerchief – she didn't remember him, but this happened often: when you're one person dealing with fifteen or twenty passengers you don't remember them all, but they remember you.

'Which flight?' she had asked him with a quick smile.

His face remained serious. 'It *is* Donna Shapiro?'

'Yes.'

Then he smiled, and it changed his face; he suddenly reminded her of her Dad. 'I'm a friend of Aldo's. Aldo Vinicari.'

'Aldo – oh, sure. Hi.'

'He sends his very best wishes, Donna.'

'Well, thanks. They – they were fantastic flowers. Orchids. Did he get my card? I thanked him for them.' She shrugged helplessly. 'I guess a card didn't seem really kind of adequate.'

The man's olive-brown eyes softened. 'It wasn't even necessary. Would you let me offer you lunch, Donna?'

'That's a nice thought, Mr – ?'

'Pinocchio. No relation,' he said, probably for the thousandth time with a patient smile. 'Friends call me Lucky.'

'Okay, but – thanks anyway, Mr – Lucky, but I have to skip lunch today. Everything's hopping.' It was true: after Lorraine's return from France the office had become even more galvanised than when Dean had rejoined the firm. 'How's little Joey?'

The man reached for her hand suddenly, and held it for a moment, till she began feeling embarrassed. 'Little Joey,' he said with his eyes growing bright, 'is fine.' He released her hand. 'I'm sorry I can't have the pleasure of giving you lunch, Donna. Some other time. But Aldo said when I was around this part of the world, I should give you his good wishes.'

'Thanks. Please tell him "hi" for me. And tell Joey.' She felt again the first fierce clutching of the small fingers as she broke the surface with him, then the limpness coming into his body as they headed for the canal bank.

'Of course,' Mr Pinocchio said. 'I'll tell them. And how are things with you, Donna? Are you okay?'

'Me? Sure. Fine.'

'No problems in your life? Nobody bothering you?'

'Huh? No. I'm fine.' She wondered whether it'd seem rude if she looked at her wrist watch; she had a hundred things to do in the next hour.

'Okay. But Aldo said to tell you that if you have any problems, anything at all – ' he said this very seriously, watching her eyes, 'whatever it is, we fix it for you.' He took both her hands this time, and gave them a gentle pressure. 'You must remember, Donna, you have friends, always. Very powerful friends.' Then he stood back suddenly and flashed her a generous smile. 'I'll tell them you're fine.'

She had watched him vanish among the lunch-time crowds on the pavement. So long as little Joey was okay, that was all she was interested in. She hadn't told anyone about what had happened; there wasn't any reason to; and she was still getting a kick at the way Judy Pollack looked at her whenever they met, her bright little button eyes focusing on her like a laser probe. 'Ya mean he hasn't sent you anything else since then? Just that crummy bunch of passion weeds a whole week ago? Take my advice, Donna, and finish with him. But let me know when you do, huh? I mean immediately.'

In the centre of the laboratory, François Farrier turned the revolving organ again, selecting a phial, uncorking it, holding it two inches from his nose – no closer, Lorraine noted every time – inhaling once and putting the stopper back and replacing it with the hand of a lover. It was an hour now since they'd come in here to put this *wunderkind* through his paces, as Carl Blatt had termed it. 'Okay,' Carl had warned them, 'the most dangerous thing we can do is rely on his reputation by hearsay; we have to get him into the lab and fire a few hundred questions at him and test his expertise and compare it with Dietrich's, rough and tumble him and see what comes out, make sure – make damned sure – we have someone here who can really do the job and pull Floderus out of the hole.' Instead, nobody had spoken a word, even Carl; from the moment when François had glanced around the lab and moved towards the essay benches they'd all sensed something going on that they didn't want to interrupt.

Jesus, Sy Goldman was thinking from the depths of the stained armchair, we have other things to do than sit here the whole day watching this poor man's Louis Pasteur go into trance, don't we? But he couldn't remember right now what they were.

321

This guy, Carl Blatt was thinking from his tennis umpire's perch, looks like he's going to spend the first twelve months sniffing around this place like a cat sniffing around a new apartment, and then he's going to spend the next twelve months considering everything he's been sniffing, and by the time he gets around to putting *Siren Song* together that creep Vanderkloot will have bought us up and thrown us out and we'll all be jockeying for position in the breadline.

Though Carl wasn't too sure about the Vanderkloot threat. Dean had tried to make it sound serious, but Carl didn't think it came out that way. 'Look,' Dean had told them in a very private meeting, 'Vanderkloot has this – er – he has this thing for Lorraine, you know? And of course she isn't interested, so he's told her he'll hit the company. Take it over. It sounds more like backstairs Washington, but Vanderkloot's well known as a power-mad megalomaniac, and incidentally he could take over Floderus just by signing his name.'

'That guy,' Joe Fisher had said, 'is in the hands of Leinster Zoltan. Doesn't that say enough?' Zoltan was the most expensive shrink in town. They'd talked about it for no more than ten minutes and then taken a vote. Ignore Vanderkloot. There were a dozen other hurdles they had to clear if they were going to succeed with this project, and if they started kicking the top rail every time they'd never make it.

François moved away from the huge revolving organ and sat down at one of the desks and opened the files one by one, running his eye down the sheets of essay formulae with his long-fingered hands turning the pages like a monk with a manuscript. Watching him, Dean tried to see him as the company's new white hope, the genius who would make them forget Dietrich and his treachery overnight; but he kept thinking of him in bed with Lorraine, with those long manicured fingers stroking her body with the legendary expertise of those goddamned Latins. But that was crazy; how many men did she sleep with anyway? Lorraine – *the* Lorraine Floderus? Christ, she must have to fight them off!

322

Okay, but he didn't know them; this one he knew. So what difference did that make? What in hell was burning him like this? He'd laid her own sister, hadn't he, almost as a reflex action – and she knew about it: that unmistakable after-sex atmosphere had been in his apartment when she'd walked in; and Madlen had actually spelt it out for her. Didn't that even the score over François?

No.

And what score, anyway?

He hadn't felt like this since Armanda had walked out of his life. It was crazy. *Ski-bump . . . ski-bump . . . ski-bump . . . The arhythmia is functional*, the doc had told him at his last visit, *not organic. If you can get your mind calm and your new life style stabilised after the divorce, it could even go away; but all the time it's there, it's real, so don't take any chances.*

Ski-bump.

Lorraine got up from her metal-framed chair and wandered out of the lab and lit a cigarette, standing in the doorway to the car park and looking up at the grey January sky, one hand on her neck, where the tension had been building up all morning. She'd found someone to replace Dietrich and brought him all the way from Europe and now he was in there making his evaluation of what they had to offer him, and the others in there were making their evaluation of whether he looked good enough, clever enough, reliable enough to be handed the exacting and critical task of saving the company – though he didn't know, of course, that so much was at stake. So one of four things could happen. François could agree to take over the laboratory, but the others could turn him down; or they could approve of him but he could say he couldn't work here without a totally new laboratory of his own design – geniuses had a bad reputation for being impossible; or he could turn down the job and the others could turn him down likewise; or . . . he could say yes and they could say yes . . . and she could start breathing again.

There was hope, so far. They'd all been watching François

323

with an extraordinary attention; Dean was the only one who'd shown any impatience, moving around a lot and sometimes looking at his watch; but then he might just be sulking; he was making it pretty clear that she shouldn't have been in bed with anyone when he got back from New Orleans – and he had a point. And there were always other things on his mind, and just possibly Madlen was one of them. He'd seen her twice, on Madlen's own admission. (Was that the word? Madlen didn't have to admit anything; she and Dean were free people. Okay, testimony.) So was Dean becoming really interested in her, apart from the sex? Underneath Madlen's present façade of bright, deliberate bitchiness she was a lovely person, with levels of human needs and responses that Dean might find reflected in his own. He had a lot of steadiness in him, which God knew her sister needed right now; and he could be protective, once he'd gotten over the need to protect himself.

Dean, a brother-in-law . . . with Madlen back in the mainstream of life, a whole person. It was something Lorraine could wish for, and even encourage, with all her heart.

All? No. But everything had its price.

She dropped her cigarette halfway through and stepped on it and went back inside. François was hitching himself with one lean haunch on an essay bench, a batch of papers on his knee.

'*Alors*,' he said on a long breath, and everyone moved slightly in reaction. '*Il était bien, hein? Au moins, pas mal.*' He looked at them in turn, his eyes lingering on Lorraine before passing on. '*Je voudrais dire –*'

'François,' Lorraine said, 'this is New York. Remember?'

His dark head swung to look at her. '*Comment? Oh – merde, alors* . . . I am sorry.' They all noticed he was blushing suddenly. 'I forget where I am, yes. But I was –' he shrugged gallically – 'far away.'

'You were saying he wasn't bad,' Lorraine told him. 'You mean our last *parfumeur*?'

'What? Yes. Yes, I like his notes. I like the way he left

324

things. And I know what he made. *Arabesque, Black Magic, Piquant* . . . They are great names. He was good, *ce monsieur*. And I am better.' Another shrug. 'I am not – *uh* – *je n'suis pas* – *uh* –'

'Boasting,' Lorraine nodded.

'That's good,' Carl said, and began rummaging in a drawer. 'Where the hell did Dietrich keep his paper-clips?'

They were all moving around suddenly, pacing, stretching, getting the blood circulating again; and it was a while before they realized that François wasn't speaking anymore; he was just sitting watching them, waiting; and finally they got the message. He was waiting for absolute silence, their absolute attention; and one by one they came to rest.

'That is correct,' François said at last. 'I am not boasting. I simply tell you the facts. You wish me to create a new *parfum* for you. It will take time, and it will be very expensive. You believe you are taking a risk with me, no? But I wish to tell you – forget it. There is no risk.' He waited, secretly proud of his use of idiom. 'Forget it' was one of his favourite phrases from the book, *Colloquial American-English*. It dismissed the subject so neatly. 'I will create the *parfum* for you, a great one.' He slapped the papers on his knee. 'The profile is not much help to me, but it is a start, yes. You ask for a brilliant top note, a resonant middle note, and a classic base note.' He shrugged. 'Many *parfums* are so.'

'Not classic,' Sy Goldman said. 'Classy. With class.'

'Oh?' François looked to Lorraine for help.

'*Haute monde*,' she tried.

'*Mais* snob?'

'*Non. Pas nécéssairement.* Think of champagne, caviar, cigars, limousines, le Concorde.'

'*Ah! Avec de la classe!*'

'Right,' Lorraine nodded, smiling.

So that's got that over, thought Sy gloomily, and if we're going to go all around the mulberry bush to get back to the same word, this thing's going to take an awful lot of time.

'In any case,' François was saying, 'I cannot create a perfume from a formula; it is the other way around; I create for the woman, then I design the formula for her.' He was leaning forward, looking into their faces, his voice becoming vibrant. 'I do not want to know what she looks like. Do we make perfume only for beautiful women? *Au contraire!* I do not care what she is, or what other people think about her, or what she thinks about herself. That is nothing, you see. It is the wrong track. I do not even care how she feels.' He paused, to make sure they were listening. 'I need to know only one thing about a woman when I create a perfume for her. I need to know how she *wants* to feel.'

He got off the bench and began moving around. 'We have hundreds of *essences* here, thousands, look at them! And if we put on a – a – *si nous étions aveugles – ?*' he appealed to Lorraine.

'If we put on a blindfold,' she nodded.

'Yes, a blindfold. If we did that, and chose the nearest dozen flacons here, and mixed them together, we would create a perfume. We could to this thing thousands of times, and make a thousand perfumes. But as you know, we would not find what we were looking for; it would be like mixing up all the words of a book: we would only have a lot of words, with no meaning. And the reason why we have to know what a woman wants to feel, before we can create for her, is that we must allow her to make a discovery.' He shrugged expressively. 'We do not really know ourselves, *hein?* We are so busy thinking about ourselves that we cannot look, we cannot listen. But we are there, somewhere; and what I say to you is this. When a woman smells the *parfum* – this one among all the others she has tried – and smiles suddenly and says yes, *this* is for me, she says only half the truth. Oh yes, she will buy it; we will have done the job. But what she really is meaning is, this *is* me. We have allowed her to discover herself – in our *parfum*. This is how she *wants* to feel. She wants to feel herself. Is this complicated? Of course. But it is the truth. I have proved it a thousand times. So did this *monsieur* here, your *parfumeur*, when he created

326

Picaresque and those others.'

Nobody was moving, or looking anywhere but at the lean rather slight figure in the blue French-cut suit, the jacket too long and the shoulders too sloping, as he moved across and across the laboratory, gesturing, shrugging, pausing to make sure he had their attention. Even Dean, Lorraine noticed with relief, wasn't fidgeting anymore.

'It is like music. When we try to think of a new tune, it is not necessary to know how many notes there are on the piano, *hein?* Or what the strings are made of, or how much tension they have, things like that. It is an instrument, you see.' He touched his head with both hands. 'The tune is in here. The music.' Then he gestured to the enormous organ of phials. 'There is the instrument.' His long hands moved to his head again. 'The *parfum* is in here.'

He began walking up and down more quickly now. 'Oh yes, there are other considerations; perfume has been made simply for women to smell; Guerlain was standing on a bridge over the Seine, on an evening before the first world war; it was twilight, and he was filled with the *nostalgie* that twilight brings, and he made *L'Heure Bleu*. He named another *parfum* for a Japanese girl, who was in love with an English navy officer in the Russian war with Japan; her name was *Mitsouko*; the *parfum* is still selling today. He made a *parfum* to honour the book by Saint-Exupéry, about he brave *aviateurs* of the airmail routes across the Andes, and the women who loved them.' With a rare smile – 'No, *Vol de Nuit* does not smell of gasoline . . . but it smells of excitement, of daring.' Another shrug. 'Guerlain was *un grand maître, bien sûr*. But he was a painter; he painted scenes, in his perfumes. I am different; I try to find the woman; to find her spirit, her soul.'

He hitched himself onto a bench again. 'But that is for me to do. You want to know about other things – costs, availability, the time necessary to do this thing. I am a creator of perfume, but also I am a practical man. If, *par exemple*, we want to use musk in the blend, it will have to be synthetic. Imagine the expense of getting the real supply; it needs hunting expeditions across the Himalayas, you know? The musk deer browses on the snow-line of the mountains in Tibet, and at night; it is difficult to hunt; and it must be killed, for the essence. And then the essence has to go by caravan through China to Burma, or from the southern Himalayas through India. Imagine! It is crazy, that. Those days are over. I am not here to cost your company a fortune, you see.'

'How much?' Sy Goldman's voice came suddenly, and some of them laughed, releasing tension.

François didn't hesitate. 'Five million francs.'

Sy made a quick calculation. A million dollars. They'd budgeted for two. He sat up straighter in his chair.

'You're going to take short cuts?' Carl Blatt asked François, blinking more rapidly.

'Short – ?'

'Make economies,' Lorraine said.

François shook his head. 'No. That is what it will cost.'

Dean spoke for the first time. 'I haven't had time to look over your track record. How experienced are you?' *Siren Song* wasn't going to be sold for twenty bucks an ounce in the supermarkets.

'I am a qualified *parfumeur* for ten years.'

'That's not long.'

François lifted his chin slightly. 'It has been long enough, *m'sieur*, for me.'

'Sure,' Dean nodded off-handedly. 'I only question whether it's been long enough for the perfumer who's going to work for us.' His tone was perfectly level as the two men stared at each other across the room.

Okay, Donna thought, now we have the message. This is why Dean hasn't been speaking to Lorraine all morning. Surprise. But not a big surprise; that François packs an awful lot of libido.

'I can only offer you my reputation,' François said quietly.

Cross-legged on the floor, Joe Fisher went into meditation, and fast. This wasn't what they'd come here for. This François was a fucking genius; you could tell it just by

328

looking at him when he was talking perfume. It was his life, his soul; he ate it, drank it and pissed it. What had gotten into Dean?

'I've heard your reputation,' Dean nodded briefly, while Sy Goldman thought, only this guy has the knack of making that word 'heard' sound like a false rumour. 'We're just trying to judge for ourselves. Your expertise, your real knowledge of fragrances, your ability to work with them.'

Lorraine closed her eyes for a moment. Even during her years in Hollywood she'd never realised or maybe let herself realise the role sex played in the modern business world, in every aspect of human endeavour, where there didn't seem any place for it. Just because Frederick Vanderkloot had the hots for her as a woman, the fortunes of a fifty-million-dollar company were in hazard. And just because she happened to be in bed with François when Dean had landed in New York, there was going to be a clash of macho personalities that could end in François going straight back to France. Jesus Christ, couldn't men ever think above their jock-straps?

Sitting with her eyes closed in an unconscious attempt to shut out reality, she had that onrushing sense of defeat that was now so familiar; every time she thought she'd managed to get it right at last, she found she'd got it wrong. Again.

The French guy's just coming across too arrogant, Joe Fisher thought, but geniuses are like that, doesn't Dean know? Thing is, Dean doesn't think he's a genius, because Dean hasn't the experience this guy has. It figures. Aw . . . *shit*.

'It is difficult,' François was saying, his voice as level as Dean's, 'for you to understand the extent of my ability –' he was picking his way carefully through the obstacles of his new language, knowing how stupid one could sound if one got even a word wrong – 'because you have no experience yourself in the work I do. I mean basically, the simple necessity to – necessity of knowing one smell from another, out of several thousand. That is the basis of my experience, *m'sieur*, the basis for all that I do. The fact that it only took

329

me ten years to learn it has no importance. In music, the infant prodigal learns even quicker; and my – ' he broke off suddenly, blushing with self-anger. '*Prodigy*, yes.' In a moment he went on, 'And my talent has much to do with music.'

Everyone waited, most of them looking down, though Donna and Sy were looking at Dean. Lorraine sat with her eyes closed, feeling sickened.

After a long silence, Dean said: 'I see. That's fine. Thank you.'

Joe's scalp crept. So that's it.

Oh my God, Carl Blatt was thinking, *this* early? Dean had got precisely the right tone in his voice. *I see. That's fine. Thank you.* You may stand down now; the case is closed.

François hadn't mistaken it. With a slight shrug he went across to the organ and took a single phial, bringing it to Dean and taking the glass stopper out. 'Can you tell me, *m'sieur*, what this contains?'

Dean wouldn't be led into a trap so simple. 'No. It's not my job.'

François nodded, restoppering the phial. 'It is what I am saying. It is not your job; but it is mine; and it is my job, I think, that is being questioned.' He put the phial back and went to a desk and picked up a heavy bound volume, turning and looking around at the others, all except Dean. He chose Sy Goldman, the big man in the deep chair who looked experienced and impartial. 'This contains all the formulae of the essays along the shelves there. Each essay is of course numbered, and you will find each number in the book, quite easily.' He looked around him again. 'Mademoiselle Donna, would you please take a flacon down and bring it to me?'

'Sure. From here?'

'Yes,' François said with his back turned towards the shelves, and waited. 'And please hold your hand to conceal the number from me, but show it first to the *m'sieur* here with the book.'

Sy looked at the number and nodded. 'I have that.'

'Thank you. Donna, please take the top out. The cork.'
'The stopper. Sure.'
'But keep the number concealed, *hein?*'
'Okay.'

François moved her hand to bring the flacon two inches from his nose, and inhaled, closing his eyes. 'Jasmine,' he said at once, 'and terpineol, with dianthus and – and violet.' He inhaled again, slowly. 'Methyl salicylate. Mimosa absolute. Cuminic aldehyde. Orange. Cassie absolute.' He moved the phial away and inhaled two or three times, and then brought it close again. 'Eugenol. Hydroxy citronellal. And orris.' He gave the phial to Donna. 'Bring another, please. From anywhere.'

Everyone was looking obliquely towards Sy in his armchair. He glanced up briefly. 'Correct. Number 1009.'

Donna brought François another flacon, showing the number to Sy first and waiting till he'd turned the pages of the book.

'There were many synthetic perfumes in the first one,' said François. 'It was good. It was a classic. But too synthetic. I will be using more natural absolutes; we have all we need in Grasse.' He began inhaling, intoning. 'Inone alpha. Guaiac wood, and Geraniol palmarosa . . .' He moved the phial away three times, and named twelve scents, the last of them trichlor phenyl methyl carbinyl acetate. 'It is a synthetic rose otto. On most women it would remain one hour, maybe two, but no more. It has no endurance.'

As Donna brought another phial, Sy Goldman nodded solemnly. 'Contents correct.'

Like I said, Joe was thinking, this guy is a fucking genius.

There was an absolute silence in the laboratory as François distinguished the ingredients of four more essays, now becoming lost in his thoughts and speaking half to himself. 'Good, but not indoloid; the superimposition of jasmin is clever, but no white lilac perfume is complete without indole . . . This one is very nice, but too masculine, because of the *fougère* – it is sophisticated, but too deep-noted for a woman . . . This will be number 237, *hein?*'

331

'Correct,' Sy Goldman nodded, looking up at him with a certain awe.

'Thank you, *m'sieur*. Now this one is very interesting, because it also is heavy and clinging, since it is a chypre, yet it is not too masculine for a woman; *au contraire*, when a woman will wear this, the men are attracted. But she would need to want a feeling of enormous romance, intrigue, the sense of a historic palace scandal . . .' He was smiling now, totally lost to the people around him. 'Because of the oak-moss, I would have used slightly less than ten per cent of alcohol, because it is too volatile. A few years ago, my uncle used to distill the lichen over cedarwood oil; the *parfum* was sensational, but it discoloured with age, and he stopped doing that thing . . .'

'Correct,' Sy kept saying as each phial was put back. 'Absolutely correct as to contents.'

Little Carl Blatt was leaning forward on his high stool, staring at the Frenchman as if mesmerised. Joe Fisher wore the seraphic smile of a saint, slipping in and out of light meditation without even trying; he had always been particularly susceptible to the presence of a genius. Once Lorraine caught a glance from Donna, who had the compressed smile of a cheer-leader who'd been told to shut up.

Dean Powers hadn't moved his position; nor had he looked away from the lean dark *parfumeur*, except when Sy reported his findings. The clock on the wall was nearing the hour of noon, but nobody noticed.

'Ethyl cinnamate . . .' François ended a list of ingredients in number 171. 'I like this one better; he has used sweet orange in the top note, as well as bergamot and lemon – not so many synthetics here, you see – and he has used cyclamen and musk ketone for the base note; yes, this one I like, but I would have used perhaps orange absolute for the middle note, as well as the tuberose . . .'

And then, as Donna replaced the fourth phial on its shelf in the organ, François put his hands behind his back and began pacing slowly from wall to wall of the laboratory, his

332

dark head down and his feet in their black polished shoes taking short precise steps across the synthetic tile floor. Despite his youth and his slight stature, he became the very image of a distinguished lecturer of the *Académie Française* as he spoke in the pedantic, donnish tones of an undisputed authority.

'*Mesdames, messieurs* . . . I bear the name of Farrier. I am of the house of Farrier, of Grasse. Four hundred years ago my family was creating perfumes for the women of the royal courts of France, Italy, and England. At the invitation of the Medicis, the *parfumeur* Tombarelli of Florence came to live in Grasse, and make perfumes. In the reign of Louis XV, the taste for aromatic flowers, herbs and spices spread throughout the courts of Europe. My family, the family of Farrier, created these things by royal appointment. My family is still creating perfume in the same town, today.'

He paused for a moment reflecting, picking up a beaker from the essay bench and holding it to the light, putting it down again. 'This morning I have been asked to perform a cheap party trick for you, to make a little guessing game to show that I know my business. I could see you were impressed, but for me it was absurd, it was a nothing. I could go through a thousand flacons here and tell you what is in them, but it would be very boring for me.' He shrugged expansively, and his tone was dulled with cynicism. 'So, *mesdames, messieurs*, the little dog has done his tricks, *hein?* I hope you are satisfied.'

Donna sat holding her breath. There was a tone of something in this young man's voice that suggested an enormous wrong, an insult to the house of Farrier deadly enough to bring forth its hosed and doubleted ghosts with plumed hats waving and swords drawn.

'In other circumstances,' François went on in his academic tones, 'and with other people, I would have walked out of here immediately.' He looked at them in turn, standing still suddenly in the centre of the laboratory. 'But you bring me to New York, to the city I love, and you invite me to work for your small but *renommé* company. So I do

333

things for you that I would not do for other people. But you have to trust me, and trust my reputation, if I am to do the best work for you. And if you do that, I will create for you *un grand parfum*, perhaps the greatest you will ever have known.' Then he pulled from *Colloquial American-English* one of its choicest plumbs. 'I am not here in New York to horse around.'

CHAPTER 28

THAT WAS MONDAY morning.

Monday evening, Lorraine made her routine call to the Lotus Club and asked if she could talk to Madlen.

'I'm sorry, she just stepped out.'

'Thank you. Please tell her I called.'

'Why, certainly. Oh – just a moment, Miss Floderus, I have a number here where she can be reached. Would you like to write it down?'

'Yes.' As Lorraine reached for the gold Parker she felt a sudden hope. It was the first time Madlen had ever left word for her. She wrote the first three digits, then the next two, and stopped writing them down. 'Thank you, I have that.' She hung up and crossed the number out. It was Dean Powers'.

That was okay. She felt hope of a different kind. This would be, as far as she knew, the third time Dean was seeing Madlen. Dean had a lot of faults, but he wouldn't hurt Madlen, knowingly. She was safer in his hands, God knew, than in Angelo Baccari's there at the club.

Tuesday morning they held the meeting.

They met in Lorraine's office – Dean, Sy, Joe, Carl, Donna – and locked the doors. Nadine was told no calls unless they were urgent; Donna sat near the phones ready to take any call that came through and decide for Lorraine how urgent it was.

Today the atmosphere was different than it had been two weeks ago, when Dean had been absent. It was less gung-ho, less sanguine, less inspired. They all of them felt this meeting was going to be the really deciding climax to everything that had gone before, and would seal the fate of Floderus Incorporated one way or the other. But there was a balance involved, and maybe, Sy Goldman thought, it was a healthy one. They were all inspired by what they'd seen of François Farrier in the laboratory yesterday, except Dean; and maybe his brooding, conservative view of the situation might easily save them from making a final and disastrous mistake.

'I don't understand the rush,' he said from the window-sill where he was perched.

'I thought we did that bit,' Joe said.

'I think we should do it again.'

'Okay.' Joe Fisher shrugged amiably. He knew there was only one thing to be done, and by the time they left here today they'd have to make up their minds to do it; he felt a sense of fatal commitment, with the fates on his side.

It was François himself who had brought them together here so soon after their meeting at the laboratory. After his studied rebuke of Dean Powers they'd asked him some more about the projected cost of creating Siren Song, and how he was coming up with a figure of only one million dollars.

'Because I work quickly,' he'd told them simply. 'It is my way. I like working to a deadline. And I can ask them to do things for me in Grasse that they would not do for anyone else. And also I will be using fewer essences, because that is the way to create a great perfume. To make a dramatic statement, you use few words, but strong ones, powerful ones. It will take me less time, much less time, than it would take someone less talented. This is always the way. To save time, of course, is to save money.'

'What time frame,' Carl asked him, 'are you talking about? Two years? Three?'

François stopped pacing and looked at him steadily. 'You are in a hurry?'

'I wouldn't say that.'

'What time frame are *you* thinking about?' François

asked him.

'How about right now?'

'Right now?' François searched his mind, and *Colloquial American-English*, for more than one meaning for the phrase, but couldn't think of any. Right now meant what it said, right now.

'We mean,' Lorraine explained, 'as soon as possible.' She knew exactly what was in Carl Blatt's mind; if they were to keep the shareholders with them until they could launch the new fragrance and give the company's image on Wall Street a shot in the arm, they would have to be quick.

'As soon as possible,' nodded François, and began pacing again while they watched him.

Joe Fisher came out of meditation and focused his mind on François, sending his thoughts like a beam of energy into the dark head of the Frenchman. *C'mon, François, make it a year. You can do it in a year, with all you've got going for you. Twelve months, okay. You listening to me? Twelve months . . . Twelve . . . Twelve . . .*

The silence drew out, and when Dean made a slight sound with the papers on his knee, everyone glared at him as if he'd uttered a primal scream.

'You Americans,' François said after a long time, and left it at that; and this time there wasn't that note of rueful affection in his voice.

We've put him on the spot, Sy thought. He's been coming across so good that we think he can produce miracles. It happened.

'Always the rush,' François said, then shrugged. 'But it is your way, and I am here to do things your way, if it will not affect the quality of the things I do.' He walked from one wall to the other, twice, past the essay benches and the filing cabinets and the huge organ and the doors to the distillation rooms and the three long desks with their word processors and computers and telephones. Then he stopped and looked up.

'How many assistants will I have here, please?'

'Seven in your personal team,' Carl told him. 'Around

337

twenty in the processing rooms.'

'And they are – they are very competent people?'

'Top of their profession,' Dean said, feigning slight surprise.

'I will not ask them for party tricks, you see. I take your word.' François shrugged again. 'Very well. Three months.' He began pacing again, more slowly, lost in thought.

Sy spoke first. 'Three months what, François?'

'*Hein?* For my deadline.'

'No,' Carl said, 'we want to know how long it would take you to create the new fragrance. Ready for marketing.'

François looked impatient. 'Yes, yes, yes. I understand. You will have your new *parfum* in three months from now. That is what I tell you.'

So now they were holed up in the chairman's office as if – thought Joe Fisher – they'd been hurled here by an explosion.

'You say you don't understand the rush,' Joe told Dean Powers. 'Okay, the rush is because I think we have to do this thing just as soon as we possibly can; and François has said three months. Three months brings us to the merry month of May, a perfect time for the presentation of a new fragrance, with spring still in the air and the promise of summer vacations to come; but the main thing is that if we can do it sooner instead of later, why the hell not? It's psychologically right, I mean for us; and we're the people who are going to be working on this thing till we drop dead in our tracks the day before the big presentation and have to be carried in there by pall-bearers.'

He lifted himself to his feet from his lotus position without using his hands and began walking around. 'I'm talking about the rhythm of events, okay? We made the decision to create a new fragrance and we made it out of our innate ebullience and enthusiasm and goal-seeking drive, which is the only way to make any successful decision; and then that creep Dietrich walked out on us and brought the whole thing down around our heads; and *then* Lorraine went and waved her magic wand over there in Europe and suddenly we have

338

what I soberly consider to be about the biggest goddamned opportunity that any business enterprise has had in its lap since we bought Manhattan from the Indians.' He stopped in front of Dean. 'So now we're going to shove it in the fridge and cool it off and sit on our hands and watch the leaves come off the calendar till we're buried alive?'

They talked for another hour.

'My considerations are entirely practical,' Dean was saying at the end of it. 'There just isn't adequate *time* to plan the ad campaign and the coast-to-coast promotions and personal appearances and word-of-mouth publicity among the distributors, aside from the physical and logistical problems of marketing and actually shipping the product across the country in time for a concerted and synchronised launching. Dammit, we haven't even designed the bottles, or the boxes, or the overall counter packaging and display material!'

Joe sank to the floor again, hoping the others might see the symbolism.

They talked for another hour.

'I see Joe's point of view,' Carl Blatt was saying as he trotted from the windows to the bookshelves and back, a paper-clip spinning between his fingers like a propeller. 'It's like getting behind a snowball and pushing; you stop to consider things too long and it just rolls back on your feet.' It was Carl, Lorraine remembered, who had first proposed creating a new fragrance as the only hope of getting the company profitable again; and despite his respect for Dean Powers he was still for going ahead, and right now. 'Sure, time would be critically short for the promotion we have to do; but not impossibly so; it depends on how hard we're all prepared to work; as far as I'm concerned I'm ready to bring a camp bed into my office.'

Joe followed him up. ' "There is a tide in the affairs of men that if taken at the flood leads on to fortune . . ." '

Lorraine looked at Sy Goldman, who remained deep in his armchair and said nothing. He'd make his decision when he was good and ready.

'There just isn't any room,' Dean said in a tone of exasperation, 'for all this unbridled romanticism. While you're talking about pushing snowballs and quoting Shakespeare I'm having to face facts and figures. And let me say this: I don't have enough faith in that French wonder-boy; he talks about his family like it's the monarchy, but I'm not terribly impressed. Can he really come up with a *great* perfume in just three months? I think we need to ask ourselves what would happen if we went right ahead and worked our hides off for three months and got the whole of the industry on its toes and breathlessly waiting for the big presentation – and then couldn't produce the new fragrance. Right now we could get a decent price for this company, providing Vanderkloot held off; but if we let ourselves be romanticised into a two-million-dollar coast-to-coast promotion campaign for a product we couldn't produce, we'd be a laughing-stock, and *have* to sell out. And the price would be a joke too.'

Point, thought Sy Goldman.

Donna hadn't contributed a word since they'd come in here, except to ask if she could get anyone some more coffee. Watching Lorraine now and then, she wondered how the hell this young woman could sit here and listen to an argument that was going to decide once and for all the fate of her company; did she realise how critical the discussion was? Yes indeed, she did. Lorraine might feel she should be acting the part of a confident, imperturbable Manhattan mogul who could take a crashed company in her stride, but she wasn't doing that. As she moved her beautiful head to watch one speaker after another, her eyes were registering her every reaction, brightening as Joe or Carl brought out an argument for going ahead, clouding as Dean or Sy threw down a warning of almost certain disaster.

Donna remembered very clearly the time when she and Lorraine had been talking here in this room two weeks ago, and Lorraine had said, *Don't you think that just sometimes it's possible to do the impossible?* And Donna had thought about it and said, *Yes, we can do the impossible, if that's what*

340

we want to do.

Lorraine was still asking these people the same question, but the answer wasn't coming quite as fast. They were a house divided: Lorraine, Carl, and Joe against Dean and Sy, with Dean bringing more weight to bear than any of the others could: the weight of his longer experience, his impressive logic, and his reasoned arguments.

Watching her boss sometimes, Donna wondered why she wasn't shaking herself to pieces inside as the future of Floderus Incorporated was tossed like a ball between the others, hour after hour. Maybe she was.

The meeting ended quite suddenly, and Lorraine herself was responsible, whether she intended it or not. Picking up one of the outside telephones she dialled a twelve-digit number and said when the line opened: *'Ici Mademoiselle Lorraine Floderus, de la maison Floderus et Cie, New York. Je voudrais parler à Monsieur Jacques Farrier, s'il vous plaît. Oui, j'attendrai.'* She looked across her desk at Dean while she waited. 'Dean, do you agree that Jacques Farrier is one of the four greatest authorities on the manufacture of perfume in the world?'

He tilted his well-sculpted head. 'Maybe. But what the hell is this?'

'I simply want – just a minute.' She spoke in English as Farrier came to the phone; he was fluent, and she wanted Dean and the others to understand what was going on. After the exchange of courtesies – it was a cold rainy day in New York, and Madame Farrier's arthritis was a little better – she asked him: 'Jacques, you know François better than I do. He assures me he can create our new fragrance within three months. Do you believe that's possible?'

There was a pause. 'If he says he can do it, yes, he will do it, without any question. He has done it before. And remember he is very grateful to you for taking him to New York. It is a tremendous incentive, *ma chère* Lorraine. Yes, he can do it. And he will.'

Lorraine was astonished at the intensity of the relief and hope that was surging through her; during the past hours the

341

continuous tension had been getting to her, until she'd begun to believe that all was lost. On a deep breath she asked Farrier to hold on for a moment, and held the phone out to Dean. 'Would you like to talk to him? I'd rather you had it first hand.'

He moved to the chair where he'd left his briefcase, picked it up and walked at a steady pace to the door. 'You'll have to excuse me, Lorraine. I don't need Farrier or anyone else to make up my mind for me. We've argued this thing into the ground and we know where we stand. I just don't have enough faith in your romantic young perfumer to rush the company and my job. You go ahead if you want to; but I'd rather not be associated if you do. Sorry.'

After he'd closed the door Lorraine talked to Jacques Farrier again for a few moments, apologising for holding him up, then said goodbye and put the phone down slowly, clasping the nape of her neck in both hands and closing her eyes and saying to no one in particular, 'What happened?'

Sy Goldman spoke from the depths of his chair.

'You pushed him. He doesn't like that.'

Wearily she asked, 'Do you think he'll reconsider?'

'No.'

That evening, Lorraine didn't go home to shut herself in with her despair; she went along to the *dojo* and threw Billy all over the floor.

He was one of the huge blacks, and the first time he looked up at her from the mat his face was so astonished that Lorraine did something she hadn't done for a long time: she laughed.

Sadie came over. 'That looked okay, Lorraine, but there was less technique than anger in it, which I don't like. We don't want anger in here; it's the wrong vibes. How much did you let her do it, Billy?'

'Jesus,' he said as he got up, 'I –'

'And don't blaspheme. You know the rules.'

'Yes *Sensei*. I didn't let her do it at all. She went right out and did it.' He gave a big sunny grin, as proud as if he'd done

342

it himself.

'So what's the anger all about, Lorraine?'

Lorraine wanted to say, I just lost a fifty-million-dollar company. But it wouldn't sound right. 'It was a rough day, *Sensei*.'

'You weren't angry at Billy?' Sometimes a student would take a roughing-up personally, and react.

'Hell, no.' Sadie let that one go by; it wasn't the name of the deity and for a hundred bucks a month you couldn't expect saints.

'Okay. Do it again.'

Lorraine tried and failed.

'Try again.'

She failed again.

'It's partly because I'm watching you now, and partly because you're not using your hips enough to sweep you around; you're concentrating too much on jackknifing his knee, an' that's using up your energy. That's the easy bit, see, the knee; even with a guy this size there isn't a lot of force required, and you're overdoin' in. Concentrate on building up that sweep and *think* him down, *see* him down, *look* at him lyin' there with that silly grin off of his face. *Project what's going to happen, in your mind,* an' believe me there ain't nothin' in this world that can stop you, least of all this big creep. An' stop grinnin', Billy, and *don't let her*, you understand, or I swear I'll feed you to Tiger.' She took Lorraine's arm, turning her away and walking in a small circle with her, coming back. 'Relax, okay? Go limp, like this, the marionette, remember? Shake your body out. Right. Now, make up your own mind when you want to go at him, don't wait for me to tell you. Take your time and *project the future* for yourself and remember by this time Billy's just about hysterical with apprehension. Do it when you feel ready.' She walked away to talk to the other black belt instructor, and when she looked around there was Billy on the floor again looking real surprised.

Ten minutes from the end of the session, after the main class had gone through basics, Sadie put Lorraine and Billy

343

together again and said, 'Okay. Do it like you did before, except this time there's one little difference. Billy ain't near hysterical with nerves anymore. He's good an' strong now, and remember he turns in at two hundred pounds, one hundred of which is muscle, and he's six foot three, and he's *fast.*' Sadie, five foot four, looked up at him. 'Now get your thinking right, Billy. You're not expectin' her to try this on you, but as soon as you see she's makin' a start, you're going to react. You're goin' to try to stop her from takin' you down.' She turned to Lorraine. *'And nothing's goin' to change, see.* You've done it before an' you can do it a thousand times in a row and it don't matter *anything* that Billy's going to react, because you're goin' to do the same thing all over again, you're goin' to project the future, and the future is the same old Billy lyin' down there on the mat lookin' surprised out of his mind. *See* him there. And *put* him there. When you're ready.' She walked away again, and when she turned around Billy was still on his feet and Lorraine was standing there looking disgusted.

'You were *thinking*,' Sadie told her sternly. 'You were thinking, by golly, if he turns in at two hundred pounds there ain't no chance I got of puttin' him on the floor.' She stared into Lorraine's eyes with that liquid mud-brown stare that for a moment made everything else go away and the air became silent and time skid to a stop. Then she said, 'When you're ready.'

She walked away from the two of them and she'd gone maybe ten paces when she heard an almighty thump on the mat and her mouth twisted into a short laugh of satisfaction. Then she heard a different sound, and turned around and went back and found Lorraine crying like a kid with the tears pouring down her face and making dark spots on her white *gi* while Billy stood there saying look, I never did anything to her, honest, she just took me down an' I never did anything . . .

'This is just *exhilaration*,' Lorraine told them when she could speak properly. 'It's just —'

'It's okay, Billy,' said Sadie. 'She's just kinda pleased with

344

herself.' She walked away and called the class to line up and recite the creed and break for the night.

As they were leaving, Lorraine said, 'Billy, do you have any plans for the rest of the evening?'

'I guess I don't.'

'Okay, I'm going to take you across there for the biggest pizza you ever saw. I haven't been winning much, lately, but tonight it was different.' She took his arm. 'Come on, I'll be your bodyguard, in case anybody tries mugging you out there on the street.'

The next day Judy Pollack was sitting in her glass-fronted office in her new rainbow-colored Terylene blouse and thinking how absolutely godawful it looked whenever she caught her reflection, and trying to forget it and concentrate on her work.

'You know something, Betty Lou? We were too late to get to the shelter.'

Betty Lou looked up from her word processor. 'What shelter?'

'The air raid shelter. Don't you recognise nuclear fallout? And don't say what nuclear fallout. Everyone on the executive floor is holed up in their own office and not going out to see anybody else; Donna is fielding so many of Lorraine's routine visits and calls that she's practically running the company; and every time I try calling anybody I get my head chewed off and spat out in the spitoon. It's frightening.' She hit her typewriter with five memos and gave them to Betty Lou and went along to the main floor for a coffee. It was something to do with Dean Powers. Dean and Lorraine. They'd provided the nuclear fission again.

Away from Betty Lou, Judy allowed herself a few minutes of black despair. Because it wasn't funny anymore. For the past twelve months this company had seemed to be running on a pretty even keel, though business had fallen off; but in the last weeks it'd been like somebody had pulled World War II out of the files and poured it all over the building. And this was Manhattan, Nouveau York, where at any

345

given time in any given office your boss was liable to call up and say hey kids, the whole thing's over, but we're xeroxing a map for you so you can find the breadline.

Coffee of course was no help; it just gave you the running shits.

By the end of the morning Lorraine had finished trying to get through her routine chores and at the same time talking to Dean Powers in her mind, cursing him out, wheedling, giving him facts, yelling at him, whispering to him and finally telling him to get out of this building and get out of her life and stay out.

Donna had been taking the pressure off her all morning and she owed her a lunch; also she owed it to herself to spend an hour in Donna's gutsy, positive-thinking, restorative company, so that she could at least get through the rest of the day without giving in to final, paralysing depression.

Donna was coming out of the ladies' room when Lorraine began looking for her at one o'clock. Even the sight of those straight shoulders and crisp red hair was heartening.

'Donna, I'm buying you a lunch, is that okay?'

'Well, gee – 'she looked a little confused. 'Terrific, but Dean's taking me to the Danish Buffet; why don't you join us?'

Lorraine turned as she heard the lift doors opening.

'I think I'll pass, this time. Dean prefers twosomes. Have fun.'

CHAPTER 29

BY THE END OF the afternoon Lorraine was sitting at her desk considering for the first time the idea of putting Floderus Incorporated up for sale. If this was a breakthrough in her thinking, she didn't welcome it. She felt like she'd spent the past weeks letting herself be pushed gradually into a corner, and had fought back all the way, and lost.

Throughout the afternoon she'd talked to Sy, Joe and Carl, asking each of them into her office alone so she could get their individual points of view, which they could express without the inhibiting influence of other listeners. But their points of view hadn't changed very much.

'It isn't really the threat posed by Vanderkloot,' Carl had told her. 'There's absolutely nothing we can do about that, so it's easier to ignore. It's the shareholders, and the industry. Everyone's waiting for us to go on sliding downwards, and unless we can come up with a real show of resurgence in our policy, that's it. And we have to do it soon. That's why this guy François is so indispensable to us, right now. But give him a year, even, to create *Siren Song* and it's going to be too late.'

Sy Goldman had been less optimistic. Joe Fisher had been almost angry, especially with Dean. 'We can't do without him, Lorraine; he has the strength we need, the experience, the invaluable knowledge of the market. But he doesn't have our faith.' On his way out, he'd asked her hesitantly, 'Mind if I say something? Is there anything – I mean can you think why there's this thing between Dean and François? I mean, is it just – you know, a clash of personalities, or – ' he

347

shrugged, balking.

'Whatever it is, Joe, there's nothing we can do about it.'
He'd nodded ruefully and gone out.

Sell Floderus, then. There were advantages. Barry had told her she'd get out with twenty million in her personal account. That was a consolation. Freedom from worry. A trip around the world. Make a new movie, if her screen image hadn't gone cold. Or buy a small, promising company in the same field.

And run it into the ground.

During the afternoon Nadine had been in a couple of times for urgently-needed signatures; Judy Pollack had called twice and been told not to call again unless it was absolutely essential; and Donna had come in with a run-down on a newly-established advertising agency on 57th Street.

'It looks interesting,' she'd told Lorraine.

'Fine.' Her tone was cool.

'Shall I leave it here?'

'Yes. I'll look at it when I can.'

'Okay.'

Donna left the report on the end of the desk and went to the door. Lorraine was picking up a telephone as Donna turned and looked at her across the width of the room.

'Is there something else?' Lorraine asked her briefly.

'I guess you're too busy right now.'

'Is it something Dean Powers can help you with?'

'Not really.'

Lorraine put the phone down but kept her hand on it. 'Donna, I think you're intelligent enough to know whether you have to talk to me right now, or leave it till later.'

Donna hesitated, then said: 'I guess it won't take long. I just want to know if I'm fired.'

'For God's sake, what for?'

'Having lunch with Dean Powers.'

Lorraine looked away. 'It's nothing in the least important, Donna. Forget it.'

'I think it's important. You're my boss, and you asked me

348

to lunch, so there must have been something you wanted to talk about, at a time when – things are kind of critical. So I should have cancelled my lunch with Dean, right away. And I didn't.' She gave a little shrug. 'I guess everyone screws up sometimes.'

Abstractedly Lorraine said, 'I said you could forget it. Okay?' She offered a bright smile, right out of the script.

Donna wouldn't move. There was some kind of struggle going on in her mind, too. 'Lorraine, could you make it a little easier for me?'

'Am I making it difficult?'

Donna compressed her lips. 'I can handle drunks and bastards and ten-year-old adult males, but I guess I'm not so good with people I like. So I need your help.'

Lorraine looked at her in astonishment. She'd been so engrossed in her own helplessness all day that she hadn't imagined anyone had need of anything she could possibly give. She took her hand off the phone and said: 'You want to sit down?'

Donna shook her head of red hair, but came slowly into the middle of the room and stood with her arms folded. 'Tell me what you think of Dean Powers, would you?'

'He's just the biggest stud in the business,' Lorraine said wearily, and came around from her desk and stared from the south windows. For the first time she wasn't sure whether she could trust this self-assured little airline stewardess; it had been a part of Donna's training to mix with all kinds of people and regard them as simply the objects of her temporary responsibility. Maybe she'd never had time to learn to handle or even understand deeper relationships.

'That's all?' Donna asked.

'What?'

'That's all Dean is? Just a stud?'

Impatiently Lorraine said, 'Not really, but you just asked me at the wrong time.' All she could feel about Dean Powers right now was a simmering anger, but she couldn't bring herself to villify a long-standing director of the company to a new recruit, even though it would have been a wonderful

349

relief to put it on the line, out loud: *Okay, my definition of a total stud is a guy who sleeps with every junior typist he can get his hands on without even trying to keep it discreet, and who is not only sleeping with my own sister but has apparently started dating my personal aide. But that would be okay – or fairly okay – if it weren't so one-sided; but he's also slept with me, and he's such a stud that he can't stand the thought of my sleeping with anyone else; and all this would be nothing more than the material for a trashy magazine serial if it weren't that we're now going to have to give up our last hope of saving this company and send François Farrier straight back to France, because there isn't room for both of them in Floderus Incorporated. Or what remains of it.*

Donna had taken a hesitant step towards her. 'I had a very interesting time with him, at the Danish Buffet.'

Lorraine swung her head to give her a freezing smile. 'I'm absolutely delighted for you.'

'He talked the entire time about you.'

Lorraine tensed. 'About what I've done with this company?'

'No. About nothing specific, really.' Her deep brown eyes studied Lorraine reflectively for a moment as she compressed her lips again; then she made up her mind to get it over with. 'Lorraine, you hired me to give you good service; that's what anyone gets hired for; and I think it's what I'm trying to give you right now. You – I guess you've fallen in love plenty of times, like most of us; and you know how it is, when you're talking to people, that you keep coming around to talking about the person you love?' She shrugged helplessly again with her hands, not at all certain she was doing this the right way; but she sure couldn't stop now. 'Like I say, Dean didn't say anything specific. He just couldn't stop talking about you.'

Lorraine stared at her. 'Dean Powers in *love*? He doesn't even know the meaning of the word! This time you're really off base.' She smiled briefly and went back to her desk.

On her way to the Algonquin, Lorraine remembered she

hadn't made her nightly call to the Lotus Club, and stopped the Rolls Royce on Lexington, walking across to a call box.

Okay, it was a routine now; she didn't any longer hope that Madlen would come on the line and talk to her; but she knew she must never stop trying. Even Madlen could change, feel in a different and more generous mood, or find something important to say to her; and if she didn't, she'd be told Lorraine called, and enjoy the small feeling of triumph that she'd turned her down again.

'Just a minute, please.'

Lorraine waited, watching the line of people outside the movie house on the corner; ironically, it was showing her own film, *Tiger Bay*.

'I'm sorry, Miss Floderus. Your sister went out half an hour ago; but she left a number where you can find her. Do you have a pencil?'

'Yes.' But it was Dean Powers' number again. 'Thank you. Please tell my sister I called.'

Walking back to the car she thought that maybe Donna was half-right; Dean was gradually falling in love with Madlen, if anyone. Was it a case of rebound?

She'd asked Donna about this, and Donna had said no. 'I've listened to this kind of thing enough times on the airline, believe me, not to know the signs. Dean would have rebounded a long time ago with one of his little girls from the typing pool – once the rebound phase kicks off they'll do it with anyone or anything, a yellow cab, a fire hydrant, the first love-object they see.'

If Dean were capable again of real feeling for a woman, it could save Madlen; but if he were simply using her for convenient sex like the rest of them, Lorraine would slaughter him the instant she found out; Madlen was ultra-sensitive right now, and dangerously vulnerable. If Dean –

Lorraine stopped thinking about him as suddenly she saw his face. He was standing near the head of the line outside the movie house, apparently alone; certainly he didn't have Madlen with him.

It must be a look-alike. Dean wouldn't be found lining up

351

to see a second-time-around movie like *Tiger Bay*, which hadn't been made to do anything but entertain. But when she walked a little closer, she was sure. It was unquestionably Dean Powers. Was he to meet Madlen here? That idea too was laughable; Madlen wouldn't be found dead lining up to see someone she bitterly hated. Where was she, then, this evening? At the Lotus Club, presumably, enjoying the pitiable little deception: leaving Dean's number with the receptionist was meant to distress Lorraine; and that idea wasn't laughable; it was heartbreaking.

The line was moving into the theatre, and she went quickly across to the car and moved it around the block where there were half-hour parking slots. By the time she came back the lobby of the movie-house was deserted.

'One, please.' She opened her purse.

'Gee!' The girl behind the glass was staring up at her; then she called to the man standing at the ropes. He came over and stared too. Brushing his hair back, straightening his tie, just as he must have looked only a few years ago at the proms. He said with gallantry: 'Okay, Debbie, this one's on the house. Our compliments, Miss Floderus. It's a real seller, and you did a great job.'

She put just enough sex into her smile to leave him looking faint; then she was inside the theatre, standing at the back until her eyes accommodated to the semi-darkness. She still couldn't imagine what the hell Dean Powers was doing here, but she knew she had to talk to him. When she made out his clean-cut head near the end of the fourth row down, she went along and took the seat beside him as the credits started rolling and her name appeared on the screen.

'Dean,' she said low, 'would you like to come and have a drink with the real thing?'

'You looked,' Lorraine was laughing softly, 'like I'd caught you in a porn movie-house . . . you almost turned your collar up!'

Dean wasn't smiling. 'For Christ's sake . . .' he said, not

352

knowing how else to express his embarrassment. 'Look, did you say you wanted the veal or the pasta?'

'I don't mind.' She watched his frustration.

'There *is* a difference, Lorraine.'

'Choose for me,' she said, intending to madden him. Dean Powers was the key to her whole future, in terms of the company; and her deep anger over this fact could be given a little release by her teasing him; it was good to see this arrogant stud looking embarrassed, and vulnerable.

'You get the pasta,' he said, 'it's cheaper.'

'Now you're out of a job again, sure, you'll have to economise.'

'Out of a job?'

'Yes.' She checked her make-up briefly in her compact. 'We're going ahead with the project, and you've opted out. You can't very well stay in your office and see the whole thing take off over your head.'

'Damn' right I can't.'

'Are you ready to order?' the waiter asked with disinterest.

'What?'

'I said are you –'

'Oh.' He didn't even seem to know he was in a restaurant. It was the first one they'd seen, after he'd agreed to get into the Rolls and go for a 'drink'. Lorraine had said she was hungry by that time. 'Yes, we'd like the Osso Buco.'

'You like something to drink?' The man stared at the traffic through the half-curtained window above the table; the little restaurant was empty tonight except for these two; if they hadn't come in he could have been at the back reading his spy novel.

'D'you have some Chianti Classico Blanco?'

'I think.'

'Don't you know? Get me the wine list.'

'Yeh, we got some Classico. Full bottle?'

'Yes.'

Lorraine was finding it hard not to laugh aloud; someone had said that a sense of humour was the ability to see the difference between what things were and what they ought to be. Dean was more used to sitting in a much swankier place surrounded by professionals in black ties who knew exactly how to conduct the business of pandering to his tastes.

'What with you and that little man,' Lorraine smiled coolly. 'I've been in more entertaining company.'

He turned a thunderous look on her. 'You didn't come here to be entertained, for God's sake; you said you were hungry.'

It couldn't have been often in Dean's well-ordered life, she mused, when a situation had come along and found him helpless. Tonight he hadn't had any options open. He couldn't simply have gone on sitting there in the theatre watching her movie while she sat beside him; nor could he have refused to have a drink with her; the last time they'd seen each other, in her office, there hadn't been any kind of show-down; he'd simply walked away from the project, politely.

And she was still waiting to spring the most embarrassing question, at which he might easily walk away again, out of the restaurant. But she had to know; and there couldn't be an easy answer.

'If you don't feel like eating, Dean, we could just go and have a drink somewhere else.'

'You said you were hungry.' He was looking desperately for a row, for an excuse to leave her.

'I am.'

'Then we'll stay here.' The domineering male attitude. She was going to change all that, right now.

'I'm dying to know what happened. Did you have to dodge in there to hide from an old flame, or something?'

'In where?' To give himself time.

'The movie theatre.' She leaned at her ease against the red leather back of the banquette, watching him look desperately for an escape.

I . . . happened to be going past the place, and suddenly felt like being entertained for a while, get my mind off things.'

354

'And stood in line without even looking at the posters?'

'I didn't actually give a damn what was showing.'

'It's not exactly your kind of movie,' she said innocently.

'What does that mean?'

'Is that your thing? Boy meets girl, girl almost drowns in the ocean, boy saves her and they do it right there on the beach?'

Dean looked down. 'I think there's rather more to *Tiger Bay* than that.'

'True. They did it twice.' She turned her wine glass slowly on the slightly stained linen cloth. 'But of course I'm very flattered.'

'Shit,' he said, finally cornered, 'is this important?' He looked around for the waiter, for something to kick.

'Yes,' Lorraine said, 'very.'

'What?' He looked back at her, catching her tone.

'You went there to see me, Dean. My performance. Or whatever. Or you'd have moved right along when you saw the posters, or got up when you saw my name come up on the credits. And I want to know why you didn't. You don't have to answer, of course.'

'You know damn' well I do.'

'Well, since you say so, yes.' She was watching him intently now; the teasing was over. And he was watching her back, with his full attention.

'I – don't know, Lorraine. We seem to keep on kind of – running into each other's susceptibilities and bouncing off again, leaving – ' he shrugged morosely.

'Bruises?'

'I'm not that easily bruised.'

'I am.'

'Well that's – '

'You wish the Classico chilled?'

'Oh for God's sake,' Dean exploded all over the waiter, 'you're not going to serve it at room temperature, I hope!'

When the man had gone, disgruntled, Dean found Lorraine laughing gently. 'I think maybe he'll finally throw you out of here.'

'I'm a customer!'

'The kind of customer they finally throw out.'

'Jesus Christ, if –'

'Dean,' she said quietly, and waited.

'What?'

'You have to bite the bullet. What were you really doing in there? And please don't say "in where?"'

He broke some bread and was about to eat it, to give himself more time; then suddenly realised he was trapped and there was only one way out that Lorraine would accept. He'd have to tell her the truth, even though she might not know what it was; she'd recognise it when she heard it. 'I hadn't seen the movie before,' he said off-handedly. 'It had some good reviews.' He pretended to see a fly on the gathered white half-curtain across the window, and slapped it away. 'You – you had some good things said about your performance.' He waited for her to respond, but she didn't. He'd have to get this over with on his own. 'So I thought I should give it a whirl.' His tone tried to convey he was giving the obvious answer to a childish question.

Lorraine began getting angry again. 'Dean, I want to tell you something. Right now I don't like you very much, but you could change that, maybe, if you chose to be honest. I'm trying to have a grown-up conversation, you see, and you're not making it easy.'

'You really are a bitch, Lorraine.'

He'd feel better now. 'Some of the time, yes. Someone described you, today, as a ten-year-old adult male. Do you think that's a fair description?'

He looked down. 'Yes. Some of the time.'

She let out her breath; it was quite a breakthrough. 'You suddenly grew up twenty years just then. I hope you're not feeling your age.'

He spread his silverware apart, as if he were setting out his chess men. 'I – I thought the reason why we keep on bumping off each other and leaving bruises might be because I don't know you well enough. So I –' he looked up impatiently. 'For God's sake, we're not going to drink a whole litre.'

'You order whole bottle.'

'Yes, but a bottle isn't always – okay, leave it right there. No, I'll pour it.' He found Lorraine laughing silently again after the man went away.

'You'll really have to leave him an *enormous* tip,' she said into her hands, her eyes swimming.

'I'm going to kick him on my way out. Where was I?' He obviously hoped she'd forgotten, and they could talk about something else.

'You were saying you didn't know me well enough.'

'By God, I'm beginning to. You're just watching me squirm, aren't you? Setting me up?' There was a hint of self-mockery to the line of his mouth, and she welcomed it.

'Not entirely, Dean. Please go on.'

He took a deep breath, busy with the silverware again, with the light of the small shaded lamp reflecting up to his face. 'So I thought that maybe I'd see things in you on the screen that you don't show in your real life.'

'Oh, Dean . . . am I *that* hard to know?'

His jaw jutted slightly, and he didn't look away. 'You're not easy.'

'Then let's start now.' She leaned forward, her hands flat on the tablecloth. 'You can ask whatever questions you like, and I'll answer them truthfully. But let me just say one thing that might answer a whole lot of questions right off. It's my belief that you're absolutely outraged by the fact that when you came back from New Orleans I was in bed with François Farrier.' She noticed him actually flinch. 'And considering you happen to be a super-stud in the habit of sleeping with half the girls in my office and now even with my own sister, I think you're a helluva one to talk. Let's take it from there.'

'Your veal is completely cold.'

'What? Big deal.' Dean pushed his plate away. 'I don't see how I can put it more simply, Lorraine. He's young, he's inexperienced for a perfumer, and as a result he's insufferably arrogant.'

357

She leaned forward. 'Because of his insecurity?'

'It would figure. He's suddenly in a strange, much more sophisticated society – '

'Insecurity leads to arrogance, as a defence, you think?'

'My God, didn't you ever read any psychology at school?'

'So that could be your problem, Dean. It could be the explanation of your own insufferable arrogance.'

Their eyes remained locked for seconds on end; then Dean said quietly, 'I'm going now, Lorraine. I hate to leave you just sitting here, but – '

'I'd like some more wine, first. You're not being very attentive as an escort tonight.' It was more effective than a slap in the face, she knew; it destroyed his defensive self-image of a confident, well-groomed, sophisticated man-about-town. 'I really should have had mercy on you,' she went on deliberately, 'and left you there in the movie house watching my silver shadow; the real thing is proving rather more of a challenge, isn't it?' Watching his eyes as he poured the wine for her, she was able to see the effect of what she was doing; and she was surprised; she'd been attempting to drive him deeper and deeper into anger, if she could; and to a degree she had done that; three or four times in the past half hour she'd been certain he was going to walk right out on her. But in the glint of his eyes she believed she saw something beyond the anger, and she was secretly astonished. In his eyes and the line of his mouth and the set of his head and the movement of his hand as he put the straw-covered bottle back at the side of the table were the separate but distinct components of what he was feeling; and it was resignation.

'Thank you,' Lorraine said, and lifted her glass. 'How do you find the wine?'

He had to bring his thoughts back an awful long way, but he managed. 'I think it's acceptable, for last year's vintage.'

She held her wine so that he must touch her glass with his; and after a bit of delay he managed that too. 'Here's to you, Dean.'

His face went blank. 'What changed your mind?'

'You did.' She suddenly wanted to break down and cry; because it was all over, and she'd survived; and the company was going to survive. It wasn't easy just to go on sitting here trying to keep her thoughts in order. 'Dean, I'm sorry I've spoilt your meal for you; I always think it's uncivilised to bring any kind of contention to a meal table; eating is an ancient ritual, meant to bring people together in peace; yes, I did read a little psychology at school. But we're okay now; we're still sitting here, two civilised people behaving themselves in front of a waiter who is at this very moment plotting how he can cut your throat and say it was self-defence.' She began laughing now, and knew it was instead of crying, because it was just as good a way of releasing all that appalling tension she'd been building up as they'd faced each other across the table. Leaning low with her arms along the stained white cloth she shut her eyes and let the laughter come. 'And you know what you'd say if he actually cut your elegant throat, Dean? You know what your famous last words would be?' She opened her eyes for an instant and looked at his totally astonished face, which was funnier still. 'You'd – you'd say, my God, you didn't even warm the knife!' The laughter took over for almost a minute; then she gradually surfaced and reached for her compact and dabbed at her eyes with her handkerchief and tried not to look at Dean because she'd collapse all over again. 'Sorry,' she said at last. 'I'm giving you such a bad time.' She snapped the turquoise compact shut. 'Dean, you had a look of – of resignation just now; I mean before I broke out in idiotic laughter. Do you think you had anything to feel resigned about?'

He drank some wine. 'You know, I really hate quizzes.'

'Aren't they awful? But try, darling.'

He looked up quickly. 'Are you serious?'

'More than ever in my life.'

'You're being difficult to follow. You –'

'I'm a woman. Ask a woman what something looks like, and she'll throw a whole kaleidoscope all over you. But don't give up on me now.'

Dean had to think, and he found it difficult to pull just one emotion out of the whole gamut he'd been feeling since they'd sat down at the table; but it was there, all right. Resignation, yes.

'I – I began thinking, some time ago,' he said very low, 'that we might have some kind of – you know – understanding. Something in common. Something we could . . .' he opened his hands helplessly, 'make work.' He wanted very much to get it right, because this woman had stopped being the antagonising bitch she'd started out to be, and was now sitting opposite him looking particularly beautiful with her eyes red-rimmed from laughing – or had she been crying, really? – and that particularly tender expression on her mouth, and that clear, attentive regard in her eyes that made him feel it was very necessary to acquit himself well, if he could, in front of her. 'So that was it, I guess, Lorraine. I'd been thinking we had something, and tonight I saw we didn't, after all. So I felt resigned.'

She nodded. 'I hoped it might be that. I thought at first it was the resignation of the big-hitting jock who'd lost the game; it looked like that. Then I started thinking there was more to it, because you didn't stride manfully out and leave this poor little woman humiliated on the table; a real jock would have done that. And then –' she leaned forward again – 'and try not to mind if I just go on like this and let the words find themselves, because I could never think them out – and then I thought, yes, you were looking as if you'd lost something worth more than just the game; and after quite a time, I thought it might be the hope for us that I'd been feeling since that instant, which I can remember with absolute precision because I was staring at the clock in General de Gaulle airport, when you told me not to worry about the fact that Elliot Dietrich had just walked out on us and left the project for *Siren Song* in bits on the floor, and when you also told me not to worry about it but just go on down to Grasse and call it a little vacation.' The tears were coming now, and she didn't care; they felt good, and she welcomed them. 'Oh my God, did I need a friend at that moment, Dean . . . and there you were, at the other end of the line, quietly saving my sanity . . .'

The salt of her tears was tingling on her mouth and she got her handkerchief again; this was going to be the night when everything happened, and the only thing to do was roll with it and let it all hang out. In the back of her mind there was Donna, that incredibly bright little ex-flying-waitress dispensing her philosophies this afternoon, refusing to leave Lorraine's office until she'd said it all. 'It's nothing to do with rebound, Lorraine. It's something you've got for him – or to put it the right way, something he's now *seen* you've got for him. And the reason why he's behaving like a ten-year-old adult male is that just at the time when he's suddenly filled with this holy light of revelation, he calls you up and finds you screwing – pardon me – in bed with a Frenchman. Okay? It was simply bad luck, bad timing.' Donna paced around the office trying to make it clear what she was saying. 'I'm no good at fancy analogies, I'm afraid, but try this one. Dean Powers was just starting to put his head out of his shell, after the trauma of the divorce had knocked him for six, when you came along and dropped a rock on it. Okay?'

Lorraine looked up from the blurred under-water vision of the linen tablecloth, where one green pea had rolled off her plate and was sitting there with just that look of resignation she'd seen with Dean. She took a deep, shuddering breath, the way as a child she'd watched storms passing. 'Dean, more than anything in this world I want you to listen to what I'm telling you now, and know it's true. When you got back from New Orleans you wanted quite a lot to see me, because I'd come back earlier from France and we had a lot to catch up on; and I wasn't there; and it had only a bit to do with the fact that I was in bed with someone; the real hurt, for you, was that I couldn't see you, right at that time; and I understood that, at once, or almost at once, and finished up howling my head off all night and praying to all the gods I'd ever heard of that you'd call me again and we could meet and make it up; which of course you didn't, being a total idiot.'

361

She heard him laugh softly, and looked up at him, surprised. So he'd come out of it too. This guy had resilience. 'And I want you to know also, Dean, that in terms of rivalry for my affections, M'sieur François Farrier, compared with you, comes on about as strong as a performing flea, and always will; but as a master perfumer for whom I have the most enormous respect, and in whom I have the most enormous confidence that he can help us all save Floderus Incorporated, I want him to receive however much of your – your respect, you can give him, however much of your faith, and your tolerance, so we can call tomorrow another day and get on with our project and beat the hell out of the competition with *Siren Song*. I also want, right now, and more than anything in this world, to leave here with you and go to your place and have the most monumental and never-ending fuck we can manage together. And give that poor guy a thousand dollar tip or I'll never speak to you again.'

362

CHAPTER 30

'YOU DON'T LIKE circuses?' asked Judy Pollack, dead-pan. 'Oh, *I* like circuses, I always have. I always remember as a child, hanging on to my mom's skirt till she couldn't walk anymore and had to promise to take me to a circus. Life is such fun, don't you think?' Her bright black eyes snapped wide open as Joe Fisher went past her glass-walled office half-hidden behind a giant peg-board. 'You see what I mean?'

Betty Lou looked up patiently from her word-processor. 'Circuses?' she asked. You always had to ask Judy what on earth she was talking about when she launched herself into a monologue and then expected questions.

'Didn't you know,' Judy asked her, 'that we have a circus in this building?'

'Where?'

'It used to be the chairman's office, but all that's changed now.' She picked up one of the phones as it rang, listened a couple of seconds and said, 'Oh for God's sake, not again!' She told Betty Lou, 'Power overload. That's part of the circus; there can't be a single person on this floor right now who isn't pounding a typewriter or a processor or a computer or a data bank or a paper shredder. So you haven't been into the chairman's office lately? You should. You don't need to buy a ticket, even, it's free; all you do is pop your head in there and make some excuse, like, maybe, we have a man at the door who rents elephants; they won't hear you anyway, or even know you're there. The last time I looked in there, Mr Fisher was up a ladder covering the west

363

wall with peg-boards and Mr Goldman was buried in an armchair under a pile of data-bank printouts and Mr Powers was sitting at the desk with three telephones in each ear and Mr Blatt was running up and down the middle of the room in his jogging shoes and Madame Chairman was flat on the floor with a man in a white linen coat giving her neck massage. As Personnel Director I'm hourly awaiting instructions from the big top to hire fifteen clowns, upon which I intend to hire fourteen and make up the number myself.' She looked at the colourful reflection of her orange and petunia flare-bottomed coat and skirt in the glass wall. 'I guess the way I look today I'd be a smash hit, Betty Lou; there must be a place for me somewhere in this exciting world.'

'At the Palace,' Carl said, 'where else?'
'Good question.' Sy breast-stroked his way up through the printouts and made a note on his clip-board as Carl went on:
'French champagne, Beluga caviar, Havanas, maybe a discreet freebie for each lady guest, a lacquered Peretti bracelet from Tiffany's, something for no more than a hundred bucks each, but acceptable. And orchids by the bush. You know who sent those orchids to Donna?'
'No?'
'Neither do I.' Crouched on his heels in front of Sy Goldman's armchair Carl looked around. 'Since when did this pace turn into a madhouse?'
'Since a week ago.' A week ago, Dean had said okay, he'd join them after all. How had Lorraine done it? Some questions were better not asked, and some answers too obvious.
'How do you feel about it, Sy?'
New frontiers were being breached, thought Sy Goldman. He'd never heard Carl ask how anybody felt before. 'I've lost six pounds, so I don't feel so good; on the other hand it's good for me, so I feel good about that. What about the guest list?'

Carl turned on his haunches. 'Joe!' Carl shouldn't really be here; he was Development, but until François made some progress with his blending there wasn't a great deal to develop that didn't overlap other people's territory; he'd been down to the laboratory every day in the past week but the French guy had thrown him out every time. He was better off here, getting a picture in his mind of the overall project.

Joe came down from his ladder. 'What's up?'

'Guest list,' Sy said briefly. Sy was in charge of the expenses, which were currently rising through the two-million dollar level for promotion and advertising.

'Very select. Very select indeed. Nobody blah like Truman Capote or Elizabeth Taylor; we'll go for real people like Princess Caroline, Basset Winmill, Candy Van Alen –'

'The Grosvenors,' Sy nodded, 'the Roosevelts, Tom Hoving –'

'Right,' Joe said, nodding vigorously, 'the real crowd, yes, Betsy Von Furstenberg, Sir Julian Grenfell – he'll be in town then – the King of Greece, Penny Rinquist Tweedy, and the top ten ambassadors.'

Carl straightened up and walked around Sy's chair in a small circle, his synapses firing at twice their normal rate: he could feel them; his head felt like it was a firework display inside, and he hadn't started on the coffee yet. He trotted over to the percolator with his jerky marionette walk and poured a full cup. What about a personal tour by Lorraine, had anyone thought of that?   .

'You're crazy,' Lorraine said with her face against the carpet as the masseur worked on her spine.

'We're all crazy,' said Carl, blinking down at her through his granny glasses, 'but that has nothing to do with it. You're also beautiful, you're famous, you can act; and you don't think you should promote Formula X coast to coast? So now who's crazy?'

Formula X was the pseudonym they'd settle on for *Siren Song*, which was henceforth to be ultra-secret, and revealed only at the grand presentation in three months' time. Carl

365

looked around for Joe again, beckoning him over. 'How about Lorraine doing a personal tour with Formula X coast to coast, say sixteen cities in the three weeks before we open at – '

'She wouldn't do it.'

'She would if we worked on her.'

Joe crouched down beside Lorraine. 'Look, you're beautiful, you're famous, you're an actress – '

'I told her that,' Carl said.

'So we may have to tell her a thousand times; it isn't too soon to start.'

Waiting on the line for the head buyer at Saks, Biltmore Fashion Square, Phoenix, Dean Powers watched Carl and Joe and Sy and Lorraine and thought, I never realised what a team this was; the pressure's self-regenerating; even Sy hasn't refused the budget yet. But if Vanderkloot decides to drop on us . . . if François doesn't come across with the product by the time we're ready for it . . . But the thing was not to look down; just keep on walking, a step at a time, with your eyes on the far end of the rope.

The line opened.

'Yes,' he told the Saks buyer after a moment or two, 'our deadline is May the first. Three months, yes.'

'I haven't seen anything in the trades yet.'

'We haven't even started promoting; this is just a personal call to you exclusively, Barbara, for old times' sake.'

'I see black glass,' Joe said, standing back, to look at the display that covered half his peg-board wall. 'Maybe with gold.'

'Turquoise,' Carl said. Where had he seen black and turquoise? It had looked classy, dramatic, somehow Indian.

The display showed full-page ads torn out of *Vogue* and *Town and Country* and *Elite* and *Beauty Fashion* and a dozen other magazines and trade editions, showing the flacons of almost every fragrance now in the stores: Chanel's stark all-black *Antaeus Pour Homme*; Jovan's classic

366

Sculptura series of coloured frosted-glass nudes; the traditional droplet-shaped *Je Reviens*; the rectangular theme of Paco Rabanne's *Metal*, engineered like a space-age component; the shouldered translucent Calvin Klein with its gold rope at the neck.

'Frosted?' Joe asked, head on one side.

'It's mysterious, veiled, romantic,' Carl said.

'But it lacks that startling, liquid clarity of clear glass.' Joe pointed to the display. 'Droplets, tears, clear pears – they're all in clear glass; you can't get that exact effect with frosting.'

'How about a clear flacon, with the name in frosted letters? Or the colophon?'

'Oh God,' Joe said, 'the expense . . .' He swung around and called to Sy. 'What's the budget for the flacon?'

'We don't know the numbers yet.'

'I mean for the design. For the prototype.'

'I'll get back to you on that.' Sy immersed himself in his paperwork again.

'We'll promote a collector's edition,' Joe said, 'through the antique store channels.'

'A fine art flacon,' Carl nodded, 'by, maybe, Lalique.'

'Something like the *Ivoire objet d'art*. It's fantastic. Look – third from the left, fourth row down.'

'We can do better than that.'

'Of course. These things will have to be numbered and signed.'

'By Lorraine.'

'Who else?'

In Barry Corbett's old office, halfway down the corridor between Lorraine's and Judy Pollack's, Donna and Nadine Keller were fielding calls and memos for Carl Blatt, Dean Powers, Sy Goldman and Joe Fisher, sorting their incoming mail and filing urgent messages in their priority boxes for each day's end – or each night's beginning, because most of them were working all hours, often till midnight or even beyond.

This afternoon Donna found an envelope with the royal

blue embossed logo of Century Cosmetics at the top left-hand corner, and felt the blood leaving her face; she'd been told about Frederick Vanderkloot a week ago, by Lorraine herself, but had since followed the unspoken rule never to mention his name aloud; today her fingers shook as she slit open the envelope with Barry's teak-handled paper knife.

'What's that?' Nadine asked her, concerned.

'Nothing, I guess.'

'Are you okay?'

'Sure.' It was a formal, printed invitation for Lorraine to attend a cocktail party at the Waldorf in ten days' time, to mark the occasion of Century's new account with Nagashi of Tokyo. There was no personal message from Frederick Vanderkloot inside.

'You don't look very well,' Nadine persisted.

'A rabbit walked over my grave, that's all.'

A week later the peg-boards in the chairman's office were covered with slogans and copy ideas, replacing the flacon ads and then the promotion-tour maps and the guest lists and the presentation arrangements.

Only You can Say it Quite Like This . . .

Joe was spending most of his days sitting cross-legged in the full lotus position, in here or in his own office or in any place where he felt he could create images out of the insubstantial air.

L'Esprit de Toi . . .

There were fifty or sixty rough artists' sketches, some in coloured crayon, pinned up or lying across the floor in Lorraine's office, and they were changed almost every half-hour as the team of artists came and went, leaving only those ideas that had been agreed on by unanimous vote among the executive staff.

The Way She is Now . . . (To capture, Joe had said, the moment in time when she passes by.)

Most of the human figures in the sketches were obviously women, and some obviously Lorraine, half-turning in shadow, her face behind misted glass, her hair flying out in a

368

cloud, her eyes shimmering from the depths of dark velvet; Lorraine masked; Lorraine nude-shouldered; Lorraine half-smiling; Lorraine in a veil, in the shadows of a palm leaf, against the moonlit ocean surf, reflected in the ripples of a stream.

Now You Know What I Mean, Darling . . . Lorraine's eyes half in shadow, looking straight at camera, her lips slightly parted. 'If we don't use this,' Joe had said, 'it goes on my bedroom wall anyway.'

The Woman in Me . . .

'I never realised,' Joe said plaintively to Dean Powers in the cafeteria one lunch-time, 'what a fantastically all-time asset we have in Lorraine, I mean as the company's image, even the product's image. I mean, Christ, a girl like her, together with the kind of fragrance we're creating . . . Didn't anyone see?'

'Her father tried to bring her into his promotion,' Dean said, 'but she felt it would limit her potential as an actress, which I think was a correct view. And since she's been chairman of the company herself . . . I guess she didn't have the time to be a model.'

'But why didn't we think of it? Why didn't we persuade her, before?'

Dean broke his roll, looked down. 'Could be a whole lot of reasons. The thing now is to think ahead.' Nobody had thought of approaching Lorraine before because from the minute she'd taken over the job of heading the company she'd been so panic-stricken, so aware of her new responsibility that she'd turned everyone off by her façade of authoritative competence, to the point where they hadn't even seen her as a woman anymore, just a threat to everyone in sight.

She was different now.

'Don't you think she'll do a stupendous job promoting Formula X, Dean?'

'She already has. She sold it to us, didn't she?'

In Lorraine's office, in Joe's office, in Carl's office and along the corridors and in the cafeteria and the coffee-shop and in the men's room, Joe and Carl kept asking each other, okay, but what exactly *is* perfume?

'It's primitive, powerful, animal . . .'

'I see it as more subtle, the power behind the throne type of thing . . .'

'It's an *accoutrement*,' Lorraine told them sometime halfway through February as the image studies went up on the peg-boards, 'an adornment.'

'That you can't even see, sure, don't even notice till suddenly it's *there*, like – like –'

'A *presence*,' from Lorraine, nodding hard, 'yes.'

'It works on the subconscious . . . it even leaves a trace of the wearer behind her when she moves on, like –'

'A lingering shadow . . .'

'After the door has closed . . .'

'The melody lingers on?'

'No. That's the Thirties. Today we're looking for the *essence of you* kind of theme.'

During February and into March the mobile top-secret files were wheeled along the executive corridor to receive the marginal tenth of all the massed material going onto paper and into printouts and onto sketch-pads and mockups and layouts, while at the same time the other ninety per cent of the material went into the shredding machines.

This Time I Mean it . . .

'Okay, add that one to Series 6.'

Am I Dreaming?

'Of what? It's too –shred it.'

For When You Meet Him Next . . .

'Too *ingénue*; we're narrowing the age group with that one.'

Siren Song . . . Now I Know She Was Here . . .

'That would go all right with the shadowed eyes image, K4. We could try it in montage, with soft lettering in italics, maybe.'

The secret files were trundled in and out in the morning and at the day's end. The shredders chewed slogans, images, first-draft copy, matchups, mockups, montages, final-draft rejects.

370

The Way I Am Now . . .

'Didn't we throw that one out weeks ago?'

'Yes, but it keeps coming back. Let's keep it and try to match one of the second series colour shots with this lettering, or maybe this. *The Way I Am Now . . .* It's a statement, it's also affirmative; she's reached a certain stage in her life where for the first time she knows herself –'

'Has discovered herself?'

Sure, like François told us in the lab – he makes fragrances to evoke a woman's self-discovery, a self-realisation of the way she is now.'

'Okay, keep it in.'

In early April the leaves brought a mist of spring green to the trees in the parks and along the streets, and white cumulus sailed in fleets along the blue distances of the sky, caught and released by the tall glass reefs of Manhattan.

'Is he making any progress?'

Dean was slumped in an armchair at Lorraine's apartment; she was on the floor, her back against his legs, while he massaged the nape of her neck.

'Yes,' she said. She had been to the laboratory almost every day, not talking to François every time but watching the work going on. 'He's making progress.'

'Does he know how much depends on him?'

'No. It could inhibit him. It could even cripple his creative talent. He's pretty well forgotten about us by now, anyway. I've had to leave food for him sometimes; he's losing weight.' She nuzzled her head against his hands. 'And how about you, old boy, are you losing weight too?'

'Probably. But I'm gaining so many things in so many other directions.

'Are you?'

'Yes.' He bent to kiss her hair. 'Don't go away.'

'I'm not going anywhere.'

'Not till next week.'

'Oh.' A shiver of apprehension passed through her. 'Yes . . . That's not long now, is it?'

371

'D'you feel up to it?'

'Yes. Oh, yes. Don't worry.' It was going to be two weeks non-stop from coast to coast, taking in sixteen major cities with a rented Lear Jet fitted out as half-office and half-dormitory to allow enough rest for her and Donna and the tour director and her team. At the end of it she would have exactly four days to recover before the gala première at the Palace-Carlton Hotel on May 1st. 'I wish you were coming with me, Dean.' She suddenly felt the loneliness of great distances.

'So do I; but somebody has to mind the store. But we'll keep closely in touch, and wherever you are I'll be thinking of you.'

She pressed her face against his hands. 'Then that's all I need to know.'

CHAPTER 31

THE HUGE DISC of the sun lowered towards the ocean's rim, its fire spreading along the cloud-bank and then touching the water, drawing its dying flame-light from horizon to horizon, until the whole ocean seemed ablaze.

Against its glow the woman walked at the surf's edge, a dark, slender silhouette, her breasts taut under her swimsuit, her lean hips moving rhythmically to the muted music of her thoughts, her hair lying curled across her bare shoulders, her feet kicking liquid rubies from the shallows where the sun's light lay dying.

As she came closer, the shadows cleared from her eyes and they took on the glow from the sea, their light blue forming ice among the embers, their dreams softening her gaze as she saw the man coming down from the fringe of palms beyond the dunes.

A low wind came, touching her dark hair as she halted, waiting for him, her head thrown back, her hands resting on her hips, her pelvis pressed forward in invitation.

'*Lorraine* . . .' the man in the little auditorium said aloud as he switched off the projector. '*Lorraine* . . .'

'I'm not at all sure,' one of the men said.

The two of them sat together, their black suits merging with the dark of the room, their immaculate linen catching the light from the street through the tall windows. They had met here an hour ago, and had not troubled to switch on the lights when dusk had come.

'One is never at all sure, with Frederick.'

373

'No.'

The smoke of their cigars drifted upward across the window glass, curling against the glow from the Pan Am sign above Park Avenue; as one of them moved slightly, sipping his brandy, a gold link gleamed at his cuff. In their polished black shoes the blue letters were reflected upside down, advertising in miniature a major airline.

'Where is he now?'

'Watching a film.'

A quick sigh of impatience. 'In his screening room?'

'Yes.'

'What film?'

'Her film.'

'Oh.'

Silence drew out for minutes; ash fell from a cigar, unnoticed, quiet as a moth in the shadows.

'How far –' the cultured voice paused hesitantly – 'I'm not sure I know quite how to put this, Gerrard, but – how far do you think he's going to go?'

'With Floderus?'

'Well yes. Or perhaps I mean . . . generally.'

'You can trust me, you know.'

Yes, I know. All right. How's he getting on with his treatment?'

'With Zoltan?'

'Yes.' A bright shoe moved, scattering coloured light.

'How far does anyone ever get with their psychiatrist? They're simply paying through the nose for a never-ending confessional, don't you think?'

'You don't believe he'll become any less . . . intractable?'

'No.' He crossed his legs the other way. 'I have to admit I'm concerned, Gerrard. In the past year we've spent seven hundred million dollars on three new companies. We're over-extending. Floderus, of course, can be picked up for small change, but even so, it's not necessary. It's not good for the Century reputation. It's my private impression that if he weren't so obsessed with this woman he wouldn't ever dream of taking her company over. It's . . . unbusinesslike.'

374

'I agree.' He leaned forward, drawing on his cigar. 'Would you say he's dissuadable?'

Silence came again; the end of the cigar glowed, reflecting in the window glass.

'No. He's gone too far, in any case. He bought out their perfumer – what was his name? Dietrich, I rather think – and he'll probably buy out their new one. He's – '

'Oh, that was his doing, was it? What was his purpose?'

'I've known Frederick for many years, Gerrard, and inside the brilliant conglomerate operator there's a vulnerable man. His purpose, I'm afraid, was simply to spite Lorraine Floderus, to hurt her. My feeling is that he approached her, and she rejected him, perhaps brusquely. He's. . . a great deal older, of course, and she may have said something . . . that wounded him.' He paused, and in a moment said, 'One doesn't, ever, wound Frederick Vanderkloot, however slightly, and survive.'

Silence came again. In the street below the windows a siren wailed faintly, its echoes dying among the buildings.

'So you don't think we could dissuade him?'

'No. I think if he's determined, he'll buy up Floderus, and soon.'

'And you think he's determined?'

'Yes.'

CHAPTER 32

MARCH 1ST.

'Give me 297,' François said. 'And 298.'

One of his assistants, a bright girl named Kate, passed him two phials, and he removed the stoppers one at a time, inhaling. 'No.' He poured the amber liquid into the bin and sealed it again. The whole laboratory was heavy with a thousand scents, but he didn't notice it. As a musician can pick a single melody out of a background cacophony, François could detect and assess the fragrances he worked with.

'299,' he said.

Kate passed him another phial, watching his profile in adoration. But he'd lost weight since she'd first seen him; he was too thin now. He'd also lost all sense of time. Every so often they'd walk him outside, round the parking lot three times and across the patch of wasteland, while he'd talk to himself in French.

'No.' He rejected the blend and sealed the bin.

'Give me . . .' he tilted his dark head back and closed his red-rimmed eyes. 'Give me the original essay. Yesterday's.'

As he assessed the blend, its microscopic volatile particles drifted into his nostrils and made their way to the olfactory epithelium, generating an electrical signal for transmission to the brain for recognition, in the area that also recognised the colours of a great painting, the sounds of a symphony; among the thousands of receptor cells, many were going out of phase, while others were switching on again; the limbic system, the most primitive structure in this young man's brain, was busy associating emotions with the incoming

376

olfactory data.

'No.' He rejected the essay.

At the far end of the room, someone dropped a container, and someone else said, '*Sshhh . . .*'

'*Donnez-moi . . . cinq cent douze, s'il vous plaît.*'

'Pardon me?'

'*Hein?*' He swung his head to look at her, his eyes focusing with difficulty. 'Oh. Yes. Give me 512, please.'

Kate passed it to him. 'François . . .'

'Yes?'

'It's time you took a break. You've been going twelve hours.'

'Yes?' He inhaled, then poured the essay and sealed the bin. 'Then I will sleep, yes.' His thin shoulders rounded, he squinted up at the girl's adoring face. 'You are good to me. Kate. You look after me like my mother.' He took her hand. 'But I am not thinking of you like my mother. Come and make love, now.' He tugged on her hand.

'For God's sake, François. When the others have gone!'

'Then get them out of here.'

March 17th.

Wind fretted at the long low building; at some time during the day, someone had dropped an empty beer can in the parking lot, and for an hour it rolled back and forth in the gusts, like a wind-chime, until François asked, '*Putain!* What is that noise?'

A lab assistant hurried out to stop it.

'We are getting somewhere,' François told Carl Blatt, who came sometimes to see him. François lay supine on the camp bed they'd brought in for him while Carl sat on the edge, his blink-rate accelerating as he listened. 'You know what I am doing, Carl? I am using pheromones. Do not tell anybody yet; it is a secret.'

'Using what?'

'Pheromones. *Phéromones*, it is the same. It is the syn – *mon Dieu* – synthis – *non* –'

'Synthetic?'

'*Hein?* Yes – no – synthetised, yes? *Le substance synthétique érotique, hein?* The sexual attraction smell, you know? It is not in any flowers, of course; it is *phenylethylamine*, like an *amphetamine* compound, *hein?* You know in the ancient days, the women used to tuck their handkerchiefs under their arms when they danced at a ball, and then waved them under the noses of the young men? Yes? *Alors*, they were waving their *pheromones* around, okay?'

'My God.' Carl blinked very rapidly indeed. 'You mean you're putting human *sweat* into your essays?'

'Of course.'

'You can't do that!' Carl got up quickly, maybe to give himself more authority. 'François, in the United States of America, the one thing worse than communism, even atheism, is B.O.'

'What?' François opened his eyes, hearing the panic in Carl's tone. 'What do you mean, this bee-oh?'

'Body odour, for Christ's sake. *Sweat.* You can't do this, François. Not in America.'

'*Hein?* I know what I am doing. You will not smell it, I tell you.' He rose wearily from the bed, scratching his mane of dark, unwashed hair. 'But that is not correct. You will smell it, *mon vieux*, but you will not notice that you smell it, among all the other smells, you see? And I promise, Carl, it will really turn you out.'

'It'll what?'

'*Hein?* No. Turn you on. Yes. Now leave me alone, I am buzzy.'

March 29th.

Heavy rain was falling, and the twenty-seven people under the long corrugated-iron roof had to shout to each other as they worked.

'Okay,' François said halfway through the day, 'listen to me, Kate. I want you to put these numbers into your computer. Are you ready?'

'Yes.'

378

'53. 54. 23. 76 . . .' He gave her nineteen, then checked his figures, made a correction and nodded. 'I want that blend made up, please. How long will you take?'

'I'll try for an hour, François.'

'One hour, *bon.*' Slumped at his main desk near the essay hatch, he looked at Kate contemplatively. 'You are working very hard, you know? Like me. You look tired. But you also look beautiful. You know, Kate, that soon you will smell the smell we are making here, and then I will put a drop behind each of your ears, and behind your knees, and in the elbows, and between those beautiful beasts, and –'

'Breasts, François.' She was blushing; 'tits' sounded okay, out loud, but 'breasts' . . . that was kinda heavy.

'*Hein?* Oh my God. Breasts, yes, I am sorry. And then you will be the first woman in the whole world, Kate, to be wearing my new creation. How do you think of that?'

'It's kinda neat.'

'Neat? My God, it is more than that. It is *sensationelle!*'

Dean came sometimes to the laboratory, asking formally if the perfumer could see him for a moment, perfectly aware that by this time the Frenchman was in the middle of a one-man marathon, in which if he stumbled, everyone would hold their breath and pray.

'I could not have done this thing, M'sieur Dean, without the American equipment – these computers, the organ, the essay complex; I could not have done it in the same time, in a few months; sometimes one can create a *parfum* with a brainstorm, you know? A sudden inspiration. Otherwise it can take years; you know that. I do not have a brainstorm yet; but with these machines, we will be okay.'

Dean fought down the temptation that came to him every time he saw François, to put the big questions. *Will we have the perfume by the deadline?* He never asked. François knew the score, and he needed their faith in him; he needed to know they were perfectly sure of success. Already he had asked for more than a half million dollars' worth of essences to be air-freighted from Grasse in readiness for the final production to go on stream.

379

'Are they looking after you here?' Dean asked him. The camp bed stood in a corner behind makeshift curtains; François would sometimes flop onto it at any hour of the day, to snatch some sleep or to go into his own personal kind of meditation to clear his head of the hundreds of formulae that filled it every hour, day after day. At one end of the main computer room was now a cooking stove, and as Dean looked around him he saw one of the girls standing at it, stirring something in a saucepan.

'More garlic, please!' François called to her. 'I do not smell enough garlic in there!' He shrugged philosophically. 'I give cook lessons here too, you know; otherwise they give me terrible American food, and I die very soon.'

Dean broached a tricky subject. 'Carl Blatt says you're putting the smell of human sweat into the formula; is that right?'

François sighed wearily. 'People come here to ask me things; I tell them what is true; but sometimes my English is not so good, and they misunderstand; also, they are sometimes crazy, like Carl Blatt. Do you go up to a conductor who is conducting his symphony and ask him what about the music, *hein?* He will hit you with his *baton*, pretty quick. But since I work for you, I tell you, no, of course I do not mix human sweat in my formula; I mix pheromones, and that is a chemical which synthe – syn – oh, *sheet*, which is like the scent a woman gives when she is ready for sex, you know? It has been done before, in England. I tell you this because you people are my friends; otherwise I will hit you with my *baton*, very hard, you understand?'

He looked at Dean with drooping eyes and sagging shoulders, the cynical, enduring philosophy of all France in his attitude.

'I understand,' Dean nodded briefly. 'It's a deal; and in future I'll see that you're left alone.'

'Okay. Very nice.'

'Also,' Dean said with a warmth that would have surprised his friends, 'I'm beginning to like you, François.'

'I do not care less. Now please go away, I am buzzy.'

April 2nd.

Now in a late phase of experimentation, with some of the basic elements already fixed, François was working through the aldehydes again, the functional group consisting of a carbon, a hydrogen and an oxygen atom, which would provide a rich, exotic and distinctive top note; but he was using great caution, and endless rejections, because the more rich and exotic the formula became, the less sophisticated and the less subtle.

'It is a bastard art,' he told Kate, 'you know? The sense of smell does not have its own words, so we have to use the words of music, and painting. I am working at this organ, right? And I am using the palette, which is this whole range of the raw materials. We do not have our own language. *C'est une chose que je regrette beaucoup, tu sais?*' A huge shrug. '*Mais . . . qu'est-ce tu veux?*'

He talked incessantly to Kate, simply because he had to talk to someone, being French and being under pressure and secretly, increasingly excited by what he was discovering among his thousands of essences and absolutes and fixatives and essential volatile oils, sitting at the huge revolving organ and calling his instructions to his now jaded entourage of assistants; he talked to Kate in English, then in French, then to himself in French, slipping into the familiar when he talked to her – though she was unaware of the intimacy – and belabouring himself without mercy when he made mistakes and wasted time . . . *Salop! Tu es completement fou, ou quoi? Sal bête! Merde, alors, tu t'appelles parfumeur? Espèce d'idiot!*

In the main distillation rooms the physical work was going on at a gradually increasing pace as François drove himself and his whole team without respite. Three of the floor chemists quit their job and had to be replaced at short notice and at double salary; a girl working on the resinoid extraction procedures left to have a baby, timing it close and producing the infant in the ambulance on the way to the clinic and deciding, since it was a boy, to call him François.

Judy Pollack, visited the lab every day or two, sometimes in working hours to straighten out personnel problems and trouble-shoot her way through complications produced by François' insistence on keeping people here at all hours, as if they had no families or private lives. Sometimes Judy came here after her own work was finished, to stand watching the red-eyed, gaunt-looking Frenchman as he wandered around in his stained white coat, talking to nobody, seeing nothing in front of his eyes, walking into stool or cabinets and then in a sudden fever talking to everybody at once and turning the big revolving organ until the glass phials were shaking on their shelves as he made his selection and hit the computer and then sat immobile again on the top of a high stool while the essay went through its initial phases.

'*Merde, alors!* Be quick, please! I need this thing now!'

'Oh, *shit*,' a girl said, and dropped a beaker.

'I do not ask you to break things, please!'

'What the hell are we still doing here?' a young chemist asked one of the analysts. 'Why haven't we hit that goddamned Froggie over the head with a carboy and gone home?'

'Because he's a genius.'

'He's also giving me one great big fucking pain in the ass.'

He's a genius at everything he does, and that's one of the things he does.'

'*Putain!*' the familiar cry sounded from the computer room. 'When can I have the essay?'

At the Manhattan office of Floderus Incorporated there was by this time a certain change in the everyday language taking place. Judy Pollack developed the habit of ending her phone conversations with – 'Okay, I gotta go now, I'm buzzy,' and with days it became commonplace for Carl to pick up a phone and ask, 'Hey Joe, are you buzzy right now?'

'*Putain!*' Donna Shapiro was heard to exclaim as she dropped a file on her way out of the chairman's office.

'Donna,' Lorraine said from her desk, 'that's not very nice, you know.'

382

April 11th.

Dean Powers found Lorraine alone in her office, halfway through the long afternoon.

'Are you buzzy?'

'Are you serious? But sit down anyway.' She looked at him across the stack of papers that had been silting up on her desk. 'God, when did I see you last?'

He loosened his necktie. 'Good question. How've you been?'

'Okay, I guess.' During the past three months she had flown out four times to the west coast for meetings with important distributors in San Diego, Los Angeles, San Francisco and Seattle, and taken in Chicago on separate flights to help her tour director set up arrangements for her nationwide preview appearances. Dean had covered most of the south, seeing nothing of her for days on end but keeping in touch by phone. On the infrequent occasions when they had time to meet, he slept at her apartment or they took a room at a hotel to get away from it all and pretend that for one night they were on a vacation trip to town.

On one rainy evening they'd found themselves deep in some disco with black light turning the place into a surrealist version of Hades and the sound from the amplifiers blasting them into a corner.

'What the fuck are we doing in here?' Dean had yelled to her with his mouth against her ear.

'I don't know. I was just following you!'

They'd reeled their way up to street level weak with laughter and got through a civilised bottle of champagne brandy at the Red Parrot.

'Dean,' Lorraine told him now, 'you're losing weight.' She sounded concerned.

'Surprise. We all are.'

'You should get a massage more often. Saunas. Try to relax.'

'Oh, sure.'

Donna came in while they were talking, and left a small bowl of flowers on the coffee-table, going on out without

383

disturbing them; Lorraine saw an envelope on the arrangement but felt too tired to get up and see who'd sent it.

'Think it's going to be okay?'

Dean looked up from the copy of *Beauty Fashion* he'd found on the settee. 'Think what's going to be okay?'

'The whole thing.'

'Oh. Sure.' There was a silence. 'Don't you?'

Lorraine forced a smile. 'Yes. Sure.'

'Well, fine.' He looked down at *Beauty Fashion* again.

'For God's sake,' she said in a moment, 'you didn't come in here to read the trade journals, did you?'

He threw it aside, and it slipped off the cushions and finished up in a mess of splayed pages on the carpet. 'You know what day it is?'

'I don't even know what year it is, Dean.'

Hew blew out some breath. 'It's the day when he told us we'd have *Siren Song*.'

'François?' She straightened up in her chair.

'That's right.'

'Today?'

'The fifteenth.' He took off his Pierre Cardin glasses and rubbed his eyes. 'Today is the fifteenth.'

She glanced at her calendar. 'Right.'

'So do we just call him,' he asked over-casually, sliding his glasses back on, 'or . . . go on waiting till he calls us?'

'I – I don't know.' She felt a rush of apprehension, and knew at once that she must try to keep it to herself; Dean was worried enough already. 'I didn't realise how much time had gone by. Okay, so he may be a few days later than he thought, that's all. I mean it's not a really precise – he can't be expected to, you know, hit the deadline right on the dot. Can he?'

'Guess not.' He leaned back on the settee with his hands clasped at his neck. 'I'll call him tomorrow, maybe. Mind if I stay here a minute? It's the only haven of calm.'

'Sure. Take your shoes off.'

One of her telephones rang and she picked it up, talking to Carl while Dean lay on the settee with his legs dangling over

384

the end, his eyes closed.

'What are you wearing?' he asked when she put the phone down.

'Tonight?' They had to go to a party they couldn't turn down. 'The first thing I find in my hand. Why?'

'No,' he said, 'I mean now.' He sounded half asleep.

'Now? It's by John Anthony. Do you –'

'No,' he said, 'I mean what perfume are you wearing?'

'Oh. It's *Solitaire*.'

In a moment he said, 'No it isn't.'

She took a minute off for herself, clasping her own neck to ease the throbbing, watching him through her half-closed eyes. 'It's what I put on, anyway. Don't you like it?'

'What?' He sat up and swung his feet to the floor. 'Yes. But it's not *Solitaire*.' He looked around, and saw the flower arrangement Donna had brought in; then he went over to it.

'It's these,' he said, sniffing. 'But what the hell are they?'

The arrangement looked ragged, lopsided. Three red roses were crowding out some short sprigs of mimosa and jasmin, while a huge magnolia bloom took up the centre among a circle of pink geraniums, orange blossom and freesias. Coming across the room from her desk, Lorraine stood beside him; some of these flowers she didn't immediately recognise, and buried among the spagnum moss at the base of the arrangement were balls of soaked cotton wool.

'It looks a mess,' he said, puzzled; yet the gold sticker bore the name of a Manhattan florist.

'Yes,' Dean said, 'but it smells so beautiful.'

She bent lower. 'It does. Exquisite. Like *Picaresque*, but–'

'Or *Lyrique*, but more . . . intriguing . . .'

They stood breathing in the strange, subtle fragrance. 'My God,' said Lorraine, 'if only we could make–' Then she broke off and stared at him and then tore open the small envelope with her name on it and read the single word of the message before the sudden springing of tears blurred it out. 'Dean . . .' She was holding on to him. 'Oh, *Dean* . . .'

He looked at the card quickly. It read: *Voilà!*

CHAPTER 33

BY APRIL 23RD the essential essencȩs and volatile oils had reached New York from France by express air freight, and production was under way at the laboratory and its adjoining plant.

François had slept for twenty-four hours non-stop after Formula X had been completed, after which Dean and Lorraine escorted him in state to Sardi's and fêted him appropriately, though he ate very little, drank only a half-bottle of Veuve Clicquot and left them before midnight with apologies to his hosts. 'I am glad you like this formula, of course. I think it has what we meant it should have; I think it will still be worn in twenty years from now, because I was lucky, you know; I had the brainstorm after all, and you know something? The formula only has twenty-three ingredients! That is fantastic! It is how they used to make the classic *parfums* in France and Italy a hundred years ago; they did not need to use, like we use now in the States, a hundred or more ingredients; everything is so complex today, *hein?* But in my formula we have a classic, *je vous assure*. But now I must go and make sure the shipments arrive in time, and that nobody screws up the production; I will supervise it myself, of course.' He had kissed Lorraine's hand. 'I shall be in love with you forever,' he had told her with the embers of romantic tragedy in his eyes, 'but I know now that I came too late in your life; therefore I shall not challenge M'sieur Dean to a duel in Central Park, but will simply congratulate him. But in the old times it would not have ended like this, of course; for this great love it would have meant drawn swords under the trees, and to the death, *bien sûr.*' With a doleful shrug, 'But then, I am not a terribly good swordsman, so per'aps it is for the best . . .'

'You know, François,' Dean had laughed as they parted, 'you really are full of bullshit.'

'That remark alone, M'sieur, would of course have meant instant bloodshed.' He had waved gallantly from his Yellow Cab, having refused to let them drive him back to New Jersey.

By the time production had started, word was out in the trade journals that Floderus Incorporated had made a major breakthrough in discovering a brilliant young perfumer, the scion of the renowned house of Farrier de Grasse, and bringing him to America to create a new and important fragrance for them, to be presented in late spring. Within two weeks the shares of the company had risen fifteen points, leading an impromptu bull market in the cosmetics group.

Four distinctive flacons had been designed by the Franklin Mint and were in production, one of them a limited edition with the frosted emblem treated with 24-ct gold and signed in the mould by Lorraine. Packaging designs were in black and turquoise with discreet gold tasselled ropes, and showcase displays had the theme of three stylised Lorelei against a background of turquoise rock in *bas relief.* By April 20th the first flacons of *Siren Song* were going into their boxes at the New Jersey warehouse and being readied for shipment.

On April 23rd, Lorraine was photographed for the trades as she boarded the Floderus Lear Jet at Kennedy Airport, wearing a stunning turquoise and black striped dress in crêpe de chine by Regina Porter, as she began her two-week, sixteen-city promotion tour. Her entourage comprised the tour director and her assistant, a secretary from the company pool, a wardrobe fitter, a hairdresser from Francine's, and her personal aide, Donna Shapiro.

Ten minutes after take-off from New York, Donna had time to look at the mail she'd grabbed from her desk at the office an hour ago; among it was an invitation to a birthday party in Jersey City on May 11th. The card was formal, elegant, and embossed, but signed in the childish hand of Joey Vinicari, who had added: *You have to come, because you are the guest of honour.*

No way, Donna decided. That was just two days after they arrived back from the tour, and four days before the grand opening show for *Siren Song*. There wouldn't even be time to sleep. And yet . . . little Joey was going to be very disappointed; and could a guest of honour turn down an invitation anyway?

'Lorraine, do you think you could possibly give me a couple of hours off, May 11th? That'll be the Tuesday after we get back from New York.'

'My God, I hope you'll be able to grab more than a couple of hours, whenever you want to. You haven't had a day off for weeks!'

'Okay.'

Donna wrote a brief note of acceptance, and mailed it when they landed at O'Hare Airport, Chicago.

In Seattle, it rained. The downpour was so bad that Lorraine was half-soaked just getting out of the limousine and crossing the sidewalk into Saks, and her dresser – a competent and imaginative girl who had toured with big names for five years – switched to what she called Crisis Phase One and dashed across the sidewalk clutching a spare dress in a plastic bag and once inside the store changed Lorraine's wet clothes and sent her into the reception room just two minutes late, the required delay anyhow to provide a dramatic entrance.

In Los Angeles the smog guaranteed most of the party their own personal pair of bloodshot eyes, and there was a rush on the pharmacy for decongestants; at the Beverly Wilshire a party of forty-seven school-age fans held Lorraine captive for fifteen minutes in the lobby and finally released her with autograph-writer's cramp.

Cables from Dean, wherever they landed.

388

Everything here going fine. Production on schedule. Take it easy whenever you can.

Phoenix, Arizona. By a frustrating coincidence Nancy Reagan was visiting her mother at the Biltmore Estates, right by the Biltmore Fashion Square where Lorraine was appearing at Saks and I. Magnin; her limousine got mixed up with the First Lady's private motorcade on the way from the National Guard airfield, and Lorraine and Donna were stopped and questioned by plain-clothes men and forced to wait for twenty minutes until the security services in the area were satisfied. They sat with their engine and the air-conditioning running in a late morning temperature of 97 degrees.

Still on schedule. Princess Caroline has accepted the invitation for the 15th. Jacques Farrier is also coming over for the occasion, proud as hell that François has created a classic for Floderus.

In New Orleans it was steamy and humid, but Lorraine received wild applause as she appeared in the doorway of the Hyatt Regency Hotel ballroom in a sheer French chiffon cocktail dress, gathered and embroidered with a discreet beaded diamond feature at the waist, the number that Regina Porter had designed for the capital city of French American fashion. For each whistle stop Lorraine wore a different outfit, not because the people of any one city would see her twice but because the trade photographers were rising to the unique occasion on which a leading film star in her own right was presenting a commercial product destined to be patronised by the world's most discriminating arbiters of fashion.

Your picture with the security men and the limo in Phoenix has hit front page of People Today *with the caption* After You, Nancy, *did you catch it? Our full page ad appeared in* Vogue *yesterday, with a picture of you leaving Kennedy. I never realised you were quite so good-looking.*

In Denver and Oklahoma City and Fort Worth and Dallas everything went off without a hitch except that a bag with three of Lorraine's dresses in it was left behind in Oklahoma

389

City and she had to call Regina Porter, who flew a charter jet straight out to Dallas with replacements.

By the time they reached Miami on May 5th Lorraine had lost six pounds, which she couldn't afford, and was eating egg puddings and pasta and cream pastries whenever she could get them; but some of the flash pictures showed gaunt shadow lines under her neck. 'Okay,' Donna reassured her, 'but just look at those cheekbones . . . you can't have everything.'

In Washington they had fabulous luck; by one of those coincidences that happen more often in real life than in fiction, Nancy Reagan was on her way to the White House after her trip to the west when Lorraine's limo was again held up at an intersection by the First Lady's security motorcade; and the next morning *People Today*'s daily entertainment issue pictured Lorraine again, suffering the delay with gracious resignation, draped decoratively over the front fender of the Lincoln; and this time the caption read: *But How Much Does This Kind of Publicity Cost?*

On May 9th the Floderus party touched down at Kennedy Airport on schedule, and the reception committee – half concealed by sheaves of pink roses – comprised Dean, Carl, Joe, Sy and François, each of whom embraced Lorraine as if none of the others were there, or had ever existed.

'My God,' Dean told her in the limo ten minutes later, 'you've been working. Really.'

'Do I look half-dead?'

'You look wonderful. But what you did with the press! There's hardly been any room for the international news in the past two weeks.'

'I just smiled, please.'

'So now you know how much your smile is worth to people.'

'To you too?'

'I couldn't ever afford it.' He tightened his arm around her. 'You know, there just hasn't been anything going wrong. Production is *ahead* of schedule, and the west coast has started receiving the first consignments. I can't believe it.'

'I can, Dean. The amount of planning you and the others put into this project was just horrendous, and it simply paid off.'

They dined *à deux* in the early evening, at a small French bistro tucked away on 57th Street where the patron made sure they were left alone; Lorraine's picture had, as Dean said, almost crowded out the news in the popular press, and since she'd landed at Kennedy she'd worn dark glasses.

There were only three personal letters for her when they reached her apartment; two were excited congratulations from a former school friend and a life-long fan; the third was from Frederick Vanderkloot. The middle paragraph contained the gist of the message.

I sincerely regret that you chose to ignore my benevolent suggestion that Century Cosmetics might offer advantages to your company in terms of a merger or developmental assistance on a formal basis. As I believe you are aware, a closer rapport between us on more personal terms would persuade me to your thinking that your company should better remain independent, in which case I would withdraw from the corporate scene while enjoying your personal friendship; but unless this is your early decision, I shall contact my investment brokers, Schilling and Loeb, on the first day of May, and ask them to initiate a deal.

It was the final paragraph that was designed to twist the knife. *Congratulations on your successful promotion of the new fragrance, which I have been watching with great enjoyment. A classic perfume created by this brilliant young man from the house of Farrier will certainly be a feather in the cap of Century Cosmetics when we take over Floderus Incorporated. Thank you for your generosity.*

Already strained by the fatigue of the long tour, Lorraine's endurance finally broke under this new shock, and Dean only just managed to catch her as her knees buckled and she began falling.

391

CHAPTER 34

'THERE'S NOTHING WE can do?'

'Nothing.' Sy Goldman spoke from the depths of his chair, his big hands on his knees. 'Nothing at all.'

One of the telephones began ringing, and Lorraine pressed a buzzer. 'No calls, Nadine.'

'That bastard!' Carl Blatt's face was pale as he went with his jerking walk from wall to wall. 'You know what we ought to do?' He broke his paper-clip and threw the ends across the carpet.

'What?' from Joe.

'I dunno,' Carl said, 'I guess I dunno.'

Joe Fisher was squatting on his haunches, bouncing rapidly. 'A corporate letter? From the board?'

Dean said tightly, 'Saying what?'

'Well, I – you know – we think this is pretty blatant, just when we're struggling to get this company back on its feet. We'd like him to reconsider.'

Sy Goldman swung his large head. 'Joe, what the hell are you talking about? It happens all the time; and it happens at the very time when the prey company's down on its luck.'

'Okay. But it's still pretty blatant.'

Sy leaned across the arm of his chair to look at Joe. 'That's right, Joe. That's absolutely right. So?'

'I'm just – ' Joe gestured helplessly, 'you know, trying to think of something.'

'Well for Christ's sake,' Sy told him, 'so are we.'

Lorraine watched them from behind her desk. 'Sy, you don't have to – ' she broke off.

392

He turned to look at her. 'What?' Then his head swung back to look at Joe again. 'Oh, Jesus. I'm sorry, Joe. You're trying to think of something and all I can find to do is lam into you. I'm sorry.'

'That's okay.' Joe tried a quick grin, and failed.

Nadine came through on the intercom. 'Lorraine, can Donna come in?'

'Yes.'

Dean went across and unlocked the door. Donna came into the room pale-faced, her movements uncertain. 'Did anyone think of anything yet?'

'No,' Lorraine told her.

After a while Dean said slowly, 'What we do, is to go right ahead with the opening show, present *Siren Song* with everything we've got, make it a smash hit, and then retire gracefully when Century takes us over. Then, with what little we have left out of the deal, we begin all over, start a small new company, find another perfumer, and take it from there. If that's what you'd want to do, Lorraine.'

She stared at him in disbelief, until she felt tears coming and shook them away. 'If that isn't courage, then what in God's name is it?'

'Common sense, actually.'

Nobody said anything; they still had to get through the emotional barrier of realising that is was over, that Floderus was finished, before they could think about starting over.

Donna came across to Lorraine. 'I – I have to go to a birthday party this afternoon. Remember? You said –'

'Yes. Yes, Donna.' Lorraine gave her the best smile she could. 'Don't be late.'

'Okay.' She looked around, her voice barely audible. 'It's – something I can't break, at the last minute. It's someone's kid, and – he wants me there.'

'We understand,' Dean said quietly. 'Have fun.'

'Oh, sure. I'll do that. Paper hats and squeakers . . .' She dragged herself to the door. 'I'll bring you some cake.'

It was a big house near the park, with shady trees and a small rose garden and flowered walks and a pool. There must have been almost a hundred people at the party, but a strange silence fell when they saw that Joey had gone into the pool, walking into the shallow end and watching Donna all the time with a nervous grin.

'*Madre mia . . .*' breathed Aldo Vinicari, as his small son kept on walking slowly through the shimmering blue water.

'There you go, Joey,' Donna said, smiling. 'Attaboy.'

The woman with the dark hair and baroque pearls said quietly, 'He wouldn't do this for anyone else.' She had been introduced to Donna as Maria, a close friend of Aldo's.

'It figures,' Donna told her, not taking her eyes off the boy. 'It's a very traumatic experience, almost drowning, especially when they're young, and imaginative. He knows I went in for him once, so he knows I'll go in for him again if he needs me, that's all. And this is important, Maria, because otherwise he'll always be afraid of the water.' She laughed lightly. 'Joey! Don't just stand there – do something!'

Everyone had come crowding around the pool area, to watch in silence; Donna hoped nobody would start yelling encouragement to him, and turning pressure on.

'Do something what like?' Joey asked her with a shaky grin.

'Well, I dunno. Think of something. Can you fly?'

'*Fly*'

'Uh-huh.'

'Of course not!' His laughter sounded real now, not shaky anymore.

'Okay, well think of something else. Can you swim?'

He shook his head quickly. 'I don't know how.'

Donna scratched her head. 'Okay, well I know there's one thing you can do, Joey. You can float.'

'Float?'

'Right. All you do is just sink yourself down into the water and take a breath and hold it. And float.'

'Float?'

'My golly, can you hear that echo around here?' It got him laughing again. 'Joey, just lie on your back. Take that breath, like on your back, and float. Then you get the present I brought for you. Deal?'

Beside her, Aldo Vinicari glanced at his friend Maria, his eyes bright. She nodded, and held his hand. They looked back at Joey.

He stood gazing at Donna, absorbing all the vibrations he was getting from her eyes and the angle of her red head and her white smile and the way she was crouched by the pool's edge, close enough to reach him if she wanted to jump in.

'Joey,' she said, bored now, 'do you always take this long to do the simplest things?'

He looked down at the surface, then up at Donna again. 'Just float?'

'Just float. Take that breath, lie on your back, and float.'

'Okay.'

He walked in deeper, and they saw him take a monstrous breath, and sit down until the water was up to his chin.

'Now straighten your body out, Joey. Lie down.'

Then everyone was holding their breath as he straightened his legs and brought his tummy up . . . and floated, with his head half-turned to watch Donna as she crouched at the poolside smiling to him.

'You got it, Joey. Feels good, doesn't it? Like being on a water bed without the bed, just the water. Now paddle with your hands a little. Paddle downwards. Right. Push the water down and away. Not too fast. Right. Just like that. Keep on doing that. You're higher in the water now, see? Okay, now just let your breath out in a quick puff and take another one back in. Try that. And keep on paddling. Right. Okay, now you can just start breathing normally, and keep on paddling. There you go . . . There you go . . .'

Someone was crying quietly near Donna; she didn't look up to see who it was. It was probably Aldo, Joey's father. They'd had a lot of trouble with the boy, they'd said, trying to get him to take swimming lessons, private coaching, and everything they could think of to make him go in again.

'There you go, Joey . . . Now what you do is paddle a bit forwards with your hands, see . . . push the water forwards

395

as well as down, get it? Right. Absolutely. Gee, you're a born learner, you know that? Forwards and – okay, and you know something else, Joey? You're swimming. Now – don't stand up and cheer for goodness sake, it'd spoil everything. Just keep on doing that, the way – right – okay. Right to the edge of the pool. C'mon, I'm waiting for you. Yes. Like that . . .'

His head was tilted backwards now as he watched her, paddling on his back, nearer and nearer until he could feel the bottom of the pool under him, and reached up with one hand and touched hers.

Then everybody seemed to be crying, and some clapping broke out, and Joey climbed out of the water and put his thin arms around Donna and they stood hugging each other while Maria said, 'For goodness sake, Joey, you're soaking her dress like that!'

'It's okay,' Donna laughed against his wet hair, 'he's got me soaked before; it's just the way he shows his affection – right, champ?'

'He adore you,' Aldo Vinicari told her as they walked among the flower beds. 'He speak of you very often.'

He's a great kid.'

Small – about Donna's own height – and neat in his grey alpacca suit with a red carnation in the lapel. Aldo walked in a faint cloud of cologne, but a good one. 'He see your pictures, a little time ago, standing next to Lorraine Floderus, in some of the papers. That impresses him very much. But it is you, his shining star.' Feeling maybe that he might be embarrassing her by going on, he changed the subject, taking her arm in his. 'But tell me about your life, Donna. How is your life treating you? Did my friend come to see you?'

She remembered the solemn gentleman who'd talked to her as she left the office a while back, saying he was a friend of Aldo's. 'Sure. He gave me your message.'

'Good. We are your friends. Always remember that.' They walked in the shade of the leafy acacia trees. 'Tell me what is she like, Lorraine Floderus, and what is it like to work for a famous film star. Now you are here for a little time, tell me about your life, and how it goes.'

In the evening, Lorraine reached home later than usual after an exhausting meeting with Dean and the other directors, who were now agreed that there was only one thing to be done at this final stage. They would go ahead with the plans to launch *Siren Song* in four days' time as if nothing were wrong, do their best to establish their new fragrance successfully in the market, and when Century bought them out they would resign before they were fired, regroup, and work out some kind of a future.

Lorraine dropped her grey shark-skin bag onto the nearest chair and poured herself a Tio Pepe as Tilly came in from the kitchen.

'Miss Lorraine? Mr Angelo call, from the club.'

Lorraine swung to look at her. 'When?'

'Ten minutes ago.'

'All right.' She went straight to the phone and dialled, aware of the light thudding of her heart as she waited. 'Mr Baccari, please. Lorraine Floderus.' It was almost a minute before he came on the line.

'Yes,' he said heavily, 'you should come to the club, right away.'

''What happened?'

'You should come,' he repeated, 'right away.' Then the line went dead.

CHAPTER 35

OFFICER THOMAS J. CREEDY came up behind the peacock-blue Rolls Royce convertible going south on Park Avenue and switched on his roof lights and drew in to the kerb behind the Rolls just before 61st Street, reporting the speeder on his radio.

'May I see your licence, please?'

She was a knockout, a blonde, and somehow familiar; but something was wrong; maybe she was doped; her eyes were too bright.

'Please listen to me. I'm trying to get to a club on 53rd Street as fast as I can. My sister's there and I think she may have committed suicide. She's tried before, at the same place. For God's sake don't hold me up.'

Officer Creedy went on watching her for a bit, then said, 'Okay, get out of the car and we'll put a call through.' He was already talking on his radio when Lorraine came back to the cruiser and gave him the name of the club and its location. He repeated it over the air and shut down his set and told her: 'Okay, you can tuck in behind me, but don't break any rules. Technically you still owe me a ticket.'

He hit Code 4 the moment he pulled out from the kerb and drove past her across the intersection, picking up speed as she fell in behind.

There were two other patrol cars standing outside the Lotus Club when they reached there five minutes later, their coloured lights throwing reflections on the huge bronze doors and one of their sirens dying away to a moan. The doorman had come out to see what the trouble was.

Lorraine slipped from behind the wheel of the Rolls and ran across the sidewalk, grabbing the man's arm – 'Is she all right? *Is my sister all right?*'

His face went blank and he just looked around at the small fleet of patrol cars; Lorraine left him and ran through the open doors with Officer Creedy behind her.

Tony, the thin, pale-faced manager, was coming away from the bar as Lorraine ran into him. *'Is my sister all right?'*

'She's back in her room.'

Lorraine left him, running between the tables and along the corridor with the small rose-coloured lamps, to the door at the far end, throwing it open and going in, stopping dead.

'Hi,' Madlen said.

She was sitting on the gold-coloured chaise-longue in a white filmy nightdress, doing her nails, her violet eyes staring as she saw the policeman.

'What happened?' she asked.

Lorraine looked around at the huge brass bedstead under its white lace canopy, the satin covered chairs and the white lacquered dressing-table, the ivory-coloured rugs. No bloodstains anywhere; no empty pill bottles; no overturned glass.

'Madlen,' she said slowly and very softly, 'are you all right?'

'I'm fine.' She polished a nail carefully with the stick, then looked up again. 'But you didn't call this evening, and I wanted you to know I was okay.'

Lorraine stared at her, seeing in her eyes that same glow of triumph she'd seen before so many times. 'And that was all?'

'Sure.' The faintest smile touched her lips. 'I didn't want you to worry.'

The police officer coughed, and Lorraine turned, remembering he was here. She said wearily, 'I'm sorry, officer. My sister tried to commit suicide here a few months ago; she survived in intensive care. She's not quite . . . responsible again yet.'

He twisted his lips around reflectively, eyeing the baby-doll girlie on the chaise-longue, then her sister, who looked just as exotic but a lot more respectable, and who drove, in any case, a brand new Rolls Royce, which was not the kind of car you normally found zanies driving; and finally he looked at the thin mean-eyed guy in the tux who'd followed them in here.

'You know anything about this?' the officer asked him.

'We called her to come here, that's all. I don't know what gave her the idea anything was wrong.'

The policeman turned back to Lorraine. 'Look, when you're through here, I want you to pass by the precinct – 18th, on 56th – and make a report. Then you don't get the ticket. Okay?'

'Yes. I appreciate that.' What ticket? Oh yes, for speeding. That's all he had to think about. It was his job. 'Thank you for escorting me here, and I'm sorry about the other cars.'

'No problem.' He turned and went back down the corridor, passing a big guy on his way to the room at the end.

'Good evening,' Angelo said to Lorraine. Smoke rose from the cigar between his stained fingers. 'Is there any problem?' He and Tony, Lorraine noticed, had moved to stand between her and Madlen.

'When you called me,' she said, with what she knew to be remarkable patience, 'why didn't you just say my sister wanted me to know she was all right?'

He shrugged with his huge shoulders. 'She just said for me to call you, so –'

'And tell me to get here right away, before you hung up and left me with the impression she'd tried something again?' He looked carefully blank. '*Is that what she told you to do?*'

Madlen said impatiently, 'Lorraine, I really don't think you should cause all this fuss; I simply wanted you to know I was okay – because you didn't think to call – and you came storming in here with a policeman and we heard sirens outside – did you bring the whole of the police force here too?' She polished another nail, turning it in the light.

400

Lorraine took a step towards her. 'Madlen, I'm taking you home with me.'

The fragile Dresden head came up and the violet eyes grew wide. 'Home with *you?*' Her laughter was forced, and too bright. 'That's the very last place on earth I'm ever going.' But she didn't pretend to go on grooming her nails; she was staring at Lorraine, having heard something in her voice that she didn't recognise.

Lorraine took another step forward, and Tony put one hand up, stopping her. She ignored him. 'Madlen, I'm going home now. If you don't come with me, that's it. You'll never see me again. And I'll never call you again. You understand what I'm saying?'

Madlen was on her feet suddenly, her face contorted. *'You can't do that to me! You can't say things like that! You–'*

'Madlen!' It was as effective as a slap in the face. Lorraine was letting it all come out now, the suppressed rage that her sister had heard in her voice, the rage she should have let free before, a long time before. 'Madlen, listen to me. I'm going now. With you or without you. If–'

'You can't do this – I won't let you do –'

Lorraine realised suddenly that the only way to get Madlen out of here once and for all was to drag her out, but as she moved forward, Tony threw a grip on her wrist and said, 'Okay, Miss Floderus, you have to go now.' He began escorting her to the door; and then Lorraine was looking into the intense mud-brown eyes of Sadie Kaminski as time slowed down and she twisted her arm in the direction of the man's thumb to break the hold and sent a thrust-kick against the back of his knees and watched him start going down before she brought a clean crisp sword-hand swinging to the side of his neck, jerking him forward and over onto his face. Then she stepped over him.

'Come on, Madlen.' Her sister was staring at her with awe in her eyes, and didn't resist as Lorraine took her hand and began leading her out of the room past Angelo Baccari, who hadn't moved. Then as they reached the door, Madlen came to life again and began tugging and screaming.

401

'You bitch! You can't do this to me – I'm not going home with you – let me go, fuck you, let me go –'

'Come on, Madlen. I mean it.'

'Let me go! Let me go or I'll —'

Lorraine brought the flat of her right hand across Madlen's face with the sound of a whiplash and she crumpled suddenly, so that Lorraine had to lift her and carry her along the corridor, not knowing whether she'd passed out or was still pretending, and not caring either. She was taking her sister home.

In the room behind them, Angelo stood looking down at Tony on the ivory-coloured rug. 'There are things I believe,' he said through his cigar smoke, 'and there are things I don't believe. This, I don't believe.'

Lorraine lost her balance across the sidewalk as Madlen went on struggling in her arms, and they both almost pitched down.

'Let me go, you bitch! Let me go!'

Lorraine got a fresh grip on her, half-carrying her to the parking lot. A man and a woman, arm in arm, turned their heads as they heard the screaming, then walked on, a little faster, maybe thinking it was a couple of prostitutes from the club, fighting over a client.

'Let me go, damn you!' She clawed at Lorraine's face.

Then for the second time Lorraine held her sister's shoulder with one hand and brought the other sharply across her face, letting out a sob as she did it; but there was no other way; coming out of the Lotus Club they'd crossed a frontier, and they were never going back.

Madlen gasped, throwing her head back and staring at her sister as if she didn't believe it; and then, when Lorraine finally got her to the car and locked the doors and fixed Madlen's seat belt around her, the storm ended with a frightening suddenness, as if the only thing that was keeping her alive – her rage – had died, and her spirit with it. Then the sobbing began, until Lorraine pulled the Rolls into a vacant parking lot and stopped, and held Madlen while she

402

got it over with, her heart breaking and breaking again as her sister's fragile body shook itself to its paroxysms of relief; because that was what it was, and Lorraine knew it instinctively; it was no longer rage, nor frustration, nor hate; it was something that Madlen should have done, in the comfort of these arms, long ago, when the world had seemed to be ended for both of them.

'It's okay sweetheart . . . you're okay now . . .' But there was nothing she could think of that could bring any consolation. 'It's okay, darling, it's all over now, and we're friends again . . .' But the sobbing went on . . . and on . . . It was like holding a young animal, scared and injured and struggling to get free, like one of the small birds they'd sometimes found in their childhood and tried to rescue. And when at last Madlen spoke, it was to tell her something she'd longed to hear ever since their heartbreaking estrangement had begun.

'I didn't want to hate you . . .'

'I know, darling. I knew it all the time.'

'I only wanted to hurt you . . . and go on hurting you . . . till I felt better. But I don't know why.'

Lorraine held her tighter. 'Grief expresses itself in strange ways, Madlen. I guess you just needed to blame someone for – for what happened; and I was handy.'

Her sister's small fingers dug into her arm. 'I'm sorry. Oh God, I didn't really mean – '

'I know. Don't worry; it's over now, and I'm taking you home.'

She turned the ignition key, with her mind at peace for the first time since she could remember.

CHAPTER 36

AT SUNDOWN THE woman walked at the surf's edge, a dark, slender silhouette, her breasts taut under her swimsuit, her lean hips moving rhythmically to the muted music of her thoughts.

A low wind came, touching her dark hair as she halted, waiting for him, her head thrown back and her hands resting on her hips, her pelvis thrust forward in invitation as the man came down from the dunes.

'It was just here,' she said quietly, 'wasn't it?'

He looked at the shape of the rocks, offshore. 'About here, yes.'

Her head was turned to watch the shimmering sea. 'I . . . keep coming back here, to this spot. I'm drawn to it.'

He held her shoulders, concerned. 'You must stop coming here. You have to go on now; life's still waiting for you.'

'I know. I'm being morbid, I suppose. It was just here that I almost lost everything.'

Touching her chin, he gently moved her head away from watching the molten sea. 'If it means anything, you found me.'

She looked up at him for a long time, at his shadowed face outlined against the last of the day's dying light. The she said, 'Yes. It means everything . . . you mean everything in the world . . .'

He kissed her on the mouth, then drew her down with him to the yielding sand, his lean swimmer's body enfolding her as she clung to him in sudden fierce response as she remembered life, and love.

The man in the chair moved the projector switch and the screen went blank. For a time he went on sitting there. What a callow youth they'd chosen for her leading man! He couldn't even speak his lines. The popular feeling was that young men had an attraction for women, but that was a lie. They needed older men; men with power, with authority, with manners and civilised charm. They needed –

You'll be staying the night, of course.

Staying the night? No, Frederick.

I want you more than any woman I've ever known.

I . . . didn't know. I thought you were . . . too old. I'm sorry.

Too old? Too old?

Their voices screamed in his head; it was always the same; whenever he thought of her, that last, final conversation came back.

Not too old to smash her company, smash her life in New York. She didn't belong here; she was an amateur, an embarrassment in the corporate world. Tomorrow he would send for Loeb, and tell him to take over Floderus; then she could go back to whoring around in Hollywood with the other sluts there; it was all she was good for.

When he left the auditorium he found his servant waiting for him on the mezzanine floor.

'The woman's here, Mr Vanderkloot.'

'What woman?' He didn't remember having sent for one. 'Is she a new one? Has she been here before?'

'No, Mr Vanderkloot.'

Very well. This one he'd use as a stand-in for that slut of a so-called actress; he wanted something to humiliate, something to hurt. This one would do.

'I'll go to my bedroom. Bring the bitch there.'

CHAPTER 37

THE NEXT DAY THE Gala Première for *Siren Song* opened at seven o'clock in the evening on the lantern-lit terraces of the Hotel Carlton-Palace, and by seven-fifteen most of the two hundred and fifty guests had arrived.

At Carl Blatt's insistence the guest list had been kept to a strict minimum. 'We're launching an exclusive perfume,' he had insisted at the final meeting of the board members, 'and we have to make it an exclusive première.'

Representatives of the major press, trade and women's magazine showcases and marketing outlets – the most important guest group – were now being received at the doors by Lorraine, in a sheer gold lamé floor-length creation by the same designer who'd done the clothes for Lorraine's coast-to-coast tour. From there they were proceeding to the immense floral display where they were invited to take a number from the Tiffany rose bowl; the first woman guest to draw the highest number would be presented by Lorraine with a 1 oz. bottle of *Siren Song* – retailing at $200 – which she would then be invited to open in front of the assembly, to become the first women in the world to wear the new Farrier perfume from the house of Floderus.

Siren Song was to be offered by Saks Fifth Avenue exclusively for a limited time, after which it would also be shown at I. Magnin, Bloomingdale's and Neiman-Marcus. The story of the presentation and marketing plans was this evening being covered by the editors of *Vogue*, *Elle*, *Vanity Fair*, *Town and Country*, *Connoisseur* and a dozen major periodicals, while a half-hour ago the 1.5 million dollar television and magazine promotion campaign had begun with a live TV coverage of tonight's gala première.

Lorraine, moving among her guests with her stunning smile, was probably giving a finer performance than any Hollywood director had ever brought from her on the sound-stage. Only once had she broken her resolve to go through with this ordeal as if tonight's celebration meant a signal success for Floderus Incorporated; in the limousine on her way here she had told Dean, 'You once said *Swan Song* would be a better name for what we've been so busy creating. I think you were right.'

Dean held her hand all the way from her apartment, and now he gave it a gentle pressure. 'No. We created *Siren Song* and it's ours. It doesn't make any difference that Century will be taking all the profit; that's just the commercial aspect. You and François and the rest of us have created a perfume that's still going to be around years from now, even decades from now; and the name on it is yours, Lorraine, and nothing can change that, not even Vanderkloot.'

In a moment she said reflectively, 'You're right, Dean; I mustn't forget what we've done together, all of us.' She turned her face to him in the soft flickering light from the streets. 'You worked at this, harder than any of us, even me, even François; and if I let myself think back over what I did to you while you were just trying to rescue the company from the state I brought it to, I – '

'That's behind us now. Think of the future. After tonight, when Century moves in, we'll pick up the pieces and start over, if you want to.'

In slow surprise she asked, 'You're prepared to do that? I know you suggested it in front of the others, but I thought you were just – cheering me up.'

'I'd want to do anything you decide to do. Go anywhere you go.' The pressure of his hand was steady.

She was aware that something important was happening, something that was trying to free her spirit from the despair that had entrapped it since she'd known that it was all over with the company; but she couldn't switch emotions that easily; her spirit was simply refusing to believe.

'After all our . . . big scenes? You still have enough – I don't know . . . faith in me? Regard for me?'

'After all those big scenes, Lorraine, and after all the stress and the tension that's been involved in trying to save everything, we're sitting together in the back of a limo holding hands. I think there's a message there somewhere, and after this little wing-ding is over, we'll have time to work out what it is.'

The moment she'd reached the hotel she had gone to the powder room to shed the tears she'd been wanting to shed all day; but right now she didn't exactly know what they were for . . . the loss of all her father had worked for . . . self-anger that it was all her fault . . . yet, a future with Dean . . . and the hope of making good if they tried hard enough . . .? It was too much to think about; the TV cameras were in there waiting for her, and she had to look good, successful, sensational. Okay, she was ready for her entrance for *Siren Song*, final take.

'Thank you . . . thank you . . . Yes, I'm feeling wonderful, too. I'm so delighted you found the time to come, Your Excellency . . .'

Don Carlos and his orchestra, brought in from Acapulco by special arrangements under the terms of his contract there, was playing music from classic modern films, from *The Sting*, through *New York, New York* to *A Chorus Line*; and as they broke into the low sweet strains of the music for *Tango Bay* the applause rose after the first few bars, and Dean led Lorraine forward as the camera lights came on and blazed for a moment while she took her bow, her gold dress shimmering and her smile moving the hearts of all those close to her.

'I don't know how she can *do* that,' Joe Fisher said.

Donna looked at him over her glass of champagne. 'She's Lorraine.'

'I know, but . . . I mean, to find this degree of sheer unholy *guts*, when she knows . . . when we all know . . .'

'Right,' Donna said. 'That's Lorraine.'

408

They hadn't told Barry Corbett what the real situation was; he was here with his wife Ginnie, and had danced for a moment with Lorraine, congratulating her and asking her to spend a weekend with them when 'things settled down'. He seemed close to tears, probably a mixture of emotions: shame that he'd quit on the company when the going got tough, joy for Lorraine and for the memory of Willie Floderus, his late, loved friend. It had been decided beforehand that he wasn't to be told the truth this evening; it would break his heart; they'd try to find a way of letting him know more gently, later.

None of the staff had been told, not even Judy Pollack, who was here in a flaming red bolero outfit with a stuffed paraqueet in her hair; Judy had been with the firm for the past six years, working her way up from the secretarial pool, and they were going to let her enjoy this glittering bonanza before they gave her the news tomorrow.

'Betty Lou,' she said, as they wandered with the other guests along the sumptuous buffet tables, 'tell me honestly, d'you think this paraqueet deal is quite right for my hair?'

With practiced tact Betty Lou said: 'Only you could wear it, Judy.'

'Oh my God, it's as bad as that?'

At the long buffet tables the guests were savouring the delights of Beluga caviar, blue point oysters, truffles, hearts of artichokes, prawns in aspic, *pâté de foie gras*, and an array of salad creations as colourful as a flower garden in spring. The first dozen magnums of Dom Perignon were already exhausted, and corks were popping with the sound of a firework display.

Dean, immaculate in his Savile Row tuxedo with a crimson carnation in his buttonhole, never moved far from Lorraine; she was bearing up with a show of grace, animation and ease of manner that left him privately inspired. Okay, he had a good working knowledge of the industry and the market; he was experienced; his judgement was usually sound and his attitude toward problems constructive and positive; but the qualities he most lacked –

409

ease in personal relationships, public charm and persuasiveness – he now watched Lorraine expressing without effort as she moved through the crowd with a glow that lit their faces and danced in their eyes whenever she came near; no wonder the press had moved in on her promotion tour as she'd captivated city after city across the nation.

Lorraine, he said to himself, I'm falling in love again, but you haven't noticed yet; that's my fault; I lack communication; but when all this is over, there'll be time to tell you how I feel.

'Isn't she absolutely *fabulous*?' Carl Blatt asked him.

'I think so.'

They tilted their glasses together, and by luck got a glance from Lorraine, and the flash of her smile.

François Farrier was called in front of the cameras halfway through the evening; he looked very young, very romantic, very French.

'*Je suis là,*' he said with panache as the crowd fell silent, '*parce que j'aime New York. Et je suis –*'

'François!' Dean called quickly.

'*Hein? Oh. Oui.*' His shy smile was captivating. 'Yes, I am here because I love New York; I am here also because I love the women, and –' he had to wait for the spontaneous cheers to die away – 'and for the women I make *Siren Song*. It is a *geste* – a gesture of homage to all women, from *la Maison Farrier de Grasse*, and from *la Maison Floderus de New York.*' He found Lorraine close to him, and embraced her with Gallic efficiency, without even spoiling her make-up, as the applause grew to a roar and they stood together holding hands and taking their bow together.

'You must please tell me something,' he said privately to Lorraine as the camera lights dimmed and the applause died down, 'who is that exquisite girl in the silver dress, with those eyes *extraordinaires*? There are so many damn important people here tonight that I am a little shy, you know? I am out of my deeps. Tell me who is she.'

Lorraine looked across the terrace at Madlen, who was of

course surrounded by young men; and for a moment the sound of the party died away and the lights went low as she reached deep inside herself for the relief and joy that were trembling there, as she still tried to believe that the nightmare for both of them was over at last.

It was only at the last minute that she'd been able to persuade Madlen to come tonight; they'd left it so late that she'd needed time to change and make up as best she could; then Tilly had brought her here, arriving only fifteen minutes ago. Now she looked as if she were enjoying herself, with some colour back in her cheeks and the light back in her eyes.

She took François by the hand and led him across to the circle of young men, who broke apart for them.

'François,' she heard herself saying, 'it's with deep pride, and great joy, that I'd like to present my sister Madlen . . .'

Then she'd left them together.

Dean asked to dance with her again; then she took the floor with the French Ambassador, the Italian Ambassador, the British Vice-Consul, le Compte de Salignac, Lord 'Jimmy' Weston, and several distinguished members of the Senate.

Then she saw the little woman in the ill-fitting cocktail dress, standing with her short legs apart near one of the terrace bars, drinking what looked like Perrier. Lorraine went over to her, giving a little bow.

'*Sensei* . . .' she said. 'I've only just seen you.'

'I only just got here,' Sadie Kaminski said, returning the bow punctiliously. 'Some wing-ding!' The mud-brown eyes regarded Lorraine intensely. 'I guess this looks kinda like your night.'

'I'm honoured you came, *Sensei*.'

'My pleasure. But you haven't been workin' out at the *dojo* recently. How come?'

'I've been away on a promotion tour. But I practiced whenever there was time. And *Sensei* . . .' she took Sadie's arm, 'I want to tell you something. There was a man who annoyed me, the other night. He was getting in my way. So

411

you know what I did?'

The brown eyes had a sudden light in them. 'Tell me.'

'I took him down.'

A grin spread over Sadie Kaminski's face that was like the sun coming out. 'Did a clean job? No fumblin' around?'

'He hit the floor without even trying.'

Sadie laughed explosively, spilling her drink. 'That's great. Wish I'd been there. But don't let it go to your head, kid. You gotta catch up on your workouts if you wanna make progress in karate. You better be there.'

'Yes, *Sensei*. I'll be there.'

Just before nine o'clock the wife of the US Consul to Brazil showed her ticket with the winning number, and in a sudden blaze of flashlight and a roar of applause, opened the black and turquoise bottle of *Siren Song* and touched the perfume behind her ears, becoming the first woman ever to wear it. She then generously splashed the rest of it over the hands of the women who crowded around her with their delighted congratulations.

The camera lights were just going out when Lorraine's secretary, Nadine Keller, saw Donna taking a newspaper from one of the waiters, who had come quickly through the crowds with it. Opening it at page two, Donna found a headline and read the few paragraphs, then went over to the wall, where she leaned with her eyes closed and the colour draining from her face. Nadine went over to her, concerned; she'd seen this happen to Donna once before.

'Are you okay?'

Donna's eyes came open. 'What?'

'Are you feeling bad?'

'No.' Donna straightened up, not wanting to attract attention. 'A rabbit walked over my grave again, I guess. For the last time.'

Only minutes ago she'd been called to a phone, and a man's voice had told her she should send out for the late edition of the *Courier* and look at page two; then he'd simply wished her goodnight and hung up.

'Nadine,' she said, 'get Lorraine over here, would you?

412

And Dean Powers.'

'Okay.'

It was a quiet corner of the terrace, where they wouldn't attract curiosity. Dean came first, saying that Lorraine was dancing with the vice president of Saks right now, and shouldn't be disturbed.

'What's up?' he asked Donna.

'Read this.' She gave him the paper.

The report was brief, obviously for lack of any background information.

Late last night the police were called to the luxurious penthouse apartment of Frederick F. Vanderkloot III, chairman of Century Cosmetics and seven other international companies. Mr Vanderkloot's nude body was discovered in his bathroom, and conjecture is that he slipped on the wet floor striking his head on the rim of the black marble bath-tub. According to one of his servants, he had received a visitor, thought to be a young woman, or possibly a young man disguised as a woman. From one authenticated source it is believed that Vanderkloot may have had transvestite tendencies. The woman – or man – was seen to leave the penthouse at about midnight, shortly after the police pathologist has estimated the time of death, the news of which has been delayed by extraordinary efforts on the part of the victim's staff to avoid unwanted publicity, as is understandable in this unusual case.

One report suggests that Vanderkloot was involved in deals with certain casinos in Las Vegas and Atlantic City, which exposed him to hostility among business factions. It is also common knowledge that he was for some time under the care of a well-known New York psychiatrist. Enquiries are proceeding with what a police spokesman describes as 'appropriate energy'.

While Dean was reading the report, Donna managed to get a final grip on herself. She didn't know who the man was on the phone, but she remembered what had taken place at little Joey Vinicari's birthday party four days ago.

'Tell me what it is like,' his father had said as they'd

413

walked under the light green acacia trees, 'to work for a famous film star. Now you are here for a little time, tell me about your life, and how it goes . . .'

He couldn't have known, but she'd gone there straight from Lorraine's office, where everyone had been trying to get over the shock of the Vanderkloot letter; and she'd simply told Vinicari what was on her mind, letting out the tension and the anger and the misery, forgetting that he was almost a total stranger and wouldn't be interested.

'Vanderkloot . . .' he'd said in his quiet, modulated voice with its slight accent, 'yes, we know him; we hear of him sometimes. He has a certain . . . reputation; he is not kind to the women, I understand. And he has made certain . . . deals in the casino groups, making some very hard terms in some cases. Frederick Vanderkloot, yes . . . he is not very much liked . . .'

Then they hadn't mentioned him again. Strolling back to the poolside, they'd watched little Joey for a while and then Donna had made her excuses to leave. She'd even forgotten telling Vinicari anything about the problem facing the company, until now. But something he'd told her before was suddenly in her thoughts. *Remember you have friends . . . powerful friends.*

That was crazy. She'd have to forget that.

'Who told you to get the newspaper?' Dean asked her when Lorraine had been fetched over from the dance floor.

'I don't know.' She didn't want to think about it; she was letting her imagination run riot. 'I guess we'll never know.' The guy was mixed up in casino deals; that could have brought him a whole lot of trouble.

Nadine brought Carl over, and Joe, and Sy; they stood in a small group for a time on the lower terrace, not talking very much; and at some time Joe went across to the nearest bar and dropped the newspaper into the bin of empty champagne magnums, and came slowly back.

'When was he going to give his instructions,' Dean asked Lorraine, 'to negotiate the takeover?' He didn't remember the exact words of Vanderkloot's letter.

414

'Today.'

The word went around in their minds as Dean beckoned to one of the waiters.

Joe Fisher had his hands pushed deep in his pockets, looking sometimes at Lorraine as if he'd like to say something, but decided not to. Sy Goldman was standing massively in thought; Carl Blatt was watching the lights along the flowered terraces, with their reflection across his glasses giving him an enigmatic air. Donna was leaning against the low stone balustrade, hands clasped together in front of her, her red head tilted in thought.

Forget it. You didn't mean to say anything. You weren't involved. And anyway you've saved enough lives, haven't you? On that plane when it ditched. And little Joey's. Okay. You win some and you lose some. Forget it, and get on with things.

When the waiter brought the champagne that Dean had ordered, wheeling it on the decorative brass trolley, opening the magnum and pouring it into the glasses, the small group drew close together.

Joe Fisher was the only one who was able to put it into words for them all. 'Is it sometimes okay to feel good about somebody dying?'

For a while no one answered. The music drifted across the terrace, the theme from *The Way We Are*, and laughter rose from the distant throng of revellers.

Then Dean said, 'That doesn't matter, Joe. But it's okay to feel good about the living, and that's us.' He touched his glass to Lorraine's, and the others followed his gesture. 'We thought the party was over, but it's just beginning. We'll drink to that.'

415